Born in Grimsby, Lincoln
Welholme Junior School an
five years at the Grimsby Tel
in Germany, where she resid

In 1987 she moved to Spain and started to write professionally. Anita has had various short stories and articles published in British magazines and newspapers; she is, however, more widely known amongst the English-speaking community of Spain as a journalist, columnist and feature writer working for the local English-language newspapers.

Anita Bond is single, resides in Calpe, Spain, and loves dogs. Savages and Saints is her first novel.

Visit her website: **www.anita-bond.com**

Praise for Savages and Saints

"Atmospheric, clever and real, with a killer ending that will leave you wanting more."

GRIMSBY TELEGRAPH, ENGLAND

"Anita takes us from Grimsby to the Costa Blanca, two areas she knows well, but I hope she has never known anyone as evil as her baddie. Will he come to a nasty end? Just one of the many good reasons to enjoy this excellent first novel."

COSTA BLANCA NEWS GROUP, SPAIN

"An intense mix of love, joy, malice and horror propel the three protagonists from their unsuspecting youth in the English coastal town of Grimsby to the Costa Blanca."

ROUND TOWN NEWS, SPAIN

Savages and Saints

Anita Bond

To May, the
very best of wishes
Anita Bond.

Libros International

ISBN 1-905988-17-6 978-1-905988-17-4

Cover by Kelly Leonie Walsh

Published by Libros International

www.librosinternational.com

Acknowledgements

I wish to express my gratitude and sincere thanks to my dear friend Jacqueline Barnett, who was kind enough to check the first draft and who encouraged and supported me throughout the entire process of writing this book.

Thanks also belong to my brother Terry Bond, who still resides in the Grimsby area and never once complained about my daily telephone calls requesting he check or confirm street and place names.

A heartfelt thank you to all those special friends and acquaintances who have wished me well with this, my debut novel.

And, finally, I would like to acknowledge my appreciation to my editors at Libros International.

There are others who are sitting,
Grim as doom,
In the dim ill-boding shadow
Of my room.
Darkling figures, stern or quaint,
Now a savage, now a saint,
Showing fitfully and faint
Through the gloom

- Sir Arthur Conan Doyle -

This book is dedicated to

BRIAN LIDDY

without whose challenge it
might never have existed

PROLOGUE

David stirred restlessly. Despite the heat of the night, the bed felt cold without Elizabeth beside him. He could feel consciousness creeping in on his slumber and he fought to stay in the sweet oblivion of sleep. The strange, as yet unidentified, smell excited his instincts and made his nostrils twitch. He turned over in bed, pulling the sheet over his head and his legs up to his belly. He was so tired. All he wanted to do was sleep. But his befuddled brain kept hammering at his senses, forcing him to wake up and identify the origin of the aroma. Realisation swept over him like a cold shower and he sat bolt upright in bed, fully awake now, his nostrils flaring. There was no mistaking anymore what he could smell, sense, feel – fire!

Ripples of pure terror crept up David's back, making his skin tingle. This was not a land, with its parched earth and dried out forests, to be caught in a fire. His stomach rushed up to lodge in his throat. What he had secretly dreaded but refused to acknowledge, even to himself, was now becoming a savage reality. Not for the first time, he questioned his judgement in building his home in the middle of the so very dry and so very inflammable pine forests of the Spanish coastal mountainsides.

Muscles tensed, David waited for confirmation of his suspicions, still clinging to the small hope that he had been dreaming. But he was totally awake now. Sitting in the darkness of his lonely bed, he listened for the crackling and whoosh that could mean the end of everything for him. He sniffed at the air like a dog trying to pick up a trail.

He practically fell out of the bed and stumbled across the cool marble tiles of the bedroom floor and out of the sliding glass doors on to the balcony, pulling on his jeans as he did so. The urgency of his actions robbed his legs of co-ordination but he was driven on by a macabre curiosity. And then he saw the night: its blackness ripped open and made light by streaks of spreading colour - crimsons and oranges slashing the mountainside. He felt the hairs on the back of his neck immediately rise and bristle.

Worse still was the unnatural music of the forest. No longer a gentle whisper of the coastal breeze playing among the foliage and the singing of the crickets, the trees burned furiously, spitting sparks in all directions and spreading the fire at an incredible speed.

David heard a eucalyptus tree explode as its oil overheated, ignited and set the tree on fire. He saw the flames reach out and encompass the neighbouring trees. Angry was the fire as it devoured with startling rapidity all that lay in its path. It burned so brightly that it cast a weird half-light over the district. David stood motionless, observing with a strange detachment as the fire began to wipe out his property, his empire, his dream; everything he had worked so hard for, for the last ten years.

A rustling in the still untouched parts of the garden directly below him grabbed David's attention. His eyes searched among the shadows. Probably a scared animal, he thought, before letting his gaze sweep once again over the torn horizon. Spots of light on each side of his vision penetrated the darkness, giving off an eerie illumination. His beloved mountainside was ablaze.

The many separate orbs of jumping flames didn't register as anything odd at first. The air was hotter than usual and the scorching breeze carried smouldering wood particles to the far corners of his land. An acrid smell hung heavy in the air and assaulted David's lungs each time he drew in a breath.

The fire inched down the mountainside in red tendrils like lava from a spewing volcano. Instinct told him he must flee and he turned to do so but a loud crash startled him, forcing an involuntary scream from his lips. He paused, cocking his head to listen. There was definitely something, someone even, in the garden.

The foliage parted and a figure moved out of the shadows into the half-light.

'Hello, Davie, old bean.' The man spoke with the intimate tone of long-term friendship, of family.

'Oh, Cal. It's you.'

Instant relief washed over David. For a second he relaxed. It was just Calvin. And Calvin had always had this unnerving habit of turning up at all hours, and in the strangest of situations. Then David saw the canisters that Calvin was carrying, and the absurdity of his cousin slinking around in his garden, in the middle of the night, in the middle of this fire, carrying canisters that they normally used to carry petrol in, hit him.

'Cal! Call the fire brigade,' he shouted. 'Get out of the garden! Look! The fire is nearly here. We've got to get out! Cal! Cal? What are you doing ...?'

Before he'd even finished his question David's heart sank, his eyes flew to the many separate fires spreading steadily then joining together as one. And he knew. He fought his disbelief. This was the third fire this month. The dusty green pines were disappearing rapidly, being replaced by brown, wizened and smouldering skeletons of the once proud trees.

The first forest fire on the land that was now called Parklands had seemed like a godsend. It had destroyed thirty-five acres of Green Zone right in the region of where he'd been saying it would be a perfect spot for a top-class housing estate. That land had been so totally ruined by the fire that the authorities had no choice other than to re-designate it as building land. David had started on his bid to buy the land as soon as the news had become official. He'd never once questioned his good luck. But now, suddenly, he remembered how he'd cursed loudly to Calvin about not having enough land: those sixty-five acres would have been better for the housing development he had in mind. Even then, as the second fire had devoured a further thirty acres of wooded land in the same area, David had stopped wondering at his luck, stopped believing in coincidences and started watching Calvin with a new awareness. It was the same now. He had a feeling that something wasn't right here, indeed, that very same something told David that this fire also had nothing to do with coincidence.

Calvin stood beneath the balcony. He was dressed completely in black and hard to see despite being bathed in the orange glow reflected from the water of the swimming pool. He shot a laconic smile up at David. His teeth shone icy white through the amber night, looking grotesque, as if hanging alone, separate from a body. David squinted through the haze and smoke that was creeping around the house.

'Good idea of mine, don't you think?' Calvin shouted up to the balcony. 'A couple of matches is all it took to get that lot going.'

Confusion rendered David speechless as Calvin indicated the patches of wildly burning woodland behind him with the vacant gesture of an off-hand wave. 'Now don't it look pretty?' he drawled sarcastically.

Icy terror gripped David's heart. Oh, God! What has he done now? The thought hammered in his head as his eyes scanned the bright turbulent mountain and valley before him. His mouth went dry at what he saw.

'You, Cal? You've done that?' he spluttered, pointing a shaking finger at the hot tongues of fire licking at the trees and dry shrubland, spreading in zigzags down the mountainside in a direct path to his door. It was a useless question; David knew that as soon as the words were out of his mouth. He looked at his cousin. Smoke was stealthily creeping into the garden and starting to swirl around Calvin's feet. The thought occurred to him that he needed to get out of the house but he seemed rooted to the spot. He peered down from the balcony at Calvin's handsome face, a beautiful face usually full of eager innocence and helpful charm, but now turned up towards him and full of a hatred he'd never seen there before. Cold fear shot down his spine and he asked himself, and not for the first time lately, just what was going on in that head behind those laughing eyes; he wondered, sadly, just what was Calvin capable of. And just when and how and why had the kind boy who had entered his life all those years ago and made his existence so much better become this monster he saw before him now.

CHAPTER ONE

A winter's day on the edge of a town in Scotland. The rows of dingy terraced houses stopped abruptly and the wild, rugged landscape started and stretched out endlessly. The foot-worn path up the hill was slippery; the blades of wild grass stiff and frosted in the cold of the early morning. It was still dark and so Calvin made haste with caution. He turned when he reached the first bank and looked back over the town. Everything still looked normal and he wondered how long it would take. The amber glow of the street-lamps fell gently upon the little terraced house huddled in the middle of a row of identical dwellings and momentarily wiped away the peeling paint, missing roof tiles and broken, porous old bricks. It practically looked quaint in the weak glimmer.

But it wasn't quaint. Anything but. Calvin hated that house just as he hated everything and anything to do with his present life. He hated his parents – his soppy, whimpering mother and his often drunk and violent father. And as for the baby, well, that thing should never have been born in the first place.

He peered down from his hiding place behind the dried-out scrub on top of the hill. Attached to the line of houses was a row of back yards, all in different stages of decay and disorder. Dilapidated wooden sheds lodged at the bottom of the yards. Despite their obvious deterioration, some were brightly painted in an effort to rejuvenate the area. But most were a dull dark brown, unpainted and rotting away. Clothes hung, forgotten, in most of the yards, too; pegged on the washing line, stiff from the morning frost. Beyond this row of houses where Calvin had been born and spent his whole life of thirteen years was another row, and another, as far as the eye could see, all in various stages of dilapidation, grey and grubby. Some showed signs of attempts at repairs, but the whole picture presented a view of abject misery.

I deserve better than this, thought Calvin. He was starting to get really cold now, caught in the icy wind at the top of the hill, and again he wondered how long it would take.

Calvin appeared much older than his thirteen years. He was a beautiful child with hair as black and shiny as a piece of coal; it curled gently into the nape of his neck. He had the bluest of eyes in an unexpectedly sculptured aristocratic face that belied his heritage. He was slim, tall of stature and possessed a charm far beyond his years. Calvin gave about himself an aura of self-confidence, of secret knowledge, a suggestion of arrogance. He had the intensity of a bored, well-to-do Scottish laird of yesteryear. In the year of 1959, at thirteen years of age, at the top of that hill, waiting, Calvin was no longer a child.

His lessons in life hadn't been easy. Born just a year after the war, when his father had finally made it home from the hell of the prison camp, got violently drunk and demanded his marital rights, Calvin's appearance in the world had not been greeted with enthusiasm by his mother. She was a quiet little being who withdrew into silence as the years passed. His father had grown more violent and prone to sudden loud outbursts in those same years. He would sit, silent and sullen, for hours on end, in the frayed armchair next to the black-grated fire in the scullery, drinking whatever he could get his hands on. Back in those war years, reliving the fear, he was lost in a tormented world of his own. When he came out of these moods, his joy was to shout down and intimidate his wife before beating her for some imagined violation of his orders, as if his miserable existence was totally her fault.

Calvin had grown clever during these early years, learning how to quietly disappear when his father was about to embark on one of his tirades. He acquired a talent for ducking out of the way of flying fists and developed a charm that could sometimes calm the beast raging in his father's breast.

He had also learned to hate, quietly and deeply.

'Christ!' he sighed, his breath making little white puffs of cloud in the air. 'How long is it going to take?'

He knew his plan was ingenious. It just couldn't go wrong. And yet, he hadn't reckoned that it would take so long. He shifted his weight from one crouched leg to the other. He hadn't missed anything, had he? Everything was in place: the candle-stub was burning, the baby had been silenced, the windows and doors sealed up. His mind raced over each detail. For more than three months Calvin had thought about this, had thought of little else. He'd been consumed by the excitement of the outcome. Today had been the day. It was today or never.

Calvin had risen early after a sleepless night but he wasn't tired at all: hours of anticipation made him feel wide-awake, alert, totally prepared. It was Monday morning. Dad had, as was the norm, spent the weekend getting pissed and beating up on Mam. She had meekly taken his insults, his shoves and slaps and gone about her business of cleaning the house and cooking his meals as silently and unobtrusively as possible. This was hindered to some degree by the wails of the baby who demanded attention, unaware of the consequences of his screams. She looked old, much older than her thirty-seven years. Wizened and grey in every respect, she would shuffle around the house like a ghost. At 9pm, she had laid the baby down in the back bedroom with so many blankets on him that movement was impossible. Then she had gone to bed and left her husband to finish his drinking. It was around two in the morning when Calvin heard the familiar sounds of his mother going to feed the baby and then helping his dad up to bed. Within the hour the house had fallen into a deathly stillness.

As was his duty, Calvin had risen at 6am. Every morning before school, he had to go down to the bakery and bring back bread rolls. The smell of the bakery could be enjoyed from a good distance and his taste buds would start tingling before he was near enough to see the tiny shop front. He had charmed the baker to such an extent that when he told him he was not allowed to eat any of the rolls on the way home, the baker always gave him an extra one to enjoy on his journey back to the house. On his return to the hated, cold terraced house, it was one of his many chores to make a big steaming pot of tea and then wake his parents. But on this particular morning he didn't do this. He didn't go to the bakery.

The house was draped in a gloomy silence at that early hour. The excitement of his planned actions lent stealth to his movements. He crept to the door of his parents' bedroom and checked that they were indeed deep in sleep. Then he entered the baby's bedroom. Lost as the child was among the many hand-crocheted and knitted blankets, it was easy enough for Calvin to just pull them up a little and press them over the baby's face. There wasn't even a struggle. The little mite just drifted away like he had never existed. Calvin felt good about this. He didn't wish to hurt his brother, cause him pain or anything. He just wanted him gone.

Next he crept down the stairs and started to block all openings. Most were sealed up against the cold anyway. A thick blanket hung at the front door. The windows were similarly covered. In the scullery, he took a towel and stuffed it across the bottom of the window where he could feel a draught coming in. He then opened the door of the gas-cooker oven. It was the arrival of this new cooker and the demolition of the old black-grated coal fire with its twin ovens either side, that had given him the idea. He turned on the knobs that serviced the four rings on top of the stove and then turned the larger knob that sent gas hissing through the vents in the oven. Moving quickly now, he took the stub of wax candle that he had hidden in the old coal room attached to the scullery, set it upright on the scrubbed surface of the old wooden table and lit it with the matches kept tidy in a saucer next to the cooker. He pinched his Dad's woollen scarf from the back of the under-stairs cupboard door, *he won't be needing this anymore,* and left the house to walk up the hill and wait.

CHAPTER TWO

It was bitterly cold in the tiny bedroom. A thin layer of ice frosted the inside of the window making crazy patterns on the glass and distorting the first dim light of morning. It had been the slamming of the back door, as his father had left for work that had awoken David. His hands were numb with cold and he drew them under the covers, close to his body, in an effort to warm them.

His eyes wandered aimlessly over the bare room as he waited for full consciousness to return. Another day, another morning like any other. His father had simply left the house without a word to him. David had gone to bed the night before hoping this morning would be different, that his father would come to his room and gently shake him awake just like he imagined other fathers did their sons. After all, today was different. Today was David's eleventh birthday.

Wrapping the quilt around him, he padded over to the window and scraped at the ice with his thumbnail until he could see into the grey shadows of the backyard. The faint outline of the back gate swinging on its hinges made him groan out loud. Now he would have to go out and close it before getting dressed and, more importantly, before Whisky made a dash for the freedom of territories unknown and un-sniffed.

Whisky, a white and tan wire-haired mongrel, had been with them for nearly two years now. He had suddenly appeared at their door one day, wandered into the scullery and into their lives. And directly into David's father's heart. Somehow, Whisky knew never to go further than the door leading to the living-room, that the rest of the house was off-limits to him. Within two days, Whisky started spending his time just waiting for George, David's father, to return from work. The bond between them was instant and solid. And with every tail-thumping greeting that Whisky gave George, David knew he'd slipped down a notch in his father's list of favoured people. It was hard, therefore, for David to understand how his father, always cold and distant with him but patient and caressing with Whisky, could forget to close the gate.

Now that the dog was firmly enclosed in the yard, David raced back into the house and up the stairs to his mother's room. Here a fire burned in the black cast-iron grate; freshly placed coal nestled on a bed of burnt embers. It was warm and cosy in the bedroom, which was at the front of the house and partially lit by the street light outside. The beam of yellow light cut through the room illuminating the bed.

David studied the blankets that covered his mother's still-sleeping form, waiting to reassure himself that they were moving up and down with the regularity of her breathing. It was his secret fear that one day he would come into this room to make sure those blankets were rising and falling only to find them not moving.

Creeping to the bed, David looked at his mother's face. It was peaceful in sleep, relaxed, nearly pretty, but he knew that, in a few minutes when she awoke, it would be mottled and flushed and wrinkled as she gasped for breath between bouts of coughing and wheezing.

'David? Is that you, lad?' Iris asked sleepily. As she attempted to turn over in bed, she was overcome by a racking cough that swallowed up the rest of her words.

'Yes, Mam. Now just you lay still. I'll go down and put the kettle on for your tea and a steam bowl.'

He always spoke the best English he could muster when speaking to his mother, knowing she would appreciate the effort he made to drop his northern accent. Many times she had told him how she wanted only the best for him and to have the best and get on in the world, you had to speak proper English, she would always say. He watched his mother cough painfully again, nodding her head in acknowledgement of his words. She wheezed as she fought to draw in air as deeply as she could.

'You're a good lad, our David,' she managed before starting to cough again.

David turned and left the room. He was already at the top of the stairs on his way down when he heard his mother say, 'Oh, and David, happy birthday, son.'

Some twenty minutes later David, dressed and ready for the freezing half-hour trek to school, was stoking up the fire in his mother's bedroom. Iris kept reappearing from under the towel that was covering both her head and a steaming bowl of hot water and camphor to sip at her tea.

'Come 'ere, lad. Open the drawer of my bedside cabinet. There's something in it for you.'

David did as he was bid. The drawer was stuffed full of half-unwound pullovers, odd balls of wool in many different colours, and knitting needles. In the middle of the confusion was a package wrapped in tissue paper.

'Go on, lad. Take it out. It's for you, for your birthday.'

He carefully extracted the package from its woolly confines. She hadn't forgotten. David's heart sang. The fact that his mother was bedridden hadn't stopped her finding a way to make him a present for his birthday. It didn't matter what the present was, he would cherish it. For in this gift was the only love that he needed. His mother, ill, weak and bedridden as she was, meant everything to him. And this package proved that she loved him, too.

'Hey! Mam! It's great!' David exclaimed in awe as held up the multi-coloured pullover. The waistband, arm and neck bindings were made up of light grey while the back and front was a mass of intricate patterns and eye-catching colours - canary yellow, China red, royal blue and leafy green jostled for first and most predominant place. The result was a startlingly colourful garment.

In his pleasure, David threw himself at his mother to kiss her, catching her off-guard with his unexpected show of affection. Iris started to cough and disappeared once more under the towel, back to the comforting steam. David cursed his stupidity. He lifted his arms, grabbed the sides of the dark blue jersey he was wearing and pulled it over his head. Now that he was eleven, it was getting too small for him anyway. With similar haste, he donned his birthday present. Before leaving the house, he made his mother a sandwich and a flask of hot tea to keep her going until his father got back from the building site. David set off for school with a feeling of joy keeping him warm along the grey, icy streets. Not even the blast of sea breeze, which tried to turn his fingers blue and creep through his new pullover to freeze his bones, could dishearten him today.

But his happiness lasted only so long as it took him to enter his classroom and take his duffel coat off.

'What's that supposed to be?' cried Tom, pointing at the new pullover.

'Looks like someone has tried to use up all the leftover bits of wool in one go,' Steven sneered, smoothing down his navy-blue, long-sleeved, shop-bought sweater.

David's face turned bright red then, angered by the insult to his mother's work, he lurched forward, his fists clenched. He would have loved to punch the bully on the nose. But he didn't. He daren't. Steven was much bigger than he was.

'Did you see that?' Steven asked the gang of kids that had gathered in anticipation of a good show. Turning to David, he smirked. 'You just wait 'til break time, Titch. I'll show you.' And with a low-placed punch to David's back, Steven sauntered off to his desk.

David smarted at the reference to his size. He hated being so small. He was just a late developer, his mother always reminded him. One day he would be as big, bigger even, than that hateful Steven. Then he'd show him. But his bravado only lasted as long as his anger, which quickly diminished to be replaced by fear.

The rest of the morning was a blur for David. His euphoria at this being his birthday and his lovely present from his mother evaporated. Anticipation and dread of what would happen at break-time superseded his indignation at the insults about his new pullover and his height. He slouched down in his chair, filled with terror.

CHAPTER THREE

Built in 1892, by 1959, Welholme School in Grimsby had grown to be an imposing tall red and yellow brick building with a roof topped by a tower. It stretched the whole of one block of Welholme Road and taught some eight hundred children. The junior and senior schools as well as the boys and girls were kept separate. Inside the Victorian building the classrooms were painted a sober brown and cream. Small lift-top desks and wooden stools stood in orderly lines. Facing these was a larger writing desk and an adult-sized chair for the teacher. Behind this the whole wall was taken over by a blackboard.

David was standing at the blackboard, rubbing out the chalked words of the last lesson with the stiff felt-like material attached to a wooden grip. He had volunteered for this duty. He would have volunteered for anything rather than leave the safety of the school building.

Mr Holland entered the room. 'That's a fine job you have done there, Gilmore,' he said, sucking on his pipe. 'Now out and get your milk, lad, before the break is over.'

David's blood froze in his veins. 'I don't mind, Sir. I can stay here. Tidy up, maybe?'

'Out, Gilmore! Now!'

Outside in the playground chaos reigned. Hundreds of children of all ages wearing navy-blue blazers: girls in gymslips, junior boys in short trousers and long grey socks, senior boys in long trousers. Games were being played, children running around and screaming, laughing, shouting, squealing. Most of the senior boys were congregating around the boundary line between the girls' and boys' playgrounds. It was a happy scene. But not for David.

He walked out into the playground, his eyes darting right and left, his heart beating so loudly he felt sure the other children would hear, would know of his fear. He tried for all he was worth to look straight ahead, to walk bolt upright, to appear unafraid. As his eyes scanned the playground, he started to relax a little. He couldn't see Steven and his gang anywhere. Tensed muscles started to loosen; his breathing began to slow down to a normal rhythm. He started out on his way to the milk hall, a little smile creeping onto his lips. They'd obviously found someone else to bully. David's hunched shoulders, tightened up in readiness to take a few blows, began to unwind. He breathed out audibly when, suddenly, a hand landed heavily on his shoulder.

'Where do yer think you're going, Titch?'

David's heart sank into his boots as Steven swung him around. The whole gang were there: five faces sneering down at him, five faces that David wished he could wipe of out his sight and memory forever.

'To get my milk,' stammered David.

'Aw, to get his milk,' mimicked Steven, 'and in his new pulli, too. What a ponce!'

Steven flicked David's blazer to one side and grabbed hold of the pullover that his mother had so lovingly knitted for his birthday. He twisted his hand and pulled it until it became misshapen. David leant backwards, trying to get away from Steven's attack but the other boys crowded around him and pushed him into the centre of their circle. One grabbed at his hair; another boy was kicking at his shins. He felt the beginning of a sob rise in his throat but swallowed it down quickly. No matter what, he was determined not to let them see they had hurt him. He saw the fist draw back, ready to strike his face. David flinched, waiting for the punch to hit him.

Abruptly, the end-of-break bell rang out. The other boys, intent on making it look to the teacher ringing the bell like they were just having a friendly scuffle, all started to laugh and lark about, patting David on the back and shoulder in a gesture that suggested he was one of their pals. The teacher never saw the pinches delivered to David's back and arms, nor did he hear the boys hiss that there would be time enough to see to him after school.

The rest of the day dragged by for David. School dinners were taken in the classroom and instead of going outside to play afterwards, where he knew the gang would be waiting for him, he complained to the dinner ladies that he had a stomach ache and felt better inside. And so he stayed with them in the serving kitchen.

As going-home time neared, David became increasingly more agitated. He had felt the eyes of his oppressors staring into the back of his head all afternoon. He had heard nothing of the lessons. He knew that when it came time to leave the school the others would grab him, relieve him of his satchel, duffel coat and most probably his beautiful new pullover. They would scatter these items, throwing them over garden walls in the unknown streets that David would be made to walk. They would be behind him all the time, shoving and thumping him in the back, always pushing him forward. They would lead him in the opposite direction of his home, down unfamiliar roads and highways, away from everything he knew, all the time calling names after him such as titch, shorty, duck's arse, any name they could find relating to his short stature. Sometimes their jibes were worse than the punches and kicks. Then they would probably tie him up and leave him somewhere, just like they did the last time. That time they had tied him to a tree on the edge of a remote playing field.

David's terror at the thought of what was going to happen to him on this day tensed his body up so tightly he thought he would crack into tiny pieces. But he didn't crack into tiny pieces; instead, when the going-home bell rang, David's bladder immediately emptied. The urine trickled through his trousers and down his legs, making a puddle on the floor.

In the commotion of the boys all rushing towards the door of the classroom, eager to get out of the school, it was a few minutes before the teacher realised what had happened. At this age, he wasn't used to his boys peeing in their pants.

'Gilmore, you dirty bugger!' he screamed. 'What on earth do you think you are doing?'

At that moment, the headmaster, Mr Holland, walked into the classroom. He had seen this type of thing before, knew about the bullying and its sad consequences that went on in schools but that the teachers were rarely privy to. Unfortunately, that was the way things were in all schools. Pupils that were bullied just had to toughen up a bit, get some backbone. He looked down at David who, stricken with embarrassment, continued to sit quietly in a wet pool on his classroom chair.

'Pull yourself together, lad,' Mr Holland instructed David. 'And tell me what on earth's the matter.'

David raised his head; his face was full of shame.

'Nothing's the matter, Sir,' he squeaked. 'Just left it too long. I'm really sorry.' His face turned scarlet; not only at the lie, but at the thought that he was telling his headmaster that he was too stupid not to realise when he needed to go to the toilet.

'Anything you want to tell me, Gilmore?'

David would have loved to spill everything to Mr Holland, to have Mr Holland get rid of Steven's gang, to have him put an end to his misery. To tell everyone in the class to just leave him alone.

'No, Sir. Just left it too long, that's all.'

'Well, your punishment will be your discomfort at going home in wet clothes. Now get off with you.' Mr Holland watched David stumble from the classroom. An uneasy admiration for the boy's pride twinkled in his eye.

David crept along the hallway to the cloakroom. He grabbed his coat, slung his satchel over his shoulders and peered out of the boys' school entrance. They weren't there. They must be waiting outside the gate, he reasoned, the Welholme Road gate. He slinked out of the entrance, crossed the boys' playground, ran through the girls' playground and out of the Heneage Road entrance. This was a longer way home, but one he knew. Joy at having escaped his tormentors, at least for today, lent speed to his little legs.

CHAPTER FOUR

The terraced house in Cooper Road was dark and silent as David entered by way of the back door. Whisky, his dad's favourite buddy, greeted him, happy in the knowledge that he would now be fed. David let the dog out into the wilderness of the overgrown back yard and closed the wooden door against the blasts of icy air. He went through the scullery, into the small living-room, out the other side into the front hallway and called up the stairs, 'I'm home, Mam. I'll just stoke up the fire and then I'll bring yer a cuppa.'

'Yer a good lad, our David,' his mother called softly from her bed in the front bedroom but too softly for David to hear.

David poked at the smouldering fire in the grate of the old cast-iron fireplace and put some more coal on it, blowing at the embers until the flames took a proper hold. Then he went into the scullery, let the dog back in and put his bowl of food - leftovers from yesterday's tea - down for him to gobble. Two minutes later, Whisky, satisfied from his meal, crawled back in his old wooden orange box bed, and on top of his green army blanket to await George's homecoming.

David took off his wet pants, filled the deep porcelain sink with water, feeling grateful that it was winter and the fire in the living-room was burning and, therefore, there was warm water in the tank. He rubbed at them lightly with the Imperial Leather soap they all used for washing. After wringing them out, he placed them in the oven at the side of the living-room fire, just like he had seem his mam do before she got too ill to do much at all.

'Ere you are, Mam,' David handed his mother her tea.

'Try not to drop your aitches, lad.' Iris smiled to soften her words. Then, 'Ee, our David, what on earth are yer doing without your trousers?'

'Slipped and fell on the way home, Mam. Got mud and dirty slush all over them. Don't yer worry now. I've washed them and they're drying in the oven already.'

Iris laughed gently, trying not to cough. She knew that if she coughed too hard or had an attack where she couldn't get her breath, David's face would turn white and fear would fill his eyes. So she laughed gently at her son's housewifery ways.

In the last three or four years, Iris Gilmore had had to spend more and more time in bed because of her asthma. Winter was always the worst time of the year for her. The fog and the icy cold would irritate her lungs and stir up her chronic bronchitis.

'You should move to a warmer climate,' Dr Barrowman had suggested, but money was scarce enough in 1959, as people were still trying to pick up the pieces after the war and rebuild what had been shot down. A warmer climate would have to wait. For now she had David and George and they were all she really needed.

She watched David as he nudged with the poker the embers in the grate of the little fire in the bedroom, making them flare up and catch fire to the fresh coals that he had placed on top. Iris's heart filled with love as she watched her son perform this simple task, simple but not really the duty of an eleven-year-old. It occurred to her that David never complained about doing for his mother. He was a good boy, much older than his years. He'd had to carry a lot of burden on those little shoulders. She watched as the fire shot red highlights into David's thick, golden hair. To Iris he was a handsome lad, kind and generous. One day those hazel eyes are going to steal someone's heart, she felt sure of it. His face was square-shaped with strong features, a straight nose and soft, full lips. But although George always saw to it that they had more than enough to eat, David was slow at growing, his body was thin, he wasn't tall and he appeared fragile.

'Go get some trousers on, lad, before yer freeze. Then come back for our little chat.'

David rushed to the back bedroom, threw on his everyday baggy grey trousers and ran back to his mother's bedroom, buttoning them up as he did so. He used the front of his foot to push off the shoe of his other foot. And then climbed, ever so gently, onto the bed to sit facing his mother.

This was the best time of the day for David. Often his mother would take his hands and tell him how life was going to be good for him; how, with hard work, he could achieve anything he wanted to. She would tell him stories of her youth, her strict but loving father, her hard-working mother, her bully of a brother. She made these people come alive, even though David had never met any of them. Iris's mother had died soon after the war and her father had died in action, fighting to keep the old, greasy engine going on a trawler, which was on its way to fight in the Channel. And her brother had married and gone to live in Scotland.

David loved his mother and would have done anything to make her happy. It pained him to see her so ill, to watch her as she attempted to act 'normal'. Her body was weak, but her mind was strong and when she spoke her voice was like music to David's ears. Despite spending most of her time in bed, Iris always looked groomed. A lady came in once a week to help her wash and set her hair and no matter what time of day, she always wore a slight touch of lipstick. You should always have pride in your appearance, she would often tell David. Even her bed jackets were intricate works of art, soft wool crocheted into delicate patterns. David loved his mother.

George didn't love David. At least that is what David thought. He never had talks with his dad. His dad was always withdrawn around him. The only time he spoke to him was when he barked his orders, as if David was someone not really worth bothering with. In fact, George rarely had anything to do with David unless he had to. George was not really an unkindly man. He definitely loved Iris and Whisky, the daft mutt of a dog, and yet he had little time for his son. David spent years, at first trying to win his father's love and then, after hearing the conversation, trying to make up for what he had done to his mother.

Iris had married George just before he was sent off to war. Left alone at a young age in their rented terraced house, the only company she had was the other girls who also worked at the cold store. They would chatter constantly as they mended the fishing nets. Later, when bullets were more important than fish, they all went together to work at the munitions factory. But at night she was alone, looking after the house, their house, George's and hers. It was everything they had between them. And if Jerry thought he was bombing this, he could go ride his bike!

Those were cold and lonely years, often spent in the makeshift bomb-shelter in the back yard. The floor was always steeped in water, the cot damp. Her bronchitis started here and got worse each winter. But she felt wonderful when George finally came home, alive, after the war. They laughed and loved and decorated the house with the meagre amount of money they had. Those were great years. Then David was born. What should have been the happiest occasion of all turned sour when, after giving birth to her son, Iris had her first, near-fatal asthma attack. George blamed David. And David found this out when he heard his dad talking to Iris about that fateful night when, if David hadn't been born, he concluded, she might be all right now. David carried this heavy weight on his thin shoulders.

The sound of footsteps heavy on the wooden stairs was a sign for David to get off the bed. The bedroom door swung open.

'Are you still here, David?' George said. 'You should have put the tatties on by now. And got the table set. Get off with yer. I'll bring Mam down in a minute.'

David heard them deep in conversation as he went downstairs to do his chores. They talked longer than usual and tea was almost ready - boiled beef, carrots and potatoes – before they came down to the scullery, which was now warm because David had stoked up the round black coal-burner in the corner.

It was as the beef and carrots were cooking on the gas stove and Mam was seated at the table nearest to the coal-burner and Whisky was back in his bed after being thoroughly fussed over by George, that his father finally told David what he and his mother had been discussing.

'Your Uncle Tom from Scotland and his family have had a bad accident. They're all dead except Calvin, your cousin. He'll be coming to live with us.'

CHAPTER FIVE

Calvin arrived three days later. He was sitting in the living-room next to the tall black fireplace talking to George, who was sitting in the high-backed armchair on the other side of the fire when David arrived home from school. The fire had already been stoked up and David's first thought was that he wouldn't get his chat with his mother today. He felt sad about that but strangely glad about having someone else in the house, excited even. Mind you, when he saw Calvin, who was supposed to be only thirteen years old, just two years older than David, he thought he looked much older, more worldly. Maybe it's because of the accident, he pondered.

'David, this is Calvin, your cousin.'

David stood awkwardly in the doorway of the living-room. What was he supposed to do? Shake his hand like he'd seen adults do? Hug him? That certainly wouldn't do. The only hugging that went on in this family was when his mother gave him a quick embrace before he went to bed. David mumbled a hello and looked at his right foot, which he was swinging to and fro.

'Stop hanging around there and get in the room, lad!'

David inched inside the living-room door; he kept his gaze down, not wishing to upset his father any more than he'd already done.

'Now listen,' said George. 'Calvin will be sharing your bed for a couple of days until we can move him into the middle bedroom.'

David wasn't sure he liked the sound of that. He only had a single bed. And his bedroom was the smallest in the house. Why was Calvin getting the middle bedroom? It was much bigger than his!

'Right, Dad,' muttered David.

'Go and feed Whisky now, David.'

George's voice had softened a little. He tried not to be too harsh with the lad, but he just couldn't help himself. Someone had to teach him what life was really about; his mother was far too soft with him.

'Then get the spuds on and we'll have some tea. And get changed out of your school clothes, too. Aren't they saying anything about that bright-coloured pullover you're wearing?'

Without waiting for an answer, George left the room taking Calvin upstairs with him to meet Iris.

That night they all had tea together in the scullery.

'It was awful, really awful. I was just on me way to get the buns when it all went up in the air. Can you believe it?' Calvin talked a lot about the accident, explaining he was doing his daily chore of getting the bread rolls for breakfast when it happened and that's why he wasn't in the house. 'Aye, if it wasn't for those buns, I'd be a goner, too.'

Iris desperately wanted to comfort him. But what did you say to someone who had just lost their entire family, and in such a tragic way?

'I'm really sorry, Calvin. Sorry that I never met your mother. And sad that we have to meet this way. Your dad and me sort of lost touch after the war.'

'Oh, he always talked about you, Auntie Iris. Thought a lot about you, he did.'

Iris fell silent. She couldn't remember a time when she and Tom had ever got on well. She'd always thought of him as a bit of a bully. But if he'd always talked about her, as Calvin was saying, then they must have been close and she had failed to see that. She felt guilty and sad that she would now never have the chance to speak to her brother again.

It seemed Calvin wanted to talk, though. He spoke about how close-knit they all were and that the baby had been such a joy. Yes, Dad had been a bit strict but that was his way and he'd said many a time that Calvin needed a firm hand. He even got tears in his eyes at the point when he said how much he was going to miss them, and thank you Uncle George and Auntie Iris for taking him in. He'd make sure not to cause them any trouble. All at the table were deeply sorry for Calvin's loss.

Calvin scanned the faces of his new family. George's face had deep lines from nose to mouth and greying wisps of hair sticking out from his cheeks. He looked worn out and tired. Probably the fault of the fragile, pale-faced Iris who was hogging the stove and kept herself wrapped up with a thick shawl around her shoulders. He knew about weak women. Hadn't his mother been one? She was always shrieking and crying when his dad had tried to beat some sense into her. Silly bitch never stood up to him. No wonder his dad got mad. 'Never give 'em a bloody inch,' he could hear his dad shouting, his words thundering in his head. 'They always take a bloody yard. No bloody good for anything, they aren't.'

He remembered that night well. The meat pie had been slung at the wall. He could still see it slowly sliding down to the floor; could still hear his father screaming that his mam couldn't even cook him a decent meal. He'd have liked to have tasted that pie. His mam had been working on it all day. But he never got the chance. He was sent to bed without his supper that night. Wasn't his fault his mother couldn't cook. He could still remember how his stomach had growled and gurgled in protest. Stupid woman!

David was sent to bed early so George and Iris could speak to Calvin alone. They comforted him for his great loss and promised him security and protection in their home. George didn't say much, he wasn't too happy about the situation as it was but what could he do? Calvin was his wife's nephew, he was family. It stood to reason that they would take him in. Still, he didn't have to be happy about it. In all honesty, he thought, there was enough burden on him already, what with making sure the loan for the house was paid, enough food was on the table and his little building business kept going. It had taken this last thirteen or so years to get back on his feet again after the war. This extra child, well, young man really, his nephew, but a stranger, nevertheless, was nothing more than a hindrance he could have done without. Of, course, Iris would take him under her wing, love him like she loved them all, and make sure he felt welcomed. But then that was sweet, loving Iris through and through.

It was gone ten o'clock before David, already in bed, heard them all coming up the stairs.

'David's bedroom is just there, Cal.' George pointed the way down the little hall leading to the back of the house. 'Just bunk down there for a couple of nights until we get yer sorted out. I got yer registered at Welholme yesterday, as soon as I knew yer were coming, so yer can go with David in the morning. Best get yer into a routine as soon as possible. Keep yer busy. No maudlin' now, lad. Off yer go.'

'Nite, Uncle George, nite, Auntie Iris. Thank you,' came Calvin's polite reply before heading for the back bedroom.

David leaned out of bed to light the candle on his bedside table, which was really only another orange box, like Whisky's bed, but his mother had covered it with brown fabric and it looked like a shop-bought one now. The switch for the ceiling light was over by the door and it was too cold to get out of bed. Also he wasn't allowed to turn the light on after he'd gone to bed; his dad said the electricity was too expensive to waste. David liked his bedroom. On top of the brown linoleum there was a rag rug that his mother had made. The room had a single bed, a hard-backed chair for putting the clothes he was wearing on and a brass hook on the back of the door for his other clothes. The curtains were made from an old army blanket and worked very well at keeping the cold out, a lot better than the thin curtains Mam made Dad put up in summer. But despite this measure, the ice would form on the inside of the bedroom window. Yes, he liked his bedroom. It offered him security and safety from his father's black moods and he wasn't sure at all if he wanted to share it. Still, it was only for a couple of days and Calvin must feel awful at losing his parents.

'Hiya,' he said in way of welcome as Calvin walked in the door.

'Hi,' Calvin gave him a broad grin. 'Sorry about this, old chap. Still it's only for a couple of days. We can manage till then, no doubt.' Calvin loosened his tie.

Christ, thought David. He not only looks grown-up; he even speaks like a toff. Wonder where he learnt that? Calvin proceeded to take off his jacket and trousers. They were obviously new. He looked around him and threw them on the back of the chair without folding them, over David's things.

'Nice parents,' Calvin commented. 'Bet your dad doesn't knock you around like my dad used to do? Still, he won't be doing that any more.' The broad smile covered Calvin's face once again. 'Life's looking good, old chum. We're going to be like brothers; have some fun and stuff.'

Again that smile. David was mesmerised. When Calvin smiled, his aura of seriousness disappeared and his whole face lit up into a mischievous little boy's grin. A flash of great sympathy swept over David. And in that moment he knew he liked Calvin. Indeed, he just felt that he would like him even before they became friends. And something told him that life would be different now and Calvin would be the one to make it different.

'It won't be so bad,' said David moving over in the bed and holding open the covers for Calvin to crawl in. 'Look, I'm really rather small. I don't take up much room.'

'Aye, that you are; small, I mean. Don't they feed you?'

'Yeah, of course. Mam says I'll grow big later.'

'Aye, yer a wee laddie, as me father would say, but you look strong. Your mam's probably right.'

With the exception of his mother, who always said good things to him, this was the first positive thing David had heard about himself from another person. His heart leapt at the compliment. And when he thought about it, yes, he was quite strong. That probably came from carrying the coal in and out all the time.

Calvin stood on the rag rug in his underclothes. He was tall for thirteen and well formed: broad-shouldered, slim hips and long legs with prominent thigh muscles. He had black hair, which shone blue whenever it caught the light, a long straight nose, and the bluest of eyes that David had ever seen. His face was long and slim, and rather aristocratic-looking. David thought for a moment, then decided that Calvin looked a bit like the poet, Lord Byron. He'd seen a picture of that Byron chap in English Literature class at school. Yes, indeed, Calvin had that intense look about him like a brooding poet. Even to David's untrained eye, he knew that Calvin was a beautiful-looking human being. Yes, he decided, he liked Calvin and could already feel himself falling under his magical spell.

'I'm real sorry about your family, Calvin,' said David, shyly. He didn't know how to speak to someone who had just lost his whole family in one go. He knew that if it had been him, he would have been so devastated that he wouldn't have been able to speak at all.

'Aye, a sad loss. A sad loss, indeed,' chirped Calvin. 'Now, laddie, let's get some sleep.' Calvin got into bed beside David. He blew out the candle and snuggled under the covers. 'Big day tomorrow, new school, new friends, new life. Hang on to me, Davie laddie, and you'll have a good time.'

David didn't know what to answer to that. A new life sounded good; anything would be better than this old one where his dad was distant and cold to him and the kids at school bullied him. Main thing was his mother appeared to be getting stronger, and that made him happy. More often than not, she came down to join them for tea these days.

David lay there, still, in the dark room. Within minutes, Calvin's heavy breathing signalled his deep sleep. But David felt wide-awake and kept going over the day's events. He wondered what Calvin had meant by having a good time. School was not his idea of having a good time. Tomorrow, he'd have to face Steven and his gang of bullies again, just like any other day. When Calvin saw how they treated him, and how David would run away if he got the chance, he would think that his cousin wasn't as strong as he first thought. David went to sleep wishing this night, this new friendship, this feeling of camaraderie could go on forever. But he knew that with the dawn and his arrival at school, Calvin's opinion of him would change drastically.

CHAPTER SIX

David didn't get his chat with his mother again that next morning. By 8.30am he and Calvin were already on their way to school, even though the walk usually only took about fifteen to twenty minutes. It had snowed in the night and the snow lay thick on the ground, the cold seeping through David's thin-soled shoes and into his legs. He pulled his school blazer tighter around his thin chest and silently thanked his mother for knitting his new pullover in thick, warm wool. Up they walked, past the terraced houses of Cooper Road with their tiny front yards and low walls showing just the stubs of the railings that his mother had told him were sawn off to help the war effort. They crossed busy Ladysmith Road, went through the cutting of the old canning factory and up into Welholme Road. The school loomed, big and austere, before them.

'Well, here we are,' said David. 'Dad said you'll have to go to Mr Holland's office first. He's the headmaster. It's at the end of the hallway, on the right. I'll see you at break time.'

As David started to walk off, Calvin called, 'Where're you going, Davie?'

'I'll see yer in the playground at break. And don't go over there. That's where the girls' playground starts. See yer later.'

David spun round and pointed to the invisible boundary line between the two playgrounds, then turned and walked quickly away. With his head bent down, his chin nearly touching his chest, and his eyes darting left to right, he headed for the toilets, a lone building at the side of the playground. It was imperative that he get there before anyone saw him; more exactly, before Steven or any of his gang saw him. Every morning he would do this: hide behind the toilet building until the bell rang and they would have to line up in twos to enter the school in orderly lines. Even then he wasn't really safe, for they would squirm and push until they were behind him. Then they would push and shove him, trying to get him out of the line. David would do his best to ignore them, even when he felt a knee ram into his back. He always just looked straight ahead as if they didn't exist. Upon entering the school, David would rush to his classroom and to his desk where he could relax a little. Here, in front of the teacher, they had no choice other than to leave him alone. He was safe, at least until break time.

Oh, crikey, thought David. What on earth will Calvin think of me when he sees the others knocking me around and hears them calling me names? Once in the classroom, David sat, stern-faced and silent on his stool, wishing that the morning's lessons would never end.

The morning break bell sounded too soon for David. Every day at this time he was forced to make a choice: to either rush out ahead of Steven and try to find somewhere where they couldn't find him, or to wait until he was the last in the classroom and try and avoid them as he slipped out of the building. Both ways were not always successful. Today he chose to rush out of the classroom and the school building. He looked around until he spotted the duty-teacher and positioned himself nearby. They surely wouldn't start if he were standing near the teacher, he thought. However, luck wasn't with David on this frosty morning as one of the younger pupils, in his haste to get to his bottle of milk, fell and grazed his knee. The playground teacher picked him up and brushed him off, then helped the snivelling child back into the school building, leaving David alone.

David scanned the playground. He couldn't see Steven's gang, decided it looked safe and walked off in the direction of the canteen, where his milk would be waiting for him. It would be frozen, of course, but still good. The only milk they had at home was just for tea, not for drinking on its own, seeing as it was too expensive. Between the three of them – now four – they only had one pint to last the whole day. Here, at school, he got a whole third of a pint to himself and he always drank it gratefully, enjoying every last drop.

Suddenly, as he was sucking on the bottle, trying to get the frozen milk to thaw a little and slide into his mouth, the bottle was struck from his hand. Sharp fingernails caught his cheek and left three scratches there, which started to well up and bleed. The bottle fell to the ground and shattered. The frozen milk sat there in the middle of the pieces of glass. Immediately the clump of ice started to melt in the faint rays of the February sun.

'No milk for you, Titch. It might make you big and strong. And we don't want that, do we? It would spoil our fun. And what would we call you then, Titch?' Steven sneered and looked around at his mates who laughed in agreement.

'Hey! Steve, look,' called Rod, pointing at David's face. 'Let's give him another three on the other cheek to match those.'

David's hand flew to his face, touching it gently where it was starting to smart. He brought his fingers down and looked at them; they were bloody. His eyes flashed hatred at Steven. Anger was making his breath come in short, sharp little rasps. He stood firm, arms at his side, fists clenched into tight little balls. He desperately wanted to lash out at them all but knew if he did, they'd slaughter him and, anyway, no matter what they did to him, his mother would be disappointed if she saw he'd been fighting.

Another of the gang grabbed for his pullover. 'Still got this tatty thing on, Gilmore?' he spat, taking a handful of David's jumper.

Steven twisted and tugged with all his might, pulling David off balance. David's hands flew to the bully's wrists, trying to make him let go of the pullover.

'Get off, get off,' he screamed. Where's that damn teacher? The thought rushed through David's mind. He knew he was doomed. The teacher wouldn't be back soon enough to save him from a beating. And even though he would thrash and punch as best he could, they would get the better of him, they always did. They'd leave him bruised and bloody as usual. His father would then tell him off for fighting and then ignore him completely for the evening, and his mother would look at him with disappointment and ask him why he had to get into so many scrapes.

David raised his hands to ward off the blows to his head. He could feel his legs giving way beneath him. Abruptly, one hand in particular grabbed hold of him under the arm and dragged him out of the centre of the gang. David looked up, expecting to get a blow to the face.

Calvin's form loomed over him. He pushed David to one side, placed his hands on his hips, and turned to face the gang of boys that had just been beating up his cousin. He towered above them.

'Right! You bastards! Deal with me.' Calvin lurched forward, seized Steven by the throat while at the same time giving Rod a hefty kick in the shins. The other boys were so shocked at such wild treatment that they were momentarily unable to move. Calvin lashed out, his fists connecting with flesh every time. Shouts and squeals went up from the bullies. Within seconds a circle of yelling boys had gathered around them. David, fresh courage raging through his veins, threw himself into the mêlée. Urged on by Calvin's seeming invincibility, he found new and extreme strength. Together with his cousin, his Superman of a cousin, he fought the boys who had been making his life a misery. The crowd hooted and yelled their approval at what was going on before their eyes. One by one Steven's gang of hooligans left the throng surrounding the fighting boys. They had to run the gauntlet of getting through the circle of cheering boys to get away and were helped on their separate journeys by being pushed and propelled forcibly from the crowd. By the time the teacher returned to the playground upon hearing the commotion, Calvin was being carried on the shoulders of the school's strong-bodied fatty, another victim of the gang's bullying. Calvin was laughing down at those who carried him.

He raised his fist to the heavens and cried, 'Fisher and Gilmore! A team to be reckoned with.'

The crowd went crazy. David stared up in awe at his cousin. Yes, indeedy, life really was going to be different now that Calvin Fisher, his hero, had entered it.

CHAPTER SEVEN

The little terraced house in Cooper Road, Grimsby, took on a different hue for David after Calvin's arrival. For one, his father started to talk more: not to him, of course, but to Calvin. Listening to their conversations, David learnt about the life Calvin had endured prior to his moving in with them. His father, Tom Fisher, Iris's brother, had been a bully, somewhat like Steven, it seemed. He had beaten Calvin daily for the smallest of sins. Calvin only had to be five minutes late returning from school and his father, home all day after being medically discharged with a small pension from the army, would take the belt to him.

Calvin's father had a heavy cross to bear. He had been a prisoner of war. The torture he had endured during his years as prisoner of war had left him quietly screaming inside his abused body. Calvin told them how he would sit for hours at a time with a vacant look on his face, staring off into the distance, reliving past horrors too terrible to talk about. His pain had manifested itself in a brutality directed against the son he knew wasn't from his seed. The matter of Calvin's birth in 1946, when Tom Fisher was still in the cruel hands of his captors, had never been openly discussed. But as he grew older, Calvin knew.

All these intimate details were a bit embarrassing for George to stomach. He was amazed at how grown-up Calvin appeared to be for his thirteen years. He talked and acted like an adult. Needn't bloody come here with his airs and graces, he brooded. And yet, he had to admit that, as far as he was concerned, the Fishers had not been without a bob or two. They'd had a telly by 1953. That he knew for sure because Iris's sister had written about seeing the Coronation on the damn thing. Bloody boasting, that was. Maybe this was why Calvin talked so posh for a Scot, what with all that BBC plum-in-the-mouth speaking going on. And, if Calvin was to be believed, they always got all the new appliances as soon as they appeared in the shops. Well, who cares? It's all gone now: went up in the explosion, it did. Still, George felt sorry for this lad's lot. He had been blamed for what his mother had done. He had been bullied. He had been browbeaten and intimidated. And yet, this young man seemed to have loved his parents all the same. He spoke only with understanding of his father's plight. He accepted without question his father's obvious favouritism of Calvin's younger brother.

George's heart finally opened a crack to let this charming young man in. He was amazed at his resilience, at his quiet acceptance of the tragedy of his parents' deaths and at the loss of his little brother. All in all, Calvin totally won George over. George leant over from his place in the armchair next to the fireplace in the living-room to reach Calvin sitting opposite him and gently squeezed his shoulder before patting him lightly and saying, 'Yep, life can be hard, me lad. We've just gotta get on with it.'

David saw this and experienced a strange feeling in his stomach. He'd never seen his father touch anyone except his mother. He wondered if Calvin might become a problem for him when he heard him say, 'Aye, it can that, Uncle George. It can that. But I'm the lucky one. I've got a new family and a great new brother. I can't tell you how grateful I am to you and Auntie Iris.' And with these words, Calvin gave a little wink to David who was sitting on a stool in the corner of the small room.

David was fascinated with Calvin. He really was so grown-up. Tall and handsome, he had a way about him that seemed to charm the birds off the trees. Even his father liked him, spoke to him like a grown-up. Spoke to him! But most of all, Calvin seemed to like him, David. And having a friend close by would fulfil David's dreams. Calvin would be his big brother. He would learn from him. He would follow his example and ask Calvin to teach him to also be charming and grown up; because if Calvin could soften some of George's harshness, he must be the cleverest person in the world. Maybe his father would start to talk to him next.

But George didn't change one bit in his attitude towards David.

Mealtimes would see Calvin and George quietly discussing George's work. He was getting more work, now he was becoming known in the neighbourhood. All the long hours of hard labour and being prepared to take on little jobs of all descriptions was starting to pay off. But he was getting fed up of working on his own and he hoped that when Calvin left school in a couple of years, he might think about joining him in the family business, as George started to call it.

Yet David never felt jealous of his cousin, for he had brought light into David's life and although his father was still off-hand and distant from him, his mother's love, together with Calvin's friendship, more than made up for his father's behaviour. Even Iris's health seemed to improve with Calvin's arrival. Her coughing bouts became less often and she hadn't had a serious asthma attack for ages now. She was strong enough to join them each evening for tea, sometimes she even managed to cook. And it didn't irk Calvin at all that the two of them had to wash up afterwards. If only I could be more like him, thought David often. Calvin was jolly, could talk to almost anyone, was always smiling and certainly the most handsome lad in the school. David knew this because he had heard some of the girls in the playground say so.

Ah, school. How that had changed since that fateful day. Steven and his gang of thugs left him alone nowadays. David was no longer afraid of what would happen to him at the break times and on the way home. It made paying attention to what the teacher was saying a lot easier and his marks soared. He found he enjoyed his lessons, was good at Maths and came top of the class in English and Geography. Calvin had made this all possible for him. What a wonderful pal, more like a brother, really.

Break times were totally different, too. Calvin and David spent these together. They walked round the playground and when they were teased as being 'shorty and lofty' or 'the tall and the short of it' or even 'David and Goliath', Calvin would laugh his infectious laugh and put his arm around David's shoulders and say, 'They're talking about us, Davie me lad.' Before roaring with laughter.

Yes, verily, life was good.

What David didn't see, and even if he did he didn't acknowledge it, was that sometimes Calvin's mood would change abruptly. His whole stance would change in a second. He could suddenly lose his smile and his charm and his face would turn to thunder. His twinkling blue eyes would cloud over and spark off a dark emotional haze that would engulf him in a sort of veil of evil.

At these moments Calvin kept away from David. He could feel and see the hero-worship that his actions had evoked in this gullible child and decided to stay in that role of hero always for David. It was useful to him. Now he was rid of his parents and that little shit of a brother, he was on his way to being his own man. The Gilmores could make the transition easier for him. He felt quite pleased with himself and his results. He was loved by David, fussed over by Iris and admired and respected by George. Oh, yes. Calvin's talent for hiding his real self developed to perfection in those first few years at Cooper Road and Welholme School.

CHAPTER EIGHT

There had been many changes in the last couple of years since Calvin's arrival at Cooper Road. For one, there was an additional armchair near the fireplace. Of an evening, George, Iris and Calvin would sit near the cosy fire, with its large black ovens flanking either side of it, discussing the day's events and laughing at life's little oddities. David still preferred to sit on the stool in the corner. He'd join in the conversation when his mother asked him direct questions, usually about school, but preferred to remain quiet, just observing the others. Family life had definitely improved since Calvin's arrival. As soon as his cousin walked into the house, it came to life. Within minutes of entering the place, he would turn off the new television, switch the radio on, do a little jig with Iris to make her laugh, and get George a beer. He brought with him a joyfulness that none of them had known before.

Iris was up and about for a few hours every day now. It had been a while since she had had a really bad asthma attack, and as long as she kept her chronic bronchitis under control with medicine from the doctor and ate the good food they could now afford, she continued to improve noticeably. Every day they had meat, eggs and butter as well as large quantities of Flowery Pekoe Tips tea. She thrived on this fare and was able to make the evening meal each day and wash up afterwards, seeing as the lads were getting a bit too old to be doing woman's work.

George still basically ignored David, but his relationship with Calvin had gone from strength to strength, especially when Calvin had agreed to join George in his one-man building business after he finished school. He wasn't fifteen until September, and so couldn't leave school until that coming Christmas. How George looked forward to having family help him. Calvin was swiftly becoming more than a nephew. He was the son George had wished he'd had.

George's business was getting better and better. Money wasn't so scarce these days, as more jobs became available. Only the Freeman Street market area was still not completely rebuilt after the bombings. The pain caused by the loss of many of the town's men folk was finally fading into the background. Trawlers and seine-net boats were making regular trips once more, the fishermen on shore frequenting the pubs and leaving the rest of their money with the ladies of the night – that's if the wife didn't get it first. Grimsby was enjoying a new prosperity, a staggering economical rise.

Builders like George were doing all right for themselves. He'd perfected the art of changing the outside lavatories, which were to be found in most of the small terraced houses in the town, into inside bathrooms, attached to the back of the scullery. This was a wonderful improvement on the old outside bog. The neighbours, seeing this, all wanted a posh inside lavatory, and so work was pouring in. Besides this, sculleries suddenly became kitchens by having their pantries knocked out, stone tiles put down and deep porcelain sinks replaced by new smaller ones. George's order book started to swell admirably. He was a good builder. He was quick. And he was reasonably priced. Business was simply booming.

Although Calvin could have won any popularity contest and was as street-smart as anyone could be, his school marks did not reflect this. He was just biding his time at school, waiting to get on his way, feeling held back in his plans. He paid little attention to the teachers, and they consequently all but ignored him. Christmas would be the time when, as he considered it, life would really start for him. At last! Some money of his own!

David had watched all these changes with fascination. It didn't bother him too much that his father openly preferred Calvin to him. He loved Calvin so much that he could forgive him anything. He still had his little private chats with his mother in the morning before going off to school and she always made him feel special.

Life around Calvin was exciting. Although only fifteen, he had a girlfriend, or to be more exact, girlfriends. Of course, George and Iris knew nothing about this. Most evenings, all of them would go to bed early and within minutes, George's soft snoring could be heard from the front bedroom. That was Calvin's signal to creep from the middle bedroom along the hallway into David's room and out of his window. He'd slide along the roof of the new bathroom, drop down onto the dividing wall between the terraced houses, and be off for the night. Often David would not even hear his return. But Calvin was always in his bed in the mornings. So no one except David knew of these little excursions. And Calvin knew that David would always keep his secret.

One evening, they were sitting in the living-room with the radio on as usual. David was in the corner listening to the conversation between George and Calvin; Iris was in the scullery washing up – she could be heard to be singing along with the radio; and George was stroking the dog, which was now allowed in the living-room. Calvin leant over from his armchair and dragged Whisky off George's lap.

'Uncle George! You're always fussing that silly dog. How about a game of draughts?' he urged laughing.

But George had had a tiring day and so had no wish to play draughts. He yawned. 'I think I'll go up now. Be a good lad and put Whisky in the back yard before yer come up yerself.'

George heaved himself out of his chair by the fire and, calling to Iris to follow him, went upstairs to bed. Calvin put Whisky in the yard, checked that there was enough water in the dog's bowl, fluffed up the blanket in his little wooden house built especially for Whisky by George, and closed and locked the back door before going to bed himself.

David was just drifting off to sleep when Calvin came in, crossed the room and climbed out of the bedroom window. He murmured, ''Night, 'night. Have a good time.'

A few seconds later, he thought he heard Whisky giving a pained yelp. He listened for a while but, hearing nothing else, floated peacefully off to sleep.

The next morning David was woken by a commotion in the scullery. George called up the stairs for Calvin to get up. David, hearing the call, met Calvin on the stairs and they swiftly ran down to see what was the matter with George.

'Where's Whisky?' George immediately asked Calvin as he entered the scullery.

'I don't know,' came Calvin's shocked reply. 'Whatever's the matter?'

David stood there, silent.

'He's gone!' moaned George looking out at the back yard as if pleading eyes alone would bring him back.

'Gone where?' asked David.

'Oh, shut up, David. Gone, I said. He's got out of the yard somehow, you little fool. Didn't you hear anything?'

'No, Dad.' David murmured. He looked at the floor, avoiding George's eyes, afraid to say anything else to upset his dad.

'I'll go look for him, Uncle George. Now don't you worry.' And with that Calvin sped out of the back door, out of the yard and down the passage in search of the lost dog.

It was only half an hour later that Calvin returned, breathless, carrying Whisky in his arms. The dog was dead.

'Oh, Uncle George. I'm so sorry. I found him down by the dike over by Humberston Road. His collar was caught up on a branch. He must have strangled himself. Oh, Uncle George! I'm really sorry. There was nothing I could do.'

And with that, Calvin gently put the limp body of the dead dog into George's arms. George lowered his head into the fur of his beloved pet, Whisky, and wept like a child.

There was no work that day for George, nor was there any school for Calvin. Together they buried Whisky in the back yard, in the hard ground running alongside the wall where flowers should have been and only an abundance of weeds now grew. They drove a little wooden cross into the small mound of dark earth then stood solemnly in silence at the little grave, Calvin's arm around the shaking shoulders of his uncle. George sobbed without restraint. They burnt the wooden dog's house and threw the drinking bowl into the tin dustbin. And then they drank a brandy together, commiserating over their loss.

That evening, with David sitting on his stool in the corner of the room, Iris already in bed because she was having a bad day and George and Calvin seated by the fire, Calvin asked, 'Let's have a game of draughts, Uncle George. It'll take your mind off things.'

'Right yer are, Cal.' George looked at him out of red-rimmed eyes. 'You're a good lad, our Cal,' said George nodding his head absently.

Calvin went to get the black and white pieces. That will teach him not to want to play draughts with me, he thought, remembering how the damn dog had whimpered and struggled.

CHAPTER NINE

The playground rocked with the cheerful cries of kids playing, running around, screeching and shouting at each other. Little groups and cliques huddled together, whispering their secrets, making their plans for later. But David didn't see or hear any of this. His world was as grey as the concrete of the playground, as dark as the red-bricked buildings and their old-fashioned, tall paned windows. It had just rained and now the sun, peeking from behind a summer cloud, was reflecting that greyness back at him.

School was strangely lonely without Calvin. He'd been left now for some six months and David was struggling to get through his school days without his hero by his side. The bullies didn't bother him at all; in fact, no one bothered him, or even talked to him very much. He had always been the other half of 'lofty and titch' and now he was missing that celebrity status.

David had lost all interest in school. Although he had been told that if he applied himself, he was intelligent enough to go on to college, maybe even university. He would be the first in the Gilmore family to achieve such intellectual success if he did, but all David wanted to do was to finish school as soon as possible and join his dad and Calvin in the family business. They seemed to be having so much fun.

Calvin was inching towards sixteen now and worked long hard days labouring diligently alongside George. When they got home, David felt shut out as George and Calvin talked non-stop about what had to be done, what had to be ordered and what the next job was going to be. They would sit next to the old fireplace after having washed themselves in the scullery sink and changed into clean clothes, both George and Calvin enjoying a beer. 'If the lad can work, then the lad can have a drink,' George would always say to no one in particular. It was plain to see that George's affection belonged to his nephew. And he paid him well.

This meant that David rarely saw Calvin even at the weekends when he wasn't working. Calvin spent his money going out and enjoying himself. He'd earned this relaxation time, he always told David. And indeed he had. Calvin worked hard. David would join him on his jaunts in a year or so when he left school. For now he was simply lonely.

In the evenings when Calvin went out, he would sit in the armchair next to the fireplace talking to his mother. George would be snoozing in the other chair.

'You're growing up quick, our David,' said Iris, reaching over and stroking David's unruly curls one evening. 'It won't be long before you'll be out chasing the girls along with Calvin. Just be patient, love.'

'I'm all right, Mam,' replied David, moving his head away from his mother's caress. He felt too old to be seen welcoming open displays of motherly affection these days.

A silence fell over the little group. Both Iris and David sat, contented simply in each other's company. The only sound to be heard above George's steady snoring was the turning of pages as Iris read the evening newspaper they now always had delivered to their door.

'Cor blimey, our David! Take a look at this. Whatever is Grimsby coming to?' Iris folded the large pages over, dividing the size by half and handed the newspaper to David, pointing to the headlines at the top of the page. 'Read that,' she commanded.

David took the newspaper from her hand and moved nearer to the fire for its light. He read the article his mother was referring to, disbelief and disgust creeping into his face as the words spelled out the story.

'This is awful, Mam. Three cases of assault, and one girl murdered. The streets ain't safe anymore.' He coloured up in embarrassment at the thought of discussing anything sexual with his mother. But without actually saying it explicitly, that's what the newspaper had implied.

'I don't know what Grimsby's coming to,' Iris repeated. 'It were never like this before and during the war. Yer could leave yer door open and nobody ever nicked anything and a woman and kids were safe on the streets if Jerry weren't dropping bombs on 'em. Ee, by gum. I hope our Calvin's all right. He never says what he gets up to. Still, he's a good lad. Looks after yer dad, he does.' Iris saw the look of disappointment cloud David's face. 'It'll be your turn soon, me lad. Just yer see about finishing school, and then it'll be your turn. That'll be all three of me men working then. Maybe we could get one of those posh televisions, one with a nice wooden cabinet. What d'yer say, our David?'

'Yeah, Mam. That'd be nice.' David's mind was already somewhere else. He was just hoping that the girl he had seen in the playground the other day wasn't out, wasn't walking on the dangerous streets, hoping she didn't live anywhere near where the murder took place, hoping she wasn't falling into the arms of some brutal rapist right this minute.

A mental picture of the girl filled David's imagination.

It had been just a couple of weeks ago that he'd seen her for the first time. Maybe it was because he didn't usually stand around near the boundary line because the teachers made such a fuss if any boy tried to mix with the girls. But on this day he had. The headmaster had asked him to find Jimmy McKenzie and tell him to report to his office immediately. Jimmy had been standing with a group of friends near the boundary line.

'Hey, Jimmy!' David had yelled, running up to him. 'Mr Holland wants to see you in his office. What yer been up to, then?'

Jimmy left without a word. The group started to break up. That was when he saw her.

As his eyes fell upon her, he got a strange light feeling in his stomach that travelled down to his groin and made his thighs shiver. He must have been staring for quite some time for, suddenly, she looked up, directly at him. She was the most beautiful creature he had ever seen. She was small and doll-like. She had straight shoulder-length black hair, a pert little heart-shaped face, a small up-turned nose with a smattering of what looked like freckles on it and big round eyes that were so light in their colour of grey that they seemed to pierce straight into his heart. This is what it must feel like to be struck by lightning, he thought. He couldn't tear his eyes away from her. The realisation filled his very soul that this girl would be someone special to him, someone with whom he would share much, someone who would fill his future.

She was so near, just the other side of the boundary line. He desperately wanted to speak to her, to ask her name, to stand next to her, to touch her. Of course, he said nothing, just kept on staring. Speak! God damn you, he admonished himself silently. But no words would come. She smiled at him; his heart melted. Then her friend nudged her in the side and she broke out in giggles. What music to his ears! The end-of-break bell rang and her friends dragged her away. He stood watching until he couldn't see her any more. He was late to class that day.

CHAPTER TEN

In the autumn of 1962, the Mecca Dance Hall in Wintringham Road was Grimsby's most popular venue for adolescents and young adults. Everybody who was anybody went there. Above the large rectangular dance floor there was a balcony that surrounded the hall, leaving the middle free of a second storey and making a high ceiling for the dance floor. Here a large mirrored ball hung on which spotlights were directed. Moving beams of light played upon the dancers below. There was a coffee bar at one end of the balcony for those guests who were under eighteen and, therefore, not allowed in the licensed bar which was situated at the back of the stage at the opposite end of the dance hall downstairs. The coffee bars were experiencing a great success in Grimsby by the early sixties. Young adults, not yet old enough to go into licensed premises congregated there, much in the same way older adults gathered in pubs and bars. The coffee bar on the balcony in the Mecca Dance Hall was famous for its décor; lots of adjoining brown-painted papier-mâché caves. It represented caves to be found in a mountain. The effect was very life-like and oh so modern. In the low lights, each little group huddled together around the small circular tables in the caves sitting either on the red plush banks or small stools fashioned to resemble rocks. The girls showed off their best frocks, made wide by lots of net petticoats and the boys sported proper blazers with shirts, collars and always a tie. This was where the social scene was happening in Grimsby; this was Calvin's favourite haunt.

Calvin liked to keep his activities to himself. Certainly George and Iris didn't always have to know his business; in fact, it didn't do for anyone to know where he was and with whom. People were just too damn nosy these days. He really didn't like for people to know what he was doing. For one, George would always complain when he went out and came back late, like he did most weekends. He'd gripe about him not getting enough sleep and being too tired to work. George did very little other than demand more work out of him. And then there was good old Iris. She'd moan because she worried about him when he was out, what with all the crime going on in the streets these days. What a tiresome nature that woman had. All in all, George and Iris liked to interfere far too much, thought Calvin.

And so most of Calvin's week evenings were spent here at the Mecca after he'd made a show of going up to bed at the same time as the rest of the family, waited for George and Iris to fall asleep, and had climbed out of David's bedroom window. That way, as far as George and Iris were concerned, Calvin was safely tucked up in his bed. And David never made a fuss.

'Your turn in a year or so, Davie, me old chum. We'll go together then,' Calvin would console David as he pushed open the sash window ever so slowly, so it wouldn't creak and groan like it had done before he rubbed the grooves with the stub of a candle. David would turn over in bed, wishing his life away, wishing the next year could fly by.

Calvin would always visit the bar first and have a beer, just one. He certainly didn't want to get like George who swilled the stuff down like he wasn't going to get any more, ever. The bar was usually filled with men just like him, few women. Calvin liked to call himself a man, even though he was still only just turned sixteen. He looked much older, had the air of a man who knew where he was going, knew what he wanted from life and was on his way to getting it. Then he would roam the coffee bar.

People used the coffee bar and the balcony as a kind of promenade deck. Here, boys and girls, men and women, would slowly walk the entire circle, only to turn round and retrace their steps. The idea was to be seen and to see what was available in the way of partners. This was where people met each other, where courtships were formed, when the preliminaries to marriage and future life together took place. This was Calvin's hunting ground.

Calvin had been back in the bar and had three beers before he had finally found someone suitable in the coffee bar. She was sitting alone in a cave alcove, drinking coffee. Her skirt was high above her knees. He could see her thighs as she sat there. And her blouse was tight and low, exposing the top of lush pink breasts as she leaned forward to drink her coffee. Her bleached hair was teased up in a large bouffant. Calvin imagined messing that hairdo up. She was not overly attractive and she looked lonely sat there stirring her coffee around and around. She lifted her head as he made to slowly pass the table, looking him squarely in the eyes. She smiled expectantly.

'Hiya,' said Calvin, a smile creeping over his face and lighting it up. He stood straight, flipped his long black hair back out of his face and, giving her a glimpse of his magnificent blue eyes and dazzling grin, said, 'You fancy a dance?'

The girl gazed long and hard at Calvin. You heard such stories these days: stories about rape and even murder. Her mam had warned her to be careful. The murder in the newspaper just recently had shocked everyone. No one could remember the last time there had been a murder in Grimsby, she'd said. But this man didn't appear dangerous at all, at least not in that way, she laughed to herself. And she couldn't help but return his beautiful greeting with a broad smile of her own. He held out his hand. She put hers in his, mesmerised by his deep blue eyes that sparkled even in the dim light.

'All right,' she said, getting up from the table and leaving her coffee.

They went down the staircase and onto the dance floor still hand in hand. Everyone was jiving to the lively music and he made to do the same with her when the tempo changed. The lights lowered and the fast music was replaced by the mellow tones of Nat King Cole.

Calvin took the girl in his arms. 'What's your name, lovely lady?' he breathed in her ear. She lifted herself on tiptoe to whisper, 'Christine.'

'You are one beautiful lady, Christine,' he murmured before entwining her just a little tighter in his arms. Together they danced under the shimmering, twirling light of the mirrored ball. The light from the tiny mirrors would fall upon her face and Calvin would draw back to look at her. Oh, he thought, seeing her eyes closed and a smile on her face, this one will be easy.

The dance ended, he kept hold of her hand. 'Allow me to buy you a drink, Lady Christine,' he offered.

'But I'm not eighteen yet,' came the honest reply.

'But you could easily pass for eighteen,' said Calvin, safe in the knowledge acquired from past experiences that girls this age liked to be told they looked older than they were.

'Okay,' she said, colouring up at the thought of the compliment. 'By the way, what's your name?'

'John,' replied Calvin.

CHAPTER ELEVEN

The bar of the Mecca Dance Hall took up the entire far wall of the rectangular room. It had two entrances opposite the bar, one either side of the stage. The tables were standard round ones just large enough to hold a few glasses and an over-sized ashtray. Simple wooden stools and chairs surrounded them. Although the music could be heard plainly, it was still at a reasonable level, which made conversation possible. Designed more for men to stand around drinking, it didn't have the comfort or the cosy atmosphere of the coffee bar upstairs. But Christine didn't see her surroundings; she only had eyes for Calvin and stared up at him in adoration.

'So John, where are you from? I can hear an accent but not one I recognise. You come in on the trawlers?' she asked. That was usually the case when a man had a strange accent. He was probably in from Iceland and wouldn't be staying in town very long. At the thought, Christine's face clouded visibly with disappointment. They reached a table and she sat down.

'Fancy a Bacardi and coke?' the man she knew as John asked her. She nodded her agreement. She'd never drunk a Bacardi and coke before. But it was the drink of the moment so she was sure it must be nice. Anyway, drinking alcohol made her appear older and Christine desperately wanted to be perfect for this man she had just met.

When Calvin returned to the table with the two drinks, she repeated her question about where he came from. She picked up the tall glass and gulped at her drink. It was indeed tasty and she took a couple more swigs at it before putting the glass down on the table between them.

'Aye, lass. I'm a fisherman,' Calvin said. 'I'm only in for two more days. But I'll be back next month. Let's have some fun while we can.'

At this, Calvin leaned over and kissed her gently on the corner of her mouth. He pulled back to see her reaction, smiling beguilingly at her. Her thick, bright pink lipstick had smeared onto her chin but he didn't say anything.

'What are you staring at, John?' Excitement flushed her cheeks and she dropped her eyes from his face, shyness at her romantic thoughts making her look away.

With a gentle finger, Calvin lifted her head until their eyes met again; with his thumb he wiped away the smudged lipstick. 'I'm just thinking how pretty you are. And how I hope I can see you tomorrow and that maybe you might be waiting for me on my return from my next trip.' She looks a bit of a mess, Calvin thought to himself; one drink and her eyes are already bloodshot and glazed. Her smile was wobbly, too. He flashed her one of his blinding cheeky grins. 'Can I walk you home?' he asked like a gentleman.

'I live up near Freeman Street, quite a hike from here.' Christine suddenly realised that the last bus had already left. With or without this new man, she would have to walk home. Rather have some company and maybe a kiss or two than walk home alone. And this chap was really handsome! Besides the fact you never knew who you were going to meet on the streets these days; they were positively dangerous.

'That's great!' exclaimed Calvin. 'I'm near there at the Fishermen's Mission. Come on. Drink up. Let's go.'

They emptied their glasses and stood up. Christine's stool fell backward and clattered to the floor.

'No matter,' said Calvin putting his arm around her shoulders and steering her towards the door of the bar, through the dance hall and out of the building onto the streets. Christine giggled. She leant her body into the crook of Calvin's arm and put her arm around his waist. Together they set out for Freeman Street.

David was dreaming. In his dream, he stood on an open plain. He could see himself clearly. He was alone. He felt alone. A mist, a deep fog arose around him. Then he saw that Calvin and his mother stood opposite him in the swirling mist. Calvin was smiling, beckoning to

David to follow. David so wanted to go with him but he was rooted to the spot; couldn't move at all. He held out his arms. Calvin, too, held out his arms. Iris just stood there, smiling at David, all the love she had for him in her face. Suddenly an unseen force started to tear at Calvin. He was being dragged away. He screamed to David to help him. How could this be? Calvin was the strong one. Why should he ever need David's help? Calvin was pulled off balance. In that moment, he grabbed at Iris's hand and pulled her with him. 'No!' screamed David as they both started to disappear from view.

'David! Be quiet!'

It was Calvin's voice. He was climbing into David's bedroom window. David just stared into the darkness, waiting for his eyes to become accustomed to the faint moonlight flooding his room. Fully awake now, he realised he had been dreaming.

'Sorry, Cal. A bad dream.' He sat up in bed, leant over and lit the candle on his bedside table. In the flickering light, he watched as Calvin manoeuvred his way through the window into the bedroom. That's when he saw the blood on his trousers. 'What happened?' he exclaimed in a loud whisper.

'Shush!' hissed Calvin. He turned round and slowly, as quietly as possible, pulled the window down to shut it. He stood there before David who could now see how dishevelled he was. There was blood on Calvin's hand and a spot on his jacket, as well as on his trousers.

'Mam will have a fit!' said David.

'Look, old chum. Don't say anything about this to your parents. I just had a bit of a set to with another lad at the pub. All right?'

'But Calvin, look at yer. They'll know.'

'No, they won't. I'll creep downstairs and wash the blood off.' Calvin's grin spread across his face.

David, trying to keep a straight face and not laugh at his cousin's impishness, smiled at his hero. What a man Calvin was! He was already grown-up. He got out there and enjoyed life. Had fights. Stuck up for himself. David's heart filled with pride at being this wonderful man's cousin, more like little brother really. One day he'd be out there with Calvin, enjoying life.

'Shall I come down and help yer, Cal?'

‘No, Davie, me lad. You just get back to sleep now. And if anybody asks, you stick to the story that I didn’t even go out on this night. Went to bed with the rest of you and that’s where I was all night. In me bed. Anything else is our little secret.’

Calvin was already out of the bedroom door and on the landing so he didn’t hear David when he said, ‘Right, Cal. Anything you say. You were at home with us.’

He slithered down in the bed, turned over, pulled the covers up round his ears and closed his eyes, pleased that Calvin trusted him so, trusted him with this secret. Visions of Calvin and his mother being dragged away filled his mind, making him open his eyes again. ‘It was only a dream,’ he murmured to himself, closing his eyes again.

CHAPTER TWELVE

The winters in Grimsby are harsh. A raw wind always blows in from the North Sea and from mid-November onwards icicles hang from the trees and rooftops. Also the snow had come early this year, making layers of snow upon ice and ice upon snow. The roads and streets were so slippery they were dangerous. No one went out unless they had to. So everyone was surprised when a knock came at the front door that afternoon in mid-December.

They were all at home. George and Calvin were often housebound during these winter months if they didn't have work inside, for it was far too cold, and the weather made it impossible to work outside. On this particular afternoon, they were sitting by the fire, George doing the books and Calvin watching the television. Iris was in the kitchen preparing tea. David was there too, school having been closed due to bad weather, the fog and ice making the early morning journey in the dark too hazardous for the pupils. He sat swotting up for his end of term tests when the knock came at the door.

Nobody moved. They all looked at each other in astonishment but no one made to answer the door. It was Iris who came out of the scullery, walked through the living-room wiping her hands on her apron and into the hallway. The stained-glass windows of the front door didn't let you see who was standing on the other side, and so Iris was shocked when she opened the door to find a policeman standing there.

'Afternoon, madam,' he said, doffing his helmet in the old-fashioned style and letting it fall back on his head in an instant. He filled the door-frame with his bulk; he looked like a giant.

'Good afternoon, officer,' replied Iris, her heart flying up into her mouth. She had great respect for policemen and their work. But to have one knocking at the door was not good. 'What can I do for yer, officer?' she said, wiping her hands on her pinny.

'It's constable, madam. We're making enquiries about the whereabouts of any adolescents and young men who might have been out on the town on the evening of October 23rd, some seven weeks ago.'

Iris wondered what on earth something happening seven weeks ago had anything to do with them, but then who could possibly know how the police worked? It wasn't for her to question their methods. She stood to one side. 'You'd better come in, constable, you look freezing. I have two young men in the house. You can ask them your questions yourself.'

The policeman stepped into the hallway, banged his boots sharply on the foot-mat, closed the front door and followed Iris into the warm living-room. He removed his helmet and placed it under his arm where he held it firmly.

'Afternoon all,' he said.

'This gentleman wants to know what David and Calvin were doing on 23rd of October,' Iris announced. She couldn't explain it but she always felt nervous. She wondered why it was that whenever she saw or had to speak to a policeman, she somehow felt guilty. She hadn't done anything. And neither had her boys.

'That's quite a while ago, officer,' said George. 'How can anyone remember that far back? Anyway, what's been going on?'

'Yes, it is a while ago, sir; and it's constable. But we were hoping that we might find some new leads concerning an incident that happened then,' edged the policeman.

'What happened then?' piped up David.

'You be quiet, David,' George shot at him.

'Won't you sit down a minute, constable?' offered Iris, pulling a stool away from the table at which David was sitting and setting it down near to the blazing fire.

The policeman knew that he wasn't going to get much out of these people unless he told them what his enquiries were about. This was always a problem. A quick sweep of the place, taking in the bareness but cleanliness of the room with his eyes told him that these were hard-working decent people who probably never had anything to do with the police. Unfortunately, these working-class lot always fell silent when they saw the police.

'It's to do with the murder that took place late on the night of 23rd to 24th of October this year. A young lady was badly beaten and strangled.' He stopped, not wishing to divulge much more.

'How awful,' muttered Iris.

'Strangled, you say? That really is bloody awful,' George agreed with Iris. 'What night was the 23rd?' he asked, addressing the policeman.

'It was a Thursday night, sir,' the constable answered.

'Oh, well, that's cleared that up then,' answered George with a satisfied smile.

'How d'you mean, sir?' asked the policeman, leaning forward in his chair to take advantage of the heat and cocking his head to one side to look at George.

'Well, officer, er, constable, if it were a Thursday night, my lads would have been home safe in their beds. They're not allowed out on week nights and Davie, here, is not allowed out at all without us knowing where he is going. Our Calvin, now he's older. He goes out at the weekends with his friends, like.'

The policeman turned to Calvin. 'Have you heard or seen anything suspicious?' he asked, almost out of habit. But he knew he wasn't going to get any leads here. This family looked like a real decent lot.

'No,' said Calvin, looking the policeman straight in the eyes.

'We were all in bed,' said David eager to be a part of the conversation. His mind was racing though. Had they all been in bed? Not for the life of him could he remember that far back.

'Shut up, our David!' admonished George.

There was a moment's silence then the policeman said, 'Right you are then, sir.' He snapped his notebook closed.

'Would you like a cup of tea before you go out in that cold again?' offered Iris, putting on her posh voice.

A cup of hot steaming tea sounded to the policeman just like what he needed. The weather was getting to his arthritis and his feet were freezing even though he was sitting by the fire. But he knew he was making the family feel uncomfortable and he was a man of duty; a young lady, girl really, had been killed and he wanted to be a part of finding out who killed her.

'No thank you, madam. I'd better be getting along. Still got a lot of doors to knock on yet. If you do hear of anything or remember anything about that night, I would be obliged if you would please call the police station. Thank you.'

'Right yer are, officer,' said George, getting up to show the policeman to the front door. The constable didn't bother to correct him again in the use of a false title. He put on his helmet, pulled on his gloves and disappeared into the darkness of the winter afternoon.

Iris returned to the scullery and her preparations of their tea. David lowered his head into his schoolbooks again. When George returned, the living-room resumed its previous peaceful atmosphere.

'What an awful thing to happen,' muttered George, glad that the policeman was gone. He turned his attention to his accounts' book once again. Calvin went back to watching the TV. Iris called from the scullery, 'I've said it before and I'll say it again. Grimsby's not like it used to be. Whatever is the world coming to these days?'

David sat over his book at the table, his head down, making out he was reading. His thoughts, though, were far away from Geography. Cal had used his bedroom window so often to come and go that he couldn't quite remember any more just when he actually did. But he had a feeling that it must have been the 23rd because Calvin went out most Thursdays. It was a good thing his parents didn't know that. It wouldn't do for them to suspect Cal of doing anything wrong. David just knew that Cal, his Cal, couldn't possibly hurt a woman. Look how gentle he was with his mother. So, all right! There was that night he'd got into a fight. He wondered if that had been the 23rd. But that was boys' stuff. Men fought. Oh, yes, David smiled to himself. Cal would be pleased with him that he hadn't brought that fight up. He liked doing things to please Cal.

Iris was chopping carrots and thinking. Calvin obviously thought that she must be asleep when he made his excursions, but she wasn't a sound sleeper and often she had heard Calvin coming and going by way of David's bedroom window. She hadn't said anything because she didn't wish to upset George and he was a bit strict with the lad, not letting him go out on a weekday although he was a working man now. David never mentioned to her either about Calvin's nightly jaunts when they had their little chats in the mornings, when he brought her a cup of tea in bed before going to school. If she admitted that she knew Calvin regularly left the house of an evening, then David would know that she knew he was covering for Calvin. David was such a trusting little soul. She hoped that he wouldn't come a cropper one day with his childish belief in people. It could be a cruel world out there.

Calvin, on the other hand, now there's a different kettle of fish. He was so charming on the surface. But Iris saw beneath that enchanting exterior and thought she saw a ruthlessness that was quite frightening. He'd never put a step wrong in the house. Was always polite, even friendly to her. But she just didn't feel right about him, although she couldn't put her finger on what it was.

Later, in bed that night, as she lay trying to get to sleep but finding it impossible because her mind was racing, she realised that on that fateful night, on that very night that Calvin had let it be said that he was home in his bed, she knew that he wasn't. She'd had a coughing fit and had got up to get a glass of water. George hadn't woken; his snoring drowning out any noise she might have been making. And, anyway, she didn't wish to disturb him. On passing the boys' bedrooms, she had checked in on them, as a mother does. Calvin's bed was empty; David was sleeping soundly. She had gone back to bed and laid there in the darkness, listening. She had heard Calvin come home in the early hours of the morning. Had heard the muffled tones of him and David whispering, and she had recognised the sounds of his moving around in the kitchen later and the water running. His trousers had been soaking in the bowl when she had got up late in the morning. She'd finished washing them and put them by the fire to dry. Later, he'd said he'd slipped and fallen on some grass the day before and had put them to soak before going to bed, after she had already retired for the night. He'd been trying to help, he'd said. He'd remembered her saying how hard it was to get grass stains out of their clothes. She'd never thought to question his story. But now she did.

CHAPTER THIRTEEN

It was early January and winter had really set in. Icicles hung from the roofs of all buildings making the frozen water drops look like sparkling ropes of pear-shaped diamonds. Sometimes the sun would break through for a short spell, melting the ice ever so slightly; and then the nightly freeze would once again turn everything rigid. Ice over half-melted snow made pavements dangerous to walk on, and so the streets were empty except for the few who had no choice other than to make their journey. Dirty sludgy snow, pushed aside on the streets by the snowplough, had frozen in their massive mounds along the pavements' edges. The roads were covered in packed snow. No bicycles or cars were to be seen on the roads flanking the rows of terraced houses in the Cooper Road area. Daylight didn't arrive fully until around 9am, hovered sadly for a time, and was gone by 4pm, but the greyness of the heavens heavy with more snow let little light through. It was a miserable time of the year.

In the little terraced house in Cooper Road, they'd all got colds and George had warned the boys to stay away from Iris so as not to infect her. A cold for her would be much more serious due to her weak chest, he'd warned them. George had taken to sleeping on an old mattress in the living-room so as not to disturb her with his snoring or infect her with his cold. But it was hard to stay out of Iris's way in the small house and before too long, she was spending more and more time sat in bed with a bowl of hot water and camphor on her lap and a towel over her head to catch the steam.

School was still open and each day David, hardly able to walk because of the many layers of clothes he had on and the slippery pavements, would struggle through the streets to Welholme Road. The knowledge that he could leave the coming summer and finally start to work together with his Dad and Calvin kept him happy on his cold journey. For, despite his brilliant grades, David didn't want to stay at school. All he wanted was to be part of the family business, to work each day with his dad and his cousin, to belong.

Calvin's week-night jaunts had stopped simply because it was too damn cold. Twice he had slipped on the ice on the roof outside David's bedroom window and fallen off. And the walk to the Mecca Dance Hall was too long in this weather. Also, it occurred to Calvin after that visit from the policeman that it might be a good idea to stay away from the Mecca for a while. He didn't even go at weekends now.

George and Calvin were mostly home these days. Work was getting scarce, seeing as it had hardly stopped snowing for the last few days. Although George had lots of jobs on his books, he couldn't do any of them because of the weather conditions. This was always a slow time for him. And so he would sit by the fire, smoking his pipe and watching the television while he drank his whisky.

George and David didn't notice anything different at home, besides that they were all snivelling, but Calvin did. The atmosphere was different. First he suspected, but then he knew: Iris's manner was different towards him. She was a little distant, not her usual friendly self. He couldn't make out what was wrong between them and, at first, put it down to her illness. It took some time before he realised that her change towards him had started with the visit of the policeman.

Twice a day, Iris would get up to sit near the living-room fire, swaddled in blankets, because Doctor Barrowman had told her she must try to move and help loosen the phlegm on her lungs caused by her bronchitis. Although she was following the doctor's advice, she was finding it consistently more difficult to breathe freely. Just walking from the bedroom to the living-room, even when helped by George, would leave her exhausted. She would sit, staring into the fire, her thoughts her own. The old black, oven-flanked, tall fireplace had gone and in its place was a modern grey-tiled one. The clock was in the middle of the mantelpiece with two pieces of plaster of Paris sculptures that David had done at school either side of it. Iris cherished the artwork, a seal sitting up and an abstract piece. This new fireplace might look tidier, she thought, and it certainly made the room look bigger because it was a lot smaller than the old one, but the heat it generated was only half that generated by the good, old-fashioned, black cast-iron fireplace.

Calvin entered the living-room from the scullery, where he had been helping George and David make tea.

'Do you need anything, Auntie Iris?' he asked, treating her to one of his brilliant smiles.

'No, thank you, Calvin. I'll just wait for tea.' She took her eyes away from the fire and let them rest on Calvin's face. He was indeed a handsome lad, beautiful, in fact, she thought. How ever he got to be in this family, she couldn't imagine. Her brother had certainly been no Adonis and she wasn't what you would call pretty. She'd only ever seen a photo of Calvin's mother and she had looked quite run-of-the-mill, so where did this boy, man now, get this extraordinary face? Even his body was god-like. He was tall and muscular with broad shoulders and slim hips. She looked at him and wondered.

'You're not going out so much these days, Calvin,' she said without preamble, staring at him, her face expressionless.

Calvin stared straight back at her and smiled. 'Well, it's really too cold to go out every weekend, Auntie Iris. And what with this cold and all...'

'I didn't mean at the weekends, Calvin. I meant during the week when you leave the house by way of David's bedroom window.'

Calvin's eyes flashed then darkened. 'What do you mean, Auntie Iris? Has David said anything?'

'David would never say anything to either George or me, Calvin. You know he adores you. Looks up to you, he does. Which puts him in a difficult situation 'cause he's always been truthful to us until you came here.' She breathed deeply, wheezing audibly, and carried on, 'I know you were out on that night, the night the policeman was asking about. I heard you. And I couldn't find any grass stains on your trousers, come to think of it. I thought they were just muddy. But it was a very red type of mud, Calvin. Where exactly were you?'

'You must be mistaken, Auntie Iris,' said Calvin walking over to her. He reached for the blanket around her shoulders and pulled it closer together around her neck as if he were being caring and trying to keep her warm.

'Tell me,' she whispered.

'There's nothing to tell,' he smiled down at her, his blue eyes cold as steel, the blanket getting tighter and tighter around her neck.

'Hey, Cal,' George called from the scullery, his voice breaking the moment. 'No skiving off. Get in here and help.'

Iris pushed Calvin's hands away.

With a gentle stroke of her cheek, Calvin left the living-room and returned to the scullery to help with the tea.

Iris's pulse raced. Her heart was beating so strongly she felt sure it would jump out of her chest. She felt her lungs constrict as she started to wheeze. It took all her strength of mind to calm herself, to keep breathing at a regular pace and as deeply as she could, just like the doctor had advised her. She eventually quietened her mind of the terrifying thoughts that were flying through it and, in so doing, the impending threat of an asthma attack receded. 'George,' she called. 'Would you help me, dear? I think I'll take me tea upstairs tonight.'

A few days later, as George was out pricing up a job and David was at school, Calvin found himself alone at home with Iris. She was upstairs, not having left her bedroom since their last conversation. The television was on; the room was bathed in an orange glow from the burning fire. Calvin sat pondering Iris's words. She knew, he thought; or, at least, suspected something. She obviously hadn't said anything yet because David hadn't mentioned it and George was his usual self. What was he to do? It wouldn't do for Auntie Iris to spoil things for him. He was doing fine here. He got on well with George, the silly old man, and David looked up to him like a god. There was money to be had here and he deserved his share of it. He'd worked hard for them, hadn't he? Done his bit, he had. If Auntie Iris started putting suspicion into words, he might lose all this. Where would he go? He'd have to do something.

He turned the television sound up a tad and made for the stairs. Taking his time he slowly ascended, making sure to miss the third and eleventh step so no creaks could be heard. Turning at the top of the stairs, he crept along the landing towards the front bedroom. The door was open; he peered around it. Auntie Iris was sleeping, still propped up with most of the pillows, but one was on the floor where she had thrown it before settling herself down for her sleep. Calvin, ever so quietly, crept into the room and picked it up. Transferring the pillow to both hands, he held it above Iris's head. Suddenly she opened her eyes, looking straight at Calvin; immediately they filled with fear and widened in disbelief. He smiled at her, one of his especially charming smiles, before pressing the pillow over her face and holding it there, tightly, silently. Her arms and legs started to flay about, but the heavy bedclothes hindered her movements. Little muffled wails of fear and mounting hopelessness escaped through the feathers, and then ceased. All in all, Iris had hardly fought back at all and soon lay completely still.

CHAPTER FOURTEEN

They all seemed to return to the house at the same time. George drew up in his old van, driving as slow as a snail to avoid skidding in the snow. David was walking down the road on his way home from school and could be seen in the distance. Calvin was at old Mrs Carr's house across the road, shovelling the snow away from her house door. He joined George outside in the street and they entered the house together.

'Ee, you're a good lad, our Cal,' said George, seeing how his nephew had spent his time helping an aged neighbour. He put his hand on Calvin's shoulder and squeezed it affectionately.

Calvin looked up the road and waved to David. George went on ahead and entered the house. After tapping the snow off his boots, he removed them before going upstairs to let Iris know he was home. All at once, a wail of agony filled the house and filtered outside into the street, alerting Calvin, who was waiting for David to reach home. David heard the scream, and together they ran in the house and up the stairs.

'No, no,' wailed George. He was sitting on the bed holding Iris in his arms, rocking her back and forth, tears streaming down his face. Physical pain contorted his features. He yowled and screamed and bellowed at a cruel world that had taken his beloved Iris from him.

Calvin and David stood there helplessly, watching George. David thought his mother must be really ill for his father to show such emotion.

'You run and get the doctor,' instructed Calvin. 'I'll call 999. There's a box just around the corner. Go! Go!'

David turned and was out of the house, across Durban Road and on his way as fast as his legs would carry him up Stanley Street to the doctor's house. He slipped and skidded but continually picked himself up and scampered the length of the long street past the park.

The living-room of the little terraced house in Cooper Road was full of people. A little crowd was even gathering outside, despite the snow starting to fall. The front door had been opened and left open so often that the room had become quite cool, despite the fire still burning. People stood around, rather than sitting. There were the two policemen who had answered the 999 call, made by an hysterical-sounding boy just an hour ago. They'd not been sure exactly what the young lad had wanted. They were so used to getting false alarms from kids with nothing better to do that they'd not really treated the call with much urgency. But the lad had sounded upset. They'd had difficulty understanding him through his obvious distress and so decided it was best to go and see what was happening. Now they stood with their helmets in their hands and littered the room. Dr Barrowman was there, too.

'George,' said Dr. Barrowman softly, 'you always knew this could happen. I'm so sorry but her lungs just gave out. The asthma won the battle. She's at peace now.'

But George didn't want Iris at peace. He wanted her here, sitting next to the fire waiting for him to get her some tea. No, George didn't want her at peace. She was to get back here, right now. Of, course, he didn't say any of this, he just sat there on the edge of the fireside armchair, his elbows on his spread knees, his hands linked, his eyes glued to the threadbare carpet. I'll get her that new carpet she always wanted, he thought. How dare she do this to him! He'd left her only two hours before and now she'd done this! Oh, Iris, Iris, his heart screamed.

David stood in the corner of the living-room, dry-eyed and vacant, his back pressed again the wall. Calvin was in the scullery - now called a kitchen because they had knocked the old pantry down - making tea for everyone.

'What happened?' he asked the doctor as he was handing out steaming mugs of tea to everyone in the living-room.

'The asthma coupled with the bronchitis was just too much for her, son,' answered Doctor Barrowman. 'I'm really sorry, lad, but these things happen.'

Calvin gave a loud sob, surprising the doctor. He'd seemed such a quiet young man. 'So, if I'd have been here instead of outside helping Mrs Carr shovel snow, Auntie Iris might have been all right?' He hung his head in pain.

The doctor knew the family history. He had looked after Iris all the years she had lived in this house. She was a good woman of strong will but weak constitution. He felt sad at the events of the day. He looked at this young man who so obviously loved his family and had now lost his auntie, the woman who had been a substitute mother to him. His heart went out to the broken young man who stood before him.

'Look, son. There was nothing you could do; anyone could do, for that matter. Mrs Gilmore had suffered from bad asthma for years. It was bound to happen. Don't blame yourself.'

Calvin sniffled and moved off. 'How long is all this palaver going to last?' he asked himself, his head bent so no one could see the irritation in his face. He went over to David.

'You all right, Davie? I'm real sorry this has happened. Your mother was such a good mam to me. I'll never forget her.'

David's eyes finally filled with tears. He felt Calvin's arm go round his shoulders and he leant into his chest and wept.

'There, there,' Calvin muttered, holding his cousin tightly. 'I'm here; everything will be all right now.'

And all right it would be, Calvin silently praised himself. No more questions about where he'd been on that night. No more suspicious atmosphere hanging heavy in the house. No more wondering if stupid old Iris was going to run her mouth off to someone. It was about time that insipid invalid got out of their hair. If the truth be known, he'd done everybody a favour. They ought to be grateful to him.

He let go of David, giving his shoulder a final pat of sympathy, took up the tray, and started to gather up the empty mugs.

CHAPTER FIFTEEN

A lot was going on in the world in 1965: a man walked in space, US President Johnson sent troops into Vietnam, Rhodesia broke from Britain, race riots flared up in the States. In Britain, Sir Winston Churchill died, the Beatles were awarded MBEs, mini skirts came into being, the pill gave new sexual freedom to women and Ian Brady and Myra Hindley were charged with the Moors murders.

In Grimsby discotheques were starting to appear, bingo became all the rage and David and Calvin were left to run the family business when George succumbed to tuberculosis.

'What are we going to do?' asked David of Calvin. This was not how he had imagined it would be. He remembered all that time spent just wishing time away so he could leave school and join Calvin and his father in the business. Now it looked like everything would break up. How would they manage? They'd just got into a routine of working together when George had been sent to Springfield Sanatorium on the edge of town. If the truth be told, they'd known for some time that George was ill, very ill. He'd been coughing up blood for a while before he eventually went to the doctor. Six months in hospital, maybe longer, the doctor had said. And even when he came out, George wouldn't be able to resume his work as a builder for a very long time.

Everything had changed so much since Iris's death.

It had been difficult for the whole family. George had started to drink heavily, openly weeping as he sat of an evening in the armchair by the fire. He didn't go to work at all for the first couple of weeks and then, when he did, he wasn't much use to anyone. He'd direct Calvin, who by this time was pretty good at most of the building work, thanks to the jobs being quite small and simple but at least regular. And George would stay in the old wooden shack doing the books, taking the phone calls and drinking his whisky.

Calvin, together with old Joe, who George had hired more out of pity than anything else, converted old coal-rooms or outside toilets into bathrooms or built on simple extensions, or walled in gardens of those lucky enough to have detached houses. And they were good at what they did, never short of work. Their reputation was growing. But by lunchtime George was so drunk he couldn't go on any of the jobs and Calvin was left to manage on his own with just the help of old Joe. Joe was in his late fifties and wasn't much good for anything other than fetching and carrying any more because his hands shook so badly, but he knew about construction. Calvin just hoped that he, too, wouldn't go to the doctor and discover he'd got some bloody illness and mess up things. Calvin and Joe muddled along, keeping the business just ticking over, as George sat steeped in his grief and whisky in the little wooden shack in the small building yard they had rented just round the corner from Cooper Road at the end of Weelsby Street.

David had joined his father and Calvin as soon as he had left school at 15 in the summer of '63. He'd spent most of that last year standing each break time by the bloody boundary line - that white painted strip that divided the boys and girls from each other and that he'd come to hate. By this time, he was getting to an age when he understood a little why they were divided, for he filled many hours dreaming of the girl. He'd never seen her again. And although at the start of his vigilance he was filled with hope and excitement, as the time passed and the girl never reappeared, his heart grew heavy, then hope left him and finally he pushed the memory of her into the back of his mind. His certainty that they belonged together began to fade. He had felt an instant love. Never before had such powerful feelings overcome him. This yearning mystified him. He loved his mother, but this was so very different. All this had occupied his mind when he first laid eyes upon her and now he felt betrayed by his own silliness. Eventually he gave up all hope and stopped looking for her. When his mother died, his misery was complete.

David changed when his mother died. Getting older now, and not so afraid of his distant father, he would approach him when he sat in the fireside chair deep in his torment and put his hand on his father's shoulder. This was probably the first contact he had had with his father since he could remember.

'Anything I can get you, Dad?' David would ask, his voice heavy with concern. He hated seeing his father like this. Seeing him cold and aloof from him, but friendly and laughing with Calvin, was far better than the broken man he now saw bent over in the chair. With a groan of irritation, George would shake David's hand off his body, then fall again into his own little world where Iris was alive and well, even. Laughing and loving with him.

Calvin would approach George with a glass full of whisky. He'd take the empty glass out of George's hand and replace it with the full one. George would look up at him with gratitude in his face. Calvin would squeeze his shoulder and George never ever shook him off.

The house was cold and without mirth of any kind without Iris in it. The fire was only lit when it was desperately cold. The kitchen was a mess, with the three of them grabbing whatever was there to eat. Shopping was only done, mainly by David, when the cupboards were absolutely bare. George would never say anything when the house was empty of food; he'd just leave five pounds on the kitchen table. He ate less and less these days, preferring to fill his stomach with whisky. Sandwiches were the main meal of the day for the two lads. David couldn't remember when he had had a home-cooked meal with vegetables and all the trimmings.

But it wasn't just for the cooking that he missed his mother. She had been the one he could talk to, the one he could share his dreams with, the one who had listened to him and encouraged him. Only she knew of his deep desire to make something of himself; to become someone people respected and looked up to in the way that he respected and looked up to Calvin; to make his father proud of him; to have his father acknowledge his efforts and be pleased with him; to have his father love him as a father should love his son. She understood his yearning, she never rebuked his father for his lack of love where his son was concerned, but she softened his treatment of David by telling her son that deep down George loved him but simply couldn't show it. She was the buffer between him and his father. And now that she was gone, David and George were further apart than ever. David loved his father and wanted his father to love him but that seemed an impossible wish.

The main thing was, thought David often, that George felt a great connection with Calvin. When he did talk, he talked to Calvin. He discussed the business with him and it was always Calvin who organised and carried out George's wishes. Calvin always saw to it that his uncle's whisky glass was replenished, and it was Calvin who, being over eighteen, sometimes went with George to the pub for a drink. Consequently, it was again Calvin who helped George home when his legs went all wobbly on him. David's loneliness grew and he tried not to feel too envious. Main thing, he always tried to remember, was that his father found some solace in his nephew's company, if not in his. And that was good.

Things got a little better when David started to work in the business. Although George still didn't have much time for his son, Calvin always went out of his way to make David feel part of the group. David learnt quickly. Within a short time he was mixing cement and laying bricks as if he'd never done anything else. Old Joe taught him how to measure up and estimate the costs of each individual job, and David was pleased with himself that he'd paid special attention to the Maths classes at school. This part of the job he found easy. Not only was David happy to be involved in the business and be with his hero Calvin, but he found that he got real pleasure out of seeing what his hands and hard work could create. He'd only been working for two years as a builder, Calvin for four, but David was becoming really good, better than his cousin, and known for his attention to detail. What David built, was built to last.

Together, they would all go to the yard each morning. They'd discuss in the shack that served as an office what the plan was for the day, and then they'd load the van up with the required materials. Since Iris's death, George was slow in getting started. He'd often have coughing fits, which racked his body with obvious pain. If David tried to help him, he would just push him away and tell him to stop fussing. And so, with time, George worked on the building sites less and less, unless something difficult came up and his expertise was needed. Mostly, Calvin and David, with Joe fetching and carrying, could manage quite well and the customers always appeared to be pleased with their efforts and the results of their labours. It was often said to them that they might be young, but they were good. At such words of praise David rose to even better efforts; Calvin just blinded everyone with one of his brilliant smiles. He knew he was good. He had paid attention to what George had taught him and this work was all right for now, but it certainly wasn't going to be what he did for the rest of his life. He wasn't about to finish up like Joe, bent and racked with early old age from too much heavy physical work. Oh, no. Calvin had other plans. And David was a large part of those plans.

Despite appearing not to take much notice of what was going on around him, Calvin missed nothing. He saw that George always ignored his son and wondered why. He knew he'd finally find out and he did as they had talked about this when George had had a skinful and didn't care whom he was talking to.

'It's all his bloody fault,' he'd ranted drunkenly to Calvin. 'She'd been healthy, she was okay, she was full of life!' he'd insisted, his words slurred. 'And then he had to come and spoil it all.'

In his drunken state, George had forgotten his wife's disposition to delicate health and looked back at their life, picturing it as he had wanted it to be rather than as it really was.

'We danced and worked as all young couples did in those days,' he'd confided in Calvin. 'But then the war came and everything changed.'

Calvin was surprised that it never seemed to occur to George that the makeshift bomb shelter he'd built in the garden to protect Iris while he was away, could have been responsible for her illnesses turning chronic. Calvin had come to this conclusion. Christ! They were still talking about its terrible condition when he'd come to live with them. It seemed it was always steeped in muddy rain and ground water.

'Maybe it had something to do with the shelter, Uncle George,' Calvin had tried.

'She was all right when I got back,' George insisted, remembering.

Then Iris had become pregnant with David and that was when their lives had changed for the worse. With the birth of that damn kid, as

George called him, Iris's health had suffered so greatly that she became, and remained from that time onwards, an invalid. No more dancing, no more excitedly running into each other's arms, no more anything really.

Whether right or wrong, George hated his son for spoiling his life.

David never complained, despite his father's coldness towards him. Somehow, he always managed to have a kindly smile for everyone, although, in general, he gave the impression of being a serious young man. He had grown in the last two years and although he would never be considered tall, he was of an acceptable height. His physique was stocky and he looked strong. But mostly his development had taken place in his head. It was his way to quietly watch what was going on around him and then make his decisions, although he always kept his thoughts to himself. He didn't even discuss all his notions with Calvin, although his cousin was everything to him, his entire family really.

It had been his mother to whom he'd always confided his thoughts and now she was gone, no one could replace her. It had taken a lot of time, but David finally realised that there was nothing he could do to make his father love him. He would try and be the best builder in the land and earn lots of money; maybe then he could at least win his respect. Quietly, he sympathised with his father, understanding how lonely he must feel. David at least had Calvin.

Calvin worked steadily at his job. He was helpful and considerate to George and he was brotherly to David who always rewarded him with real affection; a bit like a puppy dog was David, and Calvin enjoyed the power he had over him. He had worked hard to win his way into George's affections, too. And the knowledge that he had such a strong hold over both of them pleased him. He'd fallen on his feet here. There was money to be had. George preferred him above his own son, and George didn't look like he was going to be around for that much longer. Calvin had seen the blood-stained hankies George hid in the bin. Now he'd been carted off to the sanatorium, it would surely be just a matter of time before he was at his sorry end.

By that time, Calvin knew he'd have a real hold on the business. David would need him; he'd also be old enough to go in the pubs. Oh yes, David would finally be old enough for Calvin to show him some real fun and, therefore, make him eternally grateful. Calvin's lips turned upwards in a smirk of self-satisfaction.

Everything was going according to his plan.

CHAPTER SIXTEEN

'Come on, Davie, me old bean,' called Calvin through the bathroom door. David was still getting spruced up and Calvin was becoming impatient. He paced up and down the kitchen, his eyes glued to the bathroom door. 'The pubs will be closed by the time you're ready.'

The door finally opened. 'Do I look eighteen?' David asked Calvin, as he walked out of the bathroom, slipping a blue pullover over his head and pulling it down over his open shirt.

'David, stop worrying. You're nearly eighteen anyway and you look older than you are, so stop going on about it, will you? It's time you got out of here and had some fun. That pullover makes you look well over twenty-five. And the way you act, you're an old man already,' Calvin joked good-naturedly. And sniffing the air, which was pungent with the aroma of Fabergé's Brut, he continued, 'And you've been at my after-shave, you little sod! The girls will all be after you now. They love that stuff.'

David gave a chuckle. He had indeed put some of Calvin's after-shave on and couldn't believe how strong it was. All he hoped now was that the girls wouldn't think he was a pansy. 'I'll get some of my own next week,' he muttered, grabbing his jacket off the back of the chair and slipping it on.

Calvin was a picture of the times. The *Swinging Sixties*, it was being called. He felt good about his looks and the way he dressed; his stance, which he worked on, portrayed an assured arrogance normally reserved for people of a higher class. He was wearing a long jacket with a little stand up collar, like he'd seen the Beatles wearing. He also had on new black leather boots. They had small Cuban heels and made him look even taller than his six foot one inch. His pants were extra tight. He knew he'd have no trouble pulling a bird tonight.

David was checking his jacket for his wallet and keys. He kept smoothing down his hair which he wore long these days like Calvin did. But the steam from the bath he'd just taken had made it curl more than usual and it kept escaping from the stiff style into which David had attempted to coax it. It was already curling gently around his face and at the nape of his neck.

Calvin sighed. He looks more like the type who should be train-spotting or bird-watching or something excitingly similar, he thought. Davie wasn't an ugly fellow, but just not in his category. Still, Cleethorpes would be full of holidaymakers - girls that come and go. The factories in Sheffield were closed for their annual holidays, he'd heard, and the town was full of girls, ready, willing and able. Didn't matter if you couldn't understand their rough accents, give them a drink and you could do what you liked with them. This would be a good introduction to sex for David. He was just too shy and talked silly stuff about love and such, and a girl he'd seen at school. What an idiot! He'd show David the way tonight.

They walked up to Grimsby Road and got the bus to Cleethorpes. Getting off at the top of Isaac's Hill, they crossed the road and entered the Dolphin Public House. It was only 7pm, but the pub was already heaving with people standing around, sweating and crushed together; the men swilling beer down their throats for all they were worth, the women daintily sipping at their Cherry Bs. Many of the men were still in some form of beachwear – loud patterned knee-length shorts, string vests and open sandals - while the ladies were done up to the nines – bouffant hairdos, high-heels, short skirts and lots of mascara.

'There you are, me lad. That's what's on offer this evening. Take your pick.'

David swept the bar with his eyes. The room smelled of stale beer and cigarette smoke but no one seemed to notice. Everyone appeared to be having a great time. They were standing in little groups, laughing and drinking. The women looked like they enjoyed walking round and round the room. Now and again they'd stop and join a group of men. It was indeed fascinating and all so new to him.

'Just a half of bitter,' David answered Calvin's question of what he wanted to drink. Calvin returned with two full pints.

'Here,' he shouted above the noise, handing David a pint, 'halves are for wimps and, anyway, I can't keep fighting my way to the bar.'

David watched as Calvin silently surveyed the room and the people in it. A pang of pain hit his heart as the thought occurred to him that this was what a son usually did for the first time with his father. And he wondered how his father was doing in the sanatorium.

'Not much talent in here tonight, Davie. Let's move on.' Calvin drained his glass and started for the door. David edged his way through the crowd after him. Just before leaving the bar, he managed to find a table on which to plonk his still half-full glass.

'Right, Davie. When you notice that there's nothing worth having in one pub, you move on to the next,' Calvin instructed David as they walked across the road towards the Submarine.

This bar was also packed with what appeared to be holidaymakers. David heard accents and slang totally foreign to his ears. In many cases, he couldn't even make out what some people were talking about.

'We ought to come here on a Friday, Davie. They have a striptease then. Not many women in the bar on Fridays though. Still it gets you going for getting fixed up somewhere else.'

They had a quick drink in the Sub, a half-pint this time for David as he was the one to go to the bar, and then they left.

'Where to now, Cal?' asked David as they hit the fresh air. It was still only 9.30pm.

'Let's try the Lifeboat, up here,' Calvin indicated a walk along the road running parallel to the promenade. Ten minutes later they arrived.

'This looks good,' said David as soon as he saw the place. It was a hotel and a lot nicer in its décor, which had a nautical theme – red plush seats and stools and thick red-patterned carpet in a roomy bar heavy with dark, polished wood and shiny brass.

'We change to whisky here, Davie old bean,' said Calvin as he pushed through the crowds making his way to the bar.

'Why?' asked David in alarm. He'd never drunk whisky in his life before. The odd beer now and again when his father wasn't looking, but never whisky.

'Two whiskies on the rocks,' demanded Calvin of the barman before answering David. 'Because, my sweet cousin, whisky drinkers look richer and get the women easier. No woman wants a man who can't afford to buy her a drink, now, does she?'

David didn't know the answer to that. Obviously Calvin did. But David had always thought women were there to cherish and respect, like his father had cherished and respected his mother: like he had done. Calvin obviously saw things differently. And for the first time David realised how isolated from real life he had become. Here, and all that he saw before him – the crowds, the hunting-grounds of the town – was where it all was happening. The best thing he could do, if he wanted to move with the times and be like Calvin, would be to follow his lead and do as he did.

Calvin knocked back his whisky in one gulp. David followed suit and ordered the next round. He was beginning to feel woozy now and hoped that Calvin wouldn't notice. He desperately wanted not to disappoint him, wanted to be just like him, certainly didn't want to be like some of the men he'd seen when they'd drunk one over the top. Disgusting!

Together, they turned and rested their backs against the bar. Both surveyed the room.

'Nice bit of fluff over there,' Calvin whispered in David's ear.

David looked in the direction that Calvin had indicated. The people before him seemed to be off somewhere in the distance, their voices coming together in one big noise, and they were smudged round the edges. They looked a lot better like this and he smiled contentedly. 'They all look nice to me,' he chuckled.

'Locals,' complained Calvin. 'We don't want locals. We want one of those cheeky little girls from somewhere or other that wants a bit of fun while she's on holiday and then goes back to wherever she came from and never rears her ugly head again. Drink up, Davie. We're off to The Winter Gardens.'

CHAPTER SEVENTEEN

The Winter Gardens in Cleethorpes was situated at the far end of the promenade where the parallel roads end. Opposite, the town's large open-air swimming pool could be found, next to the picturesque boating lake. This was where the tourists congregated and the single people of the area came to find a partner: sometimes for life, sometimes just for the night. You had to pay to get into the Winter Gardens and, consequently, because the drinks were more expensive here than in the pubs, the type of person that frequented the place was one who wished to see and be seen, rather than one who was just out to have a skinful and collapse in a heap.

Inside, it was an elegant building, high class, decorated in red and gold. The foyer led into a large room, flanked by dining-tables right up to the massive stage where a singer crooned to a large band. The dance floor, in the middle, was huge. Families and couples tended to sit at the tables at either side of the room, having a meal. Single people, hoping to meet someone, assembled in a group opposite the stage at the end of the dance floor nearest the entrance doors. Here Calvin and David stood, drink in hand.

'So, Davie. This is our last chance. If we don't find one here, we can go home early.'

David took in the information and dutifully started to scan the room.

'No, Davie, look on the dance floor. See those two over there, dancing together. Let's go and break them up.'

David's blood turned to ice. Dance? No one had said anything about dancing. How was he supposed to know how to dance? And the two girls in question were jiving and making a good job of it as far as he could see. He couldn't do that. Time for home, really. He must tell Cal.

'Cal, I can't,' he muttered.

Calvin downed his drink, took the whisky from David's hand and downed that too. He pushed through the people to the nearest table and deposited the glasses there before turning back towards the dance floor. Grabbing David's sleeve, he dragged him towards the girls who were giving a great performance of coordinated dancing.

'What am I supposed to say?' thought David. And then realised he didn't need to say anything as they broke up the pair and Calvin took one girl in his arms and sped off into the crowd, leaving David standing with the other girl. Seeing his hesitation, she held out her arms.

'Hiya,' she said, putting her arms around David's neck and slowing down her rhythm to a slow smooch. She felt her new partner tense up.

'My name's Angie,' she offered. 'What's yours?'

'David,' was all he could manage.

Angie's faced dropped. Oh dear. She had got a shy one here and she was hoping for a bit of action tonight, the last night of her holiday. Dawn seemed to be doing all right with the other one. She spotted them among the crowd. They were draped around each other and laughing.

David suddenly wished he hadn't drunk so much. He wanted to talk to this girl, wanted to impress her with his wit and wisdom, whatever that meant, but he had read it somewhere and knew it was important that he talk to her and amuse her. His tongue swelled up in his mouth and when he tried to speak, the words came out slurred. 'You on holiday?' he finally managed.

The music ended and Calvin and Dawn rejoined them. All introduced to each other, they made their way to the bar where they had another drink. David wondered if he had brought enough money with him.

Some time later, they where walking along the road to the parkland surrounding the boating lake. David was surprised to find he was holding Angie's hand. He was fighting off the effects of the alcohol and felt proud of himself that he was succeeding. 'Where we going?' he asked.

'Here, in the cover of the bushes,' he heard Calvin's voice reply.

Suddenly Calvin stopped. 'Go on a bit, little brother,' he murmured, pushing David forward. He embraced Dawn, kissed her passionately and pulled her to the ground.

David's heart had warmed to the comment of 'little brother' and a flush of affection for Calvin filled his being. Then he felt himself being led a bit further along the path. Angie was dragging on his arm.

'Come on, Dave,' she whispered as she pulled him into the bushes. He stumbled down beside her. Before he could catch his breath, she was all over him, covering his mouth with hers. He could hardly breathe. Her hand travelled down from his face to the waistband of his pants. She was expert in flicking the belt open and popping the button on the top of his trousers. He wanted to speak out, say something; but he didn't know what. Wasn't sure what he was supposed to say. She got his pants open and was groping inside his underpants.

And then he felt her touch him in a way that no one had ever touched him before. His groin tensed up and his legs went stiff.

'Relax,' she grunted, taking her mouth away from his and planting little kisses all the way down his body until she reached his open pants.

As he felt her mouth close over his penis his head started to spin uncontrollably. Fire erupted in his groin. He arched his back and groaned.

She moved up to be face to face with him again. 'Not done this very often, have you, soldier?' she smiled down at him.

With a quick move she had hitched up her skirt and pulled her knickers to one side. Carefully she straddled him, taking his cock in her hands and positioning it in between her legs. With a sudden thrust, she lowered herself onto him and cried out, 'Oh, yeah, soldier, get going.' She thrust and swayed and moved on top of him. David eyes widened in surprise, and he watched her movements in fascination. She was using her arms as levers and he looked at what was going on as if it weren't his body that was involved, as if all this had nothing to do with him.

Abruptly, he knew his body was involved. A fire had started at the bottom of his feet, rushed up his legs, lingered around his genitals and exploded into the crazy woman pumping about on top of him.

'Awww,' he screamed. It was a weird pain.

Angie lowered herself to kiss him but David turned his head and her kiss met his cheek. Strangely, a picture of the girl he saw in the playground so long ago filled his mind and he closed his eyes to keep the image from intertwining with this one. He felt tears prick the back of his eyelids.

CHAPTER EIGHTEEN

Springfield Sanatorium on the edge of town was a small group of wooden barrack-type buildings set in lovely gardens. Grimsby's continual rain kept everything a luscious green and this hid the misery of the place. There were eight to ten beds in each ward. White bed linen and white-painted walls gave the wards an artificial brightness. Many tried to fight off the tuberculosis there with the unending help of the nurses; many eventually died there. And so, everybody was surprised when George responded so well to treatment that, after nearly nine months, he was released from the sanatorium. He was sent off home in the company of his son and his nephew with large boxes of antibiotic tablets, each tablet as big as a two-shilling piece and half an inch thick. He was instructed to take eight a day and to rest; certainly not to think about work or attempt to do any.

They travelled back from the sanatorium in the new mustard-yellow second-hand Vauxhall estate car that Calvin and David had bought for the business so that David could go and see customers, take measurements and deliver estimates. This was the way the work had been shared out. David looked more like a builder than Calvin did, although they both worked hard on site. David was muscular and stocky, while Calvin was slim and, despite his job, somehow elegant. David looked dependable and people who were wary about parting with their money warmed more easily to David's polite and quiet manner, his obvious strength and knowledge of the building trade. His many creative ideas and suggestions all worked to inspire trust in potential customers.

Business was doing so well that not only had they bought the car, but they had also hired two young lads in a special training scheme from the local council. Part of their wages were subsidised and so Gilmore's became upmarket enough to boast the fact that the council had seen fit to trust them enough to train the builders of the future.

Financially, things were starting to look up. Although there wasn't much left over at the end of the month, they'd managed to keep their heads well above water, buy the car and pay off a large lump sum of the loan on Cooper Road. A couple more years and the house would be George's, without debt. David felt sure his father would appreciate this and finally acknowledge his hard work and good financial judgement. They were doing okay. The only time the going got tough was in winter when, due to weather conditions, they couldn't work.

David had done the books since his father went into Springfield Sanatorium. It made him happy to know that not only had they kept the business going in his father's absence, but they had built it up to be one of the most trusted in their area. Indeed, he had worked hard. Up at 6.30am each morning, he was in the yard by 7am and loading the van alongside old Joe. Calvin would finally turn up around 8am, ready to go with them to the site. This was no big deal for David who liked to give his cousin that extra bit of sleep. God knows he must need it. Most nights Calvin went out on the town and didn't get back till long after David had gone to bed. Calvin was always surrounded by eager females when he went anywhere. They clamoured to partake of his beauty and charm, and Calvin just saw it as his natural lot. But after that Cleethorpes pub-crawl, and the subsequent experience in the bushes of the boating lake, David had preferred to hang around at home and do the books and make out the order and worksheets for the next day.

All this home routine became strained when George returned from the sanatorium. David tried to interest him in doing the books and ordering the materials they needed. They also had a phone now in the house and George could help from there without overdoing it, like the doctors had insisted upon. David did his best to involve his father but it seemed, although he appeared to be grudgingly impressed by the financial growth, deep down, he was stifling an anger at the son who had done so well in his absence. Instead of being grateful and happy with his son's hard work and appreciating that David had done this solely for him, he grunted and groaned his disapproval at various extravagances like the car and the telephone in the house and the cleaning lady who came in once a week.

David took to doing his paperwork either in the wooden shack in the yard or in the kitchen, leaving George to sit silently and sullen in the living-room next to the fire, rocking his body back and forth and drinking his whisky. This drinking was definitely against the doctors' orders but David didn't know how to stop him.

'Oh, leave him be,' Calvin had often said when he'd voiced his concerns. 'What else does the old man have?'

But it was David who was mostly in the house with George, unless Calvin gave him a welcome break by taking George over to the Imperial Public House, round the corner from Cooper Road.

The walk in the fresh air would do George good: the amount he drank at the pub didn't. He'd stagger home about 11pm on such nights, supported by Calvin. David would have been upset by the whole thing, considering his father needed rest and no alcohol, but to hear his father singing, even when hopelessly slurred, to see him grinning and even laughing made him soften his attitude. Calvin was really good for his father, he surmised. Whereas he couldn't talk to him, his son, he obviously had found a true mate in Calvin, and David's heart filled with gratitude at the thought of his colourful cousin making time for his broken and miserable dad.

And so, before David's eyes, George slipped into his alcoholic ways.

It was only when David started to find half-full and empty whisky bottles hidden around the house, in the pockets of jackets hanging on the hook on the back of the doors, in amongst the detergents under the sink, behind the cushions on the chair, that he realised that his father was back in the iron grip of the bottle. He tried seeking out the bottles and throwing them away, but George always had new ones and new hiding places. When he saw Calvin handing George a full bottle of whisky he knew where they were coming from.

'Cal, you're not doing Dad a favour by bringing him his whisky, you know,' he'd complained to Calvin one night while they were having a quick after-work drink together at the Imperial before going home.

Calvin had looked him steadily in the eyes and a little smile had played at the corners of his lips. 'No, you're right there, our Davie,' he had said softly. 'It's you I'm doing the favour for.'

David hadn't known what to answer. It was true that his father was belligerent and sometimes downright mean to him these days. But David understood his father's misery – he wasn't allowed to work and therefore let his mind rest on something else other than the fact that he was ill and sitting in the house in which his beloved wife had breathed her last breath. David's heart went out to his father and he realised that Calvin was right. Their trips to the pub and George's drinking were the only things that made him less miserable than he usually was. And so, David's gratitude to his cousin just grew and grew while his own sadness at not being able to help his father at all increased at the same pace.

And so the time passed. They all, even George when he was sober and sometimes when he wasn't, continued to work diligently. It was a couple of years later, when by this time George was regularly joining them on the building sites, that David really started to worry.

CHAPTER NINETEEN

This was one of the biggest jobs Gilmore's had ever taken on – a double-storey extension on a detached house on the outskirts of town. It was a beautiful old house, with turrets and dormer windows, set in its own mature grounds. The gardens were a blaze of colour as the early spring sunshine encouraged the flowers to show themselves in all their glory. It was important that the new extension matched the character of the original house. Therefore, the materials, artificially aged, had been expensive. Still David had kept the tender as low as possible to make sure they got the job. Now all of them were having to work full-out to complete in time and earn some type of profit.

Old Joe, as he was now called in a weird attempt at showing some kind of respect, and the two lads were already clearing up for the day. They looked dusty and tired; perspiration mixed with grime had left them looking scruffy. David could see them from his position on the scaffold at the top of the house, as they scurried around tidying up for the day. Old Joe was already rinsing off the dust and cement in a bucket of cold water. The roof was nearly finished and David wondered if he could trust it to luck to leave it uncovered for the night. It certainly didn't look like rain. Deciding to take the chance, David made to descend the scaffolding by way of the ladder. The thought crossed his mind that the insurance company had insisted someone always be holding it steady at the bottom before they issued the policy. But David made to go down anyway. Then, just at that moment, Calvin appeared and, seeing David at the top of the ladder, walked over to the bottom and leant his weight against it.

'Thanks, Cal,' said David stepping off the bottom rung and wiping his forehead with the back of his hand. 'Where's Dad gone?'

Calvin eyes quickly looked away from David and then slowly

returned to his face. 'Sorry, old chap. That's where I've been. Looking for him. I noticed he'd gone, about an hour ago. Unfortunately, he took the car. We're all in the van now.'

'Never mind the car, Cal. Did you see in which direction he went? This sneaking off in the middle of the afternoon as soon as the clubs open is getting out of hand. He's had nothing to eat today and he's gone off to get blotto. We'll have to go looking for him.'

David swung between dismay and anger. His father was becoming a real problem and he didn't know what to do about it. As his son, he couldn't really tell his dad off, but that's what he felt like doing.

Calvin put his hand on David's shoulder and gave it an affectionate squeeze; he pretended concern for his cousin's wrinkled brow. 'I know, Davie, me lad. Now don't you worry. He's probably gone off to Cleethorpes to that snooker club he's joined. You remember, that's where I found him the last time? It's right near the front. One of these days, he's going to walk out that club and fall in the bloody sea.' Calvin sighed audibly. 'Let's get home quickly so I can wash up properly and I'll go straight out,' he finished.

David remembered all too well what Calvin was talking about. Looking for his father was becoming a full-time hobby, these days. George seemed to have lost all interest in the business, and his drinking had become an all-day habit starting with a shot of whisky in his morning cup of tea. David had tried all sorts of things to trick George into not drinking – hiding his bottles, making him tired on the building site so he would come home with them and, usually, fall asleep in front of the fire, and keeping him short of money.

Keeping him short of money wasn't working well though. George was still suspicious of banks and insisted they only have the one bank account – for both business and personal use. Because David saw to all the paperwork and accounts for the business, he had power of attorney over the account, but the actual bank account was in George's name, so George could get to money anytime he wanted to. And by the look of the bank statements lately, George had been plundering it for quite some time now.

David sighed, visibly shrinking into himself. He'd noticed Calvin was talking about going on his own again. And David knew that would be best. Whenever he'd gone with Calvin to find his father, there'd always been a bit of a scene before they'd managed to get George to come home with them. David just had to admit that his cousin somehow knew better how to handle George, even though he was his father. When Calvin went out looking for George, at least they'd both come home. David would search the pubs and clubs and rarely find his father but Calvin always seemed to know where to look. Admittedly, when they returned they were both the worse for wear, but at least Calvin always managed to find him and bring him home safely. 'What a good person Calvin is,' thought David, wishing he was more like his cousin. This family would be nothing without him.

They all piled into the van, David and Calvin in the front and Old Joe and the lads in the back. Within half an hour David and Calvin arrived home. Twenty minutes later, Calvin, washed and changed, was on his way into town.

He tried all the working men's clubs in Grimsby before heading for Cleethorpes. It was there, in Cambridge Street, not far from the seafront, that he finally saw the yellow Vauxhall parked just outside the club. It looked unscathed and was parked in an orderly fashion so Calvin surmised that George had probably been in the same bar all afternoon and evening. He found the entrance, just a door, directly on the street, situated between the betting shop and a ladies' clothing shop and ascended the stairs. The place was dimly lit with the exception of the snooker table, which had a large, square lamp hanging low over it. To the side was the bar. There, leaning against the bar in his working clothes, full glass of whisky in hand, face still dirt-smeared, eyes glazed and half-shut, Calvin finally found George.

'Hi, George,' Calvin said cordially.

George strained to focus and, recognising Calvin, said, 'Took yer some time to find me, eh?' A soppy grin lit up his face. His words were slurred and when he tried to stand up he swayed precariously, so, thinking the better of it, he leant his elbow back on the bar, leaving only his head bobbing up and down and swaying like one of those plastic dogs you saw in the back of cars; the ones where the heads were on hinges, not attached stiffly to their bodies, and so moved around stupidly each time the car went over a bump in the road.

Calvin ordered a whisky.

'Here you are,' said Pete, the barman, putting the double shot of Johnny Walker in front of Calvin. 'You here to pick up George, are you?'

Calvin smiled his reply and took a long swallow of the whisky. Putting down the glass, he turned to George.

'You left early today, George,' he stated simply.

'Aye, lad, that I did. Indeed, I did that.' He waved a wobbly finger in Calvin's face, attempted to swallow a belch, failed, and so giggled like a little girl. 'David and all his fancy stuff's too bloody complicated for the likes of me.' He became serious for a moment. 'Whatever happened to good old plain brickwork? That's what I want to know. We didn't do it like that in my day,' he babbled. Calvin leant closer to hear him. 'All this messing around with matching up bricks and slate. Too much bloody trouble if you ask me. We didn't do it like that in my day,' George said again. 'That lad's getting too big for his boots, I tell yer.' He raised his glass to his lips and took a good gulp, spilling most of it on his hand. 'Aye, too bloody big for his boots, he is,' repeated George, licking at his hand.

'Maybe, George,' said Calvin, taking in his uncle's sorry state. 'So you and I'll have to stick together, won't we? See that he doesn't get in the way of our nights out. Doesn't understand any fun, our lad Davie, does he now?'

'Right yer are there, Cal,' mumbled George, reaching for his glass. 'Yer a good lad, our Cal.'

'Best we keep the whereabouts of this club our little secret,' Calvin leant close into George to make the statement seem even more secretive. 'Don't want David finding us now, do we?'

'Bloody don't,' George chuckled drunkenly.

'You got your cheque book with you, George?'

'Always, Cal, always.'

'That's good. Let's pay the barman then and get off. We'll leave the car. I'll come back and get it in the morning.'

'Ee, our Cal. You don't half look after me.' George fiddled around with his back pocket and pulled out his chequebook. It was dog-eared and grubby. He opened it and looked around for someone to give him a pen.

Calvin pulled his from the inside pocket of his jacket. It was silver-plated. 'Just sign them, George. I'll fill in the rest. You'd better sign a couple to cover the costs of this.'

George strained to focus on the cheque, finding that closer was better than far away. His tongue stuck out of the corner of his mouth to aid his concentration, as he laboriously signed in the right bottom-hand corner. Calvin turned to the next cheque and pointed at the corner. George signed there, too.

'How much?' Calvin asked the barman.

'George has been generous tonight. Bought a load of rounds, he has.'

'How much?' repeated Calvin, knowing that this Pete fellow was seeing himself all right, too.

'Twenty-eight quid,' said Pete, wiping the bar-top vigorously with a cloth at some unseen fleck of dirt.

Calvin knew the man must have put at least a fiver on the bill. He coldly eyed him before lowering his head to write the cheque. 'You won't mind cashing it for a little more, then,' he challenged, pen poised, ready to start writing.

'Not at all,' Pete replied, obviously pleased things were going his way.

Calvin wrote quickly, filling in the sections of the signed cheques. In the amount box on the first cheque he wrote sixty pounds; on the second, after just a moment of hesitation, he wrote a hundred. He handed the cheque for sixty pounds to the barman, who turned round to the till to give him his change of thirty-two pounds. As he handed the money to Calvin they both looked at each other. Both knew what the other was doing.

'Come on, George,' said Calvin, taking his uncle's arm and leading him towards the door. George trotted along obediently, glad of the steadying hand.

Calvin's last thought before descending the narrow staircase out of the club and into the street was that he'd have to get to the bank to cash the other cheque tomorrow morning after picking up the car. Good old George, he thought. It was always worth the trouble of looking for him. And that's why he did it, he mused, smiling to himself as they left the club.

CHAPTER TWENTY

The living-room was practically in darkness with the exception of the light from the table-lamp, which stood on the drop-leaf table opposite the fireplace. The room had grown shabby since Iris's death. The little things, like ornaments and flowers, antimacassars and doilies, were missing. The grate of the fireplace was filled with grey ashes; no embers glowed there. It was now a room devoid of happiness. One leaf of the table was propped up and the top was littered with various ledgers and papers. On top of these, David, his head resting on his arms, slept fitfully.

He was immediately awoken as he heard the front door open and Calvin and George stumble into the hallway, singing *Nellie Dean* at the top of their lungs. He gave a great sigh of relief. Obviously Calvin had found George. And he was pleased to know that his father was home in one piece. He'd wanted to talk to his father tonight about the state of the accounts, but knew that this was another day that would go by without things being straightened out. He'd have to wait until tomorrow.

They crashed into the room. At once, David saw that Calvin was only playing the drunk to help get George into the room.

'Hiya, Dad,' David said, his face falling at the sight of his totally inebriated father.

'Now don't yer get on at me!' slurred George, waving his finger around in the vicinity of David. 'Every chap's allowed a little drink once in a while. And you, me lad, are just too big for yer boots. Ain't that so, Cal?' George turned to Calvin, lost his balance and fell against him.

'Whatever you say, George,' answered Calvin, catching George mid stumble. He motioned to David with his thumb that he would take George upstairs.

David just nodded. It was no use whatsoever trying to talk to his father tonight. 'Are you coming down again?' he asked.

'Just to get him a bucket,' said Calvin. 'I'm really tired and we'll all have to get up extra early so you can drop me off in Cleethorpes to collect the car.' He disappeared up the stairs, pushing George, who was on all fours, in front of him.

The alarm normally woke them at 6.30am each morning. David would usually make the tea and each saw to getting themselves some toast, after which they'd take the van and car, pick up Old Joe and the lads and be on the site by 8am, raring to get started. Time was money, especially as the weather often kept them at home twiddling their thumbs.

The morning after George's little outing was just such a day: it was pouring down with rain and the darkness of the sky promised more to come. They sat around the chipped Formica table in the kitchen drinking their second cup of tea. David kept thinking about the roof he'd left uncovered at the big house. Now he wished he'd spent the extra time to cover it up. That would mean a few days of good weather to let it dry out before he could finish it properly. Maybe this was the time to approach his father about the unaccounted for deficits in the bank account. He was a bit afraid about talking to his father in regard to this because, when all said and done, the business was his, George's, but his dad had just let things slip the last couple of years, and if they didn't take care of the money now, they'd soon be out of business altogether.

David looked at George from across the kitchen table. His face was grey, and wrinkled far beyond his years. He looked thin and fragile, his cheekbones prominent, his eyes sunken. David hated to bring any more grief to his door, but he had to ask him where all the money was going for all their sakes.

Cash cheques for as much as a hundred pounds were often being paid out by the bank and David didn't know what for. His father didn't look like he was living the high life, but the money was gone. Surely his bar bills weren't that much! He looked at Calvin. Calvin was a godsend. Without his help, David thought, his father might be in some back alley, drunk and beaten up by robbers. Calvin at least found George and brought him home safely. Maybe if he didn't, there would be a lot more money missing out of the account.

'Dad?' David sought to get George's attention.

'What?' George replied, lifting his head off his chin and looking David straight in the eyes. 'Don't yer think yer going to lecture me now. A man's got a right to have a drink now and again. You, yer little prissy git, never go out, so what do yer know about the real world? Work and sleep that's all you do, you boring little fart. If it wasn't for Calvin, I'd have no one to talk to here.' And he sank his head back on his hands.

'Now, George,' said Calvin, trying to soften the moment.

David's heart sank. There seemed to be nothing he could do to make his father like him even, let alone love him. It was true, he didn't go out very often because he was totally tied up in the business, doing his utmost to make not only a profit but to expand and make something of the Gilmore name. He was doing it for them all. Couldn't his father see that? Couldn't he just once be proud of him? Or at least acknowledge his hard work? He took a deep breath. Despite whatever his father thought of him, it was now or never to ask about the money. He couldn't possibly carry on pretending the business was all right if there was so much cash mysteriously missing.

'Dad,' David started again. 'There's been quite a lot of money gone out of the account in the last couple of months which I don't have any invoices for, or anything to show what they are paying for. In fact, there have been unaccounted cheques going out regularly for months now. Do you know what they were for? I need to list them somewhere in the accounts ledger.'

Fire sprang to George's bloodshot eyes. 'How dare you, you little snot! What do you think I'm doing? I can't remember the last time I wrote a cheque. It's you spending the money, I bet. Just what have you been doing with it? The business was all right when I was doing the books. It must be you messing up as usual. Too big for yer bloody boots, that's what you're getting.' George's face was crimson with fury, his mouth in a snarl.

David cringed at the attack. 'I just don't know where these cheques have gone to, Dad. There's nearly four hundred pounds missing.'

'You've lifted four hundred pounds out of the business! Don't I pay you enough? What do you mean you don't know where they have gone?' With that George pulled the chequebook out of his back pocket and threw it on the table. 'Here, clever bugger. You see how you get on with writing all the cheques. What a bloody cheek! To be accused by my own son of thieving from the business. I've never heard anything like it.' George fell silent. His eyes glistened with fury.

David felt awful. He hadn't meant to make it sound like he was accusing his father of stealing from the company. Maybe he'd made a mistake; maybe he'd added up the columns of figures wrongly. But even as he asked himself this question, he knew definitely that his additions were correct. Now he'd upset his father, driven the wedge between them even deeper, and was still no nearer to discovering where the missing money had gone. He too fell silent.

'Come on, Uncle George,' said Calvin using the title uncle for the first time in ages. 'David's just having a job balancing the books. I'm sure he didn't mean to upset you.'

David picked up the chequebook from the table and opened it. He examined the stubs, hoping to find some explanation of where the money had gone. The stubs were blank. And there were two new ones.

'What happened when you picked Dad up last night?' he asked Calvin.

'Well, I didn't like to tell you but he was brandishing the chequebook around when I walked in. I took it out of his hand and put it back in his pocket. I never thought for a moment that he'd written any cheques. He seemed too drunk to write, actually. I paid the bill out of my wages. It was quite high so he'd really had a skinful. I'm so sorry, David. I really tried my best. Just didn't get to him in time. I'm sorry.'

George said nothing to this explanation. His darting eyes and puzzled look showed he wasn't sure at all about his actions the previous evening.

'It's all right, Cal.'

David's shoulders sank in defeat. His father was angry with him. Calvin was apologising when he had nothing to apologise for and the bank account was as empty as ever with no true explanation. His dad must have just squandered it away, or given it away, if he really thought about it. Once Dad was drunk, he was a soft touch for anyone with a hard luck story. He'd often seen him empty his pockets and give the money to a comparative stranger. He reached over and took the chequebook from the middle of the table where he had left it. Dad would just have to be mad at him. If he didn't look after the money, they'd all be broke.

Calvin saw David take the chequebook and put it with his other papers on the clipboard. This was not a good thing. He'd got used to having the extra cash. If the chequebook was in David's possession, he doubted very much that he would be able to convince him to write open cheques. Something had to change here. David was becoming far too business-orientated. Thinking of little else, except work and looking after that stupid drunk of a father of his. Now if he were out of the way, David might be more willing to share the profits of the business more readily. Maybe even make him a partner. As David always said, they were more like brothers than cousins and he'd served him well, hadn't he?

CHAPTER TWENTY-ONE

'Looks like the rain is easing up.' Calvin left the kitchen table and opened the back door of the house and peered upwards into the sky. He prodded the air with his finger, pointing. 'It's certainly getting lighter over there.'

'Yeah.' George finally broke his silence. He still hadn't looked once or spoken to David after the palaver about the chequebook. And his stance made it clear that he didn't intend to speak to him at all unless he had to. 'Cal, get the flasks made up. I'll do us some sandwiches. Might as well see what we can save from the day.'

The snub had not gone over David's head. His father's obvious aloofness towards him made him sad but they would all be in trouble if he didn't watch where the money was going. The suppliers only gave them a month's credit, and often the clients didn't pay on time. Sometimes it was just so hard to make ends meet. The way they were working, there should be far more profit than what they were making. Four hundred pounds missing, the thought raced through David's head over and over again. Where had it gone? No one can drink that much, surely?

He didn't intend to sit doing nothing while the others were busy.

'I'll go get the van out the yard then,' he said to no one in particular. He grabbed his coat from the back of the cupboard door and left the house.

Calvin boiled the water for the coffee. They always had coffee in the flasks because tea tended to take on a funny taste after a couple of hours of being kept thermally warm. The flasks were different colours, and each had their own as they were inclined to drink straight from the flask rather than transfer the drink to the plastic cup which worked as a top for the flask. Instant coffee powder and sugar already in the three flasks, Calvin poured water in to the top of two and only half-filled one, George's.

'Special coffee for you, George?' Calvin already knew the answer and bent to reach under the kitchen sink to get the bottle of whisky that was kept hidden there at the back, behind the waste bin.

'Right, lad. You're a good lad, our Cal. A hair of the dog will be just what the doctor ordered.'

'Well, that should keep you going, George.'

George stopped wrapping the sandwiches and turned his head to look at Calvin. 'What do you think I did with that money?' he asked, his face screwed up in consternation. 'I can't remember giving anybody anything.'

'Now don't you worry about that, George. David's probably made a mistake in his sums.' Calvin filled up the flask until the whisky nearly sloshed out of the top. 'What you need is a few days off. You work too hard.'

'But four hundred quid, lad. It must have gone somewhere.'

'Here, Uncle George,' Calvin handed George a teacup half-full of whisky. George peered into the cup, recognised its contents, raised his eyes to smile weakly at Calvin and downed the liquid in one swallow.

At that moment, David hooted the horn of the van to let them know he was back. The rain had almost stopped completely by now.

By the time they had picked up the car, Old Joe, and the lads, and got themselves sorted out at the building site, it was going on noon. The rain had stopped and the sun was shining brightly, as though to make a mockery of the grey rain clouds it had chased away.

David's first job had been to scale up the scaffolding and check the damage to the roof. The attic was soaked. But maybe it wouldn't be too bad if this sun kept shining. One thing was for sure. He wouldn't be leaving the site tonight without either finishing the roof or covering it up. Despite the intensity of the sun, David decided to take no chances and left to get a strong plastic cover, just in case he needed it later. By the time he arrived back, they were all having a lunch break. Sitting around on upturned buckets and old crates, they ate their sandwiches and emptied their flasks. The whole procedure took no longer than half an hour.

It was getting well into the afternoon by now. The skies were beginning to darken again and it wasn't clear if it was bad weather looming or the nightfall creeping in. Old Joe and George went off to mix cement, the two young lads were fetching and carrying up the scaffolding for all they were worth and David and Calvin were busy trying to get the roof finished.

Just after 5pm, it started to rain again; lightly, more like drizzle really. David and Calvin were still working on the roof and the realisation hit them that they would not be finished on this day and would need to cover the open roof to prevent any more rain getting into the attic and possibly staining the ceilings of the rooms below. They hastened down to ground level to get the covering.

All around the site the activity was fierce as they all rushed to clear up and cover the cement and sand.

'Just a couple more hours and it would have been finished,' David complained loudly to himself. 'I'll go get the plastic, Cal. You help Dad and the others here.'

'Wait, I've got a better idea,' said Calvin. 'When we've cleared up here, you take the van and drop off Joe and the lads. I'll do this with George.'

'But it's slippery up there. And it's getting dark,' protested David.

'Look, old bean. If you leave George to go home on his own, either in the car or in the van, after dropping off everyone, he's bound to finish up in some bar somewhere. And I really am too tired to go looking for him again this evening.' Calvin gave David a patient but pained grin.

Trust Calvin to always think of everyone. He was right, of course. And it was no good him staying with George, because George never listened to him and, anyway, wasn't even speaking to him at the moment. Oh, how he wished the mystery of the four hundred pounds was cleared up. He hated having his father mad at him. All he really wanted to do was hug him and tell him everything would be all right, but David knew that George would simply not tolerate such physical contact. In all his nineteen years, not once had his father hugged him. An instant sadness filled his heart. He looked at George, who was toiling amongst the bricks and dirt, wizened and crooked from years of hard work, old before his time. He'd aged visibly since Iris's death. The tuberculosis had left him pale, thin and scrawny. He'd refused to stay home and rest as the doctors had said, saying there was too much time to think when he was at home alone. David so much wanted to do more for him, but didn't know how; no matter how he tried, there seemed to be no way to get near his father. Calvin was the one that George trusted, spoke to, laughed with, when he did laugh. He didn't want to leave him now, but knew it would be better, easier all round if he took the others home and left Calvin to look after George.

David watched his dad covering the sand with a plastic sheet, putting a brick around the edges to stop the wind taking it away. How frail he looked. He seemed to be shaking and David wondered if he was still inebriated from last night, although he didn't see how. Even though George had been on the building site most of the day, he still seemed to David to be worse the wear for drink. Maybe it was the hangover from last night.

'Dad, can you help Cal put up a rain-sheet on the roof? I'll take the van and get the others home.'

George just looked at him. He didn't speak. David tried again. 'I'll get fish and chips for tea from Craven's. You like them from there, don't you, Dad?'

'Aye,' George acknowledged grudgingly.

Old Joe in the passenger seat of the van, lads in the back, David got into the driver's seat and switched on the motor. The drizzle was turning to proper rain now and he thought of his father's weak chest and started to worry. Leaning out of the wound-down side window he bellowed at Calvin and George, 'I'll see you both when you get home. Fish and chips will be on the table waiting.'

Calvin, behind George at the bottom of the ladder, turned to show a thumbs-up sign and wave to David. George stopped in his tracks. He hesitated but didn't turn round and then made to start up the ladder. Calvin followed him.

Maybe Dad will have forgiven me by teatime, thought David. I'll get the fire lit and set the table in the living-room for a change.

Yeah, he'll like that.

With a last glimpse of his father and the knowledge in his heart that he would make things up to him at teatime, David drove off.

CHAPTER TWENTY-TWO

The rain was coming down quite hard by now. The rungs of the ladder were slippery and both George and Calvin had to hold on firmly. They reached the top and stepped on to the scaffolding. Turning round, Calvin surveyed the scenery before him.

'Look, George. Isn't it magnificent? England's green and pleasant land, despite the rain,' he laughed.

George also turned around and looked out over the fields and rolling countryside. Some people have all the luck, he thought. 'Fancy being able to live here and see all this, especially on a fine day. Does it ever stop raining?' He looked at Calvin who was reaching in his trousers' back pocket. He pulled out a silver-plated hip flask.

'Come on, Uncle George. Have a drink with me, one for the road to toast this beautiful scenery and our friendship. We have been friends, haven't we?' Calvin moved closer and put his arm around George's shoulders.

'Aye, that we have, me lad. It'd be a lonely world without yer. That bloody son of mine is a load of bloody rubbish, that he is. Should have been more like you. Accused me of stealing, he has.' George reached for the hip flask and took a number of rapid swallows.

'Don't feel bad, George. He didn't mean it.'

'Thing is, Cal, I can't remember what I did with those cheques. Must have done something. I'm the only one with a chequebook.'

Calvin gave his uncle's thin shoulders an affectionate squeeze. George didn't shrug him off. It was the first affection he had felt since Iris had left him.

'Have another drink, George,' Calvin prompted him.

George tipped his head back and poured the golden liquid down his throat. He just had time to swallow before he felt himself flying through the air. He saw Calvin standing there, his arms still outstretched from the push he had given to his chest. He saw scaffolding and parts of the building whizzing past him and yet everything was moving in slow motion. He looked up; even through the dimming light he could see Calvin leaning over the rail. He could see him clearly.

George didn't scream; shock closed his throat making sound impossible. He hit the ground with a sickening thud. The last thing he saw, as the evening moon cast its glow over the rooftop, was Calvin waving to him. And then the darkness came.

CHAPTER TWENTY-THREE

'You really are going to have to get over this, David!'

The use of his full name caught his attention and David looked up from the balance sheet he was working on to stare silently at Calvin who was pacing the living-room while drinking tea from a mug. He was spruced up and in his new jeans and leather jacket, ready to go out. He was trying to persuade David to go with him.

'It's been over two years now,' Calvin went on. 'Accidents happen. It wasn't your fault. Man! You weren't even there. How do you think I feel? I was there. I should have saved him. You're tearing me up, Davie old bean.'

Calvin abruptly stopped pacing. He turned his back to David and hung his head. The hand with his tea mug hung limp at his side, tipping the mug and nearly spilling his tea. His other hand went up to his forehead. He screwed up his eyes and rubbed at their inner corners with his thumb and forefinger. He presented a picture of abject misery. David immediately felt guilty.

'Come on, Cal. Don't get upset. There was nothing you could do. You were the other side of the scaffolding. It must have been awful for you. I'm sorry I keep reminding you of it. It's just, well, you know…' David's voice trailed off.

Calvin turned towards him and put a hand on his shoulder. 'I know, mate. I know.' He smiled down at David, who raised his head to meet his gaze. For the umpteenth time, David was amazed at how blue Calvin's eyes were. His long black lashes softened their piercing effect. Indeed, those eyes smouldered in his face and David wished he himself were more like his cousin in the looks department. Calvin was so good-looking. Over the years Calvin, always tall anyway, had grown taller and the hard work on the building sites had filled out his muscles, his shoulders and thighs bulged with them, leaving the rest of his body lean and hard. Despite being of simple working-class, his features had developed a well-to-do arrogance more readily found amongst the aristocrats. For some reason unfathomable to David, Calvin always took great care of how he dressed. Even in his working clothes he seemed to look smarter than the rest of them. People coming on the site and looking for the boss always approached him first. And he was never lost for words, not like David; he never needed time to think before he spoke, never stuttered over his words and groped around for the right thing to say. People simply warmed to Calvin immediately and he knew how to please them, what to say to them to make them feel relaxed and happy in his company.

It never failed to fascinate David how much Calvin looked like the pictures he had seen of Lord Byron, the poet. He'd stolen the book from school and kept it all these years because of that uncanny resemblance. He'd never shown it to Calvin who didn't really seem bothered about books. He gave an inward chuckle. Despite his lack of interest, though, bet if he wanted to write poetry, Calvin would be able to do that at the drop of a hat, too. He seemed able to do anything. And here he was now, trying to jolly him up by asking him to go out for a drink and he was saying no, yet again.

Calvin had walked over to touch David; he now withdrew his hand from David's shoulder. He knew David wasn't much for physical shows of affection. But he always liked to see him go all soft and silly when he acted kind towards him. Yes, show Davie a bit of sympathy and he was putty in your hands.

'So, you won't be coming tonight then? But next week, on my birthday, I don't want to hear that you are busy. And I don't want to go out on my own on that day either. You can leave your books and your calculator for a change and come celebrate with me. Is that clear, Davie? I want you to finally have some fun: all work and no play, et cetera, et cetera. You know what I mean?'

'Okay, Cal. I promise. There are a couple of things I need to sort out before then. But I promise you your twenty-third birthday will be something special. Is there anyone else you want to invite along? What about that girl from Market Street you were telling me about? You seemed quite taken with her.'

It was strange really. As handsome and charming as Calvin was, he didn't seem to have that many friends, preferring to go out alone rather than meet up with a gang. There never seemed to be a shortage of women that wanted him but most of his girlfriends never lasted more than a couple of weeks before he was back on the prowl for something new. He must have let them down gently, in his typical engaging way, for he never seemed to make any enemies. In fact, he was made welcome in most circles but he always went off on his own after an hour or so. No, Calvin didn't have friends, but lots of acquaintances. That's what was so strange. Calvin appeared to have contact with loads of folks, he knew lots of people, but he never seemed to be close to any of them. He was close to him though; David felt this. Calvin made him feel special, needed and wanted. Something he hadn't felt since his mother had died.

'Oh, she started getting too serious,' Calvin answered him. 'You know what women are like: always looking for a husband. Not me, old bean. Definitely not me.' He laughed.

'Get off with yer,' chided David with a chuckle. Then, with his mind on work again, he said, 'Remember that you are working on your own first thing in the morning. I'm off to see that job over in Scartho. Sounds like it might be a big one. And after, I need to see the solicitor to sort something out with the business.'

'Everything all right, is it?' Calvin raised an eyebrow in query. 'We're not going bankrupt or anything, are we?'

A cold shiver went up Calvin's spine. George had always looked after him, even if he didn't know just how well he'd looked after him. And David was generous, too. He always left money in the home petty cash tin, the one they hid in the oven, which was rarely used these days. David had told Calvin to help himself if he needed anything over and above his wages. And he never complained when the tin was mostly empty after the third week in the month. No, no. It wouldn't do for David to let the business go to rack and ruin.

'No, not at all. In fact Gilmore's is doing all right considering we are both under twenty-five. And if it ever stopped raining and snowing for long enough so we could work all year, we might be able to afford a proper holiday next year, you know, go somewhere in a plane, like

Spain or Italy. See how the other half live.' David smiled at the thought. They'd never been further than Scarborough, and that for only a weekend.

Content that the source of his money was not about to dry up, Calvin turned to peer in the mirror above the fireplace. He straightened his tie and ran his fingers through his hair, pulling the top hair down a little to fall on his forehead. 'Right Davie, me old sausage. You stay here and mollycoddle the books. I'll go and represent British manhood.' He moved towards the door of the living-room and passed into the hallway, calling after himself, 'But next week, mind you, I will not be put off next week.'

'All right,' David called in reply just before he heard the front door slam shut.

The house now silent, he spent a few more minutes checking figures and writing in the work's journal. He was pleased with the figures before him. They had worked hard and new jobs were always coming in from recommendations. He wondered if his father would have been pleased with what he had achieved with the business, with the Gilmore name. Of course, it had been easier for David to sink himself into work rather than think about his father as he was doing now.

With a sigh, he got up from the living-room table and went into the kitchen to get a drink. They'd both eaten tea in the little homely 'caf' on the corner of Park Street and Cleethorpes Road. Plain, simple but good grub for just five bob a go. He looked around the kitchen. It was untidy. Unwashed cups and plates littered the sink and draining board. This will have to wait until Mrs Downes comes in tomorrow, thought David. A good-natured woman, she would moan at the mess they had left her, grumble as she cleaned it away, and make them a casserole before leaving. She was a gem. There was a big old fridge humming in the corner where the pantry used to be. A pile of old newspapers stood next to it where Whisky's basket had once been. David closed his eyes at the thought of Whisky. He may have been his father's dog, but he had loved him just the same and now, they were all gone. All that he had loved in his life had left him.

He opened the fridge and reached for a beer, looked at it for a second and replaced it on the shelf. He wasn't a beer drinker, didn't like the taste, in fact he only drank it to keep Cal company. He much preferred wine but it was so expensive. What the hell, he thought. He'd worked all day, he'd done the books, he'd done his duty. Now was the time for some pleasure.

David closed the door of the fridge and pulled a bottle of red wine off the wine rack, which rested on top of the fridge. He liked red wine. Within seconds he was back on his way to the living-room, a glass of wine in one hand, the bottle in the other. He flicked the on-switch on the television and settled back in the armchair, the one in which his father had always sat, to watch the regional news.

He listened as the presenter told of a young girl's body which had been found in the marshes near Tetney, a village not that far from Grimsby. The pub at Tetney Lock was very popular and always packed with young people. Although he didn't go out that much, he'd been to the Tetney Lock pub once or twice together with Calvin. It had a great atmosphere and was one of his favourite places. A chill ran up his spine and made the hair on the back of his neck stand on end. He hoped the young woman found in the marshes was not someone he'd known: someone he'd spoken to in the pub. 'What is happening to the world today?' he could hear his mother's voice asking. She would always say that when she heard of something so horrible. And now he too wondered just what was happening with the world today or, more precisely, just what had happened to his neck of the woods where such a thing as murder was unheard of. It had always been safe here. Quite boring really, but always safe. Nowadays, you were always hearing of someone being murdered, or raped or robbed and not just round London way, but here in the North where nothing of that sort ever happened. 'What is the world coming to?' he asked himself again and smiled at the words as they echoed round his head. He closed his eyes and he could see and hear his mother saying them. Things were different now, though. So much had changed since her death.

Leaning back in the chair, David savoured his wine. He'd turned the television off after the news, which had depressed him, and put on some soothing music on the old gramophone. Iris's old Mario

Lanza records filled the room with emotion. Calvin always brought home the newest titles and the shelves were heaving with his choices – the Beatles, Sandie Shaw, Lulu, the Rolling Stones – but David still liked the music of yesteryear. Calvin never really understood that he didn't mind being alone, that these evenings that he spent with Mario Lanza or Maria Callas, with a bottle of wine and only his thoughts for company, were moments of tranquillity for him. It was a time in which he would try to make head or tail of things, to try and work out what he should do next, a time to dream.

It hadn't been easy in the months after his father's death. Calvin had been a tower of strength. He had made the funeral arrangements, taking over when he saw that David was incapable of any action. He had seen to the choice of coffin, the choice of songs in the chapel, and even arranged the flowers. David had been immobilised. He had taken to sitting in his father's chair next to the fireplace and rocking back and forth silently. Calvin had not chastised him at all for this distant behaviour, somehow seeming to understand his grief and allowing him the time to try and accept what had happened. The words 'if only' roared around his head day and night. If only he had been there; if only he had not taken the others home; if only he had been the one to cover up the roof and not his father; if only he had finished the roof in time before the rain started; if only...

It took months before David was out of this zombie-like state. He had continued to work, finding forgetfulness in the creativity he performed with his hands. He thought of nothing else, just building, just working, no matter what. But George and his pained outcry of, 'Are you accusing me of thieving from the business?' never left his mind. He was driven by some unseen force, alone, searching for a way to stop the self-blame, to take away the guilt that was becoming too heavy to bear.

On this particular evening David knew exactly what he wanted to think about. It was something that he had been planning for quite some time now. Something that was making him feel good for a change. And next week seemed the most logical time to put his plan into action.

CHAPTER TWENTY-FOUR

Scartho was very definitely an up-market area of Grimsby town. It had beautiful shady tree-lined avenues and an abundance of skilfully tended gardens with a flood of colour, whatever time of year. The road was wider than anywhere else in town; at the roundabout at the bottom of the road, the technical college sprawled over a vast area, laying haughty claim to the intelligence of anyone and everyone who ever attended this educational institution. The new indoor swimming baths, complete with new-fangled saunas, had been built here along this wide road. The vast amount of glass used in the construction reflected the opulence of the surrounding area. At the top of the road, just before it veered to the left, Scartho Hospital nestled in lush, quiet gardens. Although very little could be seen to identify it as a hospital, this district was treated with a reverence bordering on the holy. This was definitely a very posh area of town.

The continuation of this road led to semi-detached and finally detached houses; all standing proudly in their own vibrant gardens with luscious lawns and long driveways up to the house; and all of a class previously untouched by David.

It was to one of these houses that David was making his way.

He inched forward in the slow-moving traffic, seeking number 159, hand on the indicator, ready to pull in at any minute. And, suddenly, there it stood.

The house was impressive. It was a one-storeyed building, modern and representative of the best types of houses built some ten years ago. David looked around him as he pulled into the drive and manoeuvred his car along the perfectly-trimmed cypress-tree hedge. When he saw the back door of the bungalow just in front of him to the left, he stopped, turned the engine off, grabbed his measuring tape and large writing block and stepped out of the car. He tugged at the bottom of his checked blazer, his best blazer, as it happened, to pull it into place. It was growing a bit too threadbare and a little too tight for him and suddenly David wished he had made the time to buy some new clothes, clothes more suited to this area. He felt a bit nervous; a bit out of his league. He was not used to dealing with people of this calibre. Nevertheless, he straightened his spine, approached the back door and rang the bell.

'Hello,' he said to the elderly woman who opened the door. She was dressed in a floral overall and was wiping her hands on a tea towel.

'Ah, yes,' she answered him. 'You must be Mr Gilmore. Right?' She raised an eyebrow in enquiry.

'Yes, I am. I have an appointment with Mr Jensen.' David was starting to feel tense. This was part of the job he didn't really like. Meeting new people was always difficult for him. He swayed from foot to foot. He was here to speak to a Mr Jensen who had phoned him two days ago about an extension.

'Is Mr. Jensen here?'

'Yes. Please come this way. Mr Jensen is expecting you.' The woman stood to one side and motioned David into the kitchen and through to a room on the other side of the hallway. It looked like David imagined a study should look. 'Please wait here. Mr Jensen will be with you in a minute.' And with that, she closed the door and was gone.

The room was filled with books on shelves that reached from the hip-level cupboards to the ceiling. Opposite the leaded French windows was a fine writing desk in what looked like rich mahogany wood. It was leather-topped, and a grand black-leather swivel chair made up the picture. A couple of healthy ivy plants trailed from the shelves. It was a fine room: a room obviously belonging to someone of importance. David squared his shoulders.

'Good morning!' said the voice belonging to the man who strode through the door a couple of minutes later. 'Mr Gilmore?' He was dressed in baggy brown corduroy trousers and a multicoloured sloppy Joe of a sweater. He extended his hand in welcome.

David took the proffered hand and shook it firmly. There was something about this man that made him relax immediately. Maybe it was his comfortable attire or his friendly smile, or just the way that he approached him – with enthusiasm. It didn't matter what it was, David hoped desperately that whatever the man wanted doing with his home, he would be able to do it. More than that. Do it well. There was something in those first few seconds of meeting this Jensen man that made David so want to please him, to impress him. To show him that he may be from the other side of town, but he was worthy of recognition.

'You called me about an extension, Mr Jensen. What exactly is it that I can do for you?'

'Big job, Gilmore,' said Jensen moving through the door and into the hallway, beckoning David to follow him. 'I've heard some good things about your work, laddie.'

David cringed at the address. He might only be twenty-one but he was sorely fed up of people judging him by his boyish looks.

'Tell me what it is you want, Mr Jensen, and I'll tell you if Gilmore's is capable of fulfilling your desires.' His back was going up.

They'd moved into the hall and come to the bottom of a staircase which led to a closed door at the top. Ascending the stairs, Jensen opened the door onto an attic room of no consequence.

'I want you to make this into a flat: comfortable living quarters that would suit a young lady. I have a daughter of an age where she requires a place of her own. What better place than this? Near to her father, in case she may need him. But separated enough for her to feel independent. What do you say, Gilmore?'

'Do you still have the plans for this house, Mr Jensen?' David was already walking through the spacious room; the sloping roof only worked to make it cosy and an interesting shape. There were already two dormer windows in one side of the roof. They overlooked the luscious gardens at the back of the house, away from the noise of the busy road. David's mind started to conjure up pictures of various possibilities. He stood still for a moment in the middle of the large space and tapped his pencil against his teeth while his mind swarmed with ideas. The attic had a floor area as large as the actual house. It was really big. Without turning to Jensen he said, 'I'm thinking you are going to need a bathroom of generous size, considering we are talking about a young lady here, and maybe a separate dressing room which could be incorporated into the eaves, so as not to waste space. That would leave enough room to make a spacious bed-sitting room, which could be open-plan, divided by opened shelving, or similar. At the sitting end of the room, a small kitchenette could be incorporated. We have the two windows here,' David pointed with his pencil at the dormers, 'and we could incorporate into the roof on this side,' his pencil swung over to the other side, 'a couple of skylights for extra light and fresh air.' He started to pace the room, making notes and screwing up his eyes in imagination as he pictured various possibilities.

Mr Jensen left the attic only to return a few minutes later with a large copy of the original house plans. He unfolded them and laid them on the floor. Both he and David crouched over them. Jensen was breathing down David's neck.

'Any chance I could take these with me for a day or so, Mr Jensen?' David straightened up to get away from Jensen's breath on his neck. 'I could draw you up some plans then, to show you my ideas, and give you an estimate of the costs of the work.'

Jensen also stood up. 'That would be all right by me, Gilmore. How much time do you think you'll need? I've had another couple of builders look at the job and they have promised to have their estimates to me by the end of the week.'

'You'll have ours by the end of the week then too, sir.' David's heart sank. It wasn't a sure job then. Looking round, it would be the biggest conversion they had ever taken on, but it was more than that; something was screaming in his head that he must get this job, no matter what.

'Right, Gilmore. I'll see you on Friday night with your estimate and let you know by Monday what I'm going to do. All right?' Jensen smiled the smile of a man who knew he had David in his hand. Jensen was used to such power.

CHAPTER TWENTY-FIVE

From Jensen's house in Scartho, David drove straight to the solicitor's office in Yarborough Road on the other side of town. The length of the journey gave him time to think about Jensen's house. This was where the money was. A conversion really, rather than an extension. The structure was already there. Okay, there was plumbing to install, insulation and heating, but electricity was already up there as were the two dormer windows. David wondered about the other firms and what their quotes would be like. One thing was for sure. If Gilmore's could get this job and people saw their van with its logo painted on the side driving through and working at a house in the area, they would surely get more offers of work here in the upper-class part of town. That could only mean one thing – a step upwards.

With butterflies in his stomach at the thought of improvement and bettering their financial prospects, David made his way into the offices of Chapman and Sons. If he got the Jensen job, this day would stay in his memory forever. He chuckled to himself at his thoughts. So, and now to see the solicitor.

The only other time he had seen a solicitor was when his father had died and there were legalities to be sorted out with the business and the house in Cooper Road. David considered himself a simple, working-class man who just didn't hobnob with solicitors and such, and talking to such people always made him feel a bit awkward, a little out of place. Mind you, he pondered, the longer he was in business, the more often he was having to deal with planning offices, architects, accountants and the like. But today David had something that he wanted to do with Gilmore's. He had thought about it a long time now and the only way to make such an adjustment to the firm was to get it done by a solicitor to make sure it was official. So here he was, sitting in the waiting-room, getting ready to speak to Mr

Chapman, *his* solicitor. He twiddled with his tattered leather document-holder while he waited.

The news had just finished and Calvin was getting ready to go out again. 'What did you say the name was of that girl you were seeing a couple of weeks ago?' David called through the kitchen to the bathroom.

'What?' Calvin's face appeared at the door, toothbrush in his mouth.

'It's been on the news that a girl was found murdered in the marshes near Tetney. They gave her name as Christine Chappers. Didn't you go out with a Christine Chappers?'

'What?' Calvin repeated, stopping his brushing motion and taking the toothbrush out of his mouth. He disappeared from the doorway and David could hear him rinsing out his mouth. 'Christine Chappers is dead?' Calvin came out of the bathroom.

'Just said so on the news,' confirmed David.

'Bloody hell!' exclaimed Calvin. 'I only saw her the other week. Not really my type, of course. But a nice girl, nevertheless. Who would want to kill her? Have they caught anybody?'

'No,' David answered simply. Poor Calvin, he thought. How terrible to learn that someone you have known, gone out with, in fact, had been killed. A shudder went up David's spine.

Calvin plonked himself in the armchair next to the fireplace in the living-room. 'Bloody hell,' he repeated.

'Hang on, Calvin,' David rose from his chair. 'Give me five minutes and I'll go with you tonight for a drink.' David knew how sensitive Calvin was. He would brood and blame himself for not looking after this Christine woman if David wasn't around to take his mind off things. Calvin was like that. Had a thought for everyone but himself. And this was a chance to talk to Calvin about the new job, about making it good and as inexpensive as possible to secure the contract.

Yes, Calvin really was a great help and he needed to talk to him and get his opinion. They worked well together. Calvin never interfered with the planning and accountancy side of things, but he was good at organising the other workers and keeping everything running smoothly on the site. Often Calvin had laughed that Gilmore's was only a success because he, Calvin, did the mindless building, and David did the nice bit of planning the jobs and carrying the responsibility. David knew, though, that he was only joking.

What a team they made. The thought warmed David's heart. Calvin was just so very good with people. It didn't matter that he didn't want to get involved with the business side of the firm. As long as he had enough money to go out and enjoy himself, Calvin seemed to be happy. David blessed the day when Calvin had entered his life. Without him he would have no family at all now. Next week, Calvin would know the depth of his gratitude. This night, however, he would just feel David's caring company.

Calvin's birthday had arrived. David wished he knew more people to invite to celebrate the event. Old Joe had said he was too tired after a day's work and the two young lads, well, they were pleased to just get off work and certainly didn't want to hang around the 'old' bosses in their free time. So it was just Calvin and David that made their way to the Kingsway Hotel in Cleethorpes for a celebratory meal. After a banquet, comprising prawn cocktails and succulent roast beef with all the trimmings, followed by trifle with extra cream, sherries to start with, wine with the meal and brandies with the coffee, both Calvin and David were feeling rather mellow. This was the time that David had waited for, the time to let Calvin into the good news and give him his birthday present.

'Cal? You know that job I went to see last week, the one in Scartho?'

'You mean the one you got all nervous about?'

'Yeah, that's the one,' David chuckled, not noticing the snipe. 'Well, we got it! Start in two weeks, when we've finished Brewer's place.'

Calvin could never quite understand why David got so excited over getting a job. There would always be work for them. Hadn't David proved this to him? They'd never been out of work. In fact, he thought David pushed them far too hard, one job directly after another. Still, as long as the money was coming in, that alone was important, wasn't it? And David always saw that money was there for him; what more did he want? He had a good life, no responsibility and no worries. He wanted for nothing. Looking across the table at David, he could feel the affection. Silly bugger still thinks I'm his hero. Well, let him think that. Daft sod. He's good for a few more years. This meal had been great, too. He would certainly keep to this level of dining out in the future. No more fish and chips and the fancy Chinese food that was so popular these days but left you feeling hungry again after a couple of hours. Here, the tablecloths were starched, the cutlery was shiny and the glasses sparkled like diamonds. The waiters had suits on and wore bow ties, and treated you like someone important. And that's what Calvin was, someone important. Other people should notice that, too.

David reached into the inside pocket of his jacket and pulled out a folded paper. He was feeling so excited, he could hardly contain himself. 'This is for you, Cal. Happy birthday.' He straightened out the paper and handed the official-looking document across the table to Calvin.

'What's this, old bean?' Calvin took the document from David's hands. He went quiet while he read it then looked up at David in surprise.

'No, no, Cal. Don't say anything. You deserve it. You are the only family I have. It's only right, mate.'

Calvin's eyes reverted back to the document, right to the part where it stated that the business formerly known as Gilmore's Constructions was now officially to be known as Gilmore and Fisher Constructions.

Calvin smiled across the table at David. Not only was he someone of importance, now he even had the documents to prove it.

CHAPTER TWENTY-SIX

The year of 1969 was a year of violence, unrest and achievements in the world. The film star Sharon Tate was brutally and sadistically slain in Hollywood; three hundred thousand Nigerians faced famine; two hundred and fifty hippie squatters were evicted by the police from a mansion in London's West End; fertility drugs became fashionable; the Kray twins were jailed. It was a year for off-beat, drop-out films such as *Midnight Cowboy, Easy Rider* and *Women in Love*. Judy Garland finally killed herself. Violence erupted in Ireland. John Lennon preached love by having reporters photograph him in bed with his wife Yoko Ono. Women's skirt lengths went down to the maxi. And a man walked on the moon.

The whole of the civilised world was talking about human eggs being fertilised in a test-tube; the election of Golda Meir as Prime Minister of Israel; the young girl who drowned when Senator Edward Kennedy crashed his car on Chappaquiddick; the terrorist bombings in Milan and Rome; the feeling of camaraderie as European lands rebuilt their countries after the war had flown. Things were changing. Reports of brutality and cruelty hardly turned anyone's heads these days. The world was becoming a cesspit of violence and indifference.

In Grimsby, things were also changing.

The end of the Swinging Sixties saw Grimsby as a town of great prosperity. The seiners and the trawlers went out to fish and came back loaded with record-breaking catches. Between trips, the pubs and clubs were full of fishermen making merry. Money flowed in the small businesses of the town, work was readily available; life was good. But even here, too, brutality and cruelty crept in.

There had been four murders in the last couple of years. The police were talking of a serial killer but no leads had been found. The names of the victims faded off as the police failed in catching the perpetrator and the news hardly even bothered to follow up with their reports, so insignificant became the crimes as they went undetected.

By December of that year, David and Calvin were working hard on the extension in Scartho. It had to be finished by the 18th because Mr Jensen's daughter was returning from Iceland where she had been living for the last two years. Now, in its final stages, Jensen was permanently hovering around and holding up progress with his extra ideas and demands. The majority of the work had gone without a hitch or interference from Jensen because, as the owner/skipper of a big trawler, he was gone for most of the month. But, oh boy! When he was in the house he hovered and questioned and argued with what was going on. Although he seemed more than pleased with what Gilmore and Fisher had done to his attic, he paced nervously around muttering to himself about whether his daughter would be happy with it or not. It became abundantly clear that his daughter's happiness was his only real concern.

'So, what's she been doing in Iceland then?' asked Calvin cordially as he was grouting the tiles in the new bathroom.

Jensen had been home for two days now and had informed them that he was not going out on the next trip. His first mate was covering for him while he stayed at home to welcome his daughter, Elizabeth. He was so excited at the prospect of his daughter returning that David and Calvin even spoke of it at home. They'd discussed how Jensen hadn't mentioned a wife at all. The only woman about appeared to be the housekeeper, the woman that had opened the door that day to David. But this Elizabeth appeared to be the most important person on the planet if Jensen's worries were anything to go by.

Jensen arched his back in pride. 'She's been staying with her grandmother for a while,' Jensen answered Calvin's question.

'You're originally from Iceland, then?' Calvin swept the grout over the tiles.

'Yeah. But my daughter was born here. She's a real Grimberian.' Jensen grinned at the phrase.

'Does her mother live here, too?' asked Calvin, full well knowing he was shooting in the dark.

'You've missed a bit,' Jensen pointed to the wall before walking out of the bathroom.

He came upon David who was deep in conversation with a woman from the town's largest department store: the one where the wealthy shopped. Jensen, somewhat late in the game, had told David that he wanted the flat decorated and finished off with curtains, carpets, etc. David, not having been asked for these finishing touches before, never wavered a minute. 'Right, Mr Jensen. I'll get on it right away,' he'd said.

He went to the manager of the department store expecting to be turned away but the manager was more than happy to help him. And David learned that there was more to his job than simply building walls and putting in plumbing. He also learned that where business was concerned his usual shyness left him and the pleasure of doing a deal filled him with a certain contentment.

The apartment looked fantastic. It was now completely finished and was, thought David, the best job they'd ever done, more so because they had followed it through with interior decorations. The construction work in the flat was first class; no costs had been spared, just as Mr Jensen had ordered. The former attic was now a luxurious flat with an interior fine enough to grace the pages of a glossy magazine.

All tools and rubbish had been cleared away; the cleaners had been in, everything sparkled. David and Jensen were walking through the flat, making a last inspection before David would present the final bill.

'So, Gilmore. It looks good to me but the final inspection will be done by my daughter tomorrow. My Liz is coming home then. She'll arrive by the early afternoon.' Jensen was fussing about, moving a vase of flowers, brought in by the housekeeper to make the place look more homely, from one side of the table to the other.

'Sir,' said David, his heart sinking as he realised he wasn't going to get his money today, 'there is nothing more to do. I'm sure your daughter will love it.'

'I want you here tomorrow, Gilmore,' Jensen barked. 'Liz is due home in the late morning. I want you to come early afternoon. And then, if there is anything that Liz doesn't like, you both can talk about changing it.'

In the nearly four weeks of work David had never seen Jensen so nervous. This was the skipper of a grand trawler. He commanded a fleet of men. He was somebody. He was rich; he was powerful. And yet, when it came to his daughter, Jensen just seemed to go to pieces. David wondered why.

'Right, sir. I'll be here at two o'clock. If that is all right with you.' David's curiosity at what this daughter was like overshadowed his disappointment at not getting paid. He would come back tomorrow, no problem. He wanted to see the woman who had brought this tough trawler skipper down to his knees. And made him act as if he were afraid of her.

'Calvin and I will be back at two o'clock tomorrow, Mr Jensen,' David repeated. 'And if all has proven to be satisfactory, I would like to present our bill, if that is all right with you, sir?'

'Fine, Gilmore. Fine,' mumbled Jensen, obviously far too busy with his thoughts of Elizabeth to think about the practicalities of paying bills.

CHAPTER TWENTY-SEVEN

The Jensen conversion had been a pleasant job for the firm Gilmore and Fisher. Working inside, the weather had not hindered them at all, despite it being winter. And Mr Jensen's housekeeper had kept them supplied with regular mugs of tea. The results, especially since they had brought the prestigious up-market store from Victoria Street into the equation, had led them to a finished work that was worthy of special praise.

David really felt good about himself. He also felt good about the fact that Calvin was legally connected to him. He wouldn't go off and work somewhere else now, would he? That had always been a fear of David's. Calvin was so clever, so helpful, so personable. And he liked nice things. Well, nice things cost money and now David had made sure that Calvin had the money for the things he seemed to desire. Best of all, Calvin would continue to be a part of his life, his only family, when he thought about it. And he was now here to stay because David had made sure of it. Funny thing was that, even though Calvin skived off sometimes, it didn't matter because he knew he would always come back. This safe feeling that his cousin would never leave him made giving up half of everything he owned more than worthwhile.

And now, after this great job, they were definitely moving up, and they were doing it together. Gilmore and Fisher Constructions was going to be a name at the top of the list of building firms; David would make sure of that. Because it wasn't only Calvin who liked the good life.

If he closed his eyes, David could already see the detached house on the edge of town and the building machines and supplies, discreetly parked round the back, hidden by the evergreen trees, the stables or outhouses that would surely be needed for the livestock. It would be a picture-book smallholding. David had to laugh at himself. His dreams were getting ahead of him. What would all that be worth without someone to share it with? At that thought, David's heart sank. He wasn't what one could call a lady's man. In fact, he had difficulty even speaking to a woman. He'd had a few dates, usually arranged for him by Calvin, but he'd never felt comfortable with the women. And he just wasn't the type to pick women up in bars. And yet he'd never really worried about his lack of female companionship. His mother had always told him there would be someone special for him, and he had believed her. He just wished she'd hurry up and come along. He hated to admit it, but sometimes he got lonely. His dear mother, her words were in his head every day. She had said that life had something special in store for him. And David believed her. He just wished that something special would start to materialise. George, his father had often said that hard work, and nothing else, was the key to success. His father had worked hard all his life, he remembered.

As the memory of his father filled his mind, a sadness descended upon him. His father had said some profound things along the years and David had forgotten none of them - work hard, keep out of trouble, don't steal or lie, treat women with respect, be kind to children and animals. They were still the rules of life that David followed; he so wished that his father was here today to see how well they were getting on. He would surely be proud of him now, wouldn't he?

At half past one, David and Calvin left for Scartho. As they made to pull into the driveway of Jensen's house, they got a big surprise. It was blocked by a sparkling new bright red Mini Cooper car, which had an enormous white ribbon tied around it.

'Nice,' murmured Calvin. 'Only the best for our Lizzy, it would seem.' This fellow must really be into the money big time, he pondered, his eyes taking in the big house, the open garage already housing a Mercedes, the perfectly manicured lawns and flower beds and now the new Mini. It would be nice to live like this, he concluded. He wondered if it would be worth making a play for this Elizabeth girl, no matter how ugly she looked.

'So it would seem,' answered David, but his mind was elsewhere.

What had happened that this man felt the need to do all this - the flat, the expensive furnishings and now this car? There's something sad about all this really, he thought.

They left the car on the road outside the driveway and made their way to the door.

Jensen had heard them and was already opening the back door and motioning for them to come in. 'Come in! Come in!' he cried. There was a big grin on his face. 'I think she likes it,' he said as they entered the house. They all came to stand in a little group at the bottom of the stairway. 'Elizabeth,' Jensen called up the stairs. 'The builders are here to see if you want any changes made. Can we come up?' Jensen turned to Calvin and David. 'It's her private domain, you see,' he said in explanation of his calling rather than going up to the flat.

'Coming, Dad,' came the answer.

For some reason, the voice made David tingle all over. He looked up to the door at the top of the stairs. It opened and out stepped the most beautiful creature he had ever seen. She closed the door, turned round to face them all and smiled before starting to descend the stairs. David's heart stood still; it was her! It was the girl he had seen at school that day; the one that had captured his heart so completely that being with someone else had never been an option. It was the girl whose face had lingered in his dreams all these years since.

He looked at her in awe. His throat went dry and closed up. His legs began to tremble ever so slightly. David could feel the blood rushing around his body, making him hot. His heart was beating so loudly he felt sure the others would hear it. He hadn't moved from the spot, and yet he felt as if he were floating.

'Hello,' she said as she came down the stairs towards them.

David couldn't speak. He wanted to reach out to her, hold her, kiss her, lay with her, have her next to him forever. In his mind he drifted off on a dream of romance. She was coming nearer now. This was his chance to speak. He opened his mouth but nothing came out. All he could think to do was lower his eyes and stare at his shuffling feet.

'Liz, darling. These are the men who made your flat. They have come to see if everything's all right and if you need anything changing,' Jensen said.

'Oh, hello.' She offered her hand to David first. 'What a grand job you have done! I'm so very pleased. There is absolutely nothing I would change.'

David shook her hand, marvelling at the soft skin, but try as he might he just couldn't look up. He mumbled something, thanking her for the praise, and withdrew his hand as though her touch had burnt him. He wanted to look directly at her, to make her see him, the real him: to awaken her to his desires. But all he did was shake her hand quickly, before continuing to inspect his shoes.

'I'm Calvin Fisher.' Calvin stepped forward with a dazzling smile. 'So pleased to meet you at last.' He grabbed her hand, placed his other hand over their clasped hands and held it firmly, looking directly into her eyes. His heart, too, was beating faster than normal. Wow! came the thought. This bird's gorgeous. 'Your father was so involved with the work, so hoping that his choices would please you.' What a catch! This was someone that Calvin could get very interested in. And her father was so rich too. He wouldn't mind living in this type of luxury if he had to, he mused. He smiled down into her face, crinkling the corners of his eyes as his lips opened to reveal his white teeth. He knew the girls just loved this when he looked at them as if they were the only truly important person in the whole world. Elizabeth smiled back up at him, her light grey eyes taking in this handsome stranger in one sweep. Fun, she thought, a definite sparkle jumping into her eyes, but dangerous. Calvin wondered what she was like in bed.

Jensen was pleased at Calvin's words. He put a hand on his shoulder and said, 'Come along to the kitchen and we'll have a celebratory drink. It seems you have managed to please my princess.'

Calvin, Jensen and Elizabeth moved forward along the hall towards the kitchen. David stared after them. He was still rooted to the spot, staring after the vision which had jolted his heart. He saw Calvin talking and laughing with Elizabeth in an easy way. She was looking up at him and smiling at his words. Oh no, David's chest ached suddenly. She likes Calvin. But then again, why shouldn't she? All women liked Calvin.

David gave himself a shake. Impossible dreams, he admonished himself. Of course Elizabeth liked Calvin. Everyone liked Calvin. He was such fun to be with as well as being handsome and totally charming. David felt like a non-person beside his cousin. A woman like Elizabeth who was from such a good house wouldn't be inclined to look at him, a simple builder who couldn't even get two words out clearly. In no way did he possess Calvin's charisma and quick wit. Although Calvin was also just a builder, he was somehow much more, thought David, wishing desperately that he could be more like his cousin.

How silly were his dreams. What frightened him now was that she might fall under Calvin's spell, no matter how far down the social ladder they were in comparison to the Jensens. Calvin had such an engaging manner she might dally with him for a while, and he would have to live with having her near and so far away. It frightened him to realise that he probably wouldn't be able to hide his feelings from her if she were to be in his company. All he wanted to do now was get in that kitchen, get his bill paid and get out of this house as quickly as possible. David didn't think he could stand the feeling of wanting what he could never have. He took a deep breath, squared his shoulders and made for the kitchen.

CHAPTER TWENTY-EIGHT

Elizabeth would recall that first meeting many times in the years to come. How it had all begun the moment she had stepped out of the attic conversion and looked down the staircase at the three men standing there in the hallway. There was her father looking up at her with adoring eyes and a quiet possession of her soul that angered her now that she was old enough to resent his control, and two young men, who were strangers to her. The tall man was really quite handsome in a dark brooding sort of way. His black hair flopped over his forehead and curled into the back of his neck. The jeans and white shirt clung provocatively to his broad shoulders and slender hips. He had the bluest eyes she had ever seen, quite fascinating. He somehow reminded her of an intense *Heathcliff,* some type of arrogant lord of times gone by. But despite this strange darkness lurking around him, he was indeed quite beautiful.

And Elizabeth knew his type. She had met many in her twenty-two years, even dallied with a few; they were usually great fun. But nothing more.

Then her eyes had wandered to the other man. He was smaller, five foot ten or eleven inches or so, she guessed. He had a strong-looking body, sandy-coloured hair cut short, and as far as she could make out, warm-brown eyes. As she caught his gaze, in those first few moments, his face had broken into a broad smile and she thought how handsome he looked when he lost that appearance of seriousness. There was something about him that appealed to her immediately. She had taken in with one glance the square-shaped face, the strong features, the straight nose and the full lips. It was a kind face, she decided. As quickly as he had smiled up at her, he had looked away and lowered his head. His greeting had been abrupt and stilted.

In the kitchen they'd drunk a glass of sherry while sitting around the kitchen table. Elizabeth had talked of her time in Switzerland at school and finally her prolonged visit with her grandmother in Iceland. Travelling had given her a confidence usually credited to older women. Calvin had listened intently, interjecting now and again with intelligent questions. David just sat there in awe of the gorgeous creature before him. Eventually, Elizabeth's father had motioned David into the study to sort out the bill. He was obviously not too pleased with the attention being given to his daughter by the workmen, and his only thought was to pay them off and get rid of them so he could have his Elizabeth back to himself again.

As David and Jensen returned to the kitchen they could hear sounds of laughter. 'Hey! Dad!' Elizabeth stood up and went over to her father. He put a protective hand around her shoulder. 'We were just talking about needing a bigger garage for my lovely new car. Did you see my car in the driveway, David?'

David nodded, unsure whether he should sit down or stay standing in the middle of the kitchen.

'It would be a shame to leave the new car outside in the snow and rain. We have the builders here now. What do you think, Dad?' said Elizabeth, smiling up at her father. 'Any chance of an extension to the garage to house my prize possession bought for me by my wonderful father?'

The last thing Jensen wanted was two young men around when he had finally got his daughter back after so long. But how could he not fulfil her every wish? Anything, if it would just make her stay with him. 'Well, if you really think so, Princess.'

'I do,' she answered simply.

'In that case, Gilmore, you'd better come with me and take a look. Have you got your stuff to measure up and so forth with you?'

'Yes, Mr Jensen. It's in the car. I'll just go and get it.'

Together they left the kitchen.

David did not want this. He didn't want to work on this house where his secret love was living. He didn't want to see how well she got on with Calvin. He definitely didn't want to see her laughing and joking with his cousin in a way that he wished she would laugh and joke with him. He needed to get away.

'Right, Mr. Jensen. Do you have any specific ideas yourself, or do you wish me to suggest something?'

'Whatever you think is right, Gilmore,' Jensen answered, looking towards the back door of the house with a worried frown upon his face.

'Did you get the job?' asked Calvin as soon as he got in the car.

'Yes,' answered David with little enthusiasm.

Calvin didn't notice how quiet David was. 'Did you see that chick?' he exclaimed, oblivious to David's withdrawn manner. 'Now she's certainly something. Won't be long before all the wolves are knocking at her door. I'd better make a quick move before she goes off with someone totally unsuitable for her. Now I, on the other hand…' he laughed, leaving the sentence open.

'Yes, I noticed her,' David said quietly.

'Well, thank your cousin, Davie. It was my idea to enlarge the garage. Slaved away there I did to get us that contract. Mind you, I must admit that the young lady of the house really interests me. Fancy being the son-in-law there. Cushy number that one would be, me lad. Elizabeth is really my type – beautiful, great figure and oh so rich! What d'you think, Davie? She's really something, isn't she?'

'That she is, Cal. That she is.' David copied the words his father always used when emphasising a point. His jaw ached from keeping his face non-committal. What he really wanted to do was shout at Calvin to keep his hands off Elizabeth. But instead he said, 'Jensen just wants a simple extension. Shouldn't take us more than a week.'

'Right. I'll have to move quick then. I've got a week to convince Lizzy that she can't live another day without having me,' Calvin grinned.

David just looked straight ahead, watching the traffic.

It did indeed only take them a week to extend the garage. During that time Elizabeth had usually been at home. She would bring them steaming mugs of tea and biscuits. And often she would stay a while to chat with them. David's heart just ached with love for her. He would watch her when he thought she wasn't looking. But he still found it difficult to speak to her. He just didn't know what to say. Everything he thought of sounded so stupid that he finished up not saying anything at all. Calvin, of course, didn't have such problems. He would always have something jolly to say to her to make her laugh. But whenever she spoke, she did so to them as a duo, never leaving David out of the conversation. And, as with all things that are meant to be, it came to pass that they arranged to all go out together on the weekend that the garage was finished. Elizabeth insisted on driving them in her new car. She promised to pick them up at 7pm that Saturday night.

David spent the day cleaning and tidying up Cooper Road. Calvin spent the day trying to work out how he could get rid of David. She might have insisted that they all go out together, but he wanted her for his own. Sod David!

CHAPTER TWENTY-NINE

It didn't take long for the threesome to become a regular item. This was not in Calvin's interest. But every time he tried to get Elizabeth on her own or suggest they go out just the two of them, Elizabeth would run to David and say, 'Calvin thinks we should try this or that pub. What do you think, David?' Even if he called her on the telephone, she would always ask what David thought to the suggestion. Quite honestly, Calvin could have happily choked David, but he assumed Elizabeth was just sorry for him and, in her kindness, was just trying to get David out and away from work. It stood to reason that a girl like Elizabeth couldn't possibly be interested in such a colourless little man as his cousin. Calvin knew this for sure, but sometimes his patience at her kindness would irritate him. And so they finished up visiting all the in-places of Grimsby and district together. Even weekends when they would drive out into the country and enjoy Sunday lunch at the charming little pubs along the A16 main road, did she insist that David joined them. Calvin was getting thoroughly fed up with having to share Elizabeth. He felt sure she was interested in him. Didn't she always laugh at his jokes and spend a great deal of time talking to him? Wasn't he the one who always rode in the front of the car when she drove them anywhere in that Mini Cooper of hers? Why on earth couldn't David see that he was spoiling everything for him?

Sometimes Calvin would look over at David as they were working with such anger and aggravation in his face that he wondered how long it was going to take before David finally saw his consternation and realised he was butting in on his cousin's love life. The little snot! Once he had Elizabeth, really had her, like marrying her, he could get rid of Davie, once and for all, he decided. He'd served his purpose and by the look of things, there was nothing more to get there. Davie, old bean, just seemed content to plod on. Well, Calvin deserved a better life than running around humping concrete and sand all over the place. Life owed him. Davie owed him. Elizabeth would be his meal ticket out of this shit.

Ironically, David also wished he could get away from the pair of them. And yet he could hardly bear the thought of not seeing her again. It was kind of Elizabeth when she insisted that they all go out together. She needed friends to help her fit into Grimsby society, she'd said. After being away so long, she didn't know anyone here any more and didn't know which pubs and clubs were the right places to go. Both Calvin and David would be doing her a great favour, she claimed, if they would help her adjust. And so they had taken to going out all together but it was becoming increasingly difficult for David to hide his longing for her. And he was afraid that she might notice something. And so, he'd spend a great deal of time when they were together either looking down at his glass or gazing off into the distance. He knew that if he looked directly at her, she would see in his face what was happening in his heart.

Elizabeth liked to drive them all in her new Mini, picking them up at Cooper Road and dropping them off again at the end of the evening. It seemed the schools she had attended had all worked to make her a very independent woman and David would often marvel at her self-reliant attitude. She was certainly a woman of these times. However he often wondered why she wanted him there, for she seemed to get on so well with Calvin – they were always talking together. And so he concluded that she must feel sorry for him because he hardly went out at all if he wasn't with them. Despite recognising her generosity, he nevertheless often felt like a gooseberry, definitely the fifth wheel on the wagon. But David could do nothing to resist her and, if Elizabeth wanted him with her, he was powerless to say no. They'd go out in the week a couple of times. At those times Elizabeth would meet them at the actual pub. She had no fear of walking into a pub on her own. But at the weekends Elizabeth would always drive. They mostly went to a pub in Cawthorpe, about half an hour's car journey out in the country from Grimsby. The Royal Oak was very popular, set in its own picturesque grounds, and affectionately called by its regulars *The Splash* as access was gained by driving through a little ford. It was here that things came to a head.

CHAPTER THIRTY

The house in Scartho was not the happy place Jensen had hoped it would be for his daughter. Despite the attic flat, the new car and recently-built garage extension to keep it in, Jensen could not hold on to his Elizabeth. She kept going out, often not even telling him where she was going and with whom. Well, he didn't need to wonder with whom. He knew that she was cavorting around with those two builders.

'What on earth are you thinking?' he'd screamed at her in frustration.

She'd given him one of her haughty looks and made to leave the room.

'Where d'you think you're going, young lady? I'm talking to you!'

'Then stop shouting, Father,' she'd commanded.

Who the hell did she think she was?

'Get yourself here, madam!'

That made her stop in her tracks.

'I didn't send you to all those fancy schools just to have you speaking to me like I wasn't worth the effort,' he bellowed. 'I've spent a lot of money on you, girl. Didn't even complain when you insisted on going to your grandma's instead of coming home after finishing school. It's time you learnt some respect.'

'I do respect you, Father. But I'm finding it increasingly difficult to do so while you are stood there shouting at me.'

Cheeky little sod! 'Well, you're not showing me respect by cavorting with those riffraff builders. They are not good enough for you.'

'That is for me to decide, Father. And I have the distinct feeling that, as far as you are concerned, there isn't anyone who would be good enough for me. You can't tell me what to do anymore, Dad.'

He'd seen tears starting to well up in his daughter's eyes and felt sorry for having shouted at her. She'd quietly left the room then, and he hadn't meant to say any more. But he couldn't get rid of this feeling that despite her return, he still didn't really have her. And he'd done everything to bring them closer together. He'd sent his trawler out with his first mate so he could be here with her. Those bloody builders were probably robbing him blind, but Jensen didn't really care. What he cared about was having his daughter finally admire and respect him. What on earth more did he have to do? She was twenty-two now and still he couldn't tame her. Well, she needn't think this was what he would put up with. If she didn't finally pull herself together, he'd show her who was boss. Without him, she had nothing. She should finally see what the world out there was like.

'You'll be sorry,' he'd called after her as she'd left the room. But instead of his threat making him feel better, he'd been left with a feeling of hopelessness. He'd try and talk some sense into her another time, he resolved.

Elizabeth was suffering from the atmosphere at home. She knew her father wanted to have her there more often but she just couldn't bear being with him on a one-to-one basis. He would insist that she sit next to him on the couch if they watched television together. He would repeatedly come up to the flat and ask it she was all right. If he heard music playing he would come and ask her what it was and hang around so long until she finally asked him to sit down. If he heard the television was on, he would come up and ask if he could watch the programme with her. If the flat was silent, he would knock at the door and ask what was wrong and suggest they go out together for a meal, to the cinema, shopping even. Indeed, the situation at home was getting harder by the minute for Elizabeth.

Despite their frequent rows, Elizabeth loved her father. Of course she did. She had never known her mother, who had been killed in a car accident when she was nine months pregnant with Elizabeth. The doctors had been able to save her but her mother had died. Her father had been everything to her, and, she now suspected, she had been everything to him. And so Elizabeth couldn't understand why he was acting this way. When she was younger, just a teenager, fourteen or so, she had, she must admit to herself, gone off the rails a bit. Well, what did he expect? He was never there, always at sea. Fancy clothes and trips with a minder did not make her feel loved and wanted at all. She had sneaked out to the new discotheques and, looking much older than her years, managed to get into any of the pubs and clubs around town. Getting home had never been a problem. Some chap had always given her a lift. It was nice to have a snogging session in the back seat of the car before climbing into the house by way of the open back window. It was simply a good feeling to have someone's arms around her. After the first couple of disappointments, Elizabeth grew to know that sex did not automatically mean love. She was just learning to use her natural assets of thick, shiny black hair and light grey eyes coupled together with a fresh budding figure, and a rage of hormones, when her father had come home from the sea, stepped in and broken up her life. He'd sent her off to boarding school, to sort her out, he had said. At that moment she had hated him.

There had been many holidays back to Scartho when her father had been between trips and school holidays had coincided. Those days had been good. They had been close, doing everything together like a father and daughter should do. Then she had been happy to visit museums, go to the cinema, feed the ducks in the park. And she loved going to expensive restaurants with her father, who taught her the delights of little portions of food on big plates. Even later, as she turned eighteen, she had often gone with him for drinks at his private club. She had thought that they were, at last, getting on better with each other. But this return home had not been all she expected it to be. She was older now; had her own opinions and tastes, and friends. She loved her father but needed to break free of his steel arm of protection. And when he questioned her choice of friends, her back went up in opposition. How dare he, at her age, think he can tell her who she could or couldn't go out with?

Besides her father, there was another problem on her horizon: Gilmore and Fisher. She liked them both, enjoyed their company immensely, and couldn't think of anywhere she would rather be than with them, but her father hated them. He'd made it quite plain that he didn't think them good enough for her. Calvin was a 'fly-by-night', as her father liked to call him, and that David was introverted and far too quiet, obviously hiding something evil, he'd said. To boot, the pair of them didn't look like they had two pennies to rub together.

Elizabeth was getting tired of the arguments each evening when she came home. Her father would wait up for her and moan and complain about her choice of companions, saying he didn't buy her a car to ferry that scum around. When he finally went back to sea, Elizabeth breathed a sigh of relief. Now she could do what she wanted for twenty-eight days. And what she wanted was to get to know David better. She liked his quiet manner. And the more she was around him, the more she noticed his gentle kindness and unwillingness to judge people. Calvin, on the other hand, was quick to voice his opinions about everyone he saw, whether he knew them or not. He did this in such a funny way, making her laugh, that it was difficult not to like him. But David had something special, if only she could find a way to encourage him to speak to her more.

Indeed, she spent a lot of time trying to bring David out of his shell. Often she wondered how he could be so shy after they'd known each other so long. Once, when Calvin was at the bar, waiting to order their drinks, he'd told her how he'd once seen her at Welholme School. He'd gone red when he'd asked her if she remembered him. She'd had to admit that she couldn't remember seeing him at all in the school. Before Calvin returned from the bar, though, she had leant towards him and said, 'I'm sorry I can't recall seeing you at school. Maybe I can make that up to you. I really like you, David. Can we see each other alone sometime, without Calvin?'

David had looked into her eyes. Even in the dim light of the pub Elizabeth could see in his face that he wanted her. Why couldn't he see her longing, too? Was the man blind? She was just about to tell him again how much she liked him when Calvin returned from the bar. Anything David was about to say got lost in the commotion of sorting out the drinks.

CHAPTER THIRTY-ONE

By the end of the following day, David had convinced himself that he must have been mistaken about what Elizabeth had said to him while Calvin was at the bar last night. He thought she had said that she wanted to see him alone, that he should call her. But, no, that couldn't possibly be right. The noise of the pub must have hindered him hearing her properly. All he could really remember was the gentle aroma of her perfume as she had leant closer to him. Oh yes, he remembered that all right. He'd had to cross his legs and move slightly away from her before his aroused state became obvious. How he hated it when his body betrayed him like that. He sighed. How he ached for her. He breathed in deeply, trying to recapture the scent that was hers. He only had to close his eyes and imagine her sitting next to him, smelling of flowers as she always did, to feel a happy jab in his heart. But reality soon came flooding back when he realised he was only dreaming. It was better to keep his eyes open at the present moment seeing as he was driving, he thought. 'Concentrate on what you are doing,' he heard his mother's voice say. 'All right, Mam. Don't worry,' he answered her in his head and strained to pay the right attention to the road and traffic around him.

He was on his way to order supplies for their next big job. This thought pleased him - a large extension of a property, also in Scartho. The man wanted the kitchen made bigger, a dining-room added on and a conservatory. What with all the little jobs they were also seeing to, business was really doing well. So well, that David had hired two further men to help him so he didn't have to turn any work down. This left Calvin as site manager. And a good job he was making of it too. It was a real comfort to have someone you can trust by your side, pondered David, pulling up at a traffic light. The whole thing had worked out brilliantly. Gilmore and Fisher were a real team, a team to be reckoned with. A few more years of hard work and they could start thinking about putting a manager in and maybe having one of those fancy holidays abroad. David looked out of the car window at the grey skies and damp pavements. Yes, it would be nice to lay out in the sunshine and not have anything at all to think about except what to have for dinner. Just get this job finished and that's what they'd do. Calvin certainly needed a bit of relief, he'd been working hard lately and where would David be without his right-hand man? Making him a partner in the business had been the best thing he had ever done. Right, he agreed with himself as he pulled into the supply yard, a holiday it is, in the sun, no work for two weeks.

Calvin was sat on an upturned bucket amidst the rubble of a building site having a cigarette. The advantage of not having David around was that he could have a moment's rest. David expected everyone to work at full steam all the time just because he did so himself. But David wasn't there presently and so he could sit and enjoy his cigarette, contemplate life, and ease his aching bones without having to explain to Mr High and Mighty David what he was doing. David's presence seemed to make everyone jump to attention. Indeed, even Calvin didn't like to be looking like he wasn't doing anything if David was around. He didn't, of course, give a damn about the rest of the crew. They should just be bloody pleased he had given them a job. It was nice to be your own boss. You could skive off any time you pleased and no one could do anything about it. Except David, of course. Still had to keep him happy for the time being. Two or three years of this and he could then sell up and move on. He didn't intend to stay a builder for the rest of his life - that was for sure. But, at the moment, David still had his uses.

What a drip that cousin of his was: he worked hard, very hard. He never stopped from the time he got on the site until they packed up for the evening and left. But, Jesus! Life was for living, not working yourself to death. They did all right. There was no need to kill themselves with work these days. Business was booming and David spent more time on the road doing estimates and ordering supplies than actually laying bricks. The more Calvin thought about that, the more discontented he became. True, David was better at the mathematical side of working out an estimate and he appeared to people as the reliable and dependable builder in his cheap suit or baggy jeans. Calvin knew he was just too good-looking, even in his work gear, to look like a reliable builder. No, David looked more the part. Still, Calvin didn't like all the responsibility of having to make sure the others were doing their jobs right, or all the time he had to spend actually getting his hands dirty. This building lark wasn't going to be forever, he re-assured himself, stubbing out his cigarette on the pile of bricks next to him.

David met up with Calvin on the site in the middle of that afternoon. 'How you doing?' he enquired. 'Everything looks to be going according to plan.'

'Of course it is, Davie, me old bean,' Calvin walked towards him wiping his hands on the back of his trousers. He took a cigarette out of the packet in the top pocket of his shirt and lit it. Breathing in the smoke deeply he continued, irritation creeping into his voice, 'Took your time, today, didn't you? We could have used one more pair of hands here. Looks like it's going to rain any minute. Where you been, anyway?'

'Finished up having to go to lunch with Mr Rayner and his wife. You know, the ones who want that big extension. She wanted to choose tiles and wallpaper already. Can you believe that? Not even built yet and they are decorating. We decided in the end to get Guy and Smith's in again to do the interior. Anyway, good news is we have the contract. Start as soon as possible.'

David smiled triumphantly. He always felt good when he managed to secure a contract and felt that Calvin must surely feel the same; it was all money in the pot, wasn't it? Money in their joint pot.

But Calvin wasn't in the mood for feeling grateful for having another load of work placed on his shoulders. In fact, he felt really put out. All this bloody work was getting him down. He rubbed at his forehead and looked down at the ground, hiding any indication of his true feelings. He wasn't going to admit to anyone that his head was still aching from the amount of alcohol he had drunk last night. Or that working day in day out was getting to be a real drag. Or, for that matter, that he was getting thoroughly fed up that damn David couldn't finally see that he wasn't wanted on his dates with Elizabeth. Christ! Can't this stupid little man see he's in the way? He and Elizabeth were made for each other; anyone could see that. And it was about time David realised that and bogged off. He was going to have her, come what may. He was going to marry her, live in that big house in Scartho and never touch another bloody brick in his life.

David took one look at Calvin and thought how tired he appeared to be. A break from work, for him, was more than overdue. David didn't mind working all hours because that was all he had but Calvin had loads of other interests and all this work was obviously getting him down rather than pleasing him. Yes, in that way, we really are different, thought David. He stretched out a hand and rested it on Calvin's shoulder. 'The job's going great here, Cal. You really are the best site manager. None of this would work as well as it does without you. But you look tired today. Why don't you take an hour off and go check on the other two jobs to see if they are getting on so well. I'll finish up here and see you at home.'

David was talking quickly. He could sense that Calvin was angry with him for some reason and no matter why, he hated it when Calvin was unhappy with him. 'I'll get fish and chips on the way home and I'll have a surprise for you, too.' David finished as the idea of a surprise entered his head. 'Yeah, a real surprise.' He smiled inwardly to himself, excited at his idea.

CHAPTER THIRTY-TWO

The door of the flat in the Jensen household stood open and the strains of Simon and Garfunkel singing about a bridge over troubled waters delicately filled the air and crept down the stairs to the hallway where the telephone was situated. Elizabeth was alone in the house. She sat curled up with her legs under her, on the couch in her fancy apartment. A mug of coffee was at her side and a magazine in her hands. But she sat idle. She was not reading the magazine and the coffee was getting colder and colder by the minute. Elizabeth was waiting.

She couldn't believe that after finally telling David she wished he would call her and that she'd like to see him without Calvin, he hadn't phoned. She looked at the open door. From this position she could make it to the phone downstairs in three rings. Usually, she never liked to answer the phone in less than three rings because she didn't ever wish to appear eager. But she was eager for David to call her and his silence disappointed her immensely. She stared intently at the open doorway, as if staring alone would make the telephone downstairs ring. Finally, she looked away in disgust when the phone remained mute. Why hadn't he called? Was she mistaken about that look on his face? Last night she was quite certain that he felt something more than friendship for her, too. Maybe his liking for her didn't go as deep as hers did for him. Maybe he didn't like her at all but only came out with her because of Calvin, who he appeared to idolise. Dear Calvin, Elizabeth smiled to herself at the thought. The three of them had been friends now for well over six months. Calvin was fun and loud and oh so handsome. He was totally different from David who, despite his quietness and polite ways, seemed to have a depth of kindness and warmth behind those hazel eyes of his, which crinkled up at the corners whenever he smiled at her. And he smiled at her a lot. Calvin was the night to David's day.

A picture of David flashed through her mind now. She just knew that he felt more than friendship for her and wondered for the umpteenth time why he didn't seem to want to pursue something deeper. She sighed audibly at her disappointment. She'd never felt like this before. It was a strange feeling of knowing exactly with whom she wished to be, a feeling of belonging, a weird instinct that this man was meant to be. And that feeling had come to her practically instantaneously.

It had happened on that day when she returned home. Her father was making a terrible fuss about the attic flat he had had done for her. Was it all right? Was the carpet the right colour? What did she think of the pink bathroom? He needn't have worried. She loved it and appreciated how much he was trying to let her grow up despite it being his nature to keep her close to him when she wasn't under the watchful eyes of either paid minders, schoolteachers or elderly members of the family. It was as he had called for her to come down the stairs that something strange had happened to her. She was unprepared for it. And to this day couldn't understand nor explain the sweet pain that had suddenly and totally gripped her heart. The moment she'd stepped out of the door and looked down the staircase at the three men stood below, she knew that this was a moment to remember for whatever reason. She remembered her father, nervous and bullying in his desire to have everything just right for her; she remembered Calvin, stood there in all his masculine glory. He was indeed a beautiful human being, tall, dark and brooding-looking; a dark-haired *Heathcliff* with intense blue eyes. But, for some reason, still unknown to her, David had caught her attention and the pain had increased until she thought her heart would jump out of her chest.

She would never forget that moment. David had been looking up at the door when she emerged from the flat. His polite, friendly smile had changed suddenly the moment he had laid eyes on her. First surprise had lit up his eyes, making them large and letting her see clearly their golden hazel colour; then a look of some kind of comprehension had entered his face, a kind of knowledge dawning, she wasn't sure what it was but suddenly he had broadened his smile, showing his teeth, and making little creases around those soft eyes. Elizabeth couldn't remember ever having seen that face before but she also couldn't help or stop this instant realisation that something monumental was about to happen. It was a strange feeling and it confused her slightly; this alone annoyed her because confusion was not something Elizabeth was akin to. She had control of her life now she was well over twenty-one and she had no intention of letting anything destroy that. She had waited far too long for this time of freedom.

The tall man, Calvin, as she later learned was his name, had stepped forward as she had descended the stairs and spoken to her first. The other stranger, David, had simply stood there as if in shock and, after shaking hands, they had all passed him and made their way to the kitchen that day leaving him standing there gawking. Elizabeth was used to having men stare at her, admiring her. It would have been false modesty not to admit that she was indeed quite attractive. Anyway, men seemed to think so. And she knew Calvin certainly found her so because he'd been trying ever since they first met to get her on her own.

During the many outings with David and Calvin over the last few months, Elizabeth had discovered much about their personalities. They both seemed to be decent guys and she appreciated them taking her with them when they went to the pub. Calvin had immediately made a play for her within the first week of them meeting, but he had done it amusingly and without embarrassment on either side. His acceptance of her refusal to go out with him on her own for the time being was gentlemanly. In fact, Calvin always acted like a true gentleman. This baffled Elizabeth sometimes for she knew he had working-class origins. Nevertheless, he had the manners of a fine gentleman. Indeed, Calvin was a surprising human being – beautiful, polite and helpful and yet, she had to admit to herself, there was something *dark*, something she knew she wasn't seeing clearly when it came to assessing dear Calvin. 'I'll be ready and waiting when you are,' he'd said, when she'd turned down his invitation to go out alone with him. And yes, somehow, she believed he would be. His intenseness, the passion hardly hidden by those startling blue eyes, and that beautiful black hair that curled gently into the nape of his neck like all the heroes in the soppy romantic books she used to read had interested her only for a second. She had met men like Calvin before; gone out with them; even dallied for a while in some cases. They all seemed to have an unknown factor when it came to knowing them completely, always something hidden and exciting lurking just underneath the surface. Of course, Elizabeth had never actually seen the eruption of any badness from Calvin but instinct told her that his laughing eyes, elegant looks and jolly ways hid something she couldn't quite put her finger on and didn't really want to, if the truth be told.

Now David was totally different and often Elizabeth would wonder how on earth these two men could possibly be related. Next to Calvin, David appeared to be small in stature, but seeing as most men were usually taller than Elizabeth's five foot two inches anyway, David seemed tall to her. She guessed his height at around five ten or eleven. Either way, she had to look up at him, as she did most people. His sandy-coloured hair was cropped short, business-like. She loved the way it would flop over at the front sometimes, like when the wind blew it or he leaned forward. He would absentmindedly run his fingers through it to stroke it back into place and Elizabeth's heart would skip a beat. She wanted to do that. She wanted to touch that hair. She liked David's body, too. It wasn't tall and lean like Calvin's, but stocky and muscular. She could certainly feel protected from the world in arms that looked so strong. His lips were full and generous, soft looking, and he had a little habit of moistening them by pulling the top lip over the bottom one. She loved his smile; it was dazzling and lit up his whole face. She thought he didn't smile hardly enough. But it was his eyes that captured her heart so totally, so completely, so irreversibly. When he smiled they crinkled up at the outer corners and softened his whole appearance. But even when he wasn't smiling, when he was looking at her, she felt she could look deeply into them, the golden hazel gleam seemed to let her gaze go through them to the very depths of his soul. When he spoke to her it was like there was no one else in the room; when David looked at her, Elizabeth found it difficult to breathe past the lump in her throat. But it was more than just looks. David had a kindness within him that filled her with longing. She wanted to be treated with that kindness, she wanted to be near it, to reciprocate it in kind. His shyness, his way of hesitating rather than barging in there in any situation appealed to her. She wanted to help him, to be his strength, to let him know how wonderful she thought he was. Damn him!

Elizabeth threw the magazine to the floor. She walked over to the door and slammed it shut. Even if he did call now, she wouldn't hear it and even if she did she wouldn't answer the phone anyway. How dare he not want her!

CHAPTER THIRTY-THREE

David slammed the front door and called, 'Cal! Cal!' He pushed into the living-room and was surprised and a little disappointed to find it empty. 'Cal,' he called again. The ticking of the clock on the mantelpiece echoed around the room. The house was empty; it felt cold and barren. David walked through the rooms quickly, calling. The steam in the bathroom confirmed that Cal had already had a bath and it appeared by the stillness of the house that he'd gone out.

David looked down at the bundle of fish and chips in his arms: far too much for one person. Hadn't Cal remembered he was bringing fish and chips home and had a surprise for him? Then he saw the note on the kitchen table. 'Gone for a drink. See you later, old bean.' The 'old bean' cheered him up a bit. It was Cal's nickname for him and made him feel a bit better. When Cal called him old bean it meant everything was all right. Obviously, he'd just forgotten that David was bringing supper home. Typical of Cal. Head in the clouds. Always rushing about. David smiled as the feeling of fondness washed over him. It was good for Cal to get out; he'd been working really hard just lately and needed a break.

David unpacked the fish and chips on the kitchen table. He got the salt and vinegar from the cupboard, sat down at the table and, still in his work clothes, with the house in silence, ate his supper alone. Later, after his bath, reading the paper and watching a bit of television, he read through the brochures he'd brought home with him. He'd wait until eleven or so, to see if Calvin returned straight after the pub closed and if not, he'd surprise him in the morning.

It was after midnight when he finally went to bed. He lay there in the dark, listening for Calvin's car. When he finally fell asleep, he dreamed of Elizabeth.

Calvin just managed to get the car round the corner before David drew up in the van. He'd not forgotten about David bringing home supper; nor had he forgotten that he was also going on about some type of surprise. Well, he was all out of patience for surprises just lately. Again, they'd all spent the evening together: a nice little trio of himself and Lizzie and bloody David! When was David finally going to butt out? Didn't he realise that Liz was just being polite, being kind to him? It was obvious she felt sorry for David because he'd seen how she always made an effort to talk to him when he went to the bar to get his round of drinks in, and she also worked hard to include him in every conversation when they all sat together. It was true that David seemed to be getting more and more relaxed around her, but that was because she'd spent the time trying to make him talk about himself. Not always successful there, she wasn't. David just didn't talk much. That was the way he was.

Now Calvin knew that women liked to talk. They liked to have someone listen to them when they talked and they liked it even better if a man told them about some of his worries or, even better, sad experiences. Calvin had gleaned this invaluable information from the women's magazines he'd found hanging around the chip shops, and take-aways, doctors' offices and the like. With nothing else to occupy him while waiting, he'd read the stupid things. And all in all, when it came to women, they were quite informative about the wants of the female sex. Armed with these valuable facts he'd gone forth and multiplied, so to speak. Very careful about multiplying, he was though. He carried condoms with him at all times. He smiled to himself at the biblical reference to his thoughts. His thoughts were anything but biblical, he chuckled. He used the same trick on Liz. Get them feeling sorry for you and you had them in your hands. Early on, in the first couple of weeks of their friendship, he'd told Elizabeth of the terrible tragic accident that had robbed him of his beloved family. He'd done it with a tear in his eye as David was at the bar getting the drinks in. He'd thought he'd got her when she took his hand and squeezed it. He'd felt triumphant at the gesture. Got yer, he concluded. He always told this weepy story to any prospective girlfriend. It worked wonders on the old sympathy scale. And it seemed to have worked with Elizabeth, too. So why, he wondered, hadn't he got her yet?

Before he realised where he was, he was in Scartho, knocking at Jensen's door. Liz answered the knock. Calvin noticed immediately that her eyes looked puffy.

'Lizzie, me old sunshine,' he started then changed his tone on recognising that something was evidently upsetting her. 'What's the matter, love?'

Elizabeth stood back to allow Calvin entry. She started up the stairs and Calvin followed, throwing a glance down the hallway to see if anyone else was at home. Downstairs was in darkness: they were alone.

In the flat, soft music filled the air. The couch had a blanket screwed up in the corner and a large cushion was shoved into the other corner: Elizabeth had obviously been lying there. On the coffee table was a half-empty bottle of white wine and one wineglass. Crumpled tissues littered the floor.

She sat down on the couch. Calvin got himself a glass, poured himself a wine and refilled Elizabeth's glass. He sat on the armchair next to the couch and then asked again, 'What's happened? What's upsetting you? And don't say you are not upset, because I can see you are.'

Looking intently at Calvin, Elizabeth, a little woozy from the half the bottle of wine she had already consumed, wondered if she could tell him of her dilemma. Maybe he even knew why David had ignored her suggestion to call her, she pondered. But then, did she want Calvin to know her business? She liked him immensely, as a friend. He was great fun but he wasn't really someone you could reveal your inner self to. He was, well, a bit superficial really and although that made him entertaining in a funny sort of way, did it make for someone you could tell your troubles to? He saw the world in blacks and whites. He was always forthcoming with an opinion and would argue his own case admirably, but was he sensitive enough to confide in? Was he too close to David?

'Nothing important really,' answered Elizabeth taking a deep swig of her wine. 'I was waiting for a phone call from someone, someone I'm, well, rather fond of...' she tapered off.

Calvin immediately didn't like the sound of that. Who on earth could she have met to be fond of in these few months without him knowing about it? Good Lord! They were nearly always all together. She had no time for another bloke. He felt the hairs on the back of his neck go up. He'd have to be careful how he handled this. All was not lost though, he reasoned. Many a marriage was based on the hero rushing in and saving the damsel from heartache. A quick glance at the flat, the expensive furnishings, the comfort around him only worked to make him more determined than ever to have Elizabeth for himself.

Calvin moved from the chair to the couch and put his arm around Elizabeth's shoulders. He drew her head on to his chest and rocked her gently. 'Sunshine,' he breathed onto the top of her head, 'any man that doesn't bother to call you isn't worth a fig. You are just too beautiful and bright to worry about such a thing. Why don't you get your coat on and I'll take you to that new Chinese restaurant in Cleethorpes? Afterwards we can go for a drink in the Lifeboat. What do you say to that, sunshine? It would do you good to get out.'

Elizabeth pulled back and sat up again. 'You are such a good friend, Cal,' she said, patting his hand affectionately. 'But I'm really not in the mood for going out.'

'And what are you going to do? Sit here and wait some more? That's not like you, Lizzie. Who is this moron, anyway?'

'He's not a moron, Cal. At least, I don't think he is. He's probably just not interested in me like that. He likes me as a friend, I know that for sure, but he never seems to want to go further than that and I'm beginning to believe that I am really in love with him.'

Calvin recoiled at the words. 'Now wait a minute, Lizzie. Love's a big word. You are probably yearning after some guy who is too stupid to notice you and therefore you think you are in love with him. I bet if he were scrabbling at your door, you wouldn't give him the time of day normally. You wait and see. There are people around you that love you.'

'Oh, I know that, Cal. And I'm sorry if I seem ungrateful for your friendship and affection at the moment, but this isn't a case of just not being able to get this man. I see him regularly. What's bothering me is that I have this inexplicable feeling that I am meant to be with him for ever and I can't understand why he doesn't feel the same.'

Calvin pulled Elizabeth into his arms again. 'Lizzie, it is friendship that leads to the best relationships. You know that. We are the best of friends, aren't we? Can't you think of me that way?' And he leant down to her upturned face and kissed her gently on the lips. She didn't respond. More passion, he thought. And so he kissed her again, this time increasing the intensity of his kiss. He held her tightly, so tight she couldn't get away from him now. He would show her what he could do for her. He would show her that he was the best man for her. He would show her how he could love her.

He pushed her back on the couch and pressed his body on top of hers. His breath was coming in short little pants and his penis was straining in his trousers. She can't fail to be aroused by that, he believed. And he squirmed powerfully on top of her as he pushed his tongue into her mouth.

Elizabeth was shocked into submission for the first few seconds; then she realised what was happening. She pulled her head to one side, separating her mouth from his. 'Cal! What are you doing?' she cried as she brought up her knee between his legs to cause pain and discomfort to the throbbing member poking at her through their clothes.

Calvin flinched at the agony suddenly sweeping through his loins, lost his balance on the narrow couch and fell off Elizabeth. He crashed down between the couch and the coffee table, knocking the table over on his descent. The glasses of wine toppled off and showered him with wetness. He lay there looking stupefied.

Elizabeth straightened herself up on the couch, pulled her skirt down over her knees and started to spit words of anger at him. 'How dare you! I'm telling you that I'm in love with someone and you think a good fuck will make everything all right? I thought you were my friend!' Fury made her stumble over her words.

What he was hearing was not what he wanted to hear. Scorn and hate brewed up inside him.

CHAPTER THIRTY-FOUR

Some half-hour later Calvin left the house in Scartho. He closed the front door of the house quietly and leant against it. Taking in great gasps of air, he opened and closed his fists rhythmically; his teeth were clenched tightly together. Calvin was seething.

Inside the house, he had made a good job of hiding his true feelings. He'd managed to laugh it off, so calming Elizabeth down. When he had fallen on the floor, it became quite clear to him that he was going to have a job winning Lizzie over to his side. But he was going to have her no matter what! She was his ticket to money and position and he was determined to have what he deserved. But obviously, tenderness and sympathy and hot passion weren't going to work. But it wasn't just the physical rejection that he was having to deal with at the moment. He'd sort that out soon enough. I mean, wasn't he just beautiful? No woman could ever resist him. And that slag Elizabeth would finally come running after him one day, too. Maybe not today, but definitely one day. And then he'd also make the little bitch wait. The physical rejection was bad enough but what was really bugging him was that Elizabeth had told him, when she'd finally calmed down, that she couldn't possibly have anything romantic to do with him because it was his cousin, his only family, bloody David, that she was in love with. Silly cow!

Calvin jumped in his car, revved the engine and sped up the road towards the Harvest Moon in New Waltham where he knew he would find food, drink and lots of women who'd most definitely want him. Bloody bitch! Just who the hell did Elizabeth Jensen think she was? And as for David, well, he'd fix him one day, too.

The Harvest Moon was one of the most popular pubs of the moment. They provided loud, lively music: the highlight of the evening being when the singer jumped up on top of the upright piano and gyrated provocatively while singing *Shake Baby Shake*. By this time in the evening, the room would be throbbing and the young women just one happy mass of drunken cheer screaming to push the singer on to greater heights in his sexy gyrations. This is what Calvin needed right now – eager women already aroused to an excited state.

He took in the room from his position at the bar, noting which women were with male companions and which were with girlfriends; even better was always women who were totally alone. His eyes fell upon a petite brunette. She stood alone, empty glass in her hand, watching the singer doing his act. She wasn't all that beautiful but she had long dark hair and a good figure. If he used his imagination to its full extent, she did look a little like Lizzie. He made his way through the crowd to her side.

'Hi, beautiful! Can I get you a drink?' he shouted over the noise, waving his half-full glass of whisky in the air to indicate what he was asking in case she couldn't hear him over the noise. She turned her face up towards him. Oh, great, thought Calvin, she has light-coloured eyes too, just like Elizabeth. That's an added bonus.

'Yeah, thanks,' she mouthed back at him. 'That would be great,' she said but Calvin didn't hear her. He was already leading her, hand in hand, back to the bar.

'What would you like, beautiful lady?' Calvin clicked his fingers to get the barman's attention.

'A *Cherry B*, please.' The young woman looked up at him, admiration shining in her eyes at Calvin's good looks. Her heart skipped a beat and she basked in her apparent good luck at pulling such a fine fellow. She ran a hand over her teased hair-do, making sure it wasn't out of place.

'A *Cherry B* and another whisky,' Calvin barked at the barman. He turned and smiled down at the young woman. Cherry B! A nasty, over sweet sherry-type drink with lots of alcohol. Bingo! This one was even going to be cheap. A couple of those and he'd have her eating out of his hand.

'I'm sure you must have heard this a thousand times, but you have such beautiful eyes. Real come-to-bed eyes.' Calvin lifted her hand and brushed it ever so gently with his lips. He stared down at her, attempting to make her feel as though she were the only woman in the room. She fluttered her eyelashes and giggled and blushed profusely.

'What on earth are you doing here on your own? A woman like you shouldn't be on her own. Have you been hurt by someone? Are you lonely, too, like me?'

A flicker of pain flashed over her eyes. Here was someone who seemed to see into her soul: someone who somehow could feel her pain; and so handsome, too. 'Let's go to the table over there. It will be quieter and then you can tell me all about why you have that sad look upon your face.'

It never failed to amaze Calvin how a bit of false sympathy got them every time. Were these women stupid, or what?

She leant against him as they made their way to the small, round table near the door. Calvin just hoped that she wouldn't start crying when she told him her history of heartache and disappointments. Great heavens! Ask a girl about her emotions and it was hard to get them to shut up in the end. Truth was, he couldn't give a damn about their feelings, but it never failed to work. Show some interest in them and they can't wait to spill the beans and cry on your shoulder. Again he hoped that this bitch wouldn't start to blubber. He'd had enough of weeping females for one night, thank you.

'Here, my beautiful one. Sit there.' He indicated a red-velvet stool, pushed the dirty glasses on the table to one side, placed the overflowing ashtray on the floor under the table and put her drink in front of her on the table. 'Now, tell me your name. Mine's Johnny, by the way.'

CHAPTER THIRTY-FIVE

David was awoken early morning by the slamming of the back door. He pulled on his dressing gown and went downstairs. The hands of the living-room clock glowed in the dark. It was twenty to six. Last night David hadn't drawn the curtains and now he could see it was still dark outside. There was a light on in the kitchen. He found Calvin sat at the kitchen table holding his head in his hands; his hair was tousled, his hands bloody. When he looked up, David saw that he had blood smeared on his face, too.

'Cal! What the hell's happened? Are you all right? Do you need a doctor?' David made for the phone on the counter top.

'No!' moaned Calvin. 'No doctor. I'm all right.'

David slowly laid the receiver back in its cradle. He turned to look at Calvin who sat, straightened up by now, rubbing his shoulder. 'I'll make some tea and then you can tell me what happened.'

He put the kettle on. Got a glass and filled it with water from the tap. From the bottom kitchen drawer, he took out a small brown-glass bottle and shook out two aspirins. These, together with the water, he placed in front of Calvin.

They both remained silent while David made the tea. He returned to the table. 'What's happened? Where have you been? How did you get in that state? Look at you! Even your clothes are torn. Do you know what time it is?' David stopped abruptly as he heard himself. He sounded like an angry wife questioning her husband. And didn't like his own attitude. He leaned back in his chair, took a swig of steaming tea from the mug and said, 'Cal, do you want to tell me what happened and how I can help you?'

Calvin smiled gratefully at David. You could always rely on Davie to do the right thing, he thought, act the right way and, above all, be concerned and helpful whenever anything had to do with him. Calvin knew exactly how his cousin felt about him, silly bugger. Well, here goes. 'I went for a drink in a pub in a village along the A16. I can't remember which pub it was but I just needed to get away from town and have a drink on my own. The work's been getting me down a bit lately, what with one job following on straight after the other, you know?'

David immediately felt guilty. He really had been driving them all like a madman. There'd been no time to have a rest. What with all the bad weather, you had to work when you got the chance. He had to stop pushing them all. They were doing all right, really. More than just paying the bills, they were earning good money. He just found it hard to slow down. He'd never forget the times when they were struggling to have enough money to just get by. In future he would remember that Calvin needed more time for his private life and relaxing. Crikey! How many times had Calvin moaned about all work and no play and he'd ignored him and pushed him even harder? David felt saturated with guilt.

'Well, anyway,' Calvin continued, now safe in the knowledge that he'd successfully manipulated David to the point of believing whatever explanation he gave. Indeed, as always, David would surely think everything was his fault and not Calvin's. 'As I said, I was in this pub, chatting to the locals. Got some funny ideas those country folk have, you know. Anyway, time was called and I thought that would be it for the night but the landlord just threw the bolt on the door and we all carried on drinking. Later, even the village policeman joined us. No worrying about licensing laws out there, it seems.'

David sat patiently letting Calvin tell the story in his own time. It always took Calvin a long time to come to the point and David was used to this by now so he just continued to drink his tea and listen quietly, nodding his head now and then to acknowledge Calvin's words.

'It must have been about two in the morning when I finally left there,' Calvin carried on. 'I decided to take the back roads rather than the main road 'cause I knew I'd had a bit too much to drink, what with having no supper and all.'

David's guilt grew as he thought about the fish and chips and how long it had taken him to finally go and get them.

'Have you ever been on those back roads?' Without waiting for an answer, Calvin continued, 'Well, there isn't a straight road from there to Grimsby, and just ditches and fields either side of them. To cut a long story short, old bean, I misjudged a corner and hit a tree on the other side of the road. I sat there stunned for a while 'cause I think I remember hitting my head and shoulder on the steering wheel: head hurts like hell, so I must have hit it somewhere.' Calvin rubbed at his forehead. 'And then I decided to get out of the car and check the damage. I opened the door, stepped out and slid right into the ditch. That's when I must have got all these scratches. The branches and roots of the bushes scratched the hell out of me and tore my clothes. I crawled back up the embankment. I checked the car. It didn't look too bad and when I tried it, it started again all right. I backed off the tree and pulled into the side of the road for a little sleep. Wouldn't have done to have a policeman find me driving like that, now would it? I'd have lost my licence. So I slept for a while to sober up a bit. And that's it really...' Calvin tapered off.

David reached across the table and patted his cousin's arm. Thank the Lord nothing more serious had happened. He would never forgive himself if Calvin got hurt because he'd been working him too hard. Well, that was going to change as from now on, he thought, remembering the brochures in the living-room and smiling to himself. He stood up and started making his way to the bathroom.

'I'll draw you a bath and you can have a long soak. Then we'll see if you have any wounds that need attending to. Best just leave your clothes on the kitchen floor; I'll throw them in the dustbin. They don't look as if they can be saved at all. No work for you today, Cal. When you've finished your bath, we'll have some breakfast and then you can go up to bed. I'll see to everything. Don't you worry.'

Work was the last thing Calvin was worrying about. What did he have David for? No good having a dog and barking yourself, he conceded, feeling bored and thoroughly tired at having to explain himself to bloody David. Still, this time it was necessary. That was why he'd gone into such detail, to make sure David knew where he was should anyone ask him. It was a good idea to ram that tree with the car, although he really did bash his head doing it. Bloody women! The trouble they get you into. They're all little tarts: every last one of them. Use sex, they do, to get a man where they want him and then they think they can just holler 'stop it' and you are supposed to back off and go home. Whores! That's what they are. Even Elizabeth. If she'd not been playing games with him tonight, he wouldn't have been at that pub, wouldn't have picked up that silly little cunt, wouldn't have got himself all messed up getting what she had obviously wanted to give him. Come on to you like a cat on heat, they do, and then cry wolf when you get down to business. Sod the bloody lot of them.

Calvin went into the bathroom. The bathtub was full of steaming water and looked very welcoming. He lowered himself into the comforting warmth of the water and breathed a sigh of contentment. He sat there in the bath watching David through the open bathroom door. He was gathering up his tattered clothes and stuffing them into an empty cement bag, ready to be burnt with the rest of the site rubbish. Calvin smiled inwardly to himself while at the same time thinking there goes the evidence. He watched complacently as David then busied himself with getting them breakfast. He looked on as his cousin got out the frying pan and threw a load of bacon into it. Good lad, old bean Davie, reflected Calvin. He still had his uses but he certainly wasn't having Elizabeth: that's for sure.

CHAPTER THIRTY-SIX

Before David left for work, he presented Calvin with the pile of holiday brochures that he had brought home with him the night before. 'Here, Cal. You choose something out of there. That was the surprise. We are finally having that rest we've been promising ourselves for nearly a year now. Sea, sun and sand, that's what we're having for a couple of weeks. Let me know what you fancy and I'll book it for as soon as they are able to take us. See you tonight, old bean,' he mimicked Calvin as he closed the door.

Who the hell would want to go on a holiday with dowdy David? mused Calvin. He'd probably want to experience the culture by visiting museums and ruins and the like, learn a bit of the language so he could speak to the natives and write postcards to everyone back home. Boring and even more boring. What Calvin needed was a couple of weeks off on his own, preferably together with Lizzie. His mind drifted off to last night, to the struggling, screaming girl. Bloody cows they all are. There he was giving her what she wanted, what she had asked for even, and then she tried to change her mind. Well, he was only striving to keep her quiet, never meant to harm her, really, but she wouldn't shut up. First he'd tried holding his hand over her mouth but the bloody bitch had bitten him! So he stopped ramming into her for a moment and moved both his hands to her throat. His fingers were long and strong from years of hard labour on the building sites, one good squeeze was all it took. That quietened her. And as she was finally still, he began thrusting again, long, slow, powerful thrusts this time with no squirming girl to hinder him. Her face began to look more and more like Elizabeth's as he pumped his way towards his climax. It was good. One of the best orgasms he'd ever had. He thought his loins would explode. Great stuff. Pity about the girl, though, but then she'd deserved what she got for leading him on. All this had been going through his mind as he was making his way up to bed. He drew the curtains against the morning glow, pulled the covers on the bed back and crawled in between the sheets. He was enveloped in a feeling of well-being as he laid his head on the soft pillows, closed his eyes and fell immediately into an untroubled sleep.

That feeling of well-being was soon to be shattered when Calvin, on getting up, switched the television on. The news stated that the body of a young woman had been discovered on the outskirts of Grimsby town, in the vicinity of the Waltham area. Foul play was suspected and a tall, dark-haired man who had been seen with the victim that previous evening was being sought in connection with this particularly gruesome murder. Should anyone know of any information leading to the apprehension of said man, they were to contact the police directly and not go near the person in question who was believed to be extremely dangerous.

Definitely time for a holiday, thought Calvin as he reached for the brochures. His head was hurting and he felt jittery. He searched his mind for whom on earth it could be that had seen him with that floozy. Why can't people mind their own business? There's always someone ready to interfere. Bloody busybodies!

The feelings of guilt on David's part were eased somewhat when he got home from work that day. 'Hi, Cal. Brought a Chinese takeaway for supper. That all right with you? And, anyway, how are you feeling now? You still look a bit peaky, you know.'

'Still feeling a bit peaky as well, old bean,' came Calvin's reply. 'Maybe it's like you said, just plain overwork. I'll be all right in a few days when I've had a bit of a rest.'

David went into the kitchen and through to the bathroom; he turned on the taps for his bath before returning to the living-room. 'But didn't you look at the holiday brochures, Cal? A few days rest aren't going to do you any good. What you need, no, what both of us need, is a holiday, some real relaxation.'

God! How easy it was to manipulate this idiot into the place where you wanted him. Five more minutes and he will be insisting they go tomorrow.

'But David, what about the business? There are still the two other jobs to finish off and that big extension is on the books to be started as soon as possible. We can't possibly afford the time, let alone the money, to go on holiday now. Doesn't matter how tired we might be.'

'You let me worry about the money,' said David. He knew that Calvin considered him to be a bit mean. He always made a joke about his extremely careful ways, as he called them, when it came to spending money. And David had to admit that he was cautious. That's the only way they would get on in the world. His mother had told him often enough – hard work and careful saving. But they were doing all right, more than all right really. And if he was really truthful, he had to admit that they were earning money faster than he could get it to the bank. It was good of Calvin to be concerned about their finances. But he needn't be.

'Look, Cal. I do the books, remember, and I say we can afford it. As for that extension, we are still waiting for planning permission, so they know we can't start until we get it and it looks like it will take a couple of weeks at the least before it comes through. Now, did you find somewhere you'd like to go?'

'Well, there were a couple of places that look nice...' Calvin flicked through the brochure looking for the pages that he had marked.

'I'm off for a quick bath, Cal. Dinner's in the oven keeping warm. Tell me where we are going when we eat.'

Twenty minutes later they were both sat at the dining-table in the living-room eating Chinese food out of the restaurant's tin-foil dishes with forks, surrounded by brochures offering package holidays in Spain and Mallorca and Ibiza. David was getting excited. This would be the first holiday he had ever been on. He'd hardly been out of Grimsby let alone Britain. But that's what one did these days; Skegness, Brighton and Southend were out; Spain, Portugal and France were in.

'This place called Benidorm looks all right, Davie. What do you think? And we can get a three-star hotel plus the flight and half-board all for this price.'

David shovelled a forkful of food into his mouth and looked at the photographs of the eastern coast of Spain. It looked beautiful – quite green considering that according to his Geography teacher it was a region with high temperatures and little rain. The pictures showed impressive mountains bordering on Mediterranean coastal areas where palm trees actually grew and a creeper plant of some kind appeared to splash the area with vivid colours of purple, red and yellow among the whitewashed houses. Benidorm was not so entwined with nature though. It looked in the picture like a miniature Manhattan. Skyscrapers lined the horizon all the way along a beach of golden sand so light it explained the name of the region – Costa Blanca, meaning white coast as the brochure clarified. Benidorm, it seemed, offered bars galore, restaurants aplenty, nightclubs with girlie shows, entertainment of all descriptions, discotheques open from midnight until the morning hours and ample sun and sand to sleep off the pleasures of the night while getting tanned into the bargain. It sounded a little too fast for David, but he knew Calvin would love it.

'Looks great to me, Cal. I'll go to the travel agent tomorrow. They did say, last year, if you remember, when we asked about trips abroad back then before we got too busy to go, that if we'd had passports already we could have taken advantage of their special offers. You know the ones, for people who are willing to travel with only thirty-six hours notice. If we do that, and we can now 'cause we've got passports, we'd get a massive discount. Are you up to going so quickly?'

'You bet!' exclaimed Calvin. Trust David to be thinking of getting a bargain, he thought. But what the hell! He couldn't get out of this place soon enough. It wouldn't do for him to be recognised by anyone who had been at the Harvest Moon last night. He needed to disappear for a while.

David warmed to Calvin's obvious pleasure at going on this trip. He knew he had made the right decision. This would perk Cal up no end. And then they could get down to some serious work again when they got home. 'What do you want to do tonight? Are you up to going out? You know Elizabeth usually picks us up Thursdays?'

'No, not tonight, David. Stay in with me. It's been a bit since we've had a night at home. Let's sink a few beers and watch the goggle-box. I'll feel better in the morning, I'm sure.'

'I'll give Elizabeth a call then and tell her tonight's off.'

David's heart lifted when he thought of Elizabeth and then suddenly sank when he realised he would be going away and not see her for a couple of weeks. It would be strange not to see her, speak to her, look at her and be close to her for so long. Oh, if only she felt the same way about him as he felt about her. But then, she had never mentioned ever seeing him at school so although he had never forgotten her, she couldn't even recall him. Still, he had her friendship and that was the most important thing in the world to him. He never wanted to lose that. Of course, one day she would go off with someone who could give her everything, who would be rich enough and educated enough to hold his own with her and look after her in the way she was used to. David knew it was just a matter of time before she would go out of his life and he wanted to savour every minute of it. Often he'd thought that she might be interested in Calvin. They both looked so good standing next to each other, like the perfect couple. David's heart quickened. It would be a hard pill to swallow if Calvin and Elizabeth finished up together. But then he would learn to live with it if it should happen that they became a pair. And, when he thought about it, it wouldn't be so bad; he'd have the two people he loved most in the world in his life for always then. But Cal needed him tonight and he would tell Elizabeth that they were not going out. He only hoped that she would still want to see them tomorrow when they had planned to go to the new discotheque over in Immingham.

Calvin watched David leave the room to go phone Elizabeth from the kitchen. For the first time he wished they had an extension here in the living-room because he wanted to hear what was said. Would she tell Davie what had happened between them last night? Would she refuse to go out with the pair of them? If that happened, how was he going to make her see that he was much better for her than that stupid wimp, David? Moreover, these were now small worries. What he really needed was to get away from Grimsby for a while, a long while, in fact.

David came back into the living-room, bringing two mugs of tea with him. 'Well, that's sorted out. Elizabeth didn't mind us calling off for tonight and she's promised to pick us up at seven o'clock tomorrow night. Said she'd drive. Good thing really, seeing as our car needs seeing to.'

Obviously she'd not mentioned anything to David about his little play for her. Good. He was still in the running. He would make sure he never left David alone with her; silly bitch might tell him what she feels about him and then he'd be the one shut out. David had been useful over the years when he thought about it, but now it was getting to the time to move on.

CHAPTER THIRTY-SEVEN

In 1972, Altet Airport by Alicante, in Spain, appeared like a gathering of wooden barracks in comparison to Stansted Airport in England. Both airports were foreign to Calvin and David though: neither of them ever having flown before. The flight had been an exhilarating experience for them and they had agreed that they should have done something like this sooner, despite the cramped legs and plastic food served in little plastic dishes and requiring one to eat with one's elbows firmly by one's side. They had laughed heartily. They'd collected their luggage and were now entering the Arrivals hall. People were rushing everywhere; there were nasal tones droning out over loudspeakers; children were either shrieking, crying or loudly demanding attention from their parents; there was a hustle and bustle of people carrying cases or shoving trolleys piled high with luggage. All around them there were yelps of happiness as adults and children were being hugged and greeted by their family and friends. Languages David and Calvin had never heard before and didn't recognise swirled around their heads. It was raw pandemonium. They waded through the mass towards the glass doors leading out of the building. As they emerged into the night they gasped for air as the wave of heat hit them. It was a typical Spanish night, warm and balmy and a little clammy. They couldn't believe that at two in the morning, the weather could still be so warm. Even at that time, although being dark, the glow from the lights at the airport lit up the palm trees and they could see the silhouette of the mountains just yonder.

'It's beautiful,' whispered David in awe.

'Yeah, makes a change from flat-as-a-pancake Grimsby, that's for sure,' answered Calvin.

They were tired from their journey but so excited at the newness of it all - being in an airport, any airport, booking in, tax-free shops, the big aircraft with its cramped sitting arrangements, the flight, the landing, and a strange new country. For the first time in their lives, they were hearing a language they didn't understand. They smiled a little uncertainly at each other, trying to hide their apprehension and glee. No one should think they didn't do this sort of thing all the time. They straightened their backs and attempted to appear as if they were seasoned travellers as they made their way to the coach waiting to take them to their hotel in Benidorm.

Calvin walked into the hotel room, dropped his suitcase and went over to the balcony doors. He opened them, stepped out into the starry night and looked out over the sparkling Mediterranean. The moonlight had turned it silver. 'Wow! Davie, old bean. Come and look at this.'

David was just two seconds behind him. Together they stood there in silence and gazed out in fascination. The scene before them was one of holiday magic. Looking down on a promenade running along the broad sandy beach they could see people strolling arm in arm, babies being carried or pushed in their carriages, dogs wandering around and hundreds of young folk in their age group laughing and joking as they walked along in little groups. It was as if this were the afternoon instead of the middle of the night. Along the water's edge lovers sauntered hand in hand.

Calvin broke the silence first. 'Can you believe it's three in the morning? If it weren't for the darkness beyond the reflection of the moon out on the sea, you'd think it was middle of the afternoon. Look at all them people. And listen, the bars are still open. Did you see downstairs as we came in? There's a disco-bar in the hotel. And from the sound of things, it's still going full swing. Come on, Davie, me lad. Grab the keys and let's go!' Calvin made for the door. Any tiredness he might have felt before instantly forgotten.

David would have been content to watch the world go by on this balcony for the rest of the night. How he wished Elizabeth was here with him. They'd got the booking so fast – a week in a three-star hotel in Benidorm followed by a week of self-catering in a luxury villa in a small fishing village – that it had only left enough time to see

Elizabeth once before they left. She had looked shocked at the news of their plans; then she had fallen silent for a while. He'd reminded her that he would have booked for the three of them but they were having enough trouble with her father being in disagreement with the friendship in the first place that he'd known she wouldn't want to upset him any further by coming on holiday with them. Her eyes had suddenly sparkled with what looked like tears. So David had given her hand a little squeeze; it was the first time he'd ever touched her. Fire seemed to shoot up his arm and he pulled it away quickly.

Calvin had been quieter than usual as well on that evening. David surmised he was surely going to miss Elizabeth, too. He'd chosen to sit in the darkened corner of the pub and have his drinks brought to him. Usually, it was Calvin's custom to go to the bar and have a good look round the place, maybe strike up a conversation with someone, anyone. Often they'd finished up with a job when Calvin had done this. He was good at approaching people and selling their building talents to the public. But on that last evening, Calvin had sat quiet and distant in the dim light of the corner. He must be really worn out, reasoned David. Or he was feeling as bad as himself, maybe even worse, at leaving Elizabeth for two weeks. Poor Cal. This holiday would do him good and if entertainment in loud discos was what relaxed him, then discos and bars it would be. 'Hang on, Cal. I'm coming,' he said as he followed his cousin out of the door.

Benidorm and the Spanish way of life suited Calvin perfectly. Within a couple of days of sunbathing and swimming in the warm Mediterranean waters, his skin had turned a dark brown, making his blue eyes stand out even more than usual. The colour worked to enhance his beauty even further. David would watch him as he butted into any beach game going on and invite himself to play. Always he was made welcome. He spoke to strangers with such ease, thought David enviously, wishing he also possessed that particular talent. David, on the other hand, spent a lot of time in the shade to avoid getting burnt. He thought about putting some suntan lotion on but didn't want to look like a sissy, so he took care not to stay in the sun too long. His skin turned golden and his hair lightened visibly. He enjoyed being on the beach. But mostly he had his head in a book and didn't see the stares of admiration he was getting from many of the bathing beauties around him. His eyes might have been down among the words printed on the pages in front of him but his thoughts were still in Grimsby, more exactly, in Scartho with Elizabeth.

They quickly accustomed themselves to the routine of a British holidaymaker in Spain. During the daytime they relaxed on the beach. They had lunch at one of the restaurants on the promenade, returned to the beach until around 5pm when they went back to the hotel to have a sleep and get showered and changed in preparation for the evening. Benidorm, with its '*fiesta*' atmosphere and selection of bars and restaurants offering both Spanish and foreign fare, coupled with its cafés, ice cream parlours, nightclubs and discotheques, street market stands and shops open until way after 10pm, presented a hive of activity well into the night. Discotheques first started to get busy at midnight and the trains and buses operated throughout the night and into the morning hours to provide transport to those with the energy to literally dance the night away. David was pleased that they were moving in a couple of days to the villa in Moraira.

Moraira was thirty minutes drive north up the coast from Benidorm. The travel agent had promised them that a week in the self-catering villa with its own swimming pool would give them a better idea of what Spain was really about. It didn't have the razzmatazz of Benidorm, a town that catered practically exclusively for tourists, but Moraira possessed the natural beauty of native Spain. Public transportation in this region was limited, they were told, and so they had hired a car.

The road out of Benidorm due north was somewhat primitive. The asphalt just stopped at the sides; there were no footpaths. And so, not only did a driver had to watch intensely were he was going, but he also had to be careful not to knock down any of the people walking along the sides of the road. As they travelled along the road, the bars and tall hotels slipped into the distance, giving way to stretches of wild-growing greenery dotted with detached houses all painted white. The further north they went, the greener it became. Not the same colour green of England, but a variation of different greens ranging from the lightest of the colour to a dark evergreen. This was speckled with bursts of, as David had recently learned, bougainvillaea, a climbing plant, which had vibrant coloured flowers - sometimes deep purple, sometimes bright red, and sometimes a deep peach colour. This was bordered by ragged mountains on the left and, on the right, the shimmering deep blue of the Mediterranean on which speed- and sailing-boats of all sizes bobbed about. Cruise liners and merchant ships drifted by on the distant horizon.

David shook Calvin who was dozing next to him. 'Cal, wake up and look. It's magnificent. Have you ever seen sun so bright, or houses so white, or sea so blue? And look at those...'

'Be quiet, Davie! Can't you see a man's trying to get some shut-eye here.' Calvin grinned to soften his words. Sitting up properly in his seat he asked, 'Where are we anyway? This is beginning to look like the back of nowhere.'

'We've just gone through a town called Altea. It looked real old. Just look at these mountains, Cal. Aren't they something? Don't they make you feel small, like just a dot on this earth?'

'Nothing makes me feel small, Davie, old bean. You really must do something about that lack of confidence of yours. How much further is it anyway?'

'We've got to come off this road at a place called Calpe, the woman at the car hire office said. And then just follow the road through the town and along the coast until we get to Moraira.'

Calvin slid down the passenger seat again and closed his eyes. 'Wake me when we get there,' he said. Within minutes he was snoring softly.

David glanced over at him and wondered how he could sleep when there was so much to see. Mind you, he had been at the disco until 6am this morning, so there was no wonder he was tired. He reckoned they would get to Moraira about lunchtime. They had to pick up the keys and get directions to the villa from the renting agency in the town before then or they had to wait until the office reopened at 5pm after the siesta time.

The road was a winding one, at some points actually going through the mountains like just before Calpe, when the road went through a series of three tunnels. This made David gasp in admiration at the incredible accomplishment of the engineer who made this possible and the astonishing beauty of the mountain rock through which the tunnels were cut.

He'd been told to look out for the Calpe Rock called *Peñón de Ifach*. When it came into view ahead of him, David felt a stab of emotion for this beautiful land. He'd never imagined anywhere could be so naturally picturesque. The road through Calpe took him past houses and apartment-blocks, a couple of supermarkets, lots of shop fronts, and some tall hotels off to the right where David supposed the sea to be. It all looked a little dingy; certainly it didn't have the glitter of Benidorm. Instinctively he knew that Calvin wouldn't like this as much as where they were coming from. The dual carriageway, which had carried him past the town, changed at the other side of Calpe into a narrow coastal road that twisted and turned sharply. It was hardly more than a dirt-track. The tarmac was full of potholes and just petered out on both sides. There were no gutters or footpaths. It was flanked either side by exceedingly large and opulent villas. David was fascinated. He slowed down and concentrated on his driving, wishing he could spend more time looking around him. Never before had he seen such buildings. The land to the right of him was sloping down to the sea, which he could see between the houses. These people must have fantastic views, he thought. The land to the left of him was sloping upwards and turning into hills on which villas were built in places that he wouldn't have thought possible to build at all.

Driving that coast road between Calpe and Moraira for the first time exhausted him. But it didn't take away any of the wonder he felt for this extraordinary land that captivated and enthralled him with its diversity.

He turned the last bend. No buildings were on his right and he could see down to the coastline. It was rugged. No promenade. The waves lapped lazily against massive rocks. At the end of the road, before it turned to the left to carry people away to places with weird names like Javea and Benitachell, David saw the traffic roundabout where he was supposed to park and look for the office in the main road. He laughed to himself when he thought of the term main road. The main road, he found, was one of only three roads that virtually made up the original tiny village of Moraira. He parked the car, leaving Calvin sleeping peacefully. He had enough time to walk to the bottom of the 'high street' before the renting office closed. When he got there, he saw the fishermen's boats moored on the old quay. The fishermen were sitting on the quay in the shade of a crumbling building, chatting loudly and rapidly, and working on their nets. Their hands moved quickly, pulling what looked like thick string wound on a wooden bobbin through their nets. The boats swayed languidly upon the mirror-like Mediterranean. Music played in the background. David could smell something delicious being cooked somewhere. Children were running around laughing. Seagulls screeched and the sun beat down on the scene. Turning around he saw the mountains dotted with white houses and green foliage. For a second he wondered how anyone got up there. 'Moraira,' he said the name out loud, and felt emotion bring tears to his eyes.

CHAPTER THIRTY-EIGHT

'There's nought to bloody do here,' complained Calvin. 'Two nights now we've hung around this place. Christ! Even the disco is a car ride away.'

'This was all the travel agent had, Cal,' David tried to mollify him. 'Next year we can book well in advance and then we can choose exactly where we want to be.'

'That beach is a drive away. If you don't have a car here, you can't live. And it's small. No life at all.'

David felt differently. 'It's quaint, Cal. I know it's not Benidorm, but Moraira has lots of character.'

This was the first time they'd had such conflicting opinions about anything. Calvin was missing Benidorm: the instant food at the hotel when he was hungry, the permanent flow of alcohol, the bar full of fellow tourists, the discos full of pretty girls. But it was different for David. In a strange way he felt as if he had come home. Everything about this side of Spain appealed to him. The warmth, the brightness, the friendliness of the locals. Some even tried to speak English to him.

He loved the villa they were in with its marble floors, light pine furniture, and white walls. The garden was a blaze of colour and had trees and plants he'd never seen before. The pool was a luxury he wanted to have forever. The view from the villa was breathtaking. There was the dark blue of the Mediterranean as far as his eyes could see. The coastline where small buildings and houses nestled among luscious green foliage and the three streets that made up the village of Moraira became mysterious twinkling lights in the darkness of the night. Moraira had taken hold of David's heart that very first day. The tiny shops, where customers stood in line and never complained about waiting, the little dark, vibrantly blue-tiled bars where no ashtrays were to be found and customers threw their cigarette ends, serviettes, prawns shells, olive stones and the like on the tiled floor to be swept up at the end of the day, all worked to enchant him. He loved walking about the Marina where the fishermen kept their small vessels next to the motor- and sailing-boats of the rich.

'What's wrong with you, anyway, old bean? You never seem to want to go anywhere since we came here.' Calvin made to walk down the roman steps into the swimming pool.

David sat at the poolside table still eating his breakfast. 'We've only got five more days, Cal. Crikey! Where has the time gone? Don't let's argue. How about I drop you at the beach? There's a beach bar, and it's not as crowded as Benidorm's beach.'

'Exactly. How am I supposed to pull a bird if the choice is narrowed down to a handful?'

David smiled at him and bit into his toast. 'You don't want to come with me and have a look at the area, then?'

'I can see the area, as you put it, from here,' said Calvin sarcastically, looking over the garden wall down to the village below and the vast Mediterranean. 'Drop me off at the beach. I'll get my stuff together.'

David spent the whole day driving around. Near his villa on the side of the mountain there were lots of houses all with large gardens to make them private. He learnt that house numbers in Spain hardly ever ran in sequence, that's if they had a number at all, and that houses and pools were built around grand old pine trees, rather than cutting them down. The roads through the built-up areas were narrow, never straight, and without signposts. Often he would get lost and quickly learnt to just find a road sloping down and it would eventually bring him again to the coast road. He had an incredibly cheap lunch of barbecued sardines with salad in a bar overlooking the sea. Then he turned the car towards the mountains on the other side of the main road.

David headed for a place called Teulada, a small and very Spanish town. The main street through the town was lined with small shop windows. He headed for the national highway, driving back in the direction of Benidorm. He went through a town called Benissa where he saw the top of what looked like a big church rising majestically over the rooftops of the town houses. Within minutes he felt he was travelling into the real Spain as he spied ridiculously narrow streets with washing hanging on lines draped from one house to the other across the street. Old people, mostly wearing black, were sitting on little stools outside what appeared to be the front door of their homes. They'd sit in small groups talking or if alone, they'd be whittling at something in their hands. The doors to many houses stood open and David saw the tiled floors and walls, the patterns being dark and foreign to him, and the furniture, too, was different. Many houses had shutters on the windows and they were all closed. Where the houses had blinds, these too were pulled down against the afternoon sun. There were no discos, supermarkets, shops, or clusters of white villas to be seen.

At the far end of the town of Benissa, David found a turning off to the right, towards the mountains. He drove along the winding road for a short time until he came into an open valley. Ahead of him he saw what looked to him to be a small village. To the right were fields of vines. Surrounded by mountains, the valley felt open and yet protected. It was like he had stepped back in time. He was amazed that his car managed to manoeuvre along the narrow village road, at the end of which he turned onto the mountain road, which took him, he felt sure, to heaven. When he thought he was as high as he could go he stopped, got out of the car and surveyed the scenery around him. Never before had he felt so tiny in the face of such natural beauty. He was the highest he had ever been. Were he to fall, he would be lost forever. And yet little had been done to alter the land from its natural state. Massive mountains, jagged rocks, shrub land rolling away from his eyes for miles, trees on the top of the mountain peaks, terraces where once farmers had planted grapes, ruins of what looked to be old farm houses. David wondered how on earth anyone managed to live here. No electricity, no phone, apparently no roads, not even a track from the road he was on to the old, brown-stone houses. Life must have been hard back then, he imagined, but this land must have made it all worthwhile. David ached with the splendour and magnificence he saw all around him. How he wished he could bring Elizabeth here. Live with her among the mountains in this wonderful land.

That evening David and Calvin went down to the Marina in Moraira and stood drinking a cooling beer at a bar called Captain Andy's. It was little more than a wooden shack but the place had tons of atmosphere. Andy, a young Spanish chap, spoke really good English and so his place was frequented not only by the people who had boats in the harbour but also by most of the British living or holidaying in the area. Andy also sold houses to anyone that wanted to buy a property, as, it seemed, did most of the regulars in the bar. If Andy didn't have the type of place you were looking for, he knew someone who did.

Calvin had started up a conversation with a couple of British men. David felt envious when they said they had come to Moraira three years ago and stayed. They'd been working in the building trade here and there was so much work that they couldn't see themselves ever going back to Britain.

'What, that lousy weather, the taxes, the petty rules and regulations,' one of them exclaimed when asked if he missed England by Calvin. 'Course, you have to be a bit careful, like. It takes ages to get a work permit; that's if you can get one at all. So me and me mate here are doing a bit of undercover work. You get me drift.' The man tapped the side of his nose with his finger and laughed.

'What exactly do you do, then?' asked David.

'We work for a Spanish geezer, building houses, extensions, anything but pools. You need an expert for them, like.'

'And is there enough work?' David again.

'Can't save ourselves for bloody work. Take a look at those houses over there. Every odd bod, sod, and his mother, are getting rid of their "dodgy" money it would seem. Know what I mean? And they all want to hide it in houses in this place. Can't save myself for work. Fancy a job?'

Calvin roared with laughter and offered to buy them a drink.

The men painted a picture of Spain as a land of plenty for anyone willing to work hard. Business was booming here, they said. They had more work than they could handle and anything they earned was going straight into their pockets. They'd never had it so good. Life was great in Spain. The weather meant they could work all year. There was a constant stream of British lovelies to keep them entertained and many of the Spanish girls were starting to speak English now. Never again would they return to England, they stated emphatically. Spain was the place to be.

The two men took their beer and went outside after a while leaving David and Calvin stood at the bar thinking about what they had said.

'Certainly is a change from Grimsby,' Calvin stated quietly. 'Wonder what they earn? Did you hear that about his house? And he has a boat in the harbour, he said. Must be doing well.' Calvin took a long gulp of his beer. Suddenly, the headlines of a discarded British newspaper, lying at the end of the bar, caught his eye. He picked it up and read the article rapidly. A strange feeling started to whirl in his stomach.

'...over a week now and no clues have been found to lead the police to any suspects connected with the hideous crime committed on this young girl in the Waltham area near Grimsby. Police are asking for anyone who has any information, no matter how irrelevant they deem it to be, to come forward. This is the latest in a series of murders committed over the last few years and police are considering the possibility that they might be dealing with a serial killer here. Should this be the case, they are advising all young women to be aware of the danger lurking...'

Calvin threw the newspaper back on the bar and David picked it up. His eyes fell upon the last few words of the article. At that moment a group of young people entered the bar laughing and larking about, and so he missed seeing Calvin go outside.

'...and if anyone knows who this dark-haired man is,' he read, 'who was seen talking to the victim on the night of the murder in a public house in New Waltham, they are to please call the police right away and not approach him at all, as he is considered to be highly dangerous.' The report ended and David made to read the article from the start when he noticed that Calvin had left the bar. He found him outside.

'Are you all right, Cal?' he asked upon seeing his face. 'I know it's only subdued lighting out here but you look really white. What's the matter?'

'Nought. Must have been something I ate. One of those mussels might have been off. You never know.' He smiled at David and lifted his drink to his mouth to avoid further questions. Slowly the colour started to return to his face.

'What do you think about staying here, Davie, me old bean?' Calvin surprised David with his question. 'Them two seem to be doing all right. Look, they even gave me a piece of paper with their contact address on. And they said they are in this bar most nights. We could arrange to meet them again and find out if there are any disadvantages to living and working here.'

'But, Cal,' exclaimed David, 'I thought you didn't like Moraira.' Although he'd fallen in love with the land, he hadn't actually thought of staying here. How could he move to Spain when Elizabeth was in England?

CHAPTER THIRTY-NINE

David couldn't believe he was sitting on the plane going back to England alone. So much had happened in the last few days that his head was spinning. It had been in Captain Andy's bar in Moraira that the seed had been planted to uproot their lives and move business and home to Spain. Now David was going back alone to sell the house, close the business and sell off what he could and get back to Spain as quickly as possible. Calvin had moved in with the blokes who had given them the idea, or more precisely, Calvin the idea. He was to labour for them until David returned. During that time, they would show Calvin the ropes and acquaint him with the different methods and products used in Spain. David couldn't believe it when Calvin agreed to this right away, without a backward glance at all their work and their home in Grimsby.

And what about Elizabeth? David had often felt Calvin and Elizabeth would one day become more than friends. But, when he thought about it, Cal hadn't mentioned Elizabeth during the whole two weeks, neither had he spoken to her on the phone. David had made the effort to find one of those public telephone cabins and he'd phoned Elizabeth a few times during their holiday. He'd told her of the beauty of the land, the friendliness of the people, the amazing amount of foreigners living in Moraira and the easy, slow-paced way of life. But he hadn't mentioned how much he was missing her, or how much he wished she were by his side enjoying all the things he was taking pleasure in. Neither had he mentioned staying at all. And again he wondered how he could possibly be apart from Elizabeth forever. If only she felt the same way about him. He swallowed down the lump rising in his throat.

He wondered why Calvin so suddenly and determinedly wanted to leave his old life behind. Had it been so bad? All right, there had never been much joy in the house but they had done well for themselves and the business more than paid the bills and left a tidy sum over, too. There was security in what they were doing in Grimsby. Would they have that in Spain? Christ! They couldn't even speak the language.

David's thought drifted back to the villa in Moraira, the comfort and luxury of the place, the swimming pool, the breathtaking view, and manicured gardens. Oh, how he wished to have all that to call his own.

Of course, by the end of the holiday, he'd realised that those sprawling luxury villas set in massive gardens were all owned by foreigners. And most of them weren't even lived in on a permanent basis. Now he understood why he got a week's rent at such a moderate price. The Spanish themselves appeared to reside in the small apartment blocks just outside the main area and above the shops in those three streets that made up the original village. It was plain to see that there was a lot of money floating around in Moraira. And it didn't take long before David started wondering at the fact that there weren't many smaller houses, terraced houses and the like. His natural business instinct told him that this was indeed a place where they could earn a lot of money. What the area needed was the sort of houses normal, as opposed to rich, people could afford.

But what about Elizabeth?

David had thought of nothing else since leaving Calvin in Spain and getting on the plane. He had to face up to the fact that such a beautiful and talented and well-educated woman as Elizabeth would never find it in her heart to love a simple man as he was. He'd tossed the coin in his head and realised it would be better to be totally apart from her than to stand by and watch her fall in love and go off with someone else. His heart ached at this realisation. He knew that never would he feel anything near to the passion he felt for Elizabeth for anyone else. His love for her was a physical pain that took his breath away. Tears sprang to his eyes, and he turned to look out of the aeroplane window so no one would see them.

Elizabeth was waiting at the house when he got back to Cooper

Road. He got out of the car and before he knew it, she had put her arms around him and was giving him a big hug. It felt great.

'Was your plane late? I feel like I've been waiting for hours.' She started in, then realising David was alone she asked, 'Where's Cal? Nothing's happened has it? Is he all right?'

David's elation at her obvious affection dissipated when he heard all her questions about Calvin. Of course, it was only natural she would be asking about him. It was Calvin who matched her better, he felt sure of it. He'd have to be very gentle about telling her that Calvin wasn't coming home, at least not in the foreseeable future.

'He's fine, Elizabeth. Don't worry. I have lots to tell you. Let me put the kettle on and I'll bring you up to date with everything that's been happening.'

'What's been happening? You never said something was happening. I thought you two were just on holiday.'

'Elizabeth! Wait! Tea first. I'm dying for a cuppa. Haven't had a decent one since we left.' Lord Almighty! thought David. How am I going to tell her Calvin's staying in Spain?

They were sitting in Steel's Restaurant in Cleethorpes waiting for their coffees, having just devoured large plates of delicious fish and chips, the restaurant's speciality. He'd missed having his fish cooked in a light, crispy batter, the way he was used to.

'So Calvin just upped and off, so to speak? What did you say to that? And, more to the point, what are you going to do? Are you leaving here? Are you selling up and going? What happened in Spain that made Calvin want to stay? Of course, you'll go, won't you? You always go everywhere with Calvin. Don't think I haven't seen the way you always look after him. Hanging on his every word. Always doing what he wants to do.' Tears were beginning to glint in her eyes.

She's upset that Calvin's gone, thought David. I'm going to have to be the one to console her. How on earth could he leave this woman? Indeed, Spain tugged on his heart, but not enough to make him leave Elizabeth. But leave her he would have to. He couldn't stand being near to her knowing she was loving someone else. He tried to act nonchalant. Playing for time to think he said, wiping his lips with the serviette, 'That lovely piece of cod was one of the few things I missed while in Spain.'

'What else did you miss?' Elizabeth was hoping he was going to say her, but he didn't.

'Certainly didn't miss this rain, for one thing.'

Elizabeth had had enough. It was now or never. And if he didn't want her he could just bloody well go to Spain. See if she cared. 'David?' She put her hand on his and looked into his eyes. 'Didn't you miss me? Didn't you miss me as much as I missed you?'

David's hand was tingling from her touch and his heart started to beat so rapidly he thought it might burst forth from his chest. He couldn't hold his feelings in anymore. He had to tell her. He tore his eyes away from hers and looked down at the tablecloth before saying quietly in a rush of words, 'Elizabeth, I have never missed anyone so much in my life as I missed you these last two weeks. It hurts me when you are away from me. And when you are away from me, I can think of nothing else but you. I love you and can't bear the thought of leaving you but I understand completely that your father would want someone better for you. In fact, I want someone better for you. You deserve to be happy, Elizabeth.' He stopped, out of breath. His face was bright red from his confession. He was waiting for her rejection. He just sat there swinging between wishing he had said nothing and wishing he had said things in a better way.

'Oh, David. At last, at last, you silly thing. Don't you realise how much I love you? Come here.' And in front of all the people sitting in the restaurant, Elizabeth took David's face in her hands and kissed him soundly on his lips.

CHAPTER FORTY

They made love that night. In the front bedroom of the house in Cooper Road where the street lamp outside cast a delicate glow into the room, they made wondrous, passionate and lingering love.

Now Elizabeth had a gentle radiance about her as she lay there. She was lying on her stomach, her face turned towards David. Her eyes were closed and a little smile played at the corners of her mouth. David gently stroked her back, never tiring of touching her soft skin. Soon, her breathing became regular, and then deep. Within minutes, she was soundly asleep. David watched her sleeping in the dim light of the street lamp; watched her sleeping in his bed, in his house. Never before in his whole life had he felt so happy, so completely content. But then the thoughts of the consequences started to creep into his mind and disturb his perfect picture.

Calvin would have to come home. David couldn't possibly go back to Spain now. But David couldn't abide not being near Calvin. So Calvin would just have to come home. Calvin had been the hero of his childhood; he'd kept the bullies at school away from him. He'd been the buffer between his father and himself. He'd been and was the only family he had. But even though David felt he owed Calvin a lot, things were changing for him now. Somehow he had to work out a plan that would suit all of them. Elizabeth had made it quite clear when he'd mentioned last night about maybe leaving England for a warmer land that she was happy where she was. And he knew from previous conversations over the time they had known each other that she was tired of never calling anywhere home for long. She had spent so many years moving around from boarding school to finishing school in Switzerland, to Grandma's home in Iceland, that all she wanted to do now was finally stay in one place. Calvin would just have to come home; there was no other way. He'd phone him tomorrow evening at John and Russell's place. David thought of the men they'd met at Andy's bar in Moraira: Calvin had been so quick to befriend them. Not really like Calvin at all, who, although always friendly and quick to start up a conversation, usually preferred to stay that little bit aloof from permanent friendships. Still, we are all changing these days, mused David.

He'd definitely call Calvin tomorrow night. He'd explain everything: how he and Elizabeth had become a couple and that he couldn't possibly come to Spain any more because he wanted to stay in Grimsby with her. And that was another thing: tomorrow when Elizabeth woke, he'd discuss their plans for the future. Oh God! What if there wasn't a future with Elizabeth? What if this was just one night of passion? And then, puff! Nothing more! Stop it! Stop it! David admonished himself. This habit of his of always looking on the bleak side would have to go.

Yes, there were a few things to sort out but nothing he couldn't handle. He'd start out early in the morning. He'd check that the others were getting on with the job all right. He'd check if permission for that extension in Scartho had come through. He'd get Mrs Downes to come in and give the house a good clean and wash and iron his clothes. He would make the house clean and welcoming for Elizabeth. Then he would go and see Elizabeth's father early evening, after talking to Elizabeth early in the morning. He shuddered at the thought and pulled his mind back to practical matters. Last job of the day would be to call Calvin, tell him the good news about him and Elizabeth and break the bad news that he must come home because he was needed here.

David didn't get much sleep that night. He spent most of the time swinging between the thought of a happy future and all the 'what ifs' that could come in to spoil his plans. Between watching his love slumber and making plans for their future and pondering the difficulties that could arise, he felt far too excited to fall into a deep sleep himself. He had slept on and off though, and although the amount of sleep didn't add up to much, he was so thrilled with the turn of events that when the morning light entered the bedroom and shone on his Elizabeth he was wide awake and not feeling tired at all. Her hair was spread out over the white cotton pillowcase; the sheet had slid down a little to expose a perfectly formed breast tipped with a pink nipple. David desperately wanted to kiss that nipple; he didn't, though. Silently, making sure not to wake her, he slipped out from under the covers and crept downstairs.

A few minutes later he was creeping back up the stairs with two mugs of tea in his hand. Halfway up it occurred to him how often he had done this for his mother, gladly done this. Now he was doing it for Elizabeth, and just as gladly. He hoped he could spend the rest of his life bringing Elizabeth tea in bed. He placed the cups silently on the bedside table, sat gently on the side of the bed, looked at his sleeping beauty for just a moment longer, then he kissed her gently on her mouth. She squirmed, she sighed, she gave a little giggle as David's lips left her face and started to travel down to her breast.

'Wake up, sleepy head!' he said, kissing her breast with a resounding smack.

'Umm, must I? I was having the most wonderful dream about making love with this gorgeous, golden-haired man called David. He was making me tingle all over.' She opened her eyes, looked straight at David and smiled.

'Brought you a cuppa, my love.' David reached for the mug of tea.

Elizabeth struggled into a sitting position and took the proffered mug. She sipped at it loudly. 'Hmm, that's good.'

'Elizabeth, there's something I want to ask you.'

Elizabeth suddenly seemed to register where she was. 'I've never been up here before. It's quite a nice room this. The old fireplace is still in and the wallpaper must be donkey's years old, but it all works to make the room look cosy. I like it,' she smiled.

'Elizabeth,' David started again. 'I've been thinking…'

'So early in the morning, my love? That certainly can't be good for your constitution.' She took another loud sip of her tea and reached out to stroke the lock of hair that had fallen onto his forehead, out of his eyes. How handsome he is, she thought. She loved how that lock of hair would always fall onto his forehead and make him look so vulnerable, so sweet. Oh, how she loved this man!

David caught her hand and clasped it between both of his.

'Elizabeth, please! Listen to me. I have something to ask you.'

Elizabeth stiffened abruptly. He was deadly serious. What was wrong? Did he think that last night had been a mistake and that it would be better if they both forgot all about it? She wouldn't be able to do that. She placed the steaming mug of tea back on the bedside table. 'What is it, David?' She held her breath, giving him her full attention.

David cleared his throat, looked into her lovely light grey eyes and said, 'Elizabeth, my darling, I have loved you since the first moment I saw you all those years ago at school. You don't remember that day but since then your face has been etched on my mind. I couldn't believe it when I saw you again just a year or so ago. Even more unbelievable is that you are here with me now. I love you, Elizabeth. I have always loved you and I always will. I know that I can't give you all the comforts that you are used to but I will work hard and make a good future for us and one day I hope to be well off enough to give you anything you want. I know that at the moment I don't have much but I can't imagine my life without you. Elizabeth, please marry me.'

David breathed in deeply, suddenly out of steam. He was afraid to exhale and sat there holding his breath in. He looked down at their hands intertwined. He was afraid to look at Elizabeth, afraid she would say no. He hadn't planned for this at all but after last night, he didn't want to ever again be without her.

Elizabeth pulled her hands out of his. David's heart stood still, he thought it would freeze over. Then he felt her arms go around him and pull him onto the bed beside her. She kissed him so deeply, he thought he would explode.

'Yes! Oh, yes!' she exclaimed, breaking off the kiss for just a moment.

David finally exhaled with a loud sigh. His world was complete. Life was great! He had exactly what he wanted. Nothing could hurt him now. At least, that's how he felt for the moment.

CHAPTER FORTY-ONE

Jan Jensen stormed around his living-room in his posh house in Scartho, Grimsby.

'Are you out of your tiny mind?' he yelled at Elizabeth, who stood just inside the doorway, ready for escape. Elizabeth had been privy before to her father's wrath. But not for a moment did she think his ranting and raving would ever be directed at her, and so vehemently, too.

'But, Dad! You knew I've been seeing David for quite some months now and...'

'How many times did I tell you to leave those two good-for-nothings alone? Now look what's happened: they've turned your head, that's what. I didn't send you off to finishing school to see you end up with some working-class, never-have-a-penny-in-his-life labourer.'

'That's not fair, Dad,' Elizabeth started in, ready to defend David.

'Not fair! Not fair! Let me tell you a thing or two about life, young lady. Life is not fair. And if you insist on having to do with people like that David, you are going to finish up living in a council house, your husband probably on the dole and six kids hanging around your apron strings. I didn't bring you up to have that kind of life. You are special, Elizabeth: far too special for that nobody. Which school did he go to anyway?'

Jensen threw down the cushion he had been punching and walked over to the sideboard. He grabbed the crystal decanter and poured a hefty shot of whisky into a cut-crystal glass. Turning back around to face Elizabeth he shouted, 'You needn't think he is having any of this!' Jensen waved his hand around the room. 'That's what he's after. Don't think it's you, 'cause it isn't. I'm telling you now. Wake up, you little fool.'

'Father, please!' Elizabeth was white hot with anger and she could feel the blood rushing to her face. But she knew that she must stand her ground and try and reason with her father. She also knew that her David was far too proud to ever want to take anything from her father. She somehow had to make that clear to him.

Jensen turned to look at his daughter. Seldom had she called him Father, always Dad. This bloody David was already driving them apart. Well he wasn't having it. Elizabeth was his. He had raised her; and that without a mother. He had forfeited his wife to have this child, and she was his and she was going to stay his. She would marry whom he chose for her and not some down-at-the-heels fortune-hunter like this Gilmore chap. Christ Almighty! She hadn't even chosen the good-looking one, the one with all the charm. No, stupid girl, she'd gone for the homey, average-Joe quiet one. What on earth was she thinking of? She needed a holiday; that was it. He would send her away on a European holiday. That ought to settle things. Get that idiotic idea of marrying a nobody out of her mind. That Gilmore wouldn't be able to give her all the things and costly comforts that he had given her. And he knew she'd miss that. He'd made sure she'd never ever wanted for anything. She had no idea what it was like in the real world for those who had to work all hours just to pay the bills. He had to make her see some sense.

'Elizabeth. Go to your room,' he ordered.

'I beg your pardon? Oh no, Father. The days of you treating me like a little girl are over. I will not go to my room. I'm twenty-two, nearly twenty-three, and I have a right to my opinion and own ideas. You can't control me forever.'

'I have never controlled you! I have always only done what was the best for you. Bought you the best of everything. Sent you to the best schools. Made a lady of you...'

'And for what? Have you any idea how lonely I've been all these years? You might have seen that I had the best of everything. Controlling my life and even controlling whom I spoke to and whom I lived with and where I went and with whom I could be friends, but always from a distance. You were never there! You were always off on one of your fishing trips. I never saw you! You were never there: just tutors and carers and maids. Where the hell where you?' Elizabeth was screaming now. Tears were running down her cheeks.

She hadn't meant to say all that, but it had been building up for years.

'You ungrateful little sod! Get out of my sight. All I've done for you!' Jensen took a deep gulp of his whisky.

Elizabeth turned and ran from the room and up the stairs to her flat, where she closed and bolted the door.

David was having a great day. With the fragrance of Elizabeth about him and a gaiety in his heart, he went about his duties like a man floating on air. The two job sites he'd left in the hands of his staff were in good order. The work was being done in an orderly fashion and in a reasonable amount of time despite his absence. He'd been to check if the building permission for the big extension in that house in Scartho was through yet and had been assured that it would be forthcoming within a few days. Indeed, David was in a dream world all of his own. It was as he was making his way back to the house in Cooper Road to get bathed and dressed for his meeting with Elizabeth's father that a feeling of apprehension hit him. For a few seconds, his chest and tummy felt tight, but then he thought of his Elizabeth and nothing, no matter how uncomfortable, would deflect him from his plan to ask for Elizabeth's hand in marriage. All this discomfort was worth it just to have her by his side. She had made him feel great about himself, given him a confidence he'd never possessed before. And, just as she had said, he was, and now he truly believed himself to be, an upstanding young man with a capacity for hard work and a positive future in front of him. David felt a moment of sadness, as he heard his mother's words resounding in his head. That's how she'd thought of him, too. Those words from Elizabeth could just as easily been from his mother. How he wished she were here now. How he wished she could meet Elizabeth.

He was in the bathroom; bathtub taps on full belt, sink tap running as he shaved and with the radio playing in the kitchen when the first phone call came. He was in the car, back from the bodywork shop, on his way to Elizabeth's home in Scartho, when the second phone call echoed through the empty rooms of Cooper Road.

'How dare you come to this house!' Jensen bellowed at him on answering the door to see David standing there in his Sunday best.

'I've come to speak to you, Mr Jensen,' said David, who was a little surprised at the curt and discourteous greeting. Straightening his back, he made to enter the house.

Jensen, who obviously decided it would not do to discuss his private business on the doorstep, stood to one side to let David enter his home. His mouth was turned down in a furious grimace. His eyes were flaring with anger. Closing the front door, he walked stiffly towards the living-room.

'I really have nothing to say to you, Gilmore,' Jensen started as soon as he walked into the room. David stood just inside the door, in the same spot Elizabeth had stood earlier in the day. 'What is it you want, Gilmore?'

David tried to ignore the open hostility that Jensen was showing him. He knew it would be difficult for any father to give away his daughter in marriage to another man, but he hadn't quite imagined this coldness, this obvious anger that was now being directed at him. He squared his shoulders, coughed into his fist and took a deep breath. Nervousness made him keep shifting his weight from one foot to the other.

'I'm here, Mr Jensen, to ask for your daughter's hand in marriage.' David had been practising the words all day. 'I love her very much. I have a successful business and a secure future and I promise you that I'll do everything in my power to make her happy.'

Silence.

Jensen went to the sideboard and got himself a drink. He didn't offer one to David.

'You will make her happy?' he exclaimed, taking a mouthful of the golden liquid in his glass. 'What makes you think you can make my daughter happy, Gilmore? You've got no education to speak of; you're a labourer whose only talent is laying one brick on top of the other; not even a personality to speak of. You are an imbecile and a fucking idiot if you think you are going to marry my daughter. And I'll tell you now, you needn't think marrying my daughter is going to get you any of my money. Because that's what you're after, isn't it, Gilmore? You have turned my daughter's head in the hope of getting your hands on some of this.' Jensen waved his hand around his head. 'Well you can forget that. If my daughter even thinks about having anything more to do with the likes of you, then she can get out and see what it's like having to earn her own living. And you, my lad,' Jensen had crossed the room and was poking David in the shoulder with his finger, 'can think again about getting anywhere in this town. I have contacts. You'll be finished here if you come near my daughter ever again. You wait and see. I'll finish you, let me tell you.'

David moved back two paces in an effort to avoid the finger that was poking in his shoulder. But Jensen just advanced towards him. Finally, he took hold of Jensen's hand. He held it away from his body, tightly. His grip, from years of heavy labour, was strong enough to make Jensen cry out in pain.

Jensen pulled his hand away from David's grip. 'You dare to touch me! In my own home! Get out of here! Do you hear? Get out of here before I call the police!'

David turned and left the room. His cheeks were burning. He felt sure that if he stayed another minute in Jensen's presence, he might do something he would regret. In the hallway he glanced up the stairs and saw the closed door of Elizabeth's flat. He hesitated for a second, desperately wanting to run up the stairs, grab Elizabeth's hand and run out of the house with her. But he didn't. Maybe the door was closed for a reason. Maybe she agreed with her father and now regretted her actions of the night before. His head spun with unanswered questions. Teeth clenched together, he opened the front door and left the house.

CHAPTER FORTY-TWO

David was pacing the living-room in Cooper Road, wondering what to do when he heard the car pull up outside. It was nearly midnight and he wondered who it could be. Seconds later, the knocker banged on the front door. Elizabeth stood there with a small soft canvas bag in her hands. She was weeping.

'David, can you please pay the taxi driver,' she said as soon as David opened the door.

David pulled her into the house. She looked terrible, swollen eyes and a red-mottled face. Her hair was dishevelled and she was in thin trousers and a short-sleeved blouse: certainly not warm enough for a brisk British night in late autumn. Putting his hand in his pocket, he went to pay the taxi driver his fare.

'Oh, David,' Elizabeth cried, as he walked back into the house. She was still standing in the hallway, looking totally dejected. He'd never seem Elizabeth looking anything but perfectly in control of every situation and his heart went out to her.

'Come, sweetheart. Come into the living-room where it's warm and tell me what's happened. Are you all right? Do you need a doctor or anything?' David led Elizabeth to the chair by the fireside and sat her down. He crouched next to the chair, holding and patting Elizabeth's hand.

'Oh, David,' she repeated, struggling to get control of her emotions. 'It's all been so horrible and I didn't know what to do, so I came here. I hope that was all right.'

'Of course it was all right, my darling. Do you want a drink or would you like a cup of tea? And then you can tell me all about it.'

'Cup of tea, please,' Elizabeth snivelled into her handkerchief.

He led her into the kitchen, took the bag from her hand and let it fall to the floor, and pulled out the chair from the table for her to sit on. From here he could talk to her while he made the tea.

The whole story was sordid. David wanted to get in his car, drive to Jensen's house and punch him on the nose.

'He thinks you want to marry me for his money,' she started.

David felt the anger rising in him. How dare he insinuate that he only wanted to marry Elizabeth to get at his money? How dare he think so little of his daughter, let alone so little of him?

'We had a blazing row after you had left this evening. I didn't even hear you arrive, love. It was only as you slammed the door that I knew you'd been there.'

David busied himself making the tea and let her speak without interruption.

'I went down to the living-room to ask what had happened. He was still livid and shouted at me. He told me you had asked for my hand in marriage; he'd sneered at that. And then he said that he would lock me up before he would allow me to marry you.'

'What did you say to that?' asked David, handing Elizabeth her tea and sitting down at the table opposite her.

'I told him that I loved you and I wanted to marry you. And he made fun of me! Then he said again that no way would he allow me to marry you. And when I said I was marrying you, come what may, he exploded!'

'He didn't hit you, did he?' David asked in alarm.

'No, no. He wouldn't do that. But he might just as well have. He was so angry. I've never seen him like that before. He dragged me up the stairs, threw open the door to my flat with such force I thought it was going to fall off its hinges, pulled a canvas bag down from on top of the wardrobe and ordered me to get my things packed.'

Elizabeth stopped for a moment. She took a swallow of her tea and closed her eyes as she remembered the terrible scene.

'And what did you do?' David prompted her.

'Well, I didn't really know what to do so I went into the bathroom and started getting my make-up and stuff together. Then I went to the desk and got my document folder. I put these in the bag and then started to put some underclothes into the bag.'

David's eye glanced at the bag on the kitchen floor. It didn't look at all full of clothes. Elizabeth followed the direction in which he was looking.

'That's when he grabbed me,' she howled, fresh tears running down her face. '"Oh no!" he screamed at me, "I bought those!" and he pulled the clothes out of my hand and threw them on the floor. He said that without him I have nothing and that's what I can leave with. Then he handed me the bag with my make-up and papers in and pushed me out of the door. I just managed to get the photo of my mother in my hand as he steered me out of the room. He practically dragged me down the stairs, shoved me out of the front door and slammed it shut behind me. It wasn't until then that I realised I hadn't got the keys to the car.'

'What did you do?' said David, reaching out across the table and squeezing her hand reassuringly. He was feeling really shocked at what Elizabeth was telling him and his instinct to protect Elizabeth was making him wish he could punch Jan Jensen, this bully, right in his face.

'I walked up the road to the phone box and called a taxi and came to you.'

Elizabeth put her head on her folded arms on the table and wept.

David listened to the story with utter amazement. How could a father treat his daughter in such a way? Elizabeth was quieter now but still distraught. He suggested they go to bed and try to sort things out in the morning. That night David didn't make love to Elizabeth, but held her tightly in his arms all night, rocking her into a troubled sleep. Before falling asleep himself, he remembered, for a fleeting second, that he hadn't spoken to Calvin yet. Better so, at the moment, he thought, before spiralling into an exhausted slumber.

Early the next morning, he tried to telephone Mr Jensen who, upon hearing his voice, just slammed the receiver down loudly. Some time later, Elizabeth tried to call her father. She got the same reaction.

'He'll come round, Elizabeth,' David said half-heartedly. But somehow he knew that Jensen wouldn't come round. He knew that Jensen was a man unused to being crossed: an unforgiving man who had to have his way or else.

David didn't go to work that day. He left the house for a while to check on his crew. They were doing all right for the moment. He raced back home to be with Elizabeth, to reassure her that he was there for her. Together, over a late breakfast, they talked about their future.

'Do you still want to marry me, Elizabeth?' David finally asked, hoping with his entire being that the answer would be the one he wanted to hear.

'Yes, of course!' exclaimed Elizabeth, leaning over the table to kiss him. 'I just never thought for a moment that all this would happen. What has become of the father who is supposed to love me? Where has he gone?' Tears sprang to her eyes.

'He might still come round, you know.' David tried to give her hope.

'Oh no, he won't, David. You don't know my father that well. When I have tried to oppose him in the past he has always risen up and beaten me down. Well I won't have it this time. I'm old enough to make my own decisions.' She took a sip of her tea.

'And mistakes?' David encouraged her to speak further.

'Marrying you will not be a mistake, my love. You are the best thing that has ever happened to me. I've never felt like this before. For the first time in my life, I feel like I belong somewhere, to someone. And it's a lovely feeling. One I am not prepared to give up.'

David's heart soared. These were exactly the words he wanted to hear. So there was no decision to make, really. He and Elizabeth would be married, and as soon as possible, if it was anything to do with him, and, hopefully, her father would eventually come round to accepting them as a pair. Whether he did or not, Elizabeth was his.

'Well, that's settled then. You stay here with me. We'll get married, and I'm sure your father will start to think differently when he sees how happy we are and then he'll be all right about things.'

Bloody hell, thought Elizabeth, looking directly at David but saying nothing. Sometimes he was so innocent about things. She'd always known somehow that he really was no good at all about judging people for what they truly were. She hoped he really loved her because she knew her father well enough to know that he had just completely washed his hands of her and that without David she really did have nothing. She would make him a good wife, she promised herself. David, she felt sure, thought the whole world was full of nice people. The more she thought about it, the more she became convinced that David really needed her to protect him against the rotters of the world. She loved him and would do a good job of protecting him from the reality of people's true imperfections. She'd make him happy.

CHAPTER FORTY-THREE

They fell into an easy routine almost immediately. Elizabeth kept house, cooked them their meals and answered the phone, taking down details of jobs that wanted doing and making appointments for David to go and give the people an estimate. Life was pleasantly jogging along. They didn't speak much about Elizabeth's father or how she hadn't heard from him after that dreadful night. But they did speak about Calvin. In fact, they nearly argued.

'Well, why won't he come back home, if you need him so badly? This has been going on for over six months now.' Elizabeth plonked a mug of tea down on the kitchen table in front of David who had just hung up the phone.

'That's what the trouble is,' said David rubbing at his eyes with his fists. He was tired. 'I don't know why, really. He keeps saying that he likes Spain and that the building trade is booming in Moraira and that there's lots of money to be made, even just as a labourer doing barrow jobs. He keeps on and on about me going over there. And even though I tell him how things have changed for me, he hardly comments on it. Worst of all, he refuses to come back here.'

'Well, let him stay there,' barked Elizabeth. It would suit her perfectly if Calvin stayed in Spain and she and David remained in Grimsby. She would be near her father and her hopes of a reconciliation would be more likely to be fulfilled. Cooper Road was all right, and she was grateful for having a roof over her head, but it wasn't quite what she was used to and living without the luxury she was accustomed to was starting to irritate her. Also, she didn't really fancy seeing Calvin so soon after his pathetic play for her. If the truth be told, she was a little afraid of him and would prefer it if he wasn't a big part of their lives. It suited her fine that Calvin was in Spain. And there he should bloody well stay. Without being able to put her finger on exactly what it was, she'd always been aware that something bad was rippling under the surface of that fine exterior of his. It wasn't even something she could put into words, but it felt evil. Why, oh why did David have to worry about Calvin? He'd got her now, and that's all he should worry about.

'Elizabeth, sunshine, you've got to understand that Calvin is all the family I have. He's the only one with whom I share memories of my mother and father. When he came into the Gilmore family, he brought some happiness into it. Without Calvin, sunshine, my childhood would have been horrible. I owe him. You understand? I owe him big time. Not only that, I'm used to having Cal around. We've always done everything together. We built up the business together. We're more like brothers than cousins.' Elizabeth didn't like the sound of that. Sure, as kids, they might have done everything together but now it was time for David to break free. She was all the family he needed. He'd see that eventually.

David certainly wasn't going to go into details of what a weakling he had been at school and that life had been a misery before Calvin had gone to school with him and beaten off the bullies. He also didn't want to tell Elizabeth of the strained relationship between him and his father. My God! What would she think of him? A sissy weakling, the victim of school bullies who wasn't even good enough to evoke any interest, let alone affection, from his own father. No, he didn't want Elizabeth to know all that. She should always and only know him as the strong and loving provider; the man who loves her and who took her in when her father threw her out; the man who will make her life a happy one. That's what Elizabeth should think of him.

'But you've got me now. Aren't I enough for you?' She stamped her foot.

'You are more than enough for me, my sunshine, but Cal is also family. I thought you liked him. You've always got on well with him when we all went out together.'

'That was different. I had to put up with Cal to be near you. It was always you I was interested in.'

'Well, you'll have to put up with Cal for a long time, 'cause he's my family and I don't intend not to have him around. Also, I'll have you know, he's a partner in the business and what we do in business, we do together.' David stopped. He couldn't believe he had spoken so harshly. He loved Elizabeth beyond all reason. How could he speak to her in such a way? He reached across the table and took her hand.

'Don't let's argue, my love. We'll work something out. Things have just got a bit on top of us; that's all.'

'Do you wish I'd never come?' Elizabeth sniffed audibly. Her eyes were starting to glisten with tears.

'Of course not, silly! You are everything to me. You know that. It's you and me against the world, forever. We'll never be apart. There will never be anyone else for me. I agree that things aren't going as good as they could be at the moment and that Calvin is a huge part of the problem but we'll sort that out. Mam always said that all things have a way of sorting themselves out if you give them time. Tell me, have you heard from your father yet?'

With that question, David managed successfully to take the onus of their upset off Calvin.

Elizabeth hadn't heard from her father all these months and she was extremely sad about that. She thought he might have gone to sea this week and that would mean she wouldn't hear from him for at least a month. Although she was exactly where she wanted to be, she wanted everything to be all right with her dad. She wanted her father to like and accept David. He'd said some awful things that night about David being a nothing and a nobody; far beneath her, a good-for-nothing, in fact. David was none of those things and Elizabeth thought that, with time, she would be able to prove that to him and he would have her back in his life and accept David for what he was: simply a good, loving man who made her feel loved and protected.

Elizabeth had been at Cooper Road for some six months now. David loved coming home to her and shortened his working days whenever he could. It took a while before he realised that things had changed in his working environment. First of all, the men he had working for him started to leave. They were apologetic enough about it, saying they needed to be nearer home or had been offered more money, but they left anyway, even when David offered them more money. Then David came up against the builders' yards; they stopped his credit, saying it was a new policy that all materials had to be paid for on delivery. This was new to David who had settled his suppliers' bills on a monthly basis. But credit was no longer forthcoming for him. It wasn't until he went to see about the building permission he had been waiting for to come through for a garage someone wanted him to build in Scartho, that he realised something was drastically wrong or, more exactly, someone was systematically throwing stones in his path. Already, in the last few weeks, he'd lost his men, had no credit in the town and no possibilities of getting the paperwork he needed to execute his work. He suspected he knew who was behind all this.

CHAPTER FORTY-FOUR

Calvin was under the shower, washing off the grime and the sweat of the workday. He was still living in the annex of the house occupied by the two men he and David had met at Captain Andy's Bar in Moraira. He was singing as he washed himself. He was thoroughly enjoying his time in Spain. It was true that he had done a lot of hard work, worked a lot harder than he was used to, even, but as hard as he worked was also as hard as he played, and the play was good. Spain, at least in the area where he had landed, offered a large selection of clubs, men's clubs, that is. They were the type of club where a man could find some relief for a price; where a man could have a drink and a good fuck without having to entertain and be nice to the bitch; a club where the ladies were available for a bit of rough handling, just like he liked it. Yes, he was enjoying his time in Spain.

Better still, he bought a British newspaper every day and read it from back to front; it had been a while since the murder in Waltham had been mentioned. Calvin definitely liked Spain. He felt safe here. And the girls went wild for his good looks and his body. He'd never had it quite so good and had no intention of leaving.

Still, all was not perfect in his little world. In fact, what was really pissing him off was that David had suddenly come out of his shell and made a play for Elizabeth as soon as his back was turned. Arsehole! What on earth did she see in that dowdy little man? David was boring, no fun at all. He was either counting his money and moaning about the cost of things or he was asleep in front of the telly. He was what one would call *a good man*. Goodness and bloody light shone out of his arse. Stupid woman! She must have been desperate for him. That was it. If he'd stayed there, it would have been him in between Elizabeth's legs now. It would have been just a matter of time before he had brought her round to his way of thinking. How dare she reject him? He was worth having. Little bitch should have been grateful for his attentions. Now bloody stupid David was in there banging away at her. She'd have to go, of course. It was more than time that David threw in the towel and came to Spain where the action was. He could find a bit of tail here easily enough. He should leave Elizabeth and her tight-arsed father behind in Grimsby, where they belonged. Here there was more than enough work and, more importantly, here no one was looking for a tall dark-haired man of Calvin's description.

Russell and John had been good to him, really, when he thought about it. How stupid can you get though? They were teaching him all they knew. In Spain the products were different, the way of building was different, the intense heat being a consideration never taken into account in England. The houses they were building were far more ornate than anything he'd ever seen or worked on in Grimsby. Rounded rooms, spiral staircases made of marble, arched windows – all things that would put the cost of a house out of most people's financial bracket, were practically run-of-the-mill here.

The heat was atrocious. Even at this late stage of the year, the heat was something Calvin still wasn't used to. The others worked without complaint, swigging often at a large bottle of water, their bodies, shirt-free, browned, their skin thickened against the blazing sun. Calvin kept his shirt on since he had got so burnt during the first few days on the site.

Building rules and regulations didn't seem to exist in Spain. Projects were started without permits because, as Russell told him, any paperwork needed was always forthcoming, if you knew the right people and, more importantly, knew exactly who to backhand. And if you got fined for building without permission, well the fine was sometimes cheaper than the actual licence to build.

'That must work out a bit expensive,' Calvin commented when they were discussing the legalities of a foreigner working in Spain.

'It might seem expensive to you, mate, but it saves a lot of trouble in the end. It's who you know,' Russell stressed.

They obviously knew the right people, Calvin surmised, because they always got their permits. And, what's more, they were left alone to get on with earning their money without interference. Calvin snapped this piece of knowledge up for future reference. He'd make sure to get to know the right people and what their prices were.

'Everybody's doing it,' John piped in. 'The British and the Germans working here in the trade, well, none of them are registered or licensed. It's the same with a lot of the Spanish, too. But if you keep your nose clean and make a habit of being generous to the "right people",' he gave an exaggerated wink before continuing, 'you are left alone to get on with your job, like Russell says.'

So Calvin spent a lot of time going in the Spanish bars with Russell and John, meeting the right people.

Life was easy in Spain. And if something wasn't done today, it would be done tomorrow, or the day after, or the day after that, or sometime next week. Oh, yes. That was an oddity that took some getting used to. The hectic ways of Britain were unheard of here. Yes, Spain was definitely the place to be.

In the first few months, Calvin learnt that if you went into the right bar, if you got to know the right people, had the right amount of money to buy your way into the circle of the local power-holders, and if you had the knowledge of how to build a house, you could make a lot of money in Spain.

Of course, David didn't know all this yet and Calvin was bursting to tell him. He was used to having David do all the wrangling and handling. Previously, Calvin had liked it best when he did his bit on the site and carried off his money at the end of the month. He'd like to change that now. But David was becoming a problem. All he could speak about when Calvin phoned home was stupid Elizabeth. He really ought to drop that tart and start thinking about their future. She was just a bird when all was said and done. Like any other bird, she could be replaced at a moment's notice. David seemed to have gone all soft and silly over her. Calvin, on the other hand, knew just the type of silly cunt he was dealing with here. The type that egged you on and then refused to deliver. He'd met her type before. And he'd wasted more than enough time on that piece of arse. She wasn't worth the effort. If David was giving her one now, it was probably because she was no good in the first place. Silly slut should have opened her legs when he lowered himself to offer her a good seeing to. Just goes to show how stupid she was. Calvin would be happy if he never saw her again in his entire life.

But the problem, at this moment, was convincing David to leave the slut and come to Spain. One thing was certain, whether the police where still looking for him or not, he was not going back to Grimsby, not for all the tea in China. Oh no. Spain was the place to be and Calvin knew that David was capable of making him a lot of money. He'd always done it in the past, and now it was time for that bloody cousin of his to get over here and do it again. His trump card was, and he knew this for a fact, that his wimp of a cousin thought he couldn't manage in life without having him near. Well, he needed to keep thinking like that. Calvin smiled at that thought. He knew it was just a matter of time before he'd convince David to sell up and start again in Spain.

CHAPTER FORTY-FIVE

It had been over six months now since Elizabeth had moved in with David. Their love-making was wild and passionate and often, very often. David would joke that she was wearing him out. If he came home at lunchtime to eat, she could hardly wait for him to finish his food before grabbing his hand and dragging him upstairs. David would pretend he couldn't possibly have sex in the afternoon, but his actions and his body belied those words. They enjoyed each other as often as possible and as much as possible. They were in love.

The house was looking spick and span because, with nothing left to occupy her besides satisfying her lust with David, Elizabeth had taken up housekeeping. She had spring-cleaned the simple terraced house, moved furniture around and bought some knick-knacks that made the house look more like a home. But when all was said and done, David worked long hours and Elizabeth was often alone. She was bored.

Indeed, she loved David, and adored being with him, but he was gone for most of the day and simply being the housewife wasn't for her. She was used to action, to travelling, to having fun. And David was changing, too.

The longer he was away from Calvin and the more he spoke to him on the phone, the more distant he had become with her. Yes, he'd mentioned that work was hard to come by at the moment and, as she had heard him talking on the phone, she knew that most of his staff had for some unknown reason left. But it would all soon get better. She just knew it would. If only David would stop moaning about Calvin being in Spain and them being here. After the scene with Calvin in her flat, she wasn't really interested in seeing him again, ever. She hated to admit it, because she knew that David looked up to Calvin like a schoolboy enthralled by Superman, but she didn't like him at all now. She could sense something simmering under that cool and handsome exterior of his and felt sure she and David would be far better off if Calvin stayed in Spain and they stayed in Grimsby.

Her father would be back soon from his trip and then she would go and see him and he would surely have stopped being so angry with her. He could never resist her when she made the effort to be nice to him. And she would make a great effort, because, despite her fury at him for trying to control her life, and not being ready to accept David, she really loved him and was missing him.

Elizabeth called him when she calculated he would now be home. The phone was answered before the third ring. 'Hello, Dad. It's Elizabeth here. How are you?'

'I'm fine,' came the curt reply. Jensen did not expand.

'Was it a good trip?' Elizabeth tried to touch a subject she knew her father liked talking about. 'How was the catch?'

Jensen breathed audibly through the connection, 'It was fine, Elizabeth. What do you want?' he asked coldly.

'I want us to be friends again, Dad.'

'Are you still with that good-for-nothing?'

'He's not a good-for-nothing, Dad.'

'Obviously you haven't seen sense yet. So I don't know why you are calling me. If you remember, I said don't call me until you've come to your senses. Do you want to come home, Elizabeth? Have you seen the error of your ways?'

'No, Dad. I don't want to come home. I want you to accept David. I want you to accept that we are together and going to get married. I want us all to be all right with each other.'

'What! Gilmore is still around then? I wouldn't have thought he could afford you any more; what with no work coming his way. Has he got any workers at all? Be sensible, Elizabeth. I've made sure he's got no chance in this town. Now stop fooling around and come home, where you belong.'

Elizabeth froze at the words. So that was why David had no business: why he had no staff, why the building permit for that big job in Scartho had been refused. The realisation washed over her that her father had been instrumental in trying to destroy the man she loved and his business. Even worse, he was succeeding at it. David hadn't said much to her, but she knew he was worried. He had grown quieter and many days in the last couple of weeks he had been at home, even though it wasn't raining and, normally, he would have been working. The full impact of her father's spiteful actions hit her like a cold shower. How could he? He was doing his best to ruin them, to ruin her chances of happiness, simply because another man loved her.

Elizabeth held her anger in check. She kept her voice low and polite. 'Father, it is now clear to me that you have once again tried to manipulate my life. You have tried to break me up from the man I love and am going to marry, whatever you say. You have controlled me all my life. It wasn't love that directed you, just pure possessiveness. Well, you don't own me. I have tried to make amends for our argument but I see no way that we can be friends again. I will marry David, despite all your efforts to destroy him. Together, David and I will make a life for ourselves and you will not be welcomed in it until you can accept that David and I are going to be together.' Elizabeth stopped for breath and when still nothing came from the other end of the line said, 'I'm sorry this had to happen, but you have pushed me into a corner and forced me to choose. And I choose David.'

Jensen slammed the phone down and headed for the whisky.

That evening, Elizabeth curled up in bed next to David and told him of her conversation with her father. He listened patiently, the realisation seeping through him that while Jensen was against him, his chances of making a living for himself in Grimsby were over. How did that rotten, mean son of a bitch have so much power? He didn't say this to Elizabeth, of course. He could see she was distraught at what her father was doing to him. It took a few minutes before he saw the silver lining in their dark clouds.

If Jensen had made sure he couldn't make a living in Grimsby, then he would have to move to somewhere where he could make a living. He wasn't without means. Besides having a nice little nest egg, he had the house, which was completely paid for, to sell. And the equipment from the business would bring a tidy sum, as well. More than all that, he still had his talent for building a great house. And he had his youth. And, he smiled to himself, as the icing on the cake, he now had Elizabeth completely. His Elizabeth who was weeping softly in his arms would surely go anywhere with him now that her father had made it impossible for him to earn a living in Grimsby. He'd call that number at the bar that Calvin had given him tomorrow evening and give him the good news. He lifted Elizabeth's head from his chest and kissed her gently on the mouth.

'Stop crying, my love. We'll be all right. It's time to pack and go. It's time to go to Spain.'

CHAPTER FORTY-SIX

David stood on the balcony of his home in Spain and surveyed the scene before him. All around the old pine trees stood tall, reaching for the sky. It never failed to amaze him how green this area was despite the lack of rain. Dotted here and there, well below him, were specks of white indicating other houses hidden among the foliage but private, like his own home. Further out, in the distance, glistened the Mediterranean. There were boats of varying sizes bobbing around on the large expanse of its sparkling waters. The picturesque view stretched from Moraira to Calpe: Calpe being the next town southwards along the coast of the Iberian Peninsula. On the water's edge, clusters of houses, hotels and commercial businesses vied for space. But here, nearly at the top of the mountain, there was no feeling of being hemmed in.

The house was ringed by a beautiful cultivated garden that looked mature although it had only been planted six months ago. The gardeners had done a good job, leaving the property appearing as if it had existed with its bougainvillaea and oleander bushes for decades. There was still work to be done: the completion of the pool area, the drive up to the house from the road needed tarmac, and the massive automatic wrought-iron gates still hadn't been installed. But the main dream home was finished and he loved it.

This was his favourite time of year, just before the oppressive heat of the summer. Yes, May and June were his favourite months. And this was his favourite time: evening after his work was done for the day.

He took his gin and tonic and went to sit on the plush upholstered wicker-cane settee. He sank into the soft cushions. This is where he liked to sit and watch the sun go down, to relax, sipping at his gin and tonic as the sun sank with a blaze of glory behind the mountains. This colourful game of nature never failed to remind him of how lucky he was to be here. The patio furniture around him was big and impressive, just like his house. Yes, indeed, he thought, with a contented glow in his heart, he'd come a long way in just nine years.

Although it had got off to a bad start, Spain had been good to him – to both him and Elizabeth, for they both loved the area in which they lived, the people, the mixture of nationalities and the lazy, hazy days. Mind you, that lazy, hazy day bit had taken some getting used to. But after struggling for a while to make everyone move at his pace, David finally accepted that Spain moved to a different drummer and there was nothing you could do about it but sit down, drink your gin and tonic and wait for things to happen.

And happen they had. Looking out over the treetops, across the wide expanse of green valley down to the far-off road and out onto the sparkling Mediterranean, David, mellowed by his drink and the success of the day, recalled their start in this new land.

After Jensen had successfully put him out of business, there had been no fine wedding but an austere occasion at the Registry Office in the Town Hall of Grimsby with one of the Registry Office staff and a stranger off the street as witnesses. It hadn't taken much encouragement for Elizabeth to agree to try and make a life for themselves in Spain. She was devastated by what her father was doing to both of them. For the first time in his life, David had felt really needed. And he revelled in the feeling. He answered that need by taking over all planning for their future. Elizabeth never questioned anything he decided; he was in complete control. He'd phoned Calvin to tell him of their marriage and that they were selling up and coming to Spain. That was the weirdest of things.

'Hey, Cal! It's me! Guess what? I'm married! No, we're married, is what I meant to say; me and Elizabeth. We're married and we're coming to Spain. Cal? Cal!'

Calvin had been on at him for weeks to sell up and move to Spain, but when he said he was actually going to do so, and that he was bringing Elizabeth with him, and as his wife, there had been a long silence on the other end of the line, so long that David had thought they had been cut off. When Calvin had finally spoken again, it was in a cool, unemotional voice, nothing like his pleading for David to get to Spain or his cajoling for him to hurry, but a somewhat cold and oh so terribly polite voice. The voice he usually reserved for strangers or anyone who had the audacity to annoy him.

'How nice for you, Davie. Congratulations,' was all Calvin had said to the news.

David had taken it at the time to be a bit of jealousy. Who wouldn't want to be married and happy, he'd reasoned. Calvin was so handsome and had such a great personality that David just knew it wouldn't be long before he would find his own happiness with a woman he loved and who loved him back just as fiercely – just like he and Elizabeth loved each other. And he knew any bad feelings would soon subside. He and Calvin were partners, as close as brothers. Nothing would ever change that, not even his marriage to Elizabeth.

He did wonder, but only for a fleeting moment, if Calvin was just put out with him for getting married and bringing someone else into their lives, when they were always used to it just being the two of them, or if it was because he'd wanted Elizabeth for himself. But, of course, if he had wanted Elizabeth, he wouldn't have just stayed on in Spain, would he? And since they had all been together again, Calvin had reverted to his friendly and familiar attitude towards them both, accepting Elizabeth into the fold just like she belonged there, which she did now that she was his wife.

Mind you, David had been so busy in Grimsby at that time, what with the wedding and selling the house and business, that he hadn't spent much time thinking about Calvin's reaction to the news of his marriage and intention to bring Elizabeth with him. He'd had no time to ponder his cool reaction. And when they had arrived, it had been so hectic that he'd given no thought to anything except getting somewhere to live and getting work.

Getting work had been surprisingly easy. This area of Spain where fate had taken him was expanding at such a breakneck speed in 1976 that the construction business was the best and most lucrative to be in. Holiday homes, and eventually houses meant for all year residency, were being turned out ten to the dozen. The Spanish had an artistic flair in their constructions and a special talent for visual beauty not usually found in other European houses, spending much time and money on arched windows, little turrets and the like. But David had the knowledge and skill as well as the desire to build a house that would last: to produce a building that included sturdy foundations and some type of insulation and just plain old good-quality construction techniques. He'd also talked incessantly about the lack of houses for the ordinary fellow, the simple working man. It wasn't long before his work mates and bosses alike, impressed by his talent, quick ideas and then his dreams, suggested he establish his own company.

But, despite all this support, the start had been difficult.

At that time the country was in a state of chaotic legalities after the death of Franco, who had previously governed Spain with an iron fist. Corruption abounded in local governments and the cosmopolitan areas of the coastal regions were trying to cope and integrate the influx of foreign nationals from northern Europe who were flocking to the busy areas looking to either make the country their home and/or make a quick buck or two.

Without Calvin it might never have happened that they finally got the chance to form their own building company. It was still quite an oddity for a foreigner to form any type of legal business. The bureaucratic path to a legal company was strewn with potholes that had to be filled first with lots of cash. But Calvin knew the right people to make anything possible.

Calvin had spent his time alone here making the right contacts: his drinking buddies who worked in the town halls, and the local police. He also knew the local bankers and lawyers. And they had all fallen prey to the Calvin Fisher charm.

To legally form a limited company, they'd needed a Spanish partner, someone who would be happy to receive a regular cash payment on a monthly basis for lending his name to the legal documents needed to form Gilmore and Fisher Constructions.

David remembered how astounded he'd been at the way things were done. But if he'd ever questioned the legalities of the procedure, Calvin had shushed him into silence, given him one of his blinding smiles, called him 'old bean' and promised that everything would be all right.

And it was all right in the end. Although their funds were heavily depleted by that time, they finally had the documents to prove they were a legally operating limited company. It didn't take long before they were employing and training quite a few Spaniards. And in doing so, the Gilmore/Fisher duo gained respect and admiration from the locals.

It wasn't just in his work that things had changed.

When all was said and done, no matter how much David and Elizabeth were in love, they were two people still in the phase of getting to know each other. Being together twenty-four hours a day could wear tremendously on the nerves, especially when one was used to being alone, being in command of one's time and being, when the truth be told, quite content in one's own company. Now there was always Elizabeth to consider.

And David did his best to consider Elizabeth's feelings in everything he did. He praised the day she came to him. However, the fact that her father had emotionally, as well as completely financially, cut her off weighed heavily on Elizabeth. She was used to having her own money, money that mysteriously appeared in her bank account each month courtesy of her father. Now she had no bank account to go to and it was obvious she had found it hard to ask David for money. He solved that by opening an account just for their private household needs and he made sure there was always more than enough funds available to her. She never once abused the account, financially caring for their home and private lives like an expert businesswoman.

But he noticed that for a long time she seemed to find it difficult to think of what he earned as hers as well as his. And although he kept telling her how important and instrumental she was to their success, he always suspected that she somehow felt shut out.

But it had been Elizabeth who had been the one to make the home, to see that they both ate proper food, that they had a soft place to fall when the going got rough. She was a wonderful organiser and homemaker; the best wife anyone could wish for. Maybe it wasn't so good that he'd had to leave her alone much of the time at first, even now, when he thought about it, but money didn't grow on trees; you had to work hard and long hours to achieve success. And he was successful. And that wasn't always easy in the, for them, unaccustomed heat and bright, burning sun.

Ah yes, the sun, thought David. Wow! After spending the first twenty-eight years of his life in Grimsby, David had hardly realised that such wonderful weather existed. The morning light brought the warm rays of the sun with it. He had flourished in that warmth and light. His body had become bronzed in its rays; his hair, so sun-kissed, it was nearly white. Never before had he felt so acceptable. Yes, that was it, acceptable. David would never think of himself as handsome, but Spain had been kind to him and if not handsome, in his own opinion of himself, he now felt at least acceptable. Calvin had, of course, just grown more beautiful. The sun had browned his lean muscular torso; made his black hair glisten like coal and his blue eyes look more startling and piercing than ever. David smiled to himself. When he thought about it, he had to admit that both he and Calvin had physically benefited from the change of countries. Elizabeth, too, had found some peace here.

It took Elizabeth a while to come out of her depression at her father's rejection and his subsequent actions. She'd fallen in love, been married and left the country, within a short timeframe and all without her father taking part; an unusual state really when one considered that Elizabeth's father had, until she met David, steered her life in the direction he wanted. She wasn't used to making her own decisions, and the one she had made concerning David had cost her dearly, resulting in her becoming afraid to voice any opinion at all. But David was glad to step in. He knew now that Elizabeth would be with him and do what he thought was right for always. She'd made a good wife and he'd never regretted marrying her. What's more, she'd given him two sons, the first, Alexander, being born within the first year of their arrival in Spain. Hardly two years later, Nathan had come along. He was immensely proud of his boys;

they made him feel like he was going to live forever.

Truly, life had been good to him, and he said a silent prayer.

David took a sip of his drink as his thoughts turned to his cousin. Calvin had been instrumental in introducing him into the business scene. Different from England, most business deals were conducted in the bars and restaurants after much social talk of families, holidays, local happenings, and the like, almost anything other than what you really wanted to talk about. This was difficult for David to get used to. He wasn't a man of many words and making unnecessary chit-chat came hard to him, but that is what was called for when dealing with the Spanish. He'd learned Spanish quickly with the aid of a teacher who taught him on a one-to-one basis, three times a week. Within six months, he was out there, crushing down his shy nature and speaking to the locals like Spanish was a language he had been speaking for years. Calvin was still fart-arsing around, speaking a kind of pidgin Spanish, having learnt the language in the bars rather than with a professional teacher, but his personality alone carried him far and he made many a good business deal while propping up the bar with the locals. However, David's knowledge of the language coupled with his cautionary way of working resulted in him finding some six sponsors for his planned project on a piece of land he'd seen in Calpe.

He'd talked on and off to Calvin about this piece of land. It was in the green zone, a part of the outskirts of town meant to stay green and not be built on. But when the shrub land had caught fire, one hot, dry summer day, David had made a bid at the town council for it to be re-designated as building land. Calvin worked closely with their lawyer, always saying it was better if David didn't know everything. And quite honestly, David didn't want to know everything. He was just happy to get down to building the type of homes he could be proud of. Calvin took care of the official stuff. Calvin and the lawyer together always seemed to get the best results. Somehow they managed to manipulate the system and backhand the right people. It was the way things were done. The handouts had amounted to a lot of money, David remembered, but it had worked. And David had done his bit, too. Within six months he had secured six investors – lawyers, bank managers, government employees, and the like. This of course, would never have worked in Grimsby, but it worked here and suddenly David was in possession of a piece of land on the outskirts of Calpe that was worth millions.

Together with an architect, he worked out a plan to build over one hundred and fifty houses, terraced, in the British fashion, and all with small private gardens. David's ideas were new and fresh. He saw rows of terraced houses on a complex incorporating a huge swimming pool and tennis courts, and all surrounded by parkland. His cheek, his daring, his pushiness and plain long hours of work had resulted in establishing Parklands of Calpe.

He'd built the pool first; an ambitious curved overlarge pool with a palm tree on an island in the middle. Instead of steps the swimmer could walk into the water, like walking into the ocean. Fountains and a children's special area were features. These were all David's idea. Then he'd planted parkland – rolling lawns and lots of quick-growing pine trees, eucalyptus and oleander bushes. By the time construction started on the first row of houses, because of the beautiful pool and surroundings, the buyers were fighting to get to them. It all made David feel very proud of himself: more than that, it made them very rich.

Despite these happy memories, David again recalled how difficult it had been to get a foothold in this new land. Calvin had been such a great support when they first moved to Spain. David had been overjoyed at seeing him again and it was only a short while before Calvin was back to his old self. They all got on so well at first that when they finally found a house to rent, and it had three bedrooms, Calvin moved in with them. Elizabeth wasn't really in agreement with that, but she soon came round because she knew that David wanted Calvin near him.

Since they have been in their new home, David's dream home, Calvin was at least housed away from them in the apartment underneath the main house. It had been nearly eight years before they moved out of that rented house and into this house where David now sat nursing his gin and tonic. And although he was somewhat surprised that Calvin was still with them and not married to some dark and passionate beauty, he was glad that he was now living separately from the main house but still near to him. It was nice to have a little more private time alone with Elizabeth. At least it stopped her moaning about Calvin always being with them. But what would his life have been like without Calvin: success and wealth bound them together.

David could hear Elizabeth tinkering in the kitchen preparing their evening meal. He knew she didn't like to be disturbed in her kitchen and so simply called, 'Have I time for another drink, or is it nearly ready?'

'Have another,' came Elizabeth's voice from the kitchen. 'And get me one, too, please.'

David returned to the sideboard and mixed himself a gin and tonic and made a vodka and tonic for Elizabeth. He took her drink to her in the kitchen, quickly kissed her cheek then returned with his own drink to his place on the settee on the balcony. How perfect was his world.

He could hear the crickets now. They all hummed together as the sun touched the horizon. Once again his mind wandered.

What a surprise it had been when Elizabeth had told him that he was about to become a father. She had worked so hard in those first few months, arranging their days so that they could work without a thought of how they were going to eat or have clean clothes when they needed them. Elizabeth did it all and it enabled both him and Calvin to get out there and make something of themselves. Moraira, at that time, was full of people just like them, all pushing to make a good living. Work was the theme of the day in the working-class expat community. There wasn't much else for Elizabeth to do, except look after them and the home. Sometimes she got lonely. It took a while before they moved into a social circle that allowed her to make friends and feel somewhat at home. Just when she thought she was going to have some time on her hands, along came Alexander, the apple of his father's eye, followed, some two years later, by Nathan.

And so, in the soft amber glow of the setting sun, David sat there on the balcony of his newly-built home situated on the side of a mountain amid the luscious green of the pine forest. He looked out over the valley onto the Mediterranean, which the sun had turned a vibrant red-orange as it prepared to sink under the horizon. His heart filled with happiness as his thoughts drifted back and forth along the last few years. He heard his children laughing somewhere in the garden below and the dog, which had honoured them with his attachment some six months ago when they had started to build the house, barked in play. Calvin would be coming up from his apartment soon to have supper with them. He downed the last drops of his drink, got off the settee and turned to walk through the French windows into the house. 'Is tea ready, yet? I'm starving,' he called as he made his way to the kitchen.

CHAPTER FORTY-SEVEN

' Have you checked at the town hall yet about this area, Cal?' David asked.

'Yep, it's still a no-go.' Calvin sliced a chunk off his steak and slipped it into his mouth, making it impossible for a moment to continue to speak. He chewed slowly before swallowing. 'Elizabeth, your cooking gets better by the day, I swear. Why don't you leave this lot and come and live the quiet life with me?'

Elizabeth reached for the bowl of salad and ladled some out of the dish onto Calvin's plate. 'Have some more salad, Cal,' she said. She lowered her eyes so he couldn't see her face and maybe guess what she was thinking. The words thundered in her brain. Every bloody evening! This sod has to dine with us, every bloody evening! Nine bloody years and he's still here! Just what does it take to get rid of him?

'You boys want any more salad?' She turned her attention to her sons who seemed only interested in getting their food down their throats as quickly as possible. They emptied their plates simultaneously, pushed them into the centre of the table, wiped their mouths on the backs of their hands and scraped their chairs on the tiles as they stood up.

'Where're you two going?' she called.

'We're just down the mountain, Mam. We're building a den.' They made towards the door.

'Half an hour. It'll be dark then and it's school in the morning.'

'All right, all right,' they both mumbled as they left the house, slamming the front door with a resounding bang.

And again another fine evening with Calvin for company. Elizabeth sighed. 'Kids,' she said to no one in particular and started to clear the table. 'You and Cal go sit on the balcony. I'll be there when

I've cleared this lot up.'

Taking their glasses and the rest of the wine with them, Calvin and David retired to the balcony.

Elizabeth loaded the dishwasher and contemplated her life. She stared at her reflection in the windowpane above the kitchen sink. It was turning to dusk outside and she could see her likeness clearly now. She was happy with what she saw. Despite having an ultra busy life, what with the kids and the need to drive them everywhere due to the lack of a regular bus service, and seeing to all the creature comforts of her husband and his stupid bloody cousin, Elizabeth felt good about life and how it was treating her. True, she'd been quite lonely at first, what with David working all hours. And time had not changed him. She was just glad to get to see him some days because he fell out of bed at dawn, worked all day, and fell back into bed at dusk. But things were getting better now. Turning sideways, she pulled herself to her full height, sucked in her stomach, shoved out her breasts and again inspected her reflection in the window. She nodded in approval of herself. She'd regained her figure both times after the boys and she didn't intend to have any more children so she assumed she would keep this figure. She stroked her hands over her full breasts and flat stomach. Yes, as far as her figure was concerned, she was happy. And David seemed more than happy with it; she giggled to herself, remembering their passion of last night.

She was also happy with being a mother. However, a small dark cloud hovered over the family that she meant to disperse. It was plain to see that David favoured Alexander over Nathan. Not surprising really, considering that Alexander was the spitting image of his father, with the exception that he had an outgoing personality. David loved him to distraction, never pulling him up for his harshness to his brother, never chastising him for his forgetfulness when it came to manners and civil behaviour. Alexander had a love of life that David revelled in and always wanted to share. Nathan, on the other hand, was often withdrawn and, consequently, left out of their horsing around. If not in looks, Nathan was just like his father, really, but David never saw that. Often Elizabeth wondered if Nathan felt the difference but he never said anything, never complained. What a wonder children are! As they had grown, they had shown her this new country she now called home through their eyes, and it was safe and welcoming and full of colour. It was a breathtakingly picturesque land of ragged mountains rolling down to green valleys and a sea the bluest she'd ever seen. She'd spent a lot of time with Alexander and Nathan on the beach; they loved playing in the white sand and she got time to relax. Having children made her automatically, it seemed, a part of Spain. The other mothers always talked to her and continued to do so for as long as it took for her to understand them. She was quite good at conversations in Spanish about children and the housework now.

A blot on her otherwise perfect horizon, besides the permanent presence of Calvin, was her father's lingering cool attitude. He'd relented somewhat when she'd written and told him of the birth of his first grandchild. She'd even been to visit him with the children. But he refused to see David, refused to visit them in Spain and never phoned or wrote to her, leaving the seeking of any further contact solely to her. Sadly, over time, she accepted that her father was a stubborn man who would never admit that he might have been wrong about her choice of husband: that David, although being poor and of no social standing in Grimsby when she met him, was now a 'somebody' over here in Spain, and rich to boot. And yet, thought Elizabeth, she felt sure her father would like David now, the way David had become.

They say a daughter always marries her father and that is exactly what she had done. David, so sweet, quiet and unimposing when they were first together had changed drastically over the years, starting when her father had shunned them. In the face of her father's wrath, David had not gone under but had become strong, had fought for what he wanted, had started again in another country after her father had made it impossible for him to stay in his home town, and had taken over the control of her life along the way. She didn't mind really. In fact, after having her father do it for so many years, she had to admit she was used to having someone tell her what to do, where to go, how to be. And she had chosen David so she really had no right to complain. But how was she to know that he would turn into her father, once married; that he would become so protective that sometimes she felt like she needed to break free to be able to breathe deeply on her own. No, no, she admonished herself. How could she think such things of her David? He adored her and she adored him. He wanted only the best for her, for them, and she knew it. How could she be dissatisfied with that? No, she wasn't dissatisfied, she was put out. That was it, put out. She was definitely put out with the permanent presence of Calvin.

For the last nine years as David and Elizabeth had made their own journey through life, Calvin had ridden shotgun. He was simply always there. Admittedly, he'd helped them enormously when they arrived in Spain, and for the first couple of years, she hadn't minded him living with them. Although it was sad that the only time she and David had had together without Calvin was when they were in Grimsby just before they came to Spain.

Calvin had never mentioned that day at her apartment when he'd made a grab for her and fallen, unceremoniously onto the floor, embarrassing them both. And neither had she. She thought he must have forgotten it just as she wanted to forget it. But she was never sure what that strange man was thinking. Yes, she had to admit to herself, she found him strange. He was not the wonderful person David always insisted he was but, for her, he appeared strangely distant; aloof, even with them; somehow unattached and singular, despite his handsome exterior and friendly charm. Just how much of his niceness was real and how much was false, she wondered. And what did he really think of them? Often when she'd look his way, he would be staring intently at her, a darkness in his eyes she couldn't quite decipher. At least he was now in his own apartment, albeit in the house but, nevertheless, separate from them.

This was the best thing about the house - not the fantastic location, not the white marble floors and the arches leading into open-plan rooms with large plate-glass windows, not the hand-painted tiled bathrooms or the spacious bedrooms, or the beamed ceilings and the luxury-class real-oak kitchen - no, none of this pleased her so much as the fact that Calvin was at least in a part of the house not frequented by her and her family. He was separate. He was gone. Unfortunately, not gone far enough and she hated that David insisted that he eat with them every evening.

No, Elizabeth would have been a lot happier with her lot if Calvin wasn't with them so much, but she couldn't quite put her finger on what was not right, and so she couldn't possibly take her worries to her husband who so obviously thought Calvin was the bloody bee's knees.

CHAPTER FORTY-EIGHT

Calvin sank back into the comfort of the armchair on the balcony of David's house and enjoyed the view. He could see the rock of Calpe to his right and the smooth mountain tops riddled with the lines of preliminary roads of the new Cumbre Del Sol Urbanisation starting to be built just beyond Moraira on his left. In the middle, the lights in people's homes were starting to come on and they twinkled brightly. This house was indeed in a lovely location offering open views all round; he'd felt a twang of envy. David, as ever the silly bugger, had always seen that all profits were split equally. And he'd had as much money as David. He couldn't complain about that. He'd just used it differently, that's all. But what was a man who didn't have a wife supposed to do? He'd spent most of his money at the sleazy bars situated along the main road a few kilometres north of Moraira. Yep, you could get anything you wanted there for the right price. And he had to admit those girls had managed to bleed him dry while satisfying his appetite. They'd not even complained when he'd punched them around a little. But then, that's what most women liked, wasn't it? They only pretended to want some soft loving but what they really liked was a bit of rough and he knew that a woman shouting 'no!' really meant, 'Yes, oh yes.'

His stomach was full and he felt content for the moment. Well, content to a point. This house should have been his, he should be upstairs with Elizabeth instead of downstairs in the apartment, and the boys should be his children. Bloody David! Took everything he did. As soon as his back was turned he upped and took Elizabeth. God alone knows how he won her over. It was always him she liked, anyone could tell that. She just felt sorry for David; that's all. Stupid woman! While he was here in Spain working his arse off making a headway start for them both, he went back to Grimsby and stole the woman who should have been his.

'As I was saying,' Calvin took a sip of his red wine and leant forward to place his glass on the table, it won't be long before all this land, all that you can see to the right and left of you, will be free for construction.'

'How can that be? It's still designated green zone. Look what I had to pay out in backhanders to get permission to build my own home. Look at the large piece of land I had to take so that I could get a permit to build at all. Ten thousand square metres is hell of a big garden, you know, Cal?'

Calvin looked taken aback.

'Sorry, mate,' David said immediately, 'I know you had a job arranging things. And I'm eternally grateful to you for pushing this through. Without your help, I would never have finally built this.' David wafted his hand around in the air to indicate his home.

Calvin felt like smashing his fist into David's face. 'And I wouldn't have had such a lovely sprawling apartment underneath, right in the home of my only family.' He smiled to hide his clenched teeth then took up his glass and saluted David with it before drinking deeply.

'Hey, Cal,' David said before joining the toast. 'We've come a long way since those school days, haven't we? And don't ever think I don't appreciate how much you've helped me. All this wouldn't have been possible for me without your help.'

Calvin looked at David over the rim of his glass. Daft, snivelling bastard, he thought, as he smiled at him.

David marvelled at his cousin for the umpteenth time. This man was so good at arranging things, at knowing the right people and knowing how to get what they wanted. Without him there would have been no Parklands, the building project, still in full swing that had made them so fabulously well off. He'd never imagined being so, well, rich, really. Every time David thought about it, his heart jumped into his mouth. His cousin, his Calvin, his only family, had made it all possible. It had been Calvin who'd made the contacts, he'd made the bids, he'd known who to pay money to. Financial encouragement, Calvin called it. And there had been a lot of financial encouragement going on before they'd got Parklands underway, and again before David had been able to take possession of the land on which he'd built his home. Anyway, it was Calvin who did all that side of the business and without him they wouldn't be here now. He just wished Elizabeth would stop going on about it being time for Calvin to move out. They practically rowed about it the other day.

'I'm sick to death of having to make sure I'm always covered up in my own home. I should be safe to walk around in the nude if I so desire. But bloody Calvin just walks in here as if he owns the place! And I'm fed up of it!' she'd screamed at him.

'But he's family, Elizabeth. And what we have, we have together.' David had reasoned, for lack of a better excuse for Calvin treating their private space as his own. And, anyway, Calvin was family and where he came from, family stuck together.

'He's family,' David had stated coolly, once again. 'He's just as much right to be here as us all,' he'd said before walking away from her, thoroughly sick to death of arguing with his wife about his cousin.

But, quite simply, he liked having Calvin around, although he did wonder, now and again, why his cousin hadn't found the right woman with whom to set up his own home yet. However, if Calvin wanted to be with him and be part of his family, he was more than welcome and Elizabeth would have to accept that. David reached for his glass; this old argument with his wife was always at the back of his mind. Why the hell couldn't the pair of them get on and have done with it. He'd never heard Cal being anything other than polite and friendly towards Elizabeth. But sometimes her attitude towards him was practically hostile.

David and Calvin sat in comfortable silence on the balcony and looked out to sea. They stared into the ever darkening void of the balmy, starlit night; each encompassed in their own thoughts. David, exhausted by his labours of the day, closed his eyes and leant his head back on the couch, letting himself drift off into a half-sleep, where all he could hear was the chirping of the crickets and the howling of some distant dog.

Calvin looked at his cousin, relaxed in near slumber. What an idiot, he thought, and his face, unseen by anyone at this moment, reflected his distaste. He could hear Elizabeth, the woman who had the nerve to reject him, fussing around in the kitchen. A tight knot formed in his stomach as the anger ate away at his soul. He sat back in the chair and stared up into the star-filled sky and thought back over his life in Spain.

Everything would have been a lot better if stupid David had left that tart back in Grimsby where she belonged. He knew her type. Once they'd got a hold of you, they never let go. Demanded all the attention, such people did. It had been like that when his naff brother had arrived all those years ago. His mam and dad had simply forgotten he existed and all their time was spent showing off the brat of a baby. Wasn't he enough for them? Anyway, not to worry, he'd shown them what he could do. And he hadn't missed any of them, not for one moment. He'd expected to be sent to an orphanage after that and was willing to just wait out the few years until he could finally be his own man. Yes, he'd forgotten about Uncle George and Auntie Iris. But they eventually got in the way of his life, too. These people always made him a lot of work, messed with his life until he was forced to do something about it. He'd liked George, in his way, but he'd messed things up, too, and Calvin had finally had to do something about him as well.

And David was going the same way. He'd have to sort this mess out because things were not going as he would have them go, and it was David's fault. Wife and kids were all very nice, really picture-book stuff and all, but family is what it is really about, and he and David were family, and no one else. Christ! For Pete's sake! He'd given that piece of skirt, Elizabeth, a good chance to be with him, and the stupid cow had ignored it. Shoved him back, in actuality – silly, stupid bitch. What on earth she saw in David, he'd never know. Such an insipid little man, always fawning over him and thanking him for the tiniest of favours. He didn't even know his own cousin well enough to know that he didn't do anything without some type of payback. David was too bloody nice for his own good, he was. No wonder he'd hung on to my shirttail all this time, thought Calvin.

Without me, he'd still be in Grimsby, labouring. Without me he's nothing. Calvin looked over at David and saw that he had fallen asleep and was gently snoring.

Bastard! thought Calvin. Without him, that silly little bastard would be nowhere. The thought repeated itself over and over in his mind. Hadn't he been the one to make the path clear for David to prosper? Hadn't he been the one to see that David's mother and father wouldn't hold him back any longer? David should be bloody grateful to him for all his help. And the first minute he's out of sight, David makes off with the woman that was supposed to be for him! How on earth could she be content with this wimp? Admittedly, he'd become a lot more assertive in the last few years, and liked to throw his weight around on the building site, but underneath, he knew that David was still just that little boy at school that was being bullied and needed to be rescued. Well, Calvin, ever loyal, would rescue him again.

With that thought, Calvin took another drink from his glass, smiled to himself and turned his thoughts to changing all their lives for the better.

CHAPTER FORTY-NINE

1985 was the year when Mikhail Gorbachev became the supreme power in the Soviet Union; Bob Geldorf was put forward for a Nobel Prize in honour of his Live Aid concert, which raised a staggering £40 million to help Africa's famine-stricken poor; and the sixteen-year siege imposed on Gibraltar by General Franco was ended when a Spanish police officer unlocked a pair of green iron gates at the Spanish-Gibraltar border. It was also the year of Elizabeth's thirty-seventh birthday.

And on this sunny day in June, she now fluttered around the kitchen preparing and packing for the picnic on the beach she had requested as celebration of the day. Never mind the expensive dinners in exclusive restaurants, Elizabeth wanted to commemorate her special day by having all her family with her. The kids had been allowed to skive off school for the day and David had promised, after just checking that work was going according to plan at Parklands, to be back at the house and ready to take them down to the beach by eleven o'clock. And so it was. Or nearly so.

Five minutes before they were ready to leave, Calvin came rushing up the driveway in his jeep. He jumped out of the vehicle and made a dash for his apartment calling out as he ran to his door, 'Sorry I'm late. Just give me a minute to change into my trunks and I'll be with you.' Then he disappeared into the apartment under the house.

'What's going on?' enquired Elizabeth of David, who was packing beach stuff and cooler-bags full of food into the boot of the Jaguar.

Despite it being Elizabeth's birthday, David's hackles rose on his back. He knew this was coming. Whatever was wrong with his wife? She ought to know that a family day automatically included Calvin. He was family, for God's sake!

'You said you wanted a family day, sweetheart,' he attempted to soften his words with a smile. 'Well, Calvin's family.'

'But he's not my family,' Elizabeth insisted.

'He is, and that's the end of it.' David's unsmiling face, coupled with his raised eyebrow, stopped Elizabeth in her tracks.

The kids were already in the back of the car, noisily letting it be known that they were ready to go and wanted to go NOW! 'Come on, sunshine,' David smiled as if he had no idea of her irritation. 'You said you wanted a family day down at the beach. Well, here we all are, taking you to the beach to celebrate your birthday. Come on, get in.' David motioned for Elizabeth to get in the front of the car.

Elizabeth sighed deeply; knowing there was very little she could do about the situation. Calvin would be part of her birthday celebration. Like it or not, she had better get used to it. All these years should have taught her that David didn't sneeze without Calvin being there. Sod him! Sod the both of them!

The beach was quite busy, with little groups of families dotted all over. They'd chosen a little cove off the main area in the hope that there would only be a handful of people about but that wasn't meant to be. However, the outcome of this was that Alexander and Nathan had loads of kids to play with. Within minutes of setting up on the beach, Alexander was off, with Nathan in tow, with a group of other lads searching for crabs in the small stream of seawater that inched onto the beach. The warmth of the sun, the gentle sea breeze, and the noise of children laughing all worked to mellow Elizabeth's mood.

'Have fun, you two,' she called after them. 'Remember, no swimming in the sea unless me or your dad is with you. You hear?'

'Yeah, Mam,' Alexander shouted over his shoulder. 'Stop fussing. I'm a big boy now and can swim like a fish.'

And how right he was, Elizabeth thought with a smile as she set up their little picnic area. He was big for his age and swam better than his mother or father. Elizabeth and David should have been quite ashamed at this, considering they were from a town on the North Sea, a town where the schools taught every child to swim as part of the curriculum. But not everyone takes to the water like Alexander, mused Elizabeth. Neither she nor David were very good swimmers. They both preferred to feel the bottom of the pool under their feet.

They'd brought loungers, sun umbrellas, blankets to spread on the sand and stake out their area, and enough food and drink to last all of them a fortnight at least. David and Calvin sorted out the beach furniture while Elizabeth opened the first bottle of Cava, Spain's answer to Champagne. And a very good answer it was, too.

'Happy birthday!' Calvin said, beating David to it as they prepared to take their first sip of Cava. 'And many of them.' He leaned over and kissed Elizabeth on the side of her mouth.

'Yeah, sunshine. Here's wishing you all the best of everything.' David clinked glasses with both Elizabeth and Calvin and then sipped from his glass.

Elizabeth smiled at her husband and wondered just what he was thinking when he decided to give her a music system for the house, open plane tickets for her and the kids to fly to Manchester, so they could visit her dad, and a wad of money. He was indeed generous, but she would much rather have had some slinky underwear and a ticket for the pair of them to fly off on their own somewhere, anywhere in the world, together, just the two of them.

Elizabeth loved her children fiercely like any mother, but she also loved her husband and wanted to have some time alone with him. Just the two of them, all right, not necessarily without their children, who she adored being with, but at least without her husband's bloody beloved cousin, who always was there, interrupting her life and taking away David's attention. God, how she wished that man would get out of her life! 'Elizabeth,' she heard her name being called.

Calvin handed her a packet, beautifully wrapped in shiny paper. There was a real orchid corsage on the top of it. 'Open it,' he commanded.

Elizabeth, caught off guard, reddened at what she had just been thinking. Realising her thoughts were still her own and private at that, she smiled at Calvin and took the present.

Inside the package was a beautiful diamond set in a simple yellow gold setting. It was hanging on a long delicate gold chain. Elizabeth was stunned.

'Oh, Cal. It's lovely,' she said, in all honesty.

'Just wanted to thank you for looking after me, Lizzie, me old bean.'

'No need to thank me,' she automatically said, then retaliated with, 'Hey! And less of the old bean!'

'That was nice of you, Cal,' David took the box and admired the piece of jewellery before handing it back to Elizabeth. He smiled at her and gave her a quick kiss on the cheek before turning to Calvin and saying, 'Seeing as you are being so pleasant to our Birthday Girl today, you won't mind taking care of her for an hour while I pop back to the site, will you?'

'What do you mean?' Elizabeth interjected before Calvin could answer. 'You said you would take the day off. Christ, David! It's my birthday! You promised!'

'I know, my love. And I'll be back in a jiffy. But these things happen in business. Calvin will look after you. And I really will be back before you know it. They've delivered the wrong tiles and I need to sort that out.'

'I'll go,' offered Calvin.

'No, Cal. You stay. You know I like to see to these things myself and, anyway, you are more of a beach bum than I am.' David chuckled at his own words to make sure they were taken as a joke.

'Well, hurry back,' Calvin said, stretching himself out on the lounger, 'or I'll make off with this ageing woman here.'

Elizabeth would have liked to say something but felt too choked up at David's departure to speak. Looking at his back as he made his way along the sand towards the clearing where the car was parked, her disappointment turned to anger. How could he! It's my birthday and I'm left here looking after the kids and entertaining damn Calvin. Then she felt bad because Calvin had just given her such a lovely present. He didn't seem to mind spending time with her. Why did her husband?

Elizabeth settled herself down on the lounger next to Calvin. The big umbrella shaded her from the direct sun and the gentle breeze coming off the sea caressed her skin. She closed her eyes and was drifting in a world of familiar and comforting sounds – the lapping of the sea, the laughter of children, soft classical music from someone's radio, the squalling of the seagulls. She was near sleep when she heard the first shrill scream.

CHAPTER FIFTY

At that first scream, Elizabeth sat bolt upright on the lounger and looked around her for the source of the shriek. She leant over and shook Calvin's arm. 'Cal! Cal! Wake up! Something's happened.'

Calvin sat up, rubbing his eyes. 'What's up? I'd dropped off. What's the matter?'

'Over there. Look. That woman over there is pointing out to sea. Can you see anything? Where're the boys? Cal! I can't see them.' Elizabeth's voice was getting more piercing by the second. Hysteria was invading her speech. 'Cal! Where are Alexander and Nathan?'

Calvin jumped off the lounger and looked up and down the beach. 'Now, now, Lizzie. Keep calm. They were just over here. I'll go looking for them. They can't be far.' Calvin started out towards the little stream but could immediately see that both boys were not there. He looked out to sea. Bloody kids, he thought. I could do without this. Today was supposed to be a day of relaxation.

Elizabeth rolled over and struggled with the beach bag to extract the binoculars. She placed them to her eyes and scanned the water. Her scream was piercing. 'It's them. Oh my God! Help me, please! My boys, my boys!' She leapt off the lounger and ran to the water's edge.

Pandemonium broke out on the beach. Everyone started to stand up and make their way down the beach to the water. Elizabeth felt the lifeguard rush past her. His long legs carried him quickly into the water and he started to swim furiously in the direction of Alexander and Nathan. Nathan was nearer to the shore, struggling in the water to stay afloat, but each fierce wave was pulling Alexander further and further out to sea.

Hysterical now, Elizabeth galloped into the water, intent on getting to her children. Nothing else mattered. It was irrelevant that she couldn't swim very well; all she wanted was to be with her children.

Suddenly she felt hands holding her back. She screamed in protest. Her legs gave way under her and she finished up crumpled in a heap, kneeling in water up to her chest.

'I'll get them, Liz. I'll get them,' she heard as Calvin waded off after the lifeguard.

Elizabeth backed up out of the sea. Still kneeling, feeling the waves lapping around her, she knelt there, in the wet sand, watching incredulously the scene that was playing out in front of her eyes. She wanted to move, to dash into the foam, swim out to her beloved children, snatch them in her arms and carry them back to safety, back to the house, back to her womb. How dare they go into the sea without her? Her tears clouded her vision and she tried desperately to get a hold of herself. Alexander and Nathan would need her. They would be cold and shocked, and feel silly after causing such a fuss. She had to keep calm somehow. She stood up, the picture of calm control. Pushing her fist into her mouth to stop herself screaming any more, she silently watched what was going on in the sea.

Calvin's lean strong body and practised swimming skill assured that he quickly caught up with the young lifeguard in the water. Together they reached Nathan. He was sinking down under the waves. The lifeguard took him into his arms, turning until both of them were on their backs. Nathan was unconscious. 'You go back,' shouted Calvin to the lifeguard. 'I'll get Alexander.' The lifeguard nodded and started pushing with his legs to propel him and the unconscious Nathan back to shore. Calvin took one look at the pair, then resumed his long, fierce strokes towards Alexander.

Damn stupid kid! With any luck, that's Nathan out of the way. He looked like he wasn't breathing any more. Why can't kids do as they are told? He'd distinctly heard his mother telling him not to go into the sea without a grown up. And look what he was having to do now. Despite his strength, his arms ached with pulling at the water, and the salt at the back of his throat was starting to make him feel sick. This bloody family was more trouble than it was worth. Calvin could feel his arms growing more tired by the minute. Here I am, having to work myself to a frazzle to save this stupid little bastard. Serves him right if he drowns. All he does is cause his mother trouble. Looks far too much like Davie, as well. A blight on the universe, that's for sure.

By the time Calvin reached Alexander, the boy was spluttering and crying and reaching out for him. His strength was obviously spent and he was starting to sink below the rolling waves. Abruptly, a wave erupted and lifted him to the surface. Calvin grabbed for his arm. He missed and started to look for Alexander under the water. He was furiously treading water, having a job to keep himself afloat in the fierce movement of the currents. The wave subsided and Alexander bobbed to the top again. This time Calvin did not miss when he reached for the boy. He grabbed and caught his arm and pulled him firmly under the water and held him there. He flayed around with his other arm; splashing and making it seem like he was frantically doing his best to save the child. Alexander was so tired from his struggle with the waves and powerful current that he hardly struggled. It's just so easy, thought Calvin.

First, he saw Alexander's eyes widen in horror, then realisation crept into them, and then they finally closed in acceptance. Well, that's taken care of one, he reasoned with himself. And the other didn't look too good either, maybe already dead. Turning towards the beach, Calvin lifted his arm to signal that he'd managed to get Alexander and was bringing him back to shore. He turned on his back, like he'd seen the lifeguard do, took Alexander's limp body under the arms and started to push them both to shore with the strength of his legs. He was truly tired when he reached the beach. He stumbled and crawled back onto the dry sand, coughing and spitting water, dragging Alexander's still form with him, all the while crying, 'Help Alexander! Please! Someone help Alexander!'

David was just making his way back down the beach, wondering what all the commotion was about when he walked through the crowd gathered at the water's edge to find his eldest son laid out dead on the sand. His mother was on her knees, rocking back and forth, wailing like a wounded animal. Her heart was broken and she didn't know whether to stay with her dead son or go with her other son who was still hanging on to life. The ambulance men were loading Nathan onto a stretcher. He was unconscious, cold and pallid. Elizabeth's cries didn't awaken Alexander; nor did her shakes. Someone lifted her away from the body and whispered in her ear that her other son was alive and needed her. She looked over to the stretcher on which Nathan was laid. Nathan, dear Nathan. He needed her now. Elizabeth stumbled along the shifting sand to join her living son. She grabbed his hand and walked beside the stretcher. When she saw her husband running towards her, she cried, 'Where were you? Where were you?' and then lurched past him towards the waiting ambulance.

David ran to Alexander. He stared down at the lifeless body of his beloved son. Calvin was now kneeling next to him, holding his limp hand, tears in his eyes. When he saw David, he stood up and placed himself between father and son. He grabbed David's shoulders and tried to pull him away from the tragic vision.

'Oh Davie, Davie,' he wept. 'I tried. I really tried. But I was too late. I couldn't save him. He's dead!'

CHAPTER FIFTY-ONE

Different people handle grief in different ways. Some six months after Alexander's death, David's family was still shattered. Sometimes tragedy binds people together stronger than ever before, sometimes it drives them apart. David and Elizabeth were struggling to even speak to each other in a civil manner. Nathan hardly ever spoke at all.

David's beautiful Spanish villa, his dream house that was meant to make them all happy, no longer rattled with the sounds of joyous children, and Elizabeth prepared their meals in total silence. They also ate in silence: each drowning in their own thoughts, unable to share them, unable to break free of them.

Since that dreadful day, David had been lost in a confusion of regret. "*If only's*" crowded his mind. If only he had been there. If only he had not gone to the site. If only he had paid his son more attention. If only he had learnt to swim better. If only, if only… At first, he and Elizabeth had clung together; stood together at the bedside of Nathan at the hospital and prayed together. It had been touch and go for a few days and they hadn't dared talk about Alexander, the shock of the funeral or the ripping out of their hearts.

Calvin had immediately sprung into action. And David wondered often what he would have done without him. He kept meaning to thank him, to let him know that he appreciated him taking over the running of the site and even the family to some extent. He meant to thank him, but somehow he couldn't find the words. And Calvin just carried on doing all the good things he was doing. David could see he was desperately trying to bring back some normality to them all. But David didn't even know any more what normal was. This pain behind his breastbone, this misery, this open wound in his heart; was that normal?

At night David would turn over in bed and seek the warmth of

Elizabeth's body for comfort. He felt a need for her that seemed practically distasteful. His son was dead and all he wanted to do was make love to his wife. Something inside of him kept urging him to prove that he was still alive, that he could feel something other than this dreadful painful loss. David wanted to feel love.

But Elizabeth would shake him off. Her grief took her to a place where there was no room for David. She turned her back, pushed his hands away and curled up into a tiny ball, hardly taking any room at all in the big bed. David just cuddled her from behind. He enveloped her body and hoped that soon they would be together again. He felt so alone. He felt unable to carry this burden alone. It only took a week, before he sought some reason to his life by returning to work. If there had been thirty hours in a day, David would have worked them. In work there was forgetfulness.

Elizabeth saw David leaving the house each day and returning exhausted and spent each night. She felt her husband had left her, left her to cope alone with the death of their son; he had abandoned her. All he needed to forget Alexander was his work. But it was different for Elizabeth. She was a mother and when her son Alexander died, so did her spirit. She might as well have also been dead. Once Nathan showed signs of improvement and the doctors said he would be all right, she even lost interest in him, too. Elizabeth lost all interest in everything. She ran on automatic pilot; making the meals, tidying the house, ironing the shirts she had washed. She took to drinking a large cognac with her morning coffee. The coffee would last her until lunch when she would wash down her salad or sandwich with enough wine to put her to sleep for the afternoon. It was in sleep that she found forgetfulness. By the time David got home from work, later each day, she was just a groggy mess, laid on the couch, jabbing at the TV remote and not really watching anything the television screen showed her. At night, she turned her back towards her husband. If only he had been there, not left her on her birthday, not thought more of his work than his family, then Alexander might be alive today.

Calvin was thoroughly fed up with the lot of them. Things had not gone quite as he planned. Actually, he hadn't planned to get rid of Alexander, but the opportunity presented itself, so it must have been meant to be. Main thing was there was one less of the Gilmores and, if he waited long enough, Elizabeth would be his. She would one day come out of her misery and see that he had been the hero, that he had been the one to attempt to rescue her son, that he was the one she should have married and not that shit of a husband of hers who obviously preferred to be at work than with his family.

No, indeed, it wouldn't take long before Elizabeth would be his and his alone, he reckoned. It really was time for David to sod off out of their lives and stop hindering his plans. All David wanted to do was work, work, work: as if there was nothing else to life. All right, he had to admit, David's hard work had resulted in them all having enough money to last them the rest of their lives, so why didn't he slow down a bit? Mind you, that wouldn't do either. The last thing Calvin wanted was David hanging around the house, trying to console Elizabeth. He was doing a nice job of that already.

Calvin would always come home early, scoot upstairs and ask Elizabeth if she needed anything, if he should go back into town and get them something to eat. She'd just wave her glass at him and ask him to get her another drink. He'd bring the drink to her and sit with her on the couch. He'd talk to her about the day, the people he'd seen, the work site. He'd even ask how Nathan was. He'd do his best to try and make her laugh. And though she never laughed properly, at least she looked these days as though she was listening to him. She even smiled at him now and again.

Calvin was happy with his progress, thinking it wouldn't be long now.

CHAPTER FIFTY-TWO

'Come on, Liz. Let me take you down to the harbour for a bit of lunch. I can't remember the last time you ate properly. Look how thin you are. And you know Davie won't be home for lunch. He never is these days.'

'Why aren't you at work?' Elizabeth pushed her hair out of her face. Now straggly and unkempt, the movement revealed a face that was pale, and with eyes that were dull with dark circles under them. Didn't this man realise that a housewife needs time in the day to do her housework?

'I was at work, Lizzie, my dear.' Calvin swept the house with his eyes. It didn't look like Elizabeth had been doing very much at all. 'Things are running famously,' he picked up the conversation. 'Your husband is cracking the whip as usual and the workers are all doing as they are bid. So why should I waste my time there? Now Nathan's having school dinners, and there is nothing more for you to do here. Come on, lass. Let's get out of this mausoleum.'

Calvin stood there and held his hand out to her.

Elizabeth looked at the offered hand. Why can't he piss off? Can't he see she'd rather be alone? Then she felt guilty at her thoughts. Calvin had been so good to her, to them both, really, since Alexander's death. It had been Calvin who had so heroically tried to rescue her son. He must feel awful that he failed, she thought. But not as awful as she felt at his failure. No, no, stop! It wasn't Calvin's fault! She silently admonished herself. He'd done his best and she ought to be grateful.

She caught a glimpse of herself in the ornate gilded mirror behind Calvin. What she saw shocked her. Once she had considered herself attractive, beautiful even. But now her hair was as dull in colour as her eyes. Her face was vacant of any emotion, her cheeks were sunken and she looked like an old woman no one would want. It was time, she thought. It was time to let her beloved Alexander go. But how could she let him slip away. Not so long ago he had been there laughing and joking with her, screaming out his joy of life, running down the mountain to build a den, asking his father for instructions on how to build a wall…

David's face swam before her eyes. How she wished she could reach out to him and wipe away all the coldness that had surfaced between them. What had happened? How had it happened? She wanted him so badly, and yet, if he came towards her, all she could do was push him away, turn her back, shut him out. Oh David, David, where are you? Stop it! Stop being so silly. You don't want David. He wasn't there. If he had been there, things would have been different. He's never here now, either. It wasn't David she wanted; what she really needed was a drink.

Elizabeth made to walk towards the sideboard. Calvin immediately recognised what she was doing and blocked her way.

'Oh no you don't, sweetheart,' he said gently. 'You can have wine down at the harbour. Go and get cleaned up, Lizzie. We are going for lunch.'

Elizabeth opened her mouth to protest then thought better of it. It was time that she rallied herself, that she made an effort at least to look human again, even if she didn't feel it.

'All right, Cal,' she said with a big sigh. 'I know you're right. Give me an hour to have a shower and clean up and then we can go. What about calling David. Maybe he'd come with us if you asked him.'

'You go shower, Lizzie. I'll give David a ring. Hurry up, I'm starving.'

Calvin had no intention of calling David, but he made the pretence of using the house phone to dial out. His conversation was loud and one-sided.

'All right, mate. Understand. See you later. Don't worry, I'll take care of her.'

When Calvin thought Elizabeth was out of earshot, he put the receiver down and settled himself on the couch to wait for a washed and polished Elizabeth.

They sat outside in the sunshine at a restaurant in the picturesque harbour in Moraira. The fish had been good and Elizabeth was astounded at how much she had eaten. She felt better than she had for a long time, she felt mellowed by the warm rays of sunshine and the two bottles of wine they had drunk with their meal. Looking over at Calvin she had to concede that he had been right, that she had needed to get out. Calvin had been right about a lot of things.

When she really considered it, she realised that Calvin was at home a lot more than David ever was, despite his late-night outings. It was Calvin who asked how she was. It was Calvin who brought her flowers. It was Calvin who took time to talk and play with Nathan. She really must give Nathan a bit more attention, it occurred to her suddenly. He was becoming a terribly quiet child. But it was Calvin who was uppermost in her mind.

Sat there, stomach full, softened by the alcohol, she looked at Calvin through different eyes. He really had been a rock over the last few months. He'd always been there, looking after them all and eventually just her as David wandered off back to work and Nathan back to school. This man who she didn't really like was the one who constantly talked to her about Alexander and the tragedy. Without those conversations she would never have been able to make head or tail out of what had happened. Maybe this man wasn't so bad as she believed, after all. At least he was here. Even now, he was here. And where was David? At work, that's where, where he always was: head in the sand, never ready to discuss or talk about anything other than bloody work. Elizabeth leant over and put her hand over Calvin's. 'Thanks, Cal, for being such a good friend.'

She couldn't quite remember how they got home. And she certainly couldn't remember how she got to be in a clinch on the couch with Calvin.

By the time she realised what was happening, Calvin had her pinned back on the couch and was working his way up her skirt with his hand. The shock at feeling his hand touch her flesh shocked her back to sobriety. This wasn't what she wanted. She wasn't married to Calvin. She was married to David!

'Calvin! Stop! What do you think you're doing?'

'I'm doing what you want, Lizzie. Admit it. It's me you want. David's never here. He couldn't give a damn about how you feel or what you want. But I do. Haven't I been good to you? Haven't I listened to all your problems? Haven't I made you feel important and loved? Isn't that what it's all about? Go on; admit it. I've made you feel loved, haven't I? Now it's time you made me feel loved. You owe me, Lizzie.'

His hand pushed her panties to one side and he roughly reached into her soft flesh, squeezing rhythmically.

'Calvin! Stop! What are you doing?'

Calvin stared down at her, his piercing blue eyes standing out on his sun-bronzed face.

'I'm giving you a little pleasure, sweetheart. Now stop pretending you don't like it and show some appreciation for my labours. You know I'm good. I'll make you feel like a princess. I'll show you what you've been missing all these years. It's me you want. Go on; tell me.'

His other hand reached for her breast and squeezed it until she cried out in pain.

Instantly, Elizabeth sobered up completely. It suddenly became clear to her what was actually happening. How could this be? How did it turn out that she was laid on the couch, her skirt hitched up to her waist, her blouse ripped open, and with Calvin on top of her, pinning her down with his urgent body? No! No! This is not what she wanted. This had to stop. And now!

'No! Calvin,' she screamed. 'Stop it!'

CHAPTER FIFTY-THREE

Anger lends even the weakest of us incredible strength. And anger was now coursing through Elizabeth's veins. How dare he! Who the hell did he think he was? She'd tell David about this, she would! With one great heave, Elizabeth succeeded in ripping herself away from under Calvin's roughly probing hands. She managed to part their bodies abruptly and roll off the couch, away from his squirming body onto the floor.

'Get off me, you bloody lout!' she cried. 'What the fuck do you think you're doing? I'm going to tell David about this. He'll not have you in this house again.'

Elizabeth was crawling along the marble floor. He skirt was still up around her waist, she was kneeling on the bottom of her ripped-open blouse and, try as she might, all she could do was crawl up the inside of the torn material, which hindered her getting away from Calvin.

Calvin jumped off the couch. 'Not this time, Lizzie, my dear. You are not going to push me off again, you little bitch.' He grabbed her by the waist and hoisted her once more onto the soft upholstery of the over-sized, white brocade couch. 'We're not at your father's in Grimsby now. There's no one here except you and me. You've been coming on to me for weeks now. All you bloody women think you can lead a guy on and then, when he responds in a natural fashion, just fob him off. Well, Lizzie dear, I've had enough of your games. You are going to give me what I want. And you are going to give it to me right now. Whether you like it or not.'

A shiver ran along Elizabeth's spine as anger turned to fear and she started to plead. 'Please, Cal. Stop it! You don't really want to do this. What about David? He's your friend, he's your family.'

'Fuck David! He's nobody. I'm sick to bloody death of always having to be grateful to that bastard for anything I have. Look where

I'm living. In the bloody basement!'

'Please, Cal,' Elizabeth tried again.

Calvin pulled back for a moment and looked at Elizabeth who was once again under him on the couch. This time she was on her knees, with her back to him. Her bottom was exposed, high in the air: the soft pink folds of her genitals beckoning to him. With one big hand, he held both her wrists in an iron grip and pushed her head down into the cushion of the couch. His face was satanic.

Elizabeth froze in terror.

'Hush, baby,' he crooned. 'You don't have to plead for it. I'm going to take you to paradise. That's a good girl. You lay nice and still now and just enjoy it.' His laugh was cruel.

Elizabeth knew she couldn't fight any more. Her strength was spent. Slowly, she realised that she was totally incapable of stopping what was happening to her. Her stomach flipped and she felt sick. She wanted to cry out in protest, to scream and claw at this monster on top of her but all she could do was kneel there. Apathy swept through her body. She managed to free her head to stare at the grotesque picture of her and Calvin in the living-room mirror. She looked on in silent horror as Calvin sought out and touched places of her that she had always considered solely hers. She thought of David. He was the only man who she'd allowed to touch her in these places. Now, no longer. Her mind became detached and drifted. It was all as if this terrible thing were happening to someone else. It wasn't her on the couch and it wasn't Calvin furiously pumping away at her, tearing her apart, hurting her.

It truly wasn't Calvin with her. Not a Calvin she'd ever known, anyway. This Calvin's face was contorted into that of a wild beast. His lips were pulled back in a snarl and pure evil gleamed in his eyes. He shoved the cheeks of her buttocks apart, while fiddling furiously at his own pants until he had them undone. His cock bounced out from the restraints of his underpants: red and throbbing, hard and large. With no preamble he thrust it into Elizabeth. She moaned with the pain as his swollen member grated into her dryness. Calvin felt the resistance.

'Come on, Lizzie. I'm sure you can do better than this.' He pulled out. Spit on his fingers and rubbed the spittle over his member before ramming it once more into her vagina, this time with a real vengeance. Within seconds, his facial features became relaxed, even content, as he pushed and pulled back rhythmically into Elizabeth's now unprotesting body.

Elizabeth watched him in disgust. She felt nothing any more. Her body had shut down and didn't belong to her at all now. But the audacity of this bastard and the feeling of being so powerless against him made her want to scream, to beat at this animal who was roughly just taking her against her will, to kick and curse, to pick up a weapon and quickly kill him by beating him to death. But all she could do was lie there. She discovered that the more she fought against him, the more violent he became. And she was now becoming more afraid of what he would do after he'd finished with her. This maniac was not the Calvin she had known for years. This person was unpredictable. This was not her husband's cousin who had been a part of their lives for always. This was not a normal human being. This was surely someone unhinged. And she didn't even like to imagine what he would do next.

Suddenly, it occurred to Elizabeth that she didn't want to die. Despite the pain of losing her beloved Alexander, she didn't want to die. David was a good husband. He had made a good life for her, for them. He was gentle and kind and adored her. Oh, my God! David must never find out about this, if she managed to get out of this with her life. It would kill him to know what his cousin is really like.

And as Calvin pumped away at her body on the couch in the house that David had built, Elizabeth promised herself that she would make it all up to her husband, that she would reach out to him, that she would make them whole again and wipe away the memory of what was happening to her now.

Calvin's thrusts suddenly became more urgent. He was holding Elizabeth down with one hand. The other hand was holding up her backside so that his thrusts went so deep as to rip at Elizabeth's soul. She hated him. She feared him. She wanted to scream out in pain and protest. She wanted to kill him. She wanted to wipe him out of her life. She wanted this day to have never happened.

Calvin was squeezing forcibly at the back of her neck and Elizabeth thought she might not even make it to live another day to hate this man. Her throat was closing; she was having difficulty in breathing through the material of the couch. She could feel her eyes beginning to enlarge and pop in their sockets. Oh, my God! she thought. He's really going to kill me. Then came a long, outdrawn moan and after a short spurt of quick lunges, Calvin quivered, and sweat from his forehead dropped onto the small of her back. She watched him in the mirror. His contorted features became relaxed and he too sought their reflection in the looking-glass. He smiled, looking directly into her eyes. Then he let his body slump on top of hers.

Elizabeth lay there, unable to move. Wondering what would happen next.

CHAPTER FIFTY-FOUR

Elizabeth sat in the bathtub sobbing. Half of her was relieved that she was still alive, the other half of her was fighting to regain some type of control now that Calvin was finished with her.

After the rape, he had calmly got off her, pulled up his pants, tucked his shirt in and meticulously done up the button and zip. He'd stared down at her, looking at her displayed body after his act, then told her to cover herself for she looked awful, before bending down to plant a quick kiss on her sweat-soaked head. Without another word, he then simply walked out of the house.

Elizabeth scrubbed at her body, pushing soap into her vagina as far as she could get it. She was sore and the soap made her sting. The muscles in her thighs ached. Her breasts were bruised. Her body from the waist to the knees felt numb and detached from the rest of her. But slowly the warm soapy water started to relax her muscles. She took the flannel, dipped it into the water and covered her face with it. Her sobs came hard and loud. Just what had she done to deserve that?

Elizabeth knew she had to get a hold of herself before Nathan got home from school. Also, she had made up her mind that David must never know what had happened. What if he thought it was her fault? Was it her fault? She wasn't even sure of that any more. What if he thought she had led Cal on? What if he didn't even believe her? She'd lose him if he knew, she was certain of it. She wasn't even sure if David still loved her. They had grown so far apart. Was it her fault? Was it his? She didn't know.

She did know that after Alexander's death she had ignored him, pushed him away for so long, it wouldn't come as a surprise if he had finally lost interest in her altogether. She bit on the flannel and hoped that she wasn't too late. She needed David. She needed him now.

She took the flannel, soaped it up and rubbed vigorously at her genitals. She was bleeding. She pulled her knees up towards her body and put her arms around her legs, hugging herself. Lowering her head onto her knees, she wept.

The bath water was cold by the time Elizabeth got out of the bathtub. But a different coldness had gripped her heart. She knew that she would never be the same again. It was so clear to her that what she and David had enjoyed all these years had been real love. And she had taken that for granted. When Alexander died, she had chosen to grieve alone; she had held on to her grief, this being the only thing she had left of her son, and she had refused to share it with David. She had never wanted to share his. No wonder he didn't want to be around her these days. No wonder he had preferred to be at work and out of her way. He hadn't been there when Alexander died and she had blamed him for that. Maybe he blamed himself, too. But common sense told her that even if David had been there on the beach on that fateful day, Alexander would still be dead now.

Life has a way of just happening. And what is meant to be will happen, no matter what. She would see to it that she and David found a way back to each other. He'd loved her once. That she was sure of. She would make him love her again. She would see to it that life would once again have some meaning.

As far as Calvin was concerned, besides wishing him dead, she would keep out of his way and she wouldn't say anything about the rape. Somehow, she felt that Calvin would want it that way, too. It would break David's heart to know what his cousin had done to his wife. She knew that David had spent most of his life idolising his cousin, although she never understood why. But David always put Calvin before himself in everything. He was the clever one, he would say. He was the imaginative one, the suave one, the one who got along with people: simply, just the one, as if there were no other.

Armed with this knowledge of how deep David's affections were for his cousin, Elizabeth knew that if she attacked Calvin at this moment, while their own relationship was so weak, David would probably think she was lying. Calvin was David's hero: she just couldn't break his heart with the truth.

That evening, she went and sat on the balcony with David while he was having his gin and tonic. She'd cooked something that was doing nicely on its own in the oven, and so joined him in his before dinner drink. She'd tried to persuade Nathan to join them, but he had preferred to stay in his room. He had homework, he'd said. Some colouring-in to do. She'd draw Nathan back to her later. For the moment, David was the most important person in her life.

David seemed pleasantly surprised and happy to have his wife sitting with him on the balcony enjoying the evening sounds and reddening of the sky. He was even more surprised that she was drinking a sparkling water rather than her usual vodka.

Dinnertime came and Elizabeth got up from her position on the couch next to David on the balcony of their luxury home saying, 'Well, I think I'll serve. Are you hungry, darling?'

David was just enjoying the moment. His wife was not only speaking to him, she was sitting next to him and she wasn't drinking. He didn't know what had happened to change her but he was grateful for whatever it was. As he looked at her getting ready to go into the kitchen to serve up his tea, he thought how wonderful she looked and how much he loved her.

Before Elizabeth could leave the balcony, they both heard the familiar sounds of footsteps on the marble floors.

'Hi, you two. Hope I'm not too late for dinner. I'm starving,' said Calvin, marching onto the balcony, a broad smile on his face.

CHAPTER FIFTY-FIVE

Elizabeth was lying between the silk sheets of their bed waiting for David to finish up in the bathroom. This would be the night she would welcome him back into her arms. Despite the pain she felt from Calvin's brutal attack, she desperately wanted David to make love to her. She pushed to the back of her mind the surfacing thought that she needed David to wash that swine out of her body: to wash away the memory of his hands on her, to cleanse herself of his smell. She still couldn't believe the gall of Calvin. It had been a strained and difficult evening for her. But not for him! He'd walked into their home and sat at their dining-table just like always, without any indication that anything untoward had happened that very afternoon. Calvin had spoken to David as if everything was normal, as if he hadn't just raped his wife. And he'd even spoken to her as though nothing had happened. A big non-event, as far as he was concerned, it had seemed.

The hate welled up inside her and made her stomach ache. Oh, how she hated him. And, although his silence was what she wanted, she still wondered why he was not saying anything about it to her. She'd tried to work out his motive, but, quite honestly, more important was reinstating her life with her husband. She'd think about Calvin another day.

When David climbed into bed and made to pick up his book, Elizabeth turned towards him straightaway. She saw the look of surprise on his face as she took the book out of his hands and placed it back on the bedside table. She reached across him and turned off the light, not wanting him to see her bruises. Hesitantly, like it was the first time, she took his hand and placed it on her breast. She was naked under the covers. 'I've missed you, David,' was all she said before kissing him on the lips, first gently then more ardently, leading into a passionate kiss.

David was too surprised to speak. But the kiss felt good and it took only seconds before he was responding in like.

At first they just kissed, then held each other for a long time. His heart soared. It was his Elizabeth. This woman holding him, kissing him, was his own Elizabeth. Not the Elizabeth of the last few months, not the heartbroken woman who had slumbered fitfully beside him without a thought of passion or comfort. No, not that broken woman who drank and fell into a deep, troubled sleep immediately her head hit the pillow. No, this was his Elizabeth, his wife. He pulled back from the kiss to look at her. Oh yes. This was his Elizabeth. He could see the need there, he could see the longing there, he could see the love there. Gently, he drew her into his embrace. His body was screaming out to touch her, to take her, to have her all at once, but he restrained himself. This was the woman he loved beyond all else. This was the reason he worked, lived, existed. He wanted her so badly, had missed her for so long. He wouldn't grab at her. He wouldn't just quickly make love. He would love her as she was meant to be loved – gently, with wonder, and completely.

The moon cast its silvery glow into the bedroom. David remembered thinking, before he reached out for the very reason he lived, that his wife's skin looked like fine alabaster. And he wanted desperately to touch it.

CHAPTER FIFTY-SIX

Things weren't going quite the way Calvin had hoped. It had been a few days now since he and Elizabeth had made passionate love on the couch in this very house. And it had been everything he'd ever imagined it would be. She certainly was a good fuck; one of the best he'd ever had. But now she was ignoring him and the fact that they had shared such desire. He couldn't understand why. Hadn't they both moaned in their craving for each other? Hadn't their lovemaking been wondrous? What was wrong with the woman? Obviously he, too, didn't wish to upset the boat too abruptly, but it was time they told David that he wasn't welcome any more; time they told him to find somewhere else to live. Way past bloody time David was gone from their lives.

That evening, after their wild afternoon on the couch, when he had gone upstairs to dine with them as he always did of an evening, Elizabeth had exhibited the same bridled hostility she usually showed towards him. And he couldn't really understand why. At first she had just looked at him, obviously to see what he was going to do or say. But he'd thought it better not to mention anything to David right away. There would be time for that later. What he couldn't understand, though, was that once she realised he wasn't going to say anything, she became quite aggressive. David had stood it for a while and then exploded.

'Hey, you two!' he'd complained. 'Why can't you just try to get along? I'm fed up of it, Elizabeth. What's wrong with you?'

She'd deserved that because her snipes were spiteful that night. But Calvin knew it was just show. Nevertheless, her played dislike of him came over as being even stronger than usual. He'd not taken that much notice of it really, thinking she was doing that to impress David and put him off track of their real intentions. And she probably had a guilty conscience, he'd thought. I mean, there he was taking the beloved wife of his cousin away from him. Yes, she probably felt bad for David; that was it. It couldn't have been easy giving way to her passion in the afternoon and then having to pretend that she was a pure and loving wife to old misery guts.

But what he totally failed to understand was that she was, well, there's no other way of putting it, loving towards the bugger. And she hadn't been very loving towards David for a long time, not since Alexander's death really. There was no need for her to be so flaming damned loving. He wondered what that was about. Even more surprising was that she wasn't drinking as she usually did. Yeah, that's probably what was wrong with her. She needed a drink: that's what it was. Still, there was no need for her to sit so close to David on the patio couch. And she was talking gently to him all the time, totally excluding him. He wasn't sure what her game was, but he knew he didn't like it one bit.

What's more, the game continued even after that night. And the confusion was starting to piss him off. It was ages before Calvin could get Elizabeth on her own again. For some reason she was always with David or Nathan or even out of the house. He'd tried coming home earlier but that didn't work either because David had starting doing the same. Is that man stupid? Can't stupid David see when he's not wanted? Once that bastard of a husband of hers is out the way, he and Elizabeth could finally get down to having the type of life they deserve. He'd worked hard for it. Hadn't he been the one to pave the way for David to make a lot of money in Spain? And hadn't he been the one to take the time to roam the bars and make the right contacts? And it had been him, Calvin, and no one else, who'd been the one to arrange for the ground on which Parklands was built to be reclassified as building land?

Oh no, David never wanted to know how that *actually* happened. Silly bugger thought the fire was caused by the dry weather turning the land into a tinderbox, and some daft sod having a barbecue among the pine trees. David was too stupid to think further than the end of his fucking nose. Surely he must have realised that it was him,

Calvin the Mighty, who had paved the way for any riches he now possessed.

And what were the thanks for Calvin's interventions?

First, the bastard had robbed him of Elizabeth. And then he had forged ahead, building Parklands, practically without him. Any praise for the estate always rested on David's shoulders, just because he was the one to have the ideas. Where would they be if the land hadn't been made available? It had cost a lot of money and know-how to arrange that. And it was he who knew the right people, not David. His cunning work on the project was never mentioned. True, he had an equal share of the profits, but while he had been making all things possible for David, just like he had been doing ever since he met him, David had blithely gone on, with his head in the clouds, as usual, and stolen Elizabeth from him and built this ridiculous palace of a Spanish villa! Just who the hell did he think he was? Just a miserable, stupid wimp of a Grimsby lad; that's all he was and ever would be. And it was about time he was reminded of it.

It was also time for them to part, pondered Calvin. David had served his purpose. He needed to get out of Calvin's life now.

But first this whole situation needed to be straightened out with Elizabeth. He had to admit that his lovemaking with her was all he dreamed it would be. And he wanted some more. David hadn't soured her. She was wild in his arms and he wanted to have that again, and soon. He'd have to find out what her plans were and why she was avoiding him. He'd get to the bottom of this. He'd see they had a showdown, and soon.

CHAPTER FIFTY-SEVEN

Elizabeth was at the school gates waving to Nathan. She stood there watching him until he'd entered the building and disappeared from her view. Only then did she turn and make her way back to the car. Another long day stretched ahead of her. She now hated the beautiful villa that David had built for them. Its walls still rang with Alexander's laughter. Each nook and cranny reminded her of her dead son. How her heart ached when she thought of him, and the pictures of that last day on the beach would forever be there in the shadows of her mind, playing over and over again. She hadn't been to the beach since and she never intended to go again. But even more prevalent in her thoughts now was that she knew Calvin was doing his best to catch her alone. And she didn't want that.

He'd not told David about what had happened, and neither had she. And she was convinced that even if she did tell David, he probably wouldn't believe her. Her animosity towards Calvin had become more obvious as she had flung herself back into David's life straight after the rape. But even David's pleasure at having his wife love him again could not lessen his consternation and irritation at her attitude towards the man who he thought of as being only next to God Himself. How she wished she could rid David of that conception about his cousin.

She found it strange and wondered often why Calvin hadn't said anything. He now had the power to break up her marriage with one sentence. For a long time her dislike of Calvin had been growing but now it had turned to hatred and, more than that, fear.

Elizabeth had had the opportunity to observe Calvin at close quarters for quite a few years. The more she had watched him, the more she realised she didn't like what she saw. Despite his physical beauty and amazing blue eyes that seemed to look right into you,

Calvin was the most egotistical man she had ever known. He thought life owed him. He thought David owed him. He thought the whole world was made to cater to his wishes and whims. He thought himself perfect. Indeed, Calvin's charm was massive and incredible and he was devilishly handsome with it, but once she'd spent a lot of time with him, she saw through his controlled polite veneer, which he used as a smokescreen to his true character.

Her dislike had turned to hate on that afternoon when he had forced her to have sex. When he had held her down, overpowered her, and brutally rammed into her. Even just thinking about it turned her stomach. Her skin crawled at the thought of his hands on her body. Her sleep was crowded with dreams of his face, contorted in his passion. She'd watched him from the corner of her eye staring down at her, those blue eyes of his laughing cruelly at her.

But he had said nothing to David. And now she lived in a sort of limbo. What did he intend to say and when? And why wasn't he saying anything?

Maybe he was simply going to pretend it hadn't happened at all. That would be acceptable, because that's what she wanted to do, pretend it never happened.

Elizabeth drove around Calpe wondering what to do with herself. The couple of female friends she had made were both busy today. Nathan was safely at school and she was roaming around the town rather than return home where Calvin might find her.

This is ridiculous! I can't let that bastard rule my life! With a sudden surge of indignation, Elizabeth turned the car around and headed for home.

The dog came scampering towards her as Elizabeth drove up the driveway towards the house. Him being this far down the mountain could only mean one thing: someone had let him out of the garden, someone was already at home. For a moment she hesitated. Should she go back? Should she leave now while she could? But then it occurred to her that it might be David at home. It would be a rare occasion if David were home during the day, for she knew that he hardly ever left the building site once he was on it. But it might be David, nevertheless. One thing was for sure: she wasn't going to let anyone keep her away from her home any more. She wanted to be there, to be making beds, cooking dinner, cleaning windows, anything rather than driving around aimlessly in town wondering what to do with herself. Today, she would face Calvin, if need be, and get some order into her life again.

She rounded the bend and continued up the drive towards the carport next to the kitchen entrance. The road split near the corner of the house; one road led to the carport, one inclined down towards the ground-floor apartment. It was at this point in the road that Elizabeth saw Calvin's jeep parked outside his flat. Her heart sank and she suddenly craved a stiff drink. Before she had even got out of her car, she saw Calvin trotting up the drive towards her. He followed her into the kitchen.

'Elizabeth! There you are! Where on earth have you been all the time? I never get to see you alone these days. You do realise that I've been coming back here every day, don't you?' His tone was one of reproach.

Calvin's voice had become louder the longer he spoke. His anger was pushing him to become aggressive. He obviously became aware of this bubbling rage tightening his chest muscles and so, with a deep breath and friendly smile, he changed course.

'Elizabeth,' he started again, in a gentler tone this time. 'It's good to see you. Have you been shopping? Can I help you in with anything?'

Elizabeth made no pretence at being polite.

'What are you doing here, Cal?'

'I'm here, like I've been here every day for bloody ages, actually, to finally see you. What's wrong, sweetheart? I feel like you have been avoiding me?'

'I have been avoiding you, Cal,' Elizabeth stated flatly. She turned away from him.

'But, why?' Calvin followed her as she made to walk away. He grabbed at her arm to stop her. 'Elizabeth, darling, we have to straighten things out. We have to tell David. What on earth are you doing, cosying up to him, like that?' Calvin's displeasure was starting to surface again.

Elizabeth walked far into the sprawling kitchen before realising she had put herself into a position where escape wasn't possible. The balconies off the living-room and bedrooms were on the second storey, and far too high to jump from. The front door, through the living-room and off to the right, was an elaborate affair of two heavy carved wooden doors that no one used, preferring to enter the house by the kitchen, and, as always, was firmly locked. She didn't carry front door keys.

Elizabeth fought with herself to appear calm. She plonked her handbag down on the worktop and made to wash her hands in the sink.

'What is it you want, Cal? I have things to do.'

The tea towels were at the end of the worktop, near the back door. Elizabeth walked there, picked a tea towel off the hook and started to dry her hands. At least she was now near the door and it was Calvin standing in the centre of the kitchen.

'I don't understand you,' Calvin exploded at last. 'I just don't understand bloody women! Are you now denying what happened between us?'

'Nothing happened *between* us, Calvin. What happened was that you raped me; you raped the wife of your cousin. You're nothing but a lousy stinking rapist.'

The memory was bringing new tears to Elizabeth's eyes. Her fear was momentarily being replaced by indignation.

'What do you mean, rape?' Calvin's eyes widened in surprise; then a cold anger flooded his face. 'That wasn't rape,' he said, his voice now dripping with sarcasm. 'You were gagging for it. Had been for quite some time, if I think about it now.'

Calvin's mouth turned down in an ugly smirk; his dark blue eyes flashed. 'Oh, I see,' he spat at her. 'So all you were doing was fucking leading me on, you miserable little bitch.'

He made to cross the kitchen.

Elizabeth grabbed the cast-iron frying-pan from off the gas hob. It was still full of fat from the morning fry-up. The fat splashed out of the pan onto the floor. She held it to one side of her body like a baseball bat, ready to strike, and said, her voice sounding more in control than she felt, 'Not all women want you, Mr Charming. And I definitely didn't. You come any nearer and I'll bash your bloody brains in. What you did to me is inexcusable. David has been the one to look out for you, to include you in everything he does. Without him you would be nothing. And all you do in return is rape his wife.' Elizabeth's voice had risen to a scream. 'I want you out of here. I want you out of our lives. And if you don't damn well go, I'll tell David what you did, you bastard!'

Calvin recoiled away from the swinging frying-pan. He stood perfectly still, shocked into immobility and silence by Elizabeth's outburst. This was not what he had expected. The woman was hysterical, obviously. She was spitting as she screamed at him. Her face was contorted and ugly in anger. And she looked silly standing there holding a frying-pan, ready to attack him. This was not the Elizabeth he had made passionate love to not long ago; this was a wild woman who was out of control and out to make his life difficult. No one made his life difficult. She would pay for this.

'Now we know where we stand, madam,' he said, approaching Elizabeth. He towered over her by head and shoulders. Peering down he said through gritted teeth in a low voice near to a whisper, 'You are a little slut, just like the rest of them, who wants nothing more than a good fuck now and again. Well, don't look at me the next time you itch.' His hand reached behind her head and pulled at her hair, tugging her head back, making her look directly into his flashing eyes. 'You weren't even good, let me tell you. Poor little David! Having to put up with you the last few years. Be very careful, Liz, my lovely. 'Cause I might just tell your darling David just how much you enjoyed being fucked by a real man.'

With that, he lowered his head and kissed her brutally on the mouth, grinding his teeth against hers, before bringing down his other hand to strike her across the face savagely.

Elizabeth fell to the floor, the frying-pan dropping from her hand. It clattered loudly as it hit the tiles. Her heart was beating so violently, she thought it would jump from her chest. But he was moving away, away from her.

'You'll pay for this, you bitch! Both of you will pay for this!' Calvin threatened as he stormed out of the house, leaving her in a crumpled heap on the cool tiles of the kitchen floor.

Elizabeth rocked back and forth in shock. She was holding her cheek, wiping her bleeding mouth with the back of her hand, and weeping profusely.

CHAPTER FIFTY-EIGHT

The building site was a hive of activity. Dust hovered in the air; a grey blanket in the sunbeams. Eight pristine rows of terraced houses already stood finished. They were freshly painted, sparkling white against the grime-covered pine trees and oleander bushes. Some were already occupied by owners. David stood in the middle of the site and looked around him. His men, mostly local Spaniards, worked diligently without pause between their allotted breaks. But they did so loudly and, apparently, quite happily. It was their way to be constantly talking to each other at the top of their voices, although they were standing next to each other. What with the cement mixers loudly whirling, the radio blaring out soulful Spanish songs telling of pain and tragedy, and the men all screaming in conversation with each other, the building site presented a hubble and bubble of action and motion under the bright harsh rays of the Mediterranean sun. David looked on in wonder; he loved it.

He also loved his home and family but sensed there was something wrong at home, despite Elizabeth's apparent turnabout. He couldn't quite put his finger on what was different. Still, whatever it was, whatever was wrong, would probably right itself. He believed all things righted themselves after a time if you just left them alone.

He was a changed man himself, of course. How could he not be? He missed Alexander terribly. He had been everything a father could want in a son and his death had left a gaping hole in David's heart. If only he'd been there. If only he'd put them first instead of scurrying off to the site. If only… If only...

For a time, even worse had been that he thought that he had lost Elizabeth, too. He didn't know what had happened to make her suddenly come back to him but he wasn't about to question it. All that mattered was that Elizabeth was back in his arms. She had stopped drinking so much as well. All in all, life was pretty great, if he didn't rest on the memory of his son's death too often and with the exception of his wife's inexplicable dislike of his cousin, Calvin.

Things had got so bad between Elizabeth and Calvin and he didn't know why. True, for some reason unknown to David, his wife had always been a bit cold towards his cousin once they were married. He'd put it down to her not really liking that they all lived together. But Calvin was his family. He and Calvin had always been together, and David saw no reason – not even getting married – why that should change. But lately, Elizabeth seemed to attack Cal the minute he walked into the house; their evening meals were becoming so strained, it wasn't fun anymore. How he wished whatever it was that Elizabeth had against Calvin could just go away. Calvin Fisher was the only family he'd got, besides her. He needed him; the firm needed him.

Despite this, though, he was just so pleased that Elizabeth was back to her normal self. But was she? He felt there was still something he was missing. He knew he wasn't the quickest when it came to reading between the lines, but whatever was wrong, if there was anything wrong at all, that is, he was definitely missing it. And he didn't like to miss anything if it had to do with his family; their happiness was his concern, his job.

Elizabeth seemed a little nervous lately and David couldn't work out why. Maybe it was because she'd stopped drinking so much. He'd heard that suddenly stopping drinking could bring on a case of the shakes. Maybe that's what was wrong. She had nothing else to worry about, he'd always seen to that. The bills were paid. The staff always got their wages on time. Parklands was coming along fine, and the houses were selling nearly as soon as they were built. He and Elizabeth were close again. Even Nathan was coming out of his shell and spending some time with them instead of vegetating in his room.

But he still felt there was something not quite right.

David was just checking the building plans in the makeshift wooden shack of an office when Calvin burst into the room.

'I've had enough of this fucking situation,' he shouted at David with no preamble. 'What with you and the firm and that stupid wife of yours! I've had it!'

'Hey! Hang on a minute. You can't speak about Elizabeth like that! What's up with you? What on earth's the matter?'

David had never seen Cal so worked up. It wasn't like him at all. His cousin was a man who never lost his cool. He pushed the plans to one side, patted the table to indicate that Calvin should sit down and turned to put the kettle on for tea.

'Leave the bloody tea! I'll tell you what's the matter,' said Calvin refusing to sit down and deciding to stand in the middle of the small office, his bulk making it look smaller than it actually was. He pulled himself up to his entire height, which made him considerably taller than David. 'That fucking bitch of a wife of yours doesn't know what she bloody well wants; that's what's the matter.'

'Cal, you're going too far.' David turned to face him. 'Stop talking about Elizabeth like that and explain what the hell's wrong. I'm starting to get pissed off.'

David's hackles were indeed starting to rise. Despite his admiration for Calvin, when all was said and done, Elizabeth was his wife and he didn't like anyone speaking about her in such derogatory terms. He'd never heard Calvin talk of her in such a way, even though they always seemed to have their differences. Why on earth they had their differences he couldn't be bothered to think about at the moment. And, quite honestly, he didn't care. Other people got on. Why couldn't they? He returned to making the tea.

'What's happened?' he asked, throwing two tea bags into a couple of mugs and pouring boiling water over them.

'I'll fucking tell you once and for all.' Calvin gritted his teeth and was about to tell David what a slut of a wife he had when he turned his head and saw the men working outside. They were laughing and sweating and putting up a wall quicker than he'd ever seen before. They were good. His eyes scanned the estate. It must be the best in the area, he thought. This estate was his, his doing. He'd made this. This was his doing and his alone. And he certainly wasn't going to storm off and leave this stupid bastard of a drunken labourer's son reaping all the benefits. Between them, Davie-boy and that tart of a

Liz had tried to push him out, take everything that he, and he alone, had worked for. He'd not let them get away with it! They'd probably spent hours planning this!

As he turned back to face David, Calvin was a changed person. Gone were the obvious anger, the loud mouthing-off and the aggressive stance. Calvin was back to his old self - friendly, smiling and as charming as ever. He sat down at the table and picked up the mug of tea.

'It's all work and no play, me old bean. That's what's the matter. Just need a bit of a break. Was having a skive-off at home when Liz caught me and we had a bit of a row. Sorry, old bean. I might have upset her. But you know me. I didn't mean to. All I really need is a break for a while. Think you can manage without me for a bit?' Calvin put the mug to his lips and pretended to take a long sip of the steaming tea.

'Christ, Cal, I didn't realise. Sorry, mate,' said David, starting to feel guilty about being so sharp-tongued earlier. 'Of course you should have a break. Sorry about Elizabeth, too. You've got to be patient with her, Cal. She's taken Alexander's death pretty hard. She's a bit touchy at the moment. I'm sure she didn't mean anything she said.'

David picked up his mug, drank from its contents and stayed staring at the table top as he put it back down. He wasn't good at coping with any type of argument and he hoped that Calvin wouldn't have anything more to say, especially about Elizabeth. He hated this animosity between them. If Calvin needed a holiday, he should have it.

'When do you want to go, Cal?' he said.

'I think now, right at this minute would be all right with me, David.'

David noticed the use by Calvin of his full name. He couldn't remember the last time Cal had called him by his full name. He must do everything to make this right. 'Of course, Cal,' he said. 'I'll take care of everything here. When were you thinking of actually going?'

'Now, I said. Right this minute. I'm not going back to that house where I'm obviously not wanted.' Calvin hissed. 'I'll use the credit card. Just make sure my account is regularly topped up.'

And with that, Calvin walked out of the hut, leaving the door swinging and his tea still steaming on the rickety old table.

CHAPTER FIFTY-NINE

David stormed into the house an hour earlier than usual. Elizabeth was sitting on the balcony, a vodka and tonic in her hand. 'What on earth happened between you and Cal this morning?' David bellowed, walking straight to the sideboard to get himself a drink. His glass filled, he went to the balcony to join Elizabeth who still hadn't answered him at all. 'Well?'

Elizabeth was sitting on the edge of the cane armchair. She had her elbows resting on her knees, her drink was in her hands and she was rocking her body ever so slightly back and forth. 'What did Cal say?' she asked, not looking at him.

'He said you'd had a big row and that he didn't want to be where he wasn't wanted. You do realise he's gone off, don't you?'

'What do you mean "gone off"? Gone off where?'

'It doesn't matter where. In fact he didn't say. He said he'd had enough and needed a break. What on earth did you say to him, Elizabeth, to make him so pissed off? What is the matter with you? Why can't you just get on with Cal? Hell! Everybody else likes him; it's just you who doesn't. You must have really upset him 'cause he stormed off in a right huff this morning.'

Elizabeth started to relax a little. So, Calvin hadn't said anything about that afternoon when they'd had, as he saw it, sex. He obviously wasn't going to tell David. This was her chance to get in first.

'We had a row because, well… I don't really know how to say this but, well…' Elizabeth looked down into her drink, 'he got out of line. There's no other way to say it, he came on to me,' she finished abruptly.

Silence. A long silence in which the only thing to be heard were the crickets buzzing their song.

David had gone deathly pale. Finally he spoke: 'What do you

mean, he came on to you?' He hovered there, in front of the armchair in which Elizabeth was sitting, looking down at the top of her head. 'Just exactly what do you mean?'

Elizabeth's mind raced. She had to be careful now what she said. She wanted to get rid of Calvin, have him out of her life. But she didn't want David getting too angry. She needed him on her side.

'He keeps coming back to the house when you are not here and I am alone,' she started. Well, that was the truth, she thought. 'I think he thinks that my dislike of him is only a show to cover up some deeper feelings I have for him. At least that's how he said he looked at it. When I told him that I was fed up with him always being there, always being around us and not letting us get on with our married life without him in the middle, he got angry. He said he knew that what I really wanted was him. And then he grabbed me and kissed me. Of course I pushed him off...'

Elizabeth looked up to see David just standing there, quietly staring down at her. She'd told the whole story to his feet, now she raised her head to look into his face, to see his reaction. 'And then he got even more angry and stormed out of the house, calling me all the names under the sun,' she finished lamely.

David still said nothing. This was not what he had expected to hear. When he really thought about it, he didn't know what he had expected to hear. He took a long deep drink of the gin and tonic in his hand, and then plonked himself down in the chair opposite his wife. This can't be happening, he thought. She must have got this wrong, he theorised, lighting a candle of hope in himself. No, no! She must have got the wrong end of the stick.

'Darling, you must have misunderstood Cal's intentions. He wouldn't do anything like that. Christ! He's my cousin. He's my business partner. He's like a brother to me. He's family!' David paused, staring at his drink for a moment to gather his thoughts. 'He knows how unhappy you've been,' he continued when Elizabeth said nothing. 'He was probably just trying to give you a brotherly hug and you mistook it for something else.'

Elizabeth was livid. How dare he insinuate that she was mistaken! She opened her mouth to protest, then caught herself and remained silent while she assembled her thoughts. This was a time when she had to be careful, she suddenly realised. She had a lot to lose. Not only David, but her whole life. She'd be on her own if David left her. She'd have nothing. She'd never worked at all in her life. What would she do if she were to suddenly find herself on her own? Her father wouldn't have her back. Although he was speaking to her again, he'd never forgiven her for going off with David. And her shame at having to admit to him that he'd been right would just be impossible for her to do. No, she had to make sure that everything would be all right between her and David and, unfortunately, that meant having that bastard Calvin in her life because her stupid husband could not see what was happening under his nose.

'May...maybe you're right,' she whispered. 'Maybe he was just trying to be nice. Maybe I've been wrong about him all along. Oh, David, I'm so sorry.' She started to weep, seeking out David's face and looking at him with her tear-filled eyes. She knew he couldn't bear to see her cry.

David's heart melted. He was right. Thank the Lord! It had all been a big mistake; just two people who don't get along too well with each other having a misunderstanding. A great feeling of relief washed over him. He always knew things would sort themselves out. He got up out of the armchair, crossed the balcony to Elizabeth and pulled his weeping wife into his arms.

'There, there,' he said, holding Elizabeth tightly and stroking her back. 'Everything will be all right. You know Cal's a bit hot-headed. He'll soon be back. Don't worry.'

CHAPTER SIXTY

It was some three months later before Calvin returned. David was really pleased as funds were getting low. Calvin had lived the high life during his trip, staying in the best hotels along the Costa Blanca and Costa del Sol. David saw all this on the credit card receipts that fluttered onto his office desk every month. He had travelled extensively. Oh yes indeed, when Calvin returned, David was immensely pleased.

He'd also genuinely missed him and looked forward to getting down to some new project together with his cousin; maybe a new estate on his side of the mountain. That's what he was still hoping for. Calvin had been negotiating with the local authorities to get the land surrounding his house designated as building land when he left. Calvin was a good negotiator, the best really. He knew the right people and if he didn't, he made it his business to get himself introduced to the right people. He would take these right people to long lunches where they'd spend three hours eating and chatting before getting down to real business. This was truly Calvin's talent. David had no patience for that; he was simply a builder. And it was always Calvin who sorted out the legalities, leaving him, the builder, to build. Oh yes, yes, yes, David was pleased Calvin was back.

But not only that, David was pleased Calvin was back and away from the areas that didn't really appear as safe as here in this location of the coast. Where Calvin had been there was a lot of crime going on. David read about it in the newspapers and there'd been loads of reports about it on the television. Looking at this beautiful land of sun and boisterous, happy people, he couldn't understand why criminals had to spoil it. The most that ever happened in Calpe was that a well-trained pickpocket would lift your wallet or purse off your person without you noticing it at all.

But elsewhere the types of crimes committed were much more serious. Crikey! Just two weeks ago two women had been brutally raped and murdered within a week of each other in the very area where Calvin was staying. They had been particularly brutal murders, the papers had reported. How awful! What on earth is wrong with the world? thought David. Better that Calvin is back from that place. He'd be better off at home with them. David liked to think of his family as being safe, particularly after what had happened to Alexander. The thought of losing anyone dear to him just crippled him with worry.

Elizabeth wasn't as happy at Calvin's return as her husband was. David had been going on and on about it now for a couple of days; about how pleased he was to have his family all back together again. She would never be able to think of Calvin as family. But she knew, to keep David happy, she must learn to live with Calvin around their home and in their lives as if she also wanted it. It was going to be difficult for her but she would do it. Pity the sod hadn't stayed where he was and got himself killed there like those poor girls. The more reports that came in the news telling of such atrocities, the more protective David became. His love was becoming a little stifling. She'd told him a thousand times that even if he had been on the beach that day, Alexander wouldn't necessarily still be alive. But he blamed himself still and this manifested itself in him mollycoddling her and Nathan far too much. He only felt happy when he knew where everyone was, how long they intended to stay anywhere and, most importantly, when they would be back and once again in the safety of the house on the hill. Elizabeth looked towards the couch, seeing the terrible scene of Calvin raping her playing once again before her eyes. It just worked to reaffirm that she hated this house now.

It had been, when all said and done, a good three months. She and David had lived quite happily without the presence of Calvin in their lives. She only wished David would see it that way. He was always going on about wanting Calvin to get back to Calpe so they could get on with... whatever. She had worked hard to become once again lovingly close to her husband. They were happier than ever. If only that bastard would stay out of her life. The thought of his return filled her with angst.

She couldn't quite remember when she realised that she was pregnant. David was ecstatic and started treating her like a piece of fine porcelain that had to be handled with great care. He strutted around, telling anyone who would listen of her condition and his prowess, like a proud peacock flashing off its feathers.

Elizabeth wasn't so happy about the pregnancy, though. She desperately hoped that when Calvin finally arrived back in their lives, he wouldn't take the time to work out when she had become pregnant. Inside her was growing a baby. Whose baby? she wondered.

CHAPTER SIXTY-ONE

Life dropped into a new routine with Calvin's arrival home. He no longer ate with them of an evening, preferring to go out each night and not returning till the early hours of the morning. Of course, Elizabeth knew where he was. It seemed more than ever now he was a regular customer of the girlie clubs along the national highway. At least, while he was getting his rocks off there, Elizabeth would think as she turned over in bed and prepared to go back to sleep, having been woken by Calvin's return home in his jeep, he'll be leaving me alone. She would lie there, watching her stomach grow, wondering what was growing inside of her, trying to get back to sleep, and watching David, who slept the sleep of the innocent. She knew he was a bit put out, hurt even, by Calvin's apparent distancing from them, but it certainly didn't disturb his sleep.

Elizabeth was coming into her seventh month of pregnancy. Despite her reservations, she was feeling physically well. Pregnancy suited her and she bloomed, whatever her misgivings. She had decided that it didn't matter who the father was. This baby was a blessing, a gift that would unite her with David more securely than ever. David was over the moon at her growing belly and showered her with love and affection as well as gifts and offers of fulfilling any desires she might have. She felt truly loved and thanked God that her life was now back to some type of normality.

Another happy circumstance in her life was that, since the rape, she had sought out the contact with her father and he had responded well. They talked at least once a week on the telephone, and often it would be he who called her. Elizabeth was again content. That was until Calvin came home in the middle of the day and threatened her.

'Don't think I'm stupid, Lizzie, my lovely. I can work out when that little bean got fertilised,' he'd said, pointing at her swollen stomach.

'It will, of course, be a lovely child. It will, of course, be mine. And I want it!'

Elizabeth had frozen at the words. 'What do you mean, yours? This child is David's and mine. We made it. It was made in love!'

'We'll see about that when it's born. I'll demand a test, you know. They can do that these days. If that little bastard in your belly is mine, I want to know about it. And, what's more, I want it. What would the courts think about a woman who betrays her own husband in his very own house with his cousin? You're going to lose, Liz. One way or another, you are going to lose.'

He'd waltzed out of the house and left her shaking with fear.

That night she had asked her father if she could come home to him and have her child in Grimsby. She didn't tell him of her fears. She just said that she wanted him to be a part of her life and what better way to introduce him to his new grandchild than to be there with him when the child was born. Elizabeth breathed a sigh of relief when he not only agreed but sounded really happy at the idea, saying he would get her old apartment in the attic ready for her and Nathan and that he was looking forward to them being together again.

David was a little more difficult to convince that her departure to England was a good thing. It took her a couple of days of wheedling and coaxing and constantly pointing out to him that her father needed to play a part in their children's lives. It was going to be September when she was due to deliver, still very hot, she reminded him, and the heat would make her confinement in Spain so much more uncomfortable. She needed to have this baby in England, she insisted. Her father had even agreed to have David over there with them when the child was born. She desperately wanted this, she told David.

When he saw the tears in her eyes, he knew he just couldn't deny her anything. He agreed to let her go, even agreed to finally take a holiday from his beloved building site and be there in England for the baby's birth.

A week later Elizabeth was gone.

CHAPTER SIXTY-TWO

Bloody bitch, thought Calvin as he saw David driving away from the house, taking Elizabeth to the airport. If she thinks she can avoid me, then she's got another think coming. That baby is mine. I'm sure of it. She might have called it rape. But then she would, wouldn't she; she was having a good time with me and she couldn't let David know that so the bitch screamed rape. Fucking women!

Calvin had returned to Calpe and the *family* reluctantly. He'd been having a good time where he was. The booze had flowed and life had been good. Okay, there'd been that bit of inconvenience with the couple of women he'd, well, sort of manhandled a bit, obviously weak slags because they'd given up the bloody ghost and pegged out on him. Damn women! He'd had to leave that area because of them and return to what he now called home.

Home, what was that? For Calvin it was the source of his money. He'd held himself back since returning. Bitch Elizabeth had obviously changed her mind about wanting him, probably thinking David was a better bet when it came to money. But if the truth be known, he had a lot more money than that wimp of a man. He hadn't spent loads of the stuff on building a house. House! It was a bloody mansion! When he really thought about it, Calvin came to the conclusion that it was David who was cheating him out of what was really his. The accounts were joint banking accounts and David was spending all the money they'd earned on his bloody home. And, what was worse, he'd relegated him to the bloody basement. Here he was, a man of the world, a businessman, a man who knew the ins and outs of getting what he wanted, what they wanted. Hadn't he been instrumental in getting the land on which Parklands was built free of building restrictions? Hadn't he taken the boring old councillors to lunch and wined and dined them and pushed wads of money into their sticky little hands long enough until they had got the results they had wanted? Gilmore and Fisher was really FISHER, that's what. David was just a freeloader and it was time he was gone. It was time to get rid of him. Time to start the next project and David would not be a part of this one. He would deal with Elizabeth and their child later.

It was a couple of months after Calvin's return that he put his plan into action. Elizabeth had been gone over a month now. David was planning to follow her. It was time. Once the shrub land and pine trees surrounding David's folly of a house had been burnt to the ground, there would be nothing left for the council to do other than declare it building land. Indeed, this mountainside would make a wonderful place for a new estate of detached, upmarket houses. It was also a chance to get rid of the thorn that had remained in his side for so many years. Bloody David! All he needed was for him to be out of the way, out of his life, and everything that was his would finally be in his possession.

Calvin crept out of the apartment under the villa that David had so painstakingly built. With him in his pocket he had matches and a couple of candle stubs. The night was warm and clammy. There was no breeze at the moment. Calvin looked at the stars in the mostly clear blue sky. It still wasn't truly dark and already the moon was just starting to cast its glow over the countryside. Calvin's eyes flashed. In the light of the moon they looked more blue and intense than ever. He smiled to himself in anticipation of his plan. This was his time. This he should have done years ago.

He marched into the thick bush of the forest covering the mountainside. He walked with grim determination, pushing his way through thorned bushes, ignoring them as they caught and tore at his clothes and exposed skin. He climbed over old forgotten crumbling terraces, which had once held and nurtured sturdy vines and now left only small mounds of earth where the vines had rotted into a hard mass. He walked and climbed until he was a good distance from the hated house: a house that, at the moment, housed only David, the cause of all his irritation.

He stooped down, gathered the dry bracken and twigs at his feet and made a pile of them. Then, taking the matches out of his pocket, he took one last look at the peace and tranquillity around him before holding the match to the pile. It took only a second before it caught the flame and whooshed into full blaze.

The end had started.

CHAPTER SIXTY-THREE

And now David stood on the balcony of his opulent home looking down into the garden at Calvin who no longer bothered to hide in the shadows. The house suddenly took on a neon hue, a psychedelic orange that looked strange and out of place among the still green foliage of the garden plants. But tendrils of blazing fire were creeping towards it.

'Cal! Cal, what are you doing?' screamed David as he watched in amazement then pure terror as Calvin sloshed petrol out of the canisters he was carrying onto the walls of David's house.

'I'm getting rid of you; that's what I'm doing. You didn't really think that I'd put up with any more of your swindling me out of what is mine. Did you?'

'Cal, what on earth are you talking about?'

'Don't come the little boy lost with me, Davie, old bean,' said Calvin, momentarily pausing in his efforts to douse the walls of the house with petrol. 'It might work on Elizabeth but it certainly doesn't work on me. You know exactly what I'm talking about. Ever since I joined the family, you Gilmores have done nothing but use me. First your father, then you. I've been nothing more than a paid skivvy, and a poorly paid one at that. Look at me now, living in the fucking basement of the Palace of the Lord My Cousin David. Well, I've had enough of it.'

Calvin took the lighter out of his pocket and looked up at the balcony. 'See this, Davie, my old lad? Well, this is what got you the land for Parklands. You're so stupid, you thought the fire was an act of God. What makes you think you are so special that God would just come to your aid and wipe that land clear of forest so you could build on it? I did it! You silly bugger! It was me!' Calvin started to cough. The smoke was stealthily floating around him.

Despite the heat, icy fear was seeping into David's bones. He could see the flames slashing through anything that stood before them at an alarming rate. The fire was already touching the boundaries of the immediate garden, he could hear the pines exploding, he could see the fragments of burning forest debris floating in the air, looking for a place to land and blow up into fierce flames. The thought suddenly occurred to him that if he didn't move quickly, he'd be trapped, he'd not get out. He'd die. And why wasn't Calvin moving? Why wasn't he running like hell away from the fire?

'Cal, let's talk about this some other time. We've got to get out of here. Look! Look at the fire! It's only going to be a few seconds before it reaches the house.'

'Stupid bastard!' shouted Calvin up at David. He threw down the canisters and moved right out of the shadows of the foliage and into the bright light created by the burning flames surrounding them. 'You are not leaving the house, old bean. Sorry, about that but it's time for you to snuff it. I can't say it has been a pleasure. But, nevertheless, it has been interesting.' Calvin leered up at David and moved closer to the balcony to make sure his cousin could hear every word he said.

'You are a snivelling little bastard that the world won't miss,' he continued. Suddenly, his tone turned nasty and sarcastic. 'And don't worry about your sweet wife. I'll take care of her. She was always mine anyway. It's me she really wants. It's all mine!' Calvin swung his arms around to show exactly what he meant was his. 'The house. Elizabeth. Even the fucking baby! Mine! Mine! Mine! All this will be mine when you are gone.' He coughed and spluttered on his words.

David stood rooted to the spot, held immobile by the shock of what he was hearing.

'I don't need you to build an empire,' Calvin shouted. 'This mountainside will carry the name of Fisher, not Gilmore, 'cause you'll be dead.'

He threw the lighter at the smouldering bushes right next to the house wall. They ignited instantly, flames shooting up high, through the balustrade on the balcony.

David had been stunned by Calvin's revelations. He said nothing at all as he looked down at his cousin. He was speechless. This was the cousin he had loved like a brother and whom he had thought felt the same about him. His words, his complaints, his accusations were too astounding to contemplate at this time. His survival instinct set in and it suddenly became crystal clear to him that his only job at the moment was to get out of this house and off this mountain.

David's last view of his cousin was sickening. Calvin was standing among the glowing embers of the flowerbeds, stooping to pick up anything that was burning and throwing it up at the balcony. His face was contorted in rage and he was screaming something that David couldn't hear. As he made to leave the balcony and make for the front door he took one last look down into the garden. The flames were starting to take hold of the house and the dry bushes and young trees around it were crackling in protest as they succumbed to the inevitable. Suddenly there was a whoosh as giant flames leapt up the wall right onto the balcony. David put up his hands to shield his face before turning and running into the house to avoid the inferno raging towards him.

He raced for the front door. Grabbing the brass handle, he shook it violently; but the door was locked, just like it always was. David turned to make his way back through the living-room towards the kitchen. He stopped in his tracks as he saw that the fire had entered the house and barred his way. He could see the oak wood of the kitchen was adding momentum to the flames. The hair on the back of his neck stood up and he felt sure he could feel them singe. For a moment it occurred to him that this was it. This was the end of his life. It was over. He would never see Elizabeth again. He would never hold her. He would never have the opportunity to make up to his son, Nathan, for all the years of fatherly neglect, and, what's more, he'd never see the baby, never really know if Calvin was telling the truth or just being spiteful. But what the hell, it didn't matter what Calvin had said. Calvin had a nasty habit of saying a lot of things he didn't mean when he was angry. And David knew his Elizabeth. He had to smile to himself despite his present predicament, for being so silly as to even entertain for a moment the thought that Elizabeth had slept with Calvin. Of course the baby's ours, he told himself. For some reason Calvin had gone crazy.

All David wanted now was to see his wife, he wanted to see his son again, he desperately wanted to have the chance to be a father to his new baby. Fuck Calvin! He would not let him take all this away from him. He would deal with him later. But for now he needed to find a place to outlive this fire.

David rushed to the small bedroom at the back of the house. He paused at the door and thought of the old photos and other things that were precious to him. He wanted to go and get them but the fire was already licking at the furniture, chasing him, and the house was beginning to fill with smoke. No chance to save anything. He picked up the bedside table in the room and rammed it into the windowpane. It shattered immediately. David climbed out of the window. The night breeze was coming from inland, gently pushing the blaze down the mountain rather than up. It was impossible to get away from the house he realised, as he saw the flames, like a giant red and orange carpet, swiftly rolling down the mountainside towards him.

Suddenly, he became aware that he was standing on an iron grate. It was directly under the bedroom window out of which he had just climbed. It topped an airshaft, which had been drawn up from a room far under the house. With the house being built on a mountainside, this back half was, naturally, built into the mountain. Originally, he'd planned to build the bathroom for the basement flat in the room but then it was decided that the room was too far into the mountain. And so it had just been left – hollowed out, a rock-filled dungeon.

David removed the grate from the airshaft, grateful that he'd built the shaft big enough to take his body and not used a ready-made plastic one, which would have been far too narrow. He slithered down the shaft, grazing his elbows and knees as he did so. At the bottom he wedged his feet against the frosted-glass window and shoved it in. He crawled into the dank, dark room of earth and rubble, curled up in the far corner, and hoped he wasn't waiting for death to claim him.

For the first time in a very long time, he prayed.

CHAPTER SIXTY-FOUR

The Esmeralda Hotel in Calpe was the most impressive hotel in the town in 1986. Situated on the seafront, it offered magnificent views of the Mediterranean on one side and scenic views of the mountains on the other. It was a building of marble floors, leather settees and pristine white walls. David hated it.

He had been staying at the hotel since the fire: the fire that he had managed to survive, lying in the dirt under the house that he had built on the mountainside. Calvin hadn't been so lucky. They'd found his charred remains near the wall, under the living-room balcony the day after the fire. Strangely, no one had mentioned the canisters found near his body, probably choosing to believe that he was just trying to move the canisters out of the way of the fire.

David had spent over three months grieving, but he wasn't quite sure for what he was grieving. He missed Calvin terribly. He knew that for sure. But it was not the Calvin he had seen outside his balcony on that awful night that he grieved for. He missed the Calvin he had always loved and admired. He missed the Calvin who had been his big brother, his protector, his friend, his idol to look up to. No matter what, Calvin would always stay in his mind like that. And he wouldn't let anyone say or think anything else but good about his cousin.

He still couldn't quite grasp what had actually happened up there on the mountain. And it was something he didn't even like to think about any more, really. But the nightmares wouldn't go away.

He'd missed the birth of his child and this saddened him greatly, too. And he'd missed Elizabeth more than he could say. She would be coming home this day and they would be moving into a rented property until he could build another house for them. He planned to build on the same mountainside, wanted the exact same view of the Mediterranean and the white-painted dwellings along the coast spreading between Moraira and the magnificent Rock of Calpe at his feet.

After the fire, the town councillors and friends of Calvin had gathered around him with words of sympathy and offers of help. They'd been good to him and he had learnt to make cash rewards in the way he thought Calvin always did. And so, it didn't take long for them to declare the whole mountainside new building land. David was in business again. For a price that he could cover alone, now that he was sole owner of the building company, he had secured the land and was now busy working with an architect. He was working out the best way to utilise the space, the best way to build a new estate he planned to call Calvin del Sol, Calvin of the Sun.

With the passing of time the memory softened and David decided that Calvin was just saying those stupid things to purposefully hurt him. Why? Why? his brain would scream out at times when he was alone and could do little else but relive that awful night. But he truly didn't know why and whenever the question filtered into his brain, he learnt to blot it out immediately. None of the things Calvin had said were true, of course. He knew Calvin. Calvin had been a great ally in his youth, was a great man and a good business partner and family member. He must have been ill to suddenly turn like that. Poor Calvin. David would let no one think anything other than the best about his cousin.

Now it was time to start life anew with his darling wife and new baby, as well as his son, Nathan. Elizabeth and the kids were the future and, with a bit of hard work, their happiness would be secure. He'd spoken to Elizabeth every day since the fire. They were closer now than ever before, although he'd hardly thought that possible.

David arrived early at the airport and was getting agitated by the time the plane carrying his family finally arrived. He stood at the barrier of the Arrivals gate and waited impatiently for their appearance. He didn't have to wait long. Elizabeth was one of the first to come out of the baggage claim hall. As soon as he saw her, his heart filled with love at the sight of her walking towards him, the baby in her arms and

Nathan walking at her side. How lucky he was to have this wonderful family!

'Hiya!' he said smiling at them before taking Elizabeth into his arms to give her a big kiss. This wasn't so easy because she was holding the baby between them.

'Hi, darling,' she said, smiling back at him. 'Meet your daughter.'

David held out his arms and Elizabeth placed the swaddled bundle into his hands. The baby was sleeping. She was warm and smelled sweet. He saw she had a shock of black hair and a button nose. David opened his heart and let her in. He held his daughter close to his chest. She had been born the night of the fire, earlier than expected. She was the very start of their new life together. A life where he would make up for the mistakes he had made. He looked down into her little face. Suddenly she opened her eyes and looked directly at him. She had the bluest of eyes he'd ever seen. Just like Calvin's, he thought.

Printed in the United Kingdom
by Lightning Source UK Ltd.
124715UK00001B/49-210/A

9 781905 988174